INSIDE

INSIDE

A NOVEL BY CHARLES L. ROSS

INK
INC.

Published by Ink, Inc.
Printed in the United States of America.

Second edition

ISBN-13: 978-1492237105
ISBN-10: 1492237108

PART ONE
WOMAN OF THE YEAR

NOVEMBER 6, 1981

"Anthony," she announces. "I need you over here. Now."
She hangs up. She doesn't have to say who it is. Or where I'm to go. I recognize that voice. No one but Leaf Wyks would summon me to her home at midnight, not concerned that I may be sleeping or with someone. And of course, she knows I'll go.

Twenty minutes later, I press her doorbell, but there's no response. The sliding glass, so uniquely a Los Angeles front door, is not locked.

"Leaf?" I call softly, entering the black-mirrored foyer. "Are you still up?"

On the living room coffee table are a liqueur bottle and two glasses. Tiffany, I think. In the adjacent dining area, the table is cluttered with chocolate-stained dessert dishes and empty cups.

I turn toward her bedroom.

"Are you asleep?"

She's propped up in a mist of pink silk pillows. A Daum lamp glows on the Art Deco nightstand, illuminating a magazine on the bed. It is, of course, *Inside*. The latest issue—which I haven't seen—features The White House, and I'm tempted to grab it.

Her eyes are closed, her lips parted.

She may be annoyed if I wake her, but if I slide out, I'll have to deal with her anger tomorrow when she accuses me of not showing up.

"Leaf." I touch her shoulder. Her head slumps forward.

I put two fingers on her neck. No pulse.

I stare, unable to move. I don't think I even breathe.

My hand shakes as I reach for the phone on the nightstand.

"I need the police." Aware of how rapidly my heart is beating, I'm surprised at how calm I sound. I relay all the pertinent information, and when I put down the phone I notice a pink envelope—addressed to me.

My eyes zoom in like a movie camera: I recognize Leaf's handwriting. I pick the envelope up but don't open it. Maybe I stare at it so intently in order not to look at her lifeless body.

The police will be here any moment. Suddenly I run to my car, pop the trunk and bury the envelope under the spare tire. I dash back inside and slow my breathing as police lights color the night blue and red.

A man in a suit examines Leaf's body while one of the uniform cops questions me in the foyer. There's no place to sit down. It's a small room, and he seems to stand deliberately too close to me. He's past forty, a little heavy, a foot taller than I. His nametag says Lodge. Anderson, the other cop—younger, cuter—writes in a tiny tablet with a stub of a pencil like the ones used on golf courses.

"Who is she?" Lodge wants to know.

"Leaf Wyks." I look at Anderson. "*L-E-A-F W-Y-K-S.*" I wonder how I appear to them. Do they sense the fear behind my calm helpfulness?

Lodge asks, "Who's she to you?"

"My boss. Well, actually my ex-boss."

"What's your name?"

"Anthony Dimora." I spell it, too.

"Got any I.D.?"

When I hand him my driver's license, he doesn't even glance at it, just passes it to Anderson, who copies the information, then gives it back to me.

"Where do you work?" Lodge asks.

"I *used* to work at *Inside* magazine."

"That's the magazine that was next to her on the bed," Anderson says.

Lodge ignores him. The man in the suit sticks his head in the foyer. Lodge follows him into the living room. I don't know why they bother to leave, since they don't lower their voices and I hear the man say, "Probably poison. Dead less than two hours."

"Call the station," Lodge tells Anderson when he comes back, "and tell them we need forensics. The whole team."

Anderson goes out. Lodge and I go over everything. Twice.

"Why'd she call you?"

"I told you, I don't know."

"Why'd you call the police and not an ambulance? How'd you know she died of foul play?

"I didn't know. I punched 9-1-1, and when someone answered, 'I need the police' just came out of my mouth."

"The whole team" arrives. Everyone's busy in latex gloves. Camera lights flash. Just like on *Quincy*.

Lodge and I lean against the mirrored walls in the foyer.

"These are weird." Anderson squats next to a colorful porcelain figure, about four feet tall, of a man with a grotesque face.

"It's an antique Chinese burial guard to protect the dead," I tell him.

"Didn't do such a good job tonight," Lodge says.

A woman comes in but doesn't speak. Lodge nods, I guess

giving her the go-ahead to talk in front of me.

"The liqueur's framboise," she says.

Lodge frowns.

I can tell Anderson doesn't know how to spell it.

"Raspberry, to you illiterates. My guess is it contained the poison. There are four coffee cups on the dining room table, but only two liqueur glasses on the coffee table. Someone may have stayed after everyone else left. Or someone else may have arrived later." She looks right at me.

As I ride in the back of the police car to the station, one thought keeps replaying in my mind over and over.

A lot of people will be glad Leaf Wyks is dead.

NOVEMBER 17, 1976

My first day at *Inside* Timmy Martin ambles past my office five times. He must be trying to figure out if I'm gay. I surmise he is—who else but gay men wear Izod shirts and 501 Levis with the bottom button unfastened?

I stroll the corridor too but not to check out Timmy. I want to see Leaf Wyks, the magazine's editor and, therefore, the boss of the whole show—except for Claret Bruin, who owns it. I get a glimpse of Leaf in her office. Her frosted blond hair is a bit wild and too bouffant for her head. She seems a little chunky although it's hard to tell with her sitting behind a desk. When she looks up, I move quickly away but not before noticing her oversize clear-framed glasses. She's not exactly pretty.

The next day Timmy wears a pink crocodile shirt. He ambles by seven times. Early on the third day—sky blue polo—he marches into my office carrying a coffee cup, introduces himself as Leaf's secretary and invites me to lunch.

"I know one thing for sure," I tell him in the small dining room at May's. "I am never going on vacation."

"Vacation?" Timmy looks incredulous. "You've only been at the magazine for three days, and you're already talking vacation?"

"I'm talking about *not* going on vacation. At my first real job, I worked for an art studio in Bloomfield Hills, Michigan. I went—

"You're from Michigan?" Timmy's transparent blue eyes meet mine.

I could tell him I was born in Pennsylvania and lived in Ohio for a while, but all I say is, "I went to college in Ann Arbor."

"I was born in Flint, Michigan. But we didn't live there long. In fact I don't remember it at all. My parents moved to San Diego when I was three."

The waitress serves our sandwiches.

"Anyway," I continue, "when I came back from vacation at this art studio, I found out that none of the employees had been paid for two weeks. Then three days later I arrived at work to find the building padlocked. The owners had been taking out withholding tax from our paychecks but hadn't turned it over to the government. We were out of jobs—and I had spent all my money on vacation."

"That's awful."

"It gets worse. I left Michigan because I was sick of cars and cold weather, so I moved to Los Angeles, and where do I end up working?"

Timmy lifts his shoulders in an *I-can't-imagine* gesture.

"*Motor Trend.*"

He doesn't seem to get the irony.

Timmy has a cute smile, but there's something severe about him. Most young men keep their hair long, curling over and sometimes completely covering their ears, but Timmy's is cropped as short as a soldier's. And while thick mustaches are also the fashion—mine is black—Timmy's is pencil-thin like a 1930s movie star.

"I worked at *Hot Rod* for a little while." he grins. "I loved the name but had absolutely *no* interest in souped-up cars."

"So you know Petersen owns more than a dozen magazines.

I was the assistant art director at *Motor Trend*. Last year I went on vacation to Mexico. And when I came back, I was told all the assistant art directors had been fired and there was going to be a pool of five assistants to help with all the magazines. They wanted me to be in the pool, but I refused."

Timmy puts his hand on mine, as if to comfort me, but his eyes say something else: *Let's do it*. I wonder if he's heard anything I've said.

I remove my hand from beneath his to take a sip of lemonade. "I never understood *Motor Trend*'s art director. Certain articles are more important than others. The biggest issue is presenting the new models in the fall. That article's at least twenty pages. And before that, there's a teaser issue, with drawings of new models. That story's at least fourteen pages. Then there's the Car of the Year article. Ten pages. And you know what? The art director never designed any of these stories. He gave them to me. I did most of the work. They fired the wrong person."

Timmy slurps his iced tea. "But another door opened, and here you are at *Inside*. It's so much more prestigious than *Motor Trend*."

"Yeah, but I'm just doing ads for local advertisers who don't have an agency. That's certainly not as prestigious as doing editorial layouts."

"Leaf is *very* unhappy with the current art director, so Mr. Bruin is looking to replace him." Timmy smacks his lips when he chews. I hate that. I may not be able to go to lunch with him again. "Don't say anything. Leaf told me in confidence."

"How long have you been her secretary?"

"Just over a year. I love it!" He points at his empty glass as the waitress walks by our table. "Some people look down on secretaries, especially male ones, but I know Leaf couldn't get through her day without me. I arrange *everything* for her. And I do it with a smile!"

"You do that a lot."

"Do what?"

"Smile."

"I'm a happy guy. Besides I think my smile is my best feature." He looks up at the waitress as she pours iced tea and asks, "What do you think? Do you think my smile is my best feature?"

"It's almost as sweet as this tea," she says and turns to another table.

"Of course, she hasn't seen *all* of me." He pulls his left nipple, stretching the fabric of his shirt just under the tiny crocodile.

He has a great chest. I bet he works out at the gym in West Hollywood.

"You do have a nice smile, Timmy, but I think your eyes are more—captivating. They're so transparent. Like pale glass."

"They spook some people." He takes a bite of his tuna sandwich, not waiting until he's finished chewing to ask, "How old are you?"

"Thirty-one."

"Well, you don't look over the hill." There's that smile again. Speckled with tuna. "I'm twenty-four."

Was that his foot that just grazed my leg? I've noticed, during the last three days, that he only wears very tight 501 Levis. Faded blue on Monday. Black yesterday. Dark blue today. It's obvious he doesn't have on underwear. And the bottom button is always left open. I wonder if he smacks his lips during sex.

He taps the top on my hand. "You know what I like best about my job?"

"What?" I expect a sexual reference.

"I get to hear all the gossip. All the designers—well, at least the gay ones, and most of them are—always tell me all the dirt about their rich and famous clients. And what they don't tell me, Leaf does. I always know who's sleeping with who before it hits *The National Enquirer*. And you should hear what the designers say about Leaf! Vicious! I swear, one day one of them is going to murder her."

NOVEMBER 19, 1976

About a quarter to five on Friday, I walk down the hall to Timmy Martin's office. Today instead of jeans he's wearing chinos; the polo shirt is pale green. He's cleaning off his desk and looks as if he's in a hurry, so I skip the small talk and get right to what I want to know.

"What's Claret Bruin like?"

"Blonds with big boobs."

"I meant: What's he like as a person?"

"He's a pussycat. He tries to come off as a tiger, but he just wants someone to rub his tummy."

"Do he and Leaf get along?"

"She's a blond with big boobs. But I'm not so sure he *likes* her." He shoves papers into folders and folders into drawers. "And I don't think she likes him. I *know* she doesn't respect him. But I'd say on the surface they get along, and she's certainly nice to him, especially when she wants something."

"Yeah, well, he does own the company."

"Not really. His wife Colette is the one with the money. She's blond, too. And if her boobs aren't quite as big as Mr. B prefers, her pocketbook is."

He takes a canvas bag that was leaning against a file cabinet and dumps the contents on his desk. Gym stuff: shoes, shorts, tank top, fingertip-less leather gloves and a small red plastic bag, which he turns upside down. Various toiletries roll out.

"Off to the gym?"

"Yes, but I can't find my membership card. Usually I put it in my wallet, but I was sure I slipped it in my bag last time." He runs his hand inside the canvas bag. Nothing.

I pick up one of his sneakers and pull out a business-size card. "Is this it?"

His shoulders sag with relief. "Thank you!" He starts stuffing everything back into the bag, and I figure I only have a minute to find out what I want.

"How much input will Claret Bruin have in hiring the new art director?"

"Almost total. Even though the new guy will work with Leaf, Mr. B will hire him. Believe me, this does *not* please Leaf." Timmy flings his bag over his shoulder. "I'd love to talk some more, Anthony, but I want to get to the gym before all the machines are taken. It's especially crowded on Fridays when guys are pumping up for the weekend."

And he's gone.

I stay late and, after everyone has left, begin designing a mock-up of how I would design *Inside* if I were the art director.

NOVEMBER 22, 1976

"Hey, I'm sorry I had to dash off so fast on Friday." Timmy enters my office on Monday with a cup of just-brewed coffee. Today he's wearing white Levis with a white Izod polo shirt and a white woven cotton belt. I wonder if he realizes he looks like the Good Humor Man.

"It's fun to see all the sweaty muscled boys work out," he says, "but I like to get my routine done without having to wait around for a machine. *Then* I can relax in the steam room. *If* you get my drift." His tongue licks his lower lip. "And thanks again for finding my gym card."

"No problem."

He leans against the door. "So, here's the dope on the Bruins. Claret's from the wrong side of Los Angeles—Orange County. Colette's family is from Pasadena. I'm talking money so old, God printed it. I don't know how the two of them met, but I do know Colette's mother wasn't in favor of the match, which is probably why Colette married him. You know the story. Typical Barbara Stanwyck movie. And just like on the great silver screen, Daddy keels over soon after the wedding." Timmy takes a gulp of coffee. I hadn't noticed before how prominent his Adam's apple is. "Colette's father was a spiteful son-of-a-bitch. He left his wife their mortgage-free, fifteen-room house and $500,000. Everything else—*twelve* apartment buildings, *two* hotels, *six* warehouses and *four* million dollars—went to Colette." Timmy raises his eyebrows. "So it's Colette's money that bought *Inside*, and I imagine she put her husband in charge to keep him from chasing other women. Not that it worked."

He's interrupted by Ann Peters, who whirls into my office without a knock or an "excuse me." She tosses an art board on my table. "The client didn't go for it. He said he wants it like he sketched on that envelope."

"You told me to do whatever I wanted to make it look better."

"Sorry, honey, but the advertiser's always right. I'll be by after lunch to pick up the revision."

And she's gone.

"God, what a tight-ass bitch!" Timmy looks after her with his mouth open. "How can you work with her?"

"I keep telling myself it's only temporary. But look." I pick up a torn envelope from my console. "Here's the sketch the owner of Geri's Antiques did for the ad. Way too much copy for a quarter-page ad. So I condensed it, dropped two of the out-of-focus photos so one could be large and maybe get noticed."

Timmy picks up the art board. "Your ad looks a lot better than that sketch."

"Thanks. But, hey, what do I know? I've only got a degree in graphic design." I start resizing the three photographs. "So, Timmy, is Mr. Bruin open to new ideas or is he a 'tight-ass' like Ann Peters?"

"I don't know for sure, but I think he must be pretty open. Why else would he be looking for a new art director?"

"So how do you know that he chases women?"

"Well, like those two reporters in D.C., I can't reveal my source." He rubs a finger across his lips as if he's putting on lipstick. "But I will say, they named Deep Throat after me."

I laugh. He is *so* obvious.

"I happen to know," Timmy continues, "that Mr. B is going to New York this Friday. Of course while he's there, he'll see potential advertisers. He'll wine and dine them. He'll take them to fancy restaurants and stuff himself with French cuisine and French wine and afterwards there will be a call girl waiting to French him in his hotel room."

"I think you've watched too many soap operas."

"Oh, yeah? Why is he going on a *Friday*? With the time change, he won't get into New York until after three." Timmy bends over my board, so close I can smell the coffee on his breath. "Tell me, Anthony, what ad man is going to be in his office after lunch on a Friday? What businessman is going to meet with Claret Bruin over the weekend?" He stands straight, puts a hand on one hip. "The man has plans."

"You should be a detective."

"And I have all the evidence too." He taps my board with his index finger. "You don't think Mr. B is going to balance his credit card charges himself, do you? Or have his secretary do it and maybe report an indiscreet charge to his wife?" He taps his chest. "No, Mr. B needs someone he can trust."

He must assume that because we're both gay, I'll keep his secret. "You do know all the dirt, don't you?"

"I make a point to." At the door he turns and smiles. "And I'll soon know all about *you*."

DECEMBER 13, 1976

I work for a week on the prototype issue. I use fewer but larger pictures—lots of two-page spreads. I use ideas I know would never get approved—three-page fold-outs, cut-outs—but I want to make a splash and grab Claret Bruin's attention.

I wonder if Maxine, his secretary, can see my knees shaking when I ask her to give him the prototype, which I've wrapped in a folio I made out of rice paper.

"He's still in New York," she says, "but I'll see he gets it when he gets back."

Guess what? She's blond, and as Timmy would say, "has big boobs."

About a week later, working after hours on some last-minute ads, I look up from my drawing board to see Claret Bruin standing in the doorway.

He's a big man: over six feet, broad but not overweight. A few of the curls tickling his ears are gray. He's attractive, not leading-man handsome but the best friend: good-looking enough to cause competition but not enough to win the girl in the final scene.

"Do you always work this late?"

"Very rarely."

"Obviously you don't know who I am or you would have

tried to impress me by saying you *always* work late."

"Oh, I know who you are, Mr. Bruin. If I told you I worked late every night, you might think I'm so slow I can't get my work done during office hours."

"Clever boy. Also talented." He waves my prototype of *Inside* with his right hand. "I like this. Of course, many of your ideas are unfeasible, if only because of the expense. But it shows creativity."

My throat is dry but I manage to get out two words. "Thank you."

"Do you mind if I keep it?"

"I made it for you."

He comes closer, puts his knuckles on the edge of my drawing board. They're flecked with black hair. "You certainly went to a lot of effort, and I appreciate it. But I can't offer you the job of art director. I looked at your résumé, and I don't feel you have enough experience yet. For example, the art director has to check the color proofs, and I noticed that wasn't one of your responsibilities at *Motor Trend*."

He probably expects me to say something, but I'm too crushed to speak.

He has dark eyes, almost black, but I'm afraid if I look into them he'll see my eyes are moist. I study his mouth: His lips are thin, almost invisible.

"I've hired a man who worked at *Playboy*. I doubt he's as creative as you, but he has the experience we need. His name's Larry Stein. You'll meet him. I told him to hire you as his assistant."

He holds out his hand. It's oversize, like the rest of him. But his handshake is weaker than I expect.

January 7, 1977

"Larry's given me a six-page layout to do," I tell Timmy as we jog side by side on matching treadmills. Timmy convinced me to join his West Hollywood gym, and I'm already pleased with the tiny improvements in my body. "At first I thought Larry was going to design the whole magazine and all I'd do was paste-up, but besides this one feature, he also wants me to design the departments."

"*Fob and Bob*. That's what the editors call the departments. *Fob*—F-O-B—for the articles in the Front of the Book and *Bob* for the ones in the back."

"*Fob and Bob* sounds like a vaudeville act. I guess that means the section in between showing all the homes is called *Mob*, for middle of the book."

"No, it's called *The Well*. I don't know why." Timmy adjusts his treadmill so he's on an incline. "Larry's the first Jew in the company."

"What difference does it make if he's Jewish?"

"Nothing. I'm just saying *Inside* is a very WASP environment. There aren't any blacks or Hispanics either. Not even in the mailroom. White, white, white. The art department is the only place with any ethnic people." He smiles at me. "Larry's Jewish and you're Italian."

"My heritage is Italian, but I'm American. My parents were born in America, too." I wonder if the rest of the editorial staff is as concerned about race and heritage as Timmy seems to be. "I guess I don't focus on a person's ethnic background."

"Don't get me wrong. I don't care where a person came from, I was just making an observation." Timmy wipes his forehead with his cotton wristband. "You know what else I observed? Except for Larry and Jane Covington, who handles the Fob and Bob stories, everyone in editorial is single. Leaf, Walter Downey and Ivory Cooke are divorced. Tom Hampton, the art and antiques editor, is gay, though he thinks no one knows, and he's so uninteresting no one cares. Mrs. Winter, the proof-reader, is a widow. She's a thousand years old and probably doesn't even remember her husband."

"I know Walter is the senior editor, but what does that entail?"

"He edits all the text and writes the titles. I think he's a closet case, but he has two kids."

"And what does Ivory do?"

"She's the managing editor. Jane assigns writers for the Fob and Bob articles, and Ivory handles The Well stories. She's really a traffic cop, making sure all the text flows along so that it gets to you on time to have typeset. You'll have to deal with her most. I don't want to prejudice you, but I think she's a prim pain in the ass. I bet her oh-so-refined accent is fake." Timmy reaches across to my treadmill and pushes a button so it moves faster.

At this speed, it's difficult to chat, but I manage to get out one more question. "Does Mr. Bruin get involved in the day-to-day running of the magazine?"

"He leaves editorial up to Leaf. She selects all the homes that are published. But every so often he likes her to know he's the boss, like selecting a new art director. But usually he concentrates on selling ads, wooing the national advertisers."

"I have to slow down." I'm practically panting as I try to keep up with Timmy.

"Okay, let's just walk for five minutes to cool down."

My tank top is soaked, but Timmy just has two small wet spots under his chest.

He notices me looking at him in the mirrored wall opposite us and flicks his tongue like a frog. "I've made another observation: Everyone in Editorial is better looking than average."

"Are Larry and I considered part of the Editorial Department?"

"On a chart you'd be the Art Department, but everyone who answers to Leaf is in Editorial."

"I don't think Larry is attractive. His beard hides a lack of a chin."

"He's better looking than anyone in Production or Circulation. Maybe he doesn't have a strong chin, but the beard is sort of sexy, and he has playful eyes."

"Well, I don't think I'm 'better looking than average.'"

"Look in that mirror, Anthony. Even with sweat running down your forehead, you're sexy. *Especially* with sweat running down your forehead."

I'm too short and don't have a hunky torso like Timmy. And right now, my dark brown hair is plastered with perspiration against my head. Not attractive. I've always thought my nose is too wide, my cheeks too round and my eyebrows too pointed; my mouth is a bit too small, although my lips are full. A lot of people comment favorably on my almost-black eyes. And I do like my hairy legs.

"If I make a critical comment," Timmy says, "do you promise not to get mad?"

"Depends how critical."

He points his chin to the mirror. "Look around at what everyone's wearing."

Most of the guys have on gym shorts, tank tops, crew socks and sneakers. I can usually tell the gays from the straights because the gays' shorts are briefer and their tops tighter.

"Now look what you're wearing."

Short shorts, tank top, crew socks and sneakers. "So?"

"You're too color coordinated, Anthony. The red stripe on your socks *exactly* matches the color of your shorts, and the trim on your tank matches the color of the other stripe."

"What can I say? I majored in art."

"Yeah, well, you look like Marlo Thomas."

"Gee, and I was going for Mary Tyler Moore."

"Same difference. And another thing. Don't pull your socks up. Look how everyone's socks are sagging, drooping in a real casual way."

As I step off the treadmill, I look around again. He's right. Almost. "You do realize, Timmy, that there's nothing real about their casualness? Everything is carefully planned."

"It doesn't matter. It looks hot." He bends down and pushes my socks down. "Now so do you." His hand brushes against my crotch as he straightens up.

I freeze and change the subject as I wipe my sweaty hair with a towel. "I'm excited I get to design an editorial feature in The Well. It's an apartment in Hollywood designed by Jason Hunt."

"Oh him! Jason's interiors are very expensive but they don't have real style. His clients only want to show how rich they are. He should simply paper the walls with hundred dollar bills and get it over with." I wonder if Timmy is quoting Leaf. He rushes into a one-breath monolog. "Jason's a forty-five-year-old queen who thinks he's butch because he owns a leather jacket but his wrists are so limp he couldn't fluff a pillow he's the one person who can be too thin he's got tons of money which he spends on boys. . ." at last he pauses not because he's out of air but for dramatic tension, "and he's supposedly hung like swagged drapes."

"You do know everything, don't you?"

"Bet your ass." And he slaps mine. "Let's hit the steam room."

"You go—have fun. I'm just going to take a quick shower."

"We could have fun together."

"Some other time, okay?"

"All right, but I'm going to hold you to that." He smiles. "Or you could hold it against me."

I'm so pumped—and not just my chest and arms—I head back to the magazine after I shower. If I do a good job on my first layout, Larry Stein might give me more features to design. I saw a couple of the layouts he's done so far, and they're rather uninspired.

I spread out David Ellis' transparencies on my tiny light table. Most of the shots are underexposed, and Timmy's right about Jason Hunt's décor: less than stellar. The loft-like apartment is mainly two large rooms stacked one above the other. On the first floor are a living area, a large dining table and an open kitchen. The bedroom at the top of the stairs features a red bathtub with claw legs. The ceilings are quite high, as if the space were once a warehouse.

I decide to stress the verticality. I stack the title and subtitle of the article in five short lines along with the credits over a single column of text in the center of the left-hand page. I put two small pictures on either side of the column; it looks a bit phallic, but it accents the height. With a long white column on the edge of each page, I repeat the vertical thrust, giving the layout a sense of unity. To bring out the best elements of the project, I crop some of pictures so severely I wonder if Ellis will recognize them. I'm pleased with my layout, but it really isn't good décor, and I wonder why Leaf is publishing it.

JANUARY 13, 1977

"Didn't you say you're doing the layout for the apartment Jason Hunt designed?"

I jump. Timmy's tread is so quiet, I didn't hear him enter my office. No wonder his shoes are called *sneakers*. "Yeah, I finished it."

"Leaf wants to see it. She has Jason in her office."

"I gave it to Larry."

"Okay, I'll get it from him." Timmy turns to leave, but looks back to say, "If you want to see what the most self-centered queen in West Hollywood looks like, come to my office in a few minutes and take a peek."

Less than five minutes later, Timmy spots me walking down the hall, gets up from his desk and times it so we're directly in front of Leaf's office when we meet. He positions himself so his back is to her and I have a clear view of the designer.

Jason Hunt is wearing chinos, a blue blazer and penny loafers with no socks. His thick black hair looks a bit greasy—and may be dyed. He must sense someone watching him, because he looks toward the door, then gives me a wide smile with probably two teeth too many.

I follow Timmy as he steps back into his office. "What do you think?" Timmy doesn't wait for my answer. "He certainly is not as handsome as he thinks he is."

"Of course, it's hard to say after such a quick glance, but he looks like he tries too hard," I whisper. "I don't like when older guys try to still look collegiate."

"Absolutely. And that pale skin looks unhealthy, not 'British' like he thinks." Timmy grabs his coffee cup. "They'll be in there gossiping for half an hour. Let's go to the break room, and I'll tell you all about Jason's pathetic little life."

Describing it as a "break room" is generous. The room's main purpose is to hold an enormous copier and a tall gray metal cabinet of office supplies. There's a blue-plastic water cooler and, probably as an afterthought, a small counter with a sink and a miniature refrigerator underneath. A bistro table with two wrought-iron chairs doesn't encourage group gatherings.

After Timmy fills his coffee cup, he wipes the table with a damp paper towel and sits down.

I get a cup of water and join him. "Do you think Jason dyes his hair?"

Timmy raises his eyebrows. "Does Dolly Parton sleep on her back? He also has capped teeth." He leans closer and whispers conspiratorially, "I also think he's had his eyes done."

"Why are you whispering? No one's around."

"You're right. Besides, what does it matter if someone hears?" He gulps his coffee. "Anyhoo, Jason's from Houston, and during high school he worked in a fabric store. Can you image the ribbing he must have gotten from the other kids?"

"I wonder if he was ever beat up. Maybe that's why he needed his teeth capped."

"Possible. So, after high school he worked at a furniture store that had an interior design department. I can just imagine. Texan homes give opulence a bad name." He finishes his coffee in another swig. "Jason, of course, thought he knew everything, and when he was twenty-three he moved to Los Angeles to establish his *own* design firm. Well, he chose the perfect city for his style. It's filled with celebrities who want glitz. And since he's decorated so many of their homes, he's become a bit of a celebrity too. As Leaf once said, 'As a decorator Jason Hunt has more media coverage than talent.' But she keeps publishing him."

"That apartment I did the layout for wasn't opulent. In fact, it looked almost industrial."

"Who's the homeowner?"

"Dirk Garcia."

"Oh, don't you know who he is? He was in *Hot Tamales*—mostly with his shirt off—and some producer saw his shall-we-say 'potential' and signed him for a big blockbuster that will come out this summer. I bet Dirk Garcia doesn't have even a quarter of the money as most of Jason's clients, but Jason probably wanted to get into his pants."

Just then a man in a cashmere jacket with elbow patches walks in carrying a coffee mug as if it's the Holy Grail. He looks like Alfred Hitchcock—way overweight and nearly bald. He has the pinkest skin I've ever seen.

"Hi, Walter," Timmy says. "Have you met Anthony Dimora, Larry Stein's new assistant?"

"Not officially." He extends a hand, and I stand to shake it. "Walter Downey, senior editor, better known as 'The Invisible Man.'"

"Oh, Walter, everyone loves you."

"That's only because I stay quietly in my office, emerging only for the occasional cup of tepid coffee." He fills his cup and heads back out. "Welcome aboard. I guess."

"He seems cynical."

"I heard he used to be funny before he stopped drinking." Timmy takes a box of Fig Newtons out of the cupboard. "Only one! We don't want to ruin all your hard work at the gym."

"What's Jason's own home like?"

"I haven't seen it. *Them*, I should say. He has two, one near Leaf on Stone Canyon Road and another in Palm Springs. I don't know how he can have a home in the desert and not get tanned. Maybe he never goes outside. He's probably a vampire. Anyhoo, I'm sure both of his homes are overdone. He does *everything* to excess. He drives a Ferrari and can buy enough cocaine to feel successful."

"You really don't like him, do you?"

"Well, to be perfectly honest, I'm probably still pissed off at him for something that happened at a midnight screening of *The Rocky Horror Picture Show* last year."

"I love that movie, but what happened?"

"Cole Bruin had never seen it, and—"

"Who's Cole Bruin?"

"Collette and Claret Bruin's only child." Timmy leans closer. "He's going to be *very* rich one day." When I don't say anything, he continues, "So, anyway, I asked him to go to the movie with me, and we're standing in line and Jason Hunt, who's about eight or nine people ahead of us, keeps looking back at us. After he buys his ticket, he comes over, and I think he's just going to say hello, but, no, he bought tickets for us too, so naturally we have to sit with him. And at one point during the movie, I look down and see Jason's hand rubbing Cole's crotch! Cole was supposed to be *my* date, and he ended up going home with Jason, who, I might add, is old enough to be his father."

"It's seems like you should be mad at Cole, not Jason."

"You haven't seen Cole. No one could stay mad at him. At least not for long." He refills his cup. "Come on, we better get back. Madame Editor has probably been pressing the intercom button for ten minutes."

I head to the door, and just when I think Timmy's finally

stopped making passes at me, he caresses my ass.

After Larry shows Leaf the boards for the next issue, I ask him if she had made any comment about my Jason Hunt layout.

"She said and I quote, 'This layout makes this home work.'" He takes his pipe from his breast pocket. "Good going, Anthony."

"I hope you'll give me more features in The Well to design."

"Yes, but you have to stay on top of the departments." Larry fills his pipe. "They may not be as glamorous as the features, but they're vital to the magazine since they're opposite the ads."

"I'll get it all done, Larry. It's those stupid little ads that are the problem, especially since most of them come in right when we're on deadline."

"Well, what if I hire someone part-time to do the ads?"

"That would be wonderful!"

This is the most Larry's said to me since I became his assistant. I wonder if he's uncomfortable with me being gay. I haven't told anyone but I'm not hiding it. At any rate, he needn't worry: I don't go for straight guys, and besides, he's not my type. About five-seven, he's at least thirty pounds overweight. Larry's eyes are tiny and too close together, giving him a mousey look. His beard is turning grey. I guess he's about forty. Married with two kids. Boring!

But he seems like a nice guy.

When I'm leaving for lunch, Leaf gets on the same elevator. She's quite short, probably just an inch or two over five feet. She's a bit top heavy, and four-inch high heels don't help with her balance. Today her hair is in a pageboy and looks a little too professionally applied with a dozen variations of blond. I only get a glimpse of Leaf's eyes behind her oversize glasses, but I think they're a grayish blue. Her lipstick is almost orange.

We've not been introduced so I offer my hand. "I'm Anthony Dimora, the new assistant art director."

Leaf's smile seems forced; then she looks straight ahead.

If she's trying to intimidate me, it doesn't work. "Larry told me you liked my layout for Jason Hunt," I tell her profile. "It's the first one he's let me do, so I'm glad you're pleased."

She turns, her right eyebrow arched. "What did you say your name was?"

"Anthony Dimora."

"And *you* designed the Jason Hunt layout?"

I nod as the elevator stops at the garage level.

"I see." She heads for a silver Cadillac Seville.

Does that mean Larry took credit for my design?

JANUARY 14, 1977

Since it's Friday, everyone in Editorial takes off early, and Timmy and I get to the gym by a quarter to five.

"Leaf asked about you today," he says when we're warming up with stretches. "I didn't think she'd be impressed that you worked at *Motor Trend*, so I told her you designed a fabulous mock-up of the magazine when you applied for the job."

"You knew about that?"

"Oh, sure. Mr. B showed it to me. Leaf wanted to see it, so I got it from his secretary, Maxine."

"Do you know what Leaf said when she saw it?"

"Of course I do! She was impressed. It really *is* beautiful, Anthony. You should have been art director instead of Larry Stein. Hey!" He punches my arm. "You should watch *All About Eve*. That movie will teach you everything you need to know about getting ahead."

"It's one of my favorites. Have you seen *The Women*?"

"Several times. Why?"

"Oh, you remind me a bit of one of the characters."

"Please don't say Joan Crawford! I am not *that* mean. But I'd rather be her than that mouse, Paulette Godard."

"No, Rosalind Russell."

"Sylvia Fowler."

"Or as Joan cracked, 'Mrs. *Prowler*.'"

"'I got that innuendo,'" Timmy says, misquoting a line from the film. "I like Roz in that movie. And I do know all the gossip like she does, don't I?"

I nearly say, *and you're just as quick to spread it*, but decide he might be insulted. I wonder if he shared his juicy tales with someone else before I arrived.

"Hey, see that blond kid at the free weights?"

I look in the mirror. He's tall, slender but muscled, cute but probably underage.

"That's Cole Bruin," Timmy whispers.

"The Bruins' son?"

Timmy nods.

"He looks about fourteen."

"And if that's what you want, that's what he'll be."

"What do you mean?"

"Let's just say he's been around." Timmy makes a rude gesture with his tongue. "Actually, he's sixteen."

I don't say anything at first, my mind doing the math. "Let me see if I've got this right. Last year when you asked him to see *The Rocky Horror Picture Show*, Cole was *fifteen* and he went home with Jason Hunt, who's over forty?"

"That's right. If you take a steam after our work-out, I'll ask Cole to tell you about Leaf and the mouse."

Cole Bruin looks even younger up-close in the steam room. His nipples are tiny pink buds poking out of snow-white skin. His beauty—salient cheekbones, pouty lips, chiseled nose, curly blond hair casually falling forward over denim blue eyes—is a cliché. One worth repeating.

He lies on his back with his hands supporting his head on a white tiled platform stretching along one side of the small room. His has on white gym shorts and white flip-flops. His legs are quite hairy.

I've noticed that Timmy looks good in a tank top, but I'm amazed when I see his bare chest. Its solid but not over-muscled like on a bodybuilder. He must do something to his nipples, because they stick out nearly half an inch. He sees me staring and pinches his left teat. He plops down on the platform opposite Cole, opens his towel and proudly spreads his legs. I'm tempted to say *I've sucked bigger*, but he's not someone I want mad at me.

The only place for me to sit is next to Timmy. I keep my towel closed.

Timmy makes the introductions. Cole, staring at the dripping ceiling, barely turns his head in acknowledgement. He doesn't seem interested that I work in the art department. He doesn't seem interested in the magazine at all.

"Anthony just did a layout for one of Jason Hunt's projects," Timmy says. "And I said you'd tell him about 'the mouse.'"

"You love that story, don't you?" Cole yawns.

"It's funny on so many levels."

"So what happened?" I ask.

"Well, I was over at Jason's—"

"He was in Jason's bed," Timmy interjects.

"Do you want to tell the story?" Cole abruptly sits up.

Timmy feigns closing a zipper across his lips.

"So I was in Jason's *bed*, and just as he unzipped my jeans, the telephone rang. I suggested he not answer it, but he thought it might be important. I went to the bathroom, but when I heard Jason say, 'Are you sure it's dead?' I stuck my head out. He held the phone away from his ear, and I could hear a woman on the other end shouting. Finally Jason said, 'Okay! Okay! I'll be right over.'

"The woman was Leaf Wyks, and her cat had dragged a dead mouse into her bedroom, and she expected Jason to run over and get rid of it. I couldn't believe Jason would actually consider doing it, especially with me there half naked, but he said Leaf was too important, that she could wreck his career if she wanted to. I said I could wreck his *life* by telling the police he seduced an underage boy, but he just gave me a funny look—"

"Because he knew who had done the seducing," Timmy says out of the side of his mouth.

Cole glares at him. "Jason said he'd only be gone for fifteen minutes, because Leaf lives just up the hill from him, but I told him I might not hang around waiting, so he offered me some coke. Which is what I really wanted in the first place."

There's only one dim light bulb in the room, and with all the steam in the air, I hope my face doesn't reveal how shocked I am. A fifteen-year-old boy in bed with a forty-plus-year-old man who offers him coke. I guess I'm not in Michigan anymore.

"Jason didn't return for over an hour," Cole continues, "and I'd fallen asleep, but he was all wound up and insisted on telling me every detail."

Timmy suddenly covers his crotch with his towel, but the gesture is just a ruse, because at the same time he deftly moves his left hand behind me and rubs my back. Looking down at his feet, he glides his fingers inside my towel, massaging my ass just above the crack.

Cole winks at me. "Jason said Leaf was in a faded blue terrycloth robe with ragged cuffs, but I told him to spare me the costumes and set decoration. She pushed him into her bedroom, and there was the mouse, not on the floor, but right in the center of her bed where her cat had abandoned it."

Timmy mutters, "I bet that's not the only thing that's been abandoned on that bed."

This time Cole smiles. "So Leaf handed Jason some paper

towels and a plastic grocery bag, and he scooped up the poor dead thing and put it in the trash out by the carport. When he came back, she had poured two glasses of wine. Jason thought about his career and not about the perfect ass lying in his bed"—Cole pointed at himself—"and sat down."

I'm fascinated but also distracted. I think about repositioning myself so that Timmy doesn't get the wrong idea, but what he's doing feels too good.

"By the second glass Leaf had stopped adjusting her robe every time it slipped open," Cole says. "I'm sure you've noticed that for a tiny woman she's got big knockers, and she sat there letting more and more of her cantaloupes pop out."

I dare to speak. "But didn't she know Jason was gay?"

"Oh, she knew. But he said they had made it before."

Timmy pinches my butt. "How do you think he got the first home he designed published in the magazine? What was it Jason told you, Cole?"

"'If you want to get *on* the cover, you have to get *under* the covers.'"

"Time to hit the showers." When Timmy stands up, his towel sticks out enough to let us know he's halfway to a woody.

"I don't shower at the gym," Cole says. "You never know what you can catch." Before Timmy can say something racy, he adds, "Like athlete's foot." In the locker room, he says, "I took the bus here—it took nearly an hour—so, I wonder, Anthony, would you mind giving me a ride home?"

"Do you mind waiting while I take a quick shower?"

Cole leans forward and sniffs. "I think you smell fine just the way you are."

"I have just four words for you," Timmy tells me before heading to the showers. "*Rocky Horror Picture Show.*"

In my Toyota pickup, Cole gives me an address in Beverly Hills.

"I thought you lived in Pasadena."

"My mom's *from* there, and Granny still lives there, but we're in the boring flats of Beverly Hills. We also have a house on the ocean in Malibu. Maybe you'd like to drive out there one day."

"Sure." I can't decide if he's hitting on me. I don't care that he's obviously very sexually experienced, he's still a kid—and dangerous. "You remind me of a satyr."

"What exactly is that?"

"A mythical deity with the body of a man and the legs of a goat. He's always pictured with very hairy legs."

"Well, I certainly have hairy legs." He's still in his shorts but put on a hooded sweatshirt before we left the gym.

I give him a quick glance. "He's also very randy."

"That's sort of an old-fashioned word. But accurate in my case. Are *you* old-fashioned?"

"In some ways."

"What's this satyr's face like—man or goat?"

"Man but often shown with little goat horns."

Cole feels under his thick blond hair. "Yeah, I think they're starting to spout." He twists his body so he's facing me. "Do you like satyrs?"

"They're very sexy." I deliberately shift the topic. "When you were a little kid, what was your favorite bedtime story?"

"*Peter Pan*. I wanted to be Peter Pan. I loved hearing about Never-Never Land and the Lost Boys. But unlike Peter, I *wanted* to be captured by the pirates."

"I bet you did."

"My mom would get all dressed up to go to the ballet or a party, just like Mrs. Darling, and as soon as she had kissed me good-night and gone downstairs, I'd get out of bed and open the window, hoping Peter would fly in and take me away."

"And are you still hoping someone will take you away?"

"In a turquoise Toyota pickup."

"Very funny."

"When I was about six, I insisted on a Peter Pan costume for Halloween, and our cook spent hours sewing me an all-green outfit. And instead of being grateful and saying thank you, I pouted and said, 'Where's my shadow?'"

"Did she make you a shadow?"

"Of course. I always get what I want."

"Sometimes that's not a good thing."

He turns away and stares out the windshield. When I'm on his street, Canon Drive, he says, "When I was about five, my parents took me to a local production of *Peter Pan*, and I was horrified that Peter was played by a girl. I cried all the way home, even though Mom assured me it was just a play with actors and that Peter was a boy, just like me. So I asked, 'Does Peter have a penis?' and Dad said, 'Just like you and I do.' I don't know if Mom meant for me to hear, but she whispered to my father, 'Let's hope *not* just like yours, Tinkerbell.'" He continues to stare straight ahead, and quietly says, "But I guess I did take after Dad, cause it's really small."

I stop in front of his house. A tall security gate blocks the driveway.

"Pull up," Cole says, "and I'll give you the code to punch in."

"Cole, why did you tell me this?"

"So you can get past the gate."

"No. Why did you tell me you have a small penis?"

"I don't want you to be disappointed."

I put my hand on his arm. "You're adorable. And not just physically. Everything about you." I take a deep breath. "But nothing's going to happen between us. I cannot have sex with a sixteen-year-old boy. And, I'm sorry, but you are still a boy."

"Oh, do you like older men, like I do?"

"No, I don't. Actually I find you very appealing, but it's too dangerous. For me."

"But you don't have to worry about that, Anthony. I've been with a lot—I've been with other guys and I'd never get them in trouble. *Never*."

"I can't, Cole."

"Okay." His eyes are moist. "But will you still come out to Malibu with me one day?"

JANUARY 19, 1977

I'm not invited to Picture Selection. I don't exactly know what goes on at this meeting, but the production room is right across the hall from my office, so I'll soon find out. Ivory Cooke, the managing editor, is already there, blowing cigarette smoke toward the ceiling. Larry's stuffing his pipe. They're waiting for Leaf.

Timmy sticks his head in the room. "She'll be here in a minute." Then he walks into my office and whispers, "She's in the ladies. It'll take her twenty minutes to pull up her pantyhose."

He pulls the guest chair around the drawing table so he's sitting beside me. He opens a blue folder and flips through a couple a sheets. "Pretend I'm showing you something important so we can watch them play."

I pick up a pencil and one of his papers.

"Look at her," he says quietly, nodding toward Ivory. "I'll bet you anything she spends an hour in front of her mirror every morning trying to make herself *not* look forty. Which she's not. Only thirty-eight. But she *looks* forty-five. And have you ever seen such tight lips? You'd think with all she's been through, she'd be a bit more relaxed."

"What's she been through?"

"Let's see." He counts on his fingers. "Transcendental meditation, rebirthing, Rolfing and a divorce. And she's still lost."

"What are they going to do at this meeting?"

"Well, see that stack of plastic folders? Each one contains the photography that was taken of a residence. They have to sort through all the shots and pick out which ones to use in the next issue. It can take *hours*. Leaf hates it."

Just then Leaf enters the production room smoking a cigarette. "Shall we begin?"

Larry picks up the top plastic folder and dumps the transparencies for the first residence on the three-foot by two-foot light table.

"Where's your assistant?" Leaf asks Larry. "Tell him to get in here and help us sort these out."

I'm already on my feet by the time Larry approaches my office. Behind my back, I wave bye-bye to Timmy.

Many of the shots are duplicates, just different exposures. We each take a few transparencies and attempt to put them in order. Exteriors are placed on the far left of the light table, followed by entrance hall, living room, dining room, bedrooms and any other rooms, such as dens or baths.

"Here's a living room," Leaf says, tossing a picture in the general direction.

We huddle and bump into each other, and Ivory knocks over the ashtray. Twice.

Once the duplicates are removed, seventeen shots remain.

Leaf stands at the center of the light box with Ivory and Larry on each side. I'm behind them.

Leaf asks, "Which shot of the living room do you think we should use?"

No one answers.

Ivory opens her mouth but only to blow smoke.

I wonder why Leaf asks for opinions. Doesn't she know which shots are best? But since she's asked, why don't Larry or Ivory respond?

After a full half minute of silence, I reach my arm through and point. "I think we should use this one. It shows the view and lets the reader see that the living room is open to the outside. All the other shots show that ugly rug."

"I'll buy that," Leaf says.

We go on to other rooms, other homes. Leaf continues to ask for comments but Larry and Ivory rarely make a suggestion. But I do. And Leaf agrees with almost all of my choices. Two hours later, when we're looking at the transparencies of the last house, Leaf asks, "What do you think, Anthony?"

Larry glares at me.

Ivory smokes.

JANUARY 20, 1977

The day after Picture Selection, Ivory Cooke asks me to lunch. No place fancy, just the small café on the ground level. The magazine's on the eighth floor, and we ride down the elevator in silence. We arrive exactly at noon, before all the tables are taken.

"I don't like to eat at the counter." She walks to a table in the far corner and sits so she looks out into the room. Although I'm facing the back wall, there's floor-to-ceiling glass beside us, so at least I can see outside.

It rarely gets very cold in Los Angeles, even in January, but Ivory's wearing a plaid tweed skirt and a bulky white sweater over a pale blue jersey blouse. Her hair, pulled back in a ponytail, was probably once brown, but now it's streaked a half-dozen shades of blond; but I can still see traces of gray.

A thin young waiter flits over to our table and places a tall glass of iced tea in front of Ivory. "What would *you* like to drink, sir?"

"Lemonade."

Ivory stirs two packets of Sweet'n Low into her tea and lights a cigarette while I scan the menu. When the waiter returns with my drink, Ivory says, "I'll have the chopped salad, Billy."

"With no onions and extra tomatoes?"

"Thanks." Ivory blows smoke toward the sealed window.

I order a French dip sandwich. Billy refills Ivory's iced tea. Since Ivory invited me to lunch, I expect her to lead the conversation, but she seems content to add two more packets of fake sugar. So I ask, "How long have you been at the magazine?"

"A little over six years. Longer than Leaf. Taylor Allen, the previous editor, hired me."

I wonder if she wants Leaf's job. "Is it true," I ask, "that *Inside* started out as a black-and-white journal?"

"That's right. In the twenties. I have an original issue from back then somewhere in my office." She lights another cigarette. I hope she doesn't plan on smoking while we're eating. "It wasn't until the Bruins bought the magazine in the early fifties that color was added. It used to be just regional, showing only California homes, but Taylor started publishing homes on the East Coast and Chicago."

I remember Timmy saying he thought Ivory had a fake accent. It does seem to come and go, so I ask her where she's from.

"Connecticut."

She crushes her cigarette in the ashtray just as Billy brings our food. Ivory spends so much time mixing together the neatly arranged rows of her chopped salad that I finish half of my sandwich before she takes her first bite.

Still wondering why she asked me to lunch, I pose another question. "Did Leaf make a lot of improvements to the magazine?"

"It depends what you think is an improvement." Her tone is ice. "Leaf said the magazine needed punch. Taylor was a sweet man, but unfortunately, his taste tended to the ornate. I thought Leaf would publish more contemporary homes, but her idea of punch was Hollywood." Maybe it's the light from the window, but her right eye seems a darker brown than the left one. "Leaf seems fascinated with celebrities. So starting with the November/December 1975 issue, she introduced a new series: "At Home with . . ." The first celebrity was Dinah Shore. Believe it or not, the issue sold out on newsstands."

"That must have been gratifying."

She pierces two diced tomatoes with her fork. As she slowly chews the tomatoes, her eyes lock on mine as if accusing me of taking the wrong side. "Six months later, when America celebrated the bicentennial, Leaf published the home of Senator and Mrs. Edward Kennedy. We practically doubled our subscribers."

"And yet you don't seemed pleased."

"The interiors were less than stellar. I wonder if Leaf would have published the home if the owners weren't famous."

"Have you always been interested in interior design?"

"I've *never* been interested in interior design."

I think she smiles. It's hard to tell. I switch topics. "So Leaf selects all the homes that are published in the magazine?"

"Yes."

"She never asks anyone for their input?"

"No."

"Not even Claret Bruin?"

"Especially *not* Claret Bruin."

Does that mean Mr. Bruin has no taste or that he and Leaf don't get along? I want to ask more questions but don't want to come across as too inquisitive. I finish my sandwich.

Ivory pulls her sweater tight across her flat chest. "It's always so cold in here."

"Did you work for another magazine before *Inside*?"

"I was at *Los Angeles* for about eight years."

Billy once again refills Ivory's iced tea but doesn't offer me more lemonade.

"You can take this." She pushes away her plate even though

she's not eaten even a quarter of her salad. I understand why she's so frightfully thin.

Billy doesn't ask if we want coffee or dessert, just deposits a small leather folder holding the bill. I offer to split it with her, but Ivory reaches in her purse and slips a credit card in the folder without even glancing at the total. When I thank her, she says, "It's on the magazine."

She applies a swatch of vermillion lipstick to her narrow lips. Her two front teeth are capped, and she looks in her compact mirror to make sure they don't have a lipstick smear.

She signs the credit card slip and stands up.

Lunch is over. I still have no idea why she invited me.

JANUARY 21, 1977

Except for Timmy, the editorial staff isn't very friendly. Art and Antiques editor Tom Hampton usually works with his door closed. Articles editor Jane Covington seems to be out of the office or on the phone most of the day. Eating with Ivory was a bizarre experience, but nevertheless, I decide to ask senior editor Walter Downey to lunch. He seems surprised, as if no one on staff had ever invited him to anything, then suggests we go to Molly Malone's, an Irish pub a few blocks away.

"I come here once in a while to test myself," Walter says as he selects a small wooden table pushed against a used-brick wall.

"What do you mean?"

"I'm an alcoholic. Four years, three months, two days without a drink."

"I don't understand why you'd put yourself through this."

"Most of my life is boring. Same routine everyday. Get up, go to work, edit copy, go home, have dinner and watch television. Naturally I don't keep liquor at home, and I rarely go out, so there's not much chance of being offered a drink. But when I come here it's like riding a Ferris wheel. Will I go round and round safely or will I get stuck at the top and come crashing down?"

"Well, congratulations on four-plus sober years."

"Thanks. As a kid, I was terrified of the Ferris wheel. Always afraid I'd get stuck on top and that a big storm would come and shake the car."

"Where was this?"

"Nebraska."

"I thought the Ferris wheel was rather tame," I say. "I loved the rollercoaster. I loved that feeling of zero gravity as we dove toward the ground. But my favorite moment was right before, at the summit, where we seemed to stand still for a moment, filled with terror and anticipation of the drop."

"Yes, the apprehension is often more exciting than the event. Coming to Molly Malone's and being tempted is much more exhilarating than actually having a martini."

A waitress in a green apron asks for our drinks order. Walter pauses, smiles at me, and says, "Iced tea." I have cranberry juice.

When I first met Walter, I thought he looked like Alfred Hitchcock. They both are bald with just a fringe of white hair above the ears; they share a stomach-prominent profile; but Walter is more attractive. He has only one double chin, without the sagging jowls and neck of the film director. Although Walter seems determined to give off an air of disenchanted boredom, his blue eyes twinkle mischievously.

"You described your work as routine. Don't you like editing copy?"

"It gets rather repetitive. The one aspect of my job I do enjoy is coming up with titles for the features. Each one has to be unique. The space you gave me for the Jason Hunt design was a nice challenge. I saw how you stacked the title and subtitle in five short lines. At first I wondered why you had done that, then I realized it was to stress the verticality of the loft."

"Thanks for noticing. What title did you come up with?"

"My first thought was 'The High and the Flighty,' since Mr.

Hunt can be rather frivolous, but Leaf would never have approved, and it really isn't the tone of the magazine. I settled on 'A Loft in the Big City: Open Space for a Rising Young Star.'"

"Oh, I like the play of 'a loft' and 'aloft.'"

"Well, now I have to thank you for noticing."

By the time the waitress brings our drinks and we order sandwiches, the tiny restaurant is filled. With all the hard surfaces and nothing soft to absorb sound, everyone talks a bit loud to be heard—which only adds to the noise.

"How did you know I designed the Jason Hunt feature?"

"Timmy told me."

"He seems to know everything."

"And what he doesn't know, he'll find out." Walter lights a cigarette. "You don't smoke?" I shake my head. "Good for you. Smoking is the only vice I have left."

The waitress seems frazzled as she refills Walter's drink. I wish I liked iced tea with its endless refills.

"I bought *House & Garden* and *House Beautiful* this weekend," I say, "and they're quite different from *Inside*. They seem more like how-to magazines."

"Yes, *Inside* is singular among the shelter magazines."

"I've never heard that term: *shelter magazines*. It's almost clinical. I'd think they'd be called 'home magazines.'"

"Admen jargon." Walter shrugs. "*Inside* isn't much competition to *House & Garden* and *House Beautiful*. They have hundreds of thousands more readers than we do. But, as I say, *Inside* is unique. Leaf likes to say, 'We report not promote.' What she means is we let the interiors speak for themselves. The other magazines have articles on the latest color. They promote new trends. *Inside* doesn't do that."

"Was *Inside* always like that?"

"To a certain extent. But before Leaf, the magazine didn't present entire homes. She started that with Burton Fisher."

I look puzzled, and Walter adds, "He's probably the best interior designer in San Francisco. The story goes that just after Leaf became editor, a living room Burton Fisher had designed was published in *House & Garden*, and she called him to say how beautiful it was. Well, according to Leaf, he was furious! He said it wasn't the room he designed, that he had created a simple room with minimal but oversized furniture. But the *House & Garden* editors had put a quilt on the banquette, added colorful pillows and—quote—*more flowers than a funeral parlor*—unquote. When Leaf asked if she could publish one of the other rooms, Burton said they already photographed the entire residence and Mary Jane Pool—the editor of *House & Garden*—said they'd show the bedrooms in the winter bedroom issue, the bathroom in the bath issue, the kitchen in the kitchen issue—you get the idea. Burton said by the time they showed the whole house, it would be out of style.

"And that's where you have to hand it to Leaf. She's quick. She said his work would never be out of style; his interiors were timeless, but if he had given *her* that residence, she would have published the entire house in one issue—given it ten pages *and* the cover. So of course, Burton promised his next project to *Inside*."

Lunch arrives, and Walter digs into his Rueben sandwich as if he hadn't eaten in days. Unlike Timmy, he waits until he's finished chewing before speaking again.

"So, to complete the story: Right after her conversation with Burton, Leaf announced to the staff that as soon as possible, we'd show complete homes—or at least living room, dining room and bedroom—in each issue. She also said we were no longer to use the word 'decorators.' From now on, they were 'interior designers.' When *decorators* heard about this and saw the amount of coverage Leaf was devoting to a single residence, they begged her to publish their projects. Of course, *In-*

side doesn't have even *half* the subscribers as the other shelters, but we are starting to get recognition."

"What did Leaf do before she was editor of the magazine?"

"She and her husband had a small publishing house. All the authors they published were unknown. They remained so."

"Leaf is married?"

"Was. I should have said 'then-husband' or 'husband at the time.' I'd have caught the mistake if I'd seen it written. Anyway, they divorced and folded the publishing house. I'm not certain in what order. Leaf doesn't really speak about her past. Makes you wonder if there's not something she's trying to keep secret."

MARCH 11, 1977

During picture selection for the next issue, Leaf wants to include, in a feature of a New York apartment, a photograph of a screening room, especially since the homeowner is a vice president at 20th-Century-Fox, but Larry feels the photo won't work since the large screen is blaring white.

I ask if I can do the layout for the apartment, and I not only use the questionable photo but make it a two-page spread, stripping in a black-and-white movie still onto the screen so it appears as if it had been projected.

I wonder if anyone will notice the film is *All About Eve*.

MARCH 18, 1977

Walter invites me back to Molly Malone's the day *after* St. Patrick's. "Nobody will be there," he says. And he's right.

I find out Timmy, for once, has the wrong information: Walter is not divorced. He and his wife are separated, and by quite a distance. For nearly six years, she has lived in Paris with their sixteen-year-old daughter, while their fourteen-year-old son lives with Walter in Westwood.

"I feel sorry for our children growing up apart, but I think Michelle—my wife—and I would have murdered each other if we'd stayed together."

"Do you ever see your daughter?"

"Philip—my son—and I get to France about once a year." Walter bends the paper wrapper of a straw into an accordion. "Michelle vowed to never return to America."

"Did something terrible happen to her here?"

"My alcoholism happened."

"And even though you've been sober for more than four years, she won't consider coming back, even for a visit?"

"She likes being with 'her people,' and I'm sure she has a French lover."

"How does your son take all this?"

"I imagine Philip hates me." Walter tosses the mutilated

straw wrapper in the ashtray. "It's hard to tell, since he lives in his own little world."

"If I'm doing the math correctly, it took you more than a year after your wife left for you to stop drinking. May I ask what made you quit?"

"Philip threatened to move to Paris. Talk about a sobering effect. I dropped him off at my mother's and checked myself into a clinic."

I don't know what to say—express congratulations or condolences—but fortunately the waitress comes to take our order.

"Timmy told me to ask you about Taylor Allen's death."

Walter raises his eyebrows. "How did that come up?"

"When we were working out at the gym, I told Timmy about this great *film noir* I'd seen on the Z Channel, *The Big Clock*."

"Oh, that is a good one. Ray Milland and Charles Laughton."

"So when I told Timmy it was about a murder that took place at a magazine, he said to ask you about *Inside*'s former editor."

"Did you ever see another Ray Milland movie that also takes place at a magazine, *Lady in the Dark*?"

"With Ginger Rogers as the editor. I love that movie, especially the dream sequences."

"Remember the flamboyant fashion photographer who swoons when the male movie star arrives for a photo shoot?"

"How could anyone miss him?"

"That character could have been played by Taylor Allen. When he glided through the halls, you had to look to make sure he wasn't on skates."

"Did he wear outrageous outfits?"

"Oh no. He always wore tailored suits. Almost Edwardian with a wasp waist."

With hardly anyone in the restaurant, our meals come out fast and steaming. We eat in silence for a while, then I ask, "So how did Taylor die?"

"Ah, that's the mystery." Walter takes a bite of his Irish stew, leaving me in suspense. Then he puts down his fork and folds his hands. "It was two years ago, during the Christmas holidays. When Taylor didn't show up at a party, the hostess didn't think too much about it because he could be a real prima donna. But when Taylor didn't answer his phone all weekend, she got worried and roused Taylor's landlord. They found Taylor in a fetal position on the floor of his bedroom, clutching a small piece of paper. It said, 'Because I can't forget.' By the bed, they found a glass with a trace of framboise—raspberry liqueur— and poison. The liqueur bottle hadn't been laced.

"We were all questioned, but especially Leaf. It turned out she may have been one of the last to see him alive. She said Taylor invited her to his place on Christmas Eve to drink Champagne he'd received from decorators. She said they got drunk on Dom Pérignon, and he told her the framboise was from a 'special friend,' who was coming over on Christmas to open the bottle."

"Why'd he invite Leaf? Were they friends?"

"I don't think either one of them had real friends, so they understood each other." Walter dips a piece of bread into his stew. "And Leaf was the only one at the magazine who didn't make fun of Taylor or talk behind his back. She just let him be who he was, and I think he was grateful. Of course, she wanted his job."

"What was Leaf's position at the magazine at that time?"

"Articles editor."

"And she became editor after Taylor Allen's death?"

"Yes, to everyone's surprise. Ivory, as managing editor, expected she'd be selected. But she was no match for Leaf."

"What do you mean?"

"Leaf took the last issue Taylor had edited and drew a big X across the cover in an orange grease pencil. Then she went through the rest of the magazine marking it up with more Xes. By the time she was finished, the magazine was one big X. Then she marched into Claret's office and threw it on his desk."

"And he made her editor because of that?"

"It depends on whom you believe. Maxine, Claret's secretary, said that Leaf was in his office for at least twenty minutes with the door closed. It was her feeling that Leaf got the job because she had sex with Claret. But you have to consider the source. Maxine got her job because *she* slept with Claret. And probably still does."

The waitress clears our empty plates and Walter orders dessert. "Bread-and-Butter Pudding please. If I can't drink, at least I can have sugar."

I look at the menu and just have to ask. "What's Spotted Dick?"

"Not what you think," Walter says. "It's not even Irish."

"Custard with currants." The waitress' tone indicates she's been asked too many times.

"I'll have Baileys Mousse Pie."

After she leaves, Walter says, "All that conjecture about how Leaf got to be editor is fun and gossipy, but the more interesting story is Taylor Allen's death. The police found no evidence of anyone visiting Taylor on Christmas and concluded he was despondent because his lover hadn't returned, so he committed suicide by lacing the lover's liqueur with poison." Walter shakes a finger at me. "But I think Taylor was murdered."

MARCH 21, 1977

I stand behind him as Timmy, on his back, presses one hundred and twenty pounds. After the third rep, he rubs my calf. "Add ten more pounds to each side, okay?" He does three more reps. "What'd you do Saturday night?"

"Watched the final episode of *Mary Tyler Moore*."

"Geez, Anthony! You didn't go out?"

"I didn't feel like it. What did you do?"

"Went to the baths."

"Which one?"

"To me—and countless other men—there's only one gay bathhouse: 8709."

"I heard they have a strict admittance policy, that they make certain guys lift up their shirts to make sure they're not fat. And if you're not white, they ask for three picture IDs."

"I wouldn't know. All I know is every Saturday night there's a line around the block of hot men with mustaches."

"I also heard they only let in guys under thirty. I'm sure I'd be turned away."

"You'd have no trouble getting in. You look twenty-five." Timmy stands up and pinches my nipple. "And your body's gotten in great shape." He nods toward the bench. "Your turn."

I remove thirty pounds from the bar before lying down. Timmy deliberately stands with a leg on either side of my head. He's not wearing a jockstrap and knows perfectly well where I'm looking.

"It's not that I get hard so quickly," he says, "it's that I'm hardly ever soft."

After I do three reps, I raise my head and look around. "Is there one man here you wouldn't have sex with?"

Timmy scans the gym. "The short guy in the green t-shirt."

"*One* man out of fourteen."

"Actually, it's fourteen out of fourteen. I blew Shorty in the steam room a couple of weeks ago. Pencil prick."

Three more reps. "I wonder what a psychiatrist would think of your obsession with cock."

"He'd probably unzip his pants."

I finish the last three reps. "I wanted to be a psychiatrist but didn't want to go to med school. At the time, I didn't know you could be a psychologist without a getting a medical degree."

Timmy adds more weight to the bar.

"I don't know if I can lift that."

"Sure you can. It's only ten more pounds. You want to get in 8709, don't you?"

I look up Timmy's shorts for inspiration and press the weight.

"So did you take any psych courses?"

"Intro 101."

Timmy has to help me lift the last repetition. "That's good." He waves his hand, signaling me to move over so he can sit on the bench. "So since you've studied a bit of psychology, maybe you could give me some pointers on Leaf. Most of the time, I know how to deal with her, but sometimes it's as if she's gotten up on the wrong side of the bed and finds fault with everything I do."

"Like today?"

"Yeah, how'd you know?"

"Is she usually more difficult on Mondays and Fridays?"

"I've never thought about that. Maybe." He stands. "Come on, let's do some leg stretches to cool down."

We put our towels on top of two mats and lie on our sides facing each other.

"Is Leaf involved with anyone?"

"Not that I know of, and believe me, I'd know."

As we do leg lifts, I see in the mirror that several men, including Shorty, are watching Timmy. I'm sure from their angle, he's giving them quite a show.

"A lot of psychiatry is observation," I say. "Maybe Leaf is lonely. She can be out of sorts on Monday because she's angry she was alone all weekend and on Friday because another lonely weekend looms ahead."

"She gets invited *everywhere*. She could go out every night of the week if she wanted."

"Come on, Timmy. Surely you know you can feel lonely in a crowd."

He lies flat and begins slicing his legs like scissors. A couple of guys don't even pretend to work out: They simply stare. Timmy looks in the mirror and, satisfied enough men are watching him, abruptly sits up.

"I think things are going to change for Leaf pretty soon. Mr. Bruin hired a press agent to get some publicity for the magazine. They had a meeting in Leaf's office, and the PR guy—Jake White—said you couldn't promote a magazine. People aren't interested in *things*. But people *are* interested in other people. He said the way to promote the magazine was to promote Leaf. He's said the first thing to do was change her title from 'editor' to 'editor-in-chief.' Leaf's going to be a celebrity."

APRIL 4, 1977

I don't realize I'm pouting until Timmy stops at my office door on his way to the copier. "Why so glum?"

"I asked Larry if I could be there when Leaf reviews the layouts for the next issue, and he said 'no.'"

"Why do you want to be there?"

"Well, I did four of the thirteen features and would like to hear her comments." I sound like a little boy whining because he's not allowed to stay up past his bedtime. "Also, during Picture Selection, when Leaf saw the photography of an apartment Geraldo Cortez designed, she didn't think the shots were good enough. Larry agreed and it was dropped from the issue. But I liked the interiors and suggested I take a crack at a layout before she killed the feature. I want to see her reaction to it."

"Oh, can I see the layout?"

I take several transparencies out of a small envelope. "The problem is David Elliot's photographs." I hand Timmy a shot of the living room. "As I said, I like the interiors, especially the sensuous curves of the low white leather banquettes against the black lacquered floor."

"'Sensuous' is good."

I ignore his leer and present the opening two-page spread of my layout. "See how I cropped out the ceiling and half of the floor, making the shot strongly horizontal?" I flip to the next spread. "Then, by using extra white space at the top and bottom of each page, I've created wide bands that complement the long banquettes and give the layout continuity."

"Looks good, Anthony. Don't worry about the meeting. Just stay by your phone, and when I buzz you, walk down the hall toward Leaf's office with this layout." Then Timmy picks up his papers and twirls toward the Xerox room.

I do as he suggests, and at 3:15—forty-five minutes after the meeting is suppose to begin—my phone buzzes. I grab the Cortez layout and hurry down the corridor. Just as I reach her office, Leaf looks up and says, "Come in, Anthony. We're about to begin."

Larry, sitting opposite her, frowns. I sit in the only other chair.

Larry hands her the first layout.

She flips through the boards then turns back to the second spread. "What if you put the dining room picture here and make it larger?"

Larry nods and gives her the next feature.

She looks through it twice. "I understand what you're doing in this layout, but I think it would be more logical if we switched these two photos, don't you?"

"Okay."

She finds other faults with the next four layouts. Then Larry hands her one of mine. I don't expect him to say I designed it, and he doesn't.

"This is good," Leaf says. "I like how one page flows into the next."

Larry scowls at me, so I softly say, "Thank you."

Leaf smiles.

She approves the other three layouts I designed then Larry presents the art feature.

Leaf shuffles through the pages. She looks at me. I sit with my hands folded over my lap. I hope she realizes I didn't design the layout. She turns to Larry. "What is the subject of this feature?"

"Posters from the turn of the century."

"And what is the most prominent characteristic of posters?"

Larry coughs. "Well, they usually have a single subject matter and—"

"They're BIG, Larry. Posters are BIG. Wouldn't you agree?"

"Yes," he mutters into his beard.

"Then why have you shown them so small? This one looks like a postage stamp! I suggest you talk with Tom and drop two or three posters so you'll have room to make the rest BIG! Do you think you can handle that?"

Larry nods.

Leaf turns to me. "Do you have something you want to show me?"

I pick up the Geraldo Cortez layout leaning against my chair.

She spreads it across her desk. "That's a lot of white space, Anthony. But it makes the interiors look more interesting than they are. We'll publish it in the next issue."

Leaf reaches for her cigarettes and a lighter. A sure sign we are dismissed.

APRIL 9, 1977

Saturday I have a date with a man I met at the gym, but when he calls and cancels an hour before we're to meet, I decide to take my chances at the 8709 bathhouse. I obviously arrive too early, because there's no waiting line.

As I approach the payment window, panic nearly overwhelms me. It's the exact same hollowness in my stomach that I felt as a child on the school playground, terrified not that I would be the last selected for one of the softball teams but that I wouldn't be chosen *at all*. The bath attendant doesn't smile, but he doesn't turn me away for being too old or ask me to lift my shirt to see if I'm overweight. He simply makes me sign a membership card, takes my money, hands me a white towel and pushes a buzzer to let me inside the adult playground.

It's so dark I stand perfectly still until my eyes adjust and I can find my way to the lockers. I pass the showers, where one muscled man casually soaps himself as if he's unaware he has an erection. Several guys soak in a large whirlpool. The sauna is cramped. The steam room is too foggy to see anyone; maybe that's the point.

Most of the men have white towels around their waists, but one guy has on a black jockstrap, another ripped jeans and a third man, obviously high on some drug, dances down the halls naked. I tour the entire facility before sitting down on a black leather sofa in front of a ceiling-mounted television showing porn.

A thin man with long straight red hair and a droopy mustache flops down beside me. "So what do you think?"

"About what?"

"This place." He waves his hands to include the entire space. "I saw you come in. I can always tell first-timers. They don't know where anything is, and they move around as if they're walking on eggshells."

Am I that obvious?

"So?" He waves his hands again.

"Oh, I didn't think you really wanted an answer. I thought you were just interested in letting me know how perceptive you are."

"Touché. But now I *am* interested in what you think of this place."

"It's cleaner than I imagined it would be, and I like the effort that went into creating different areas, like the jail and the maze. But most of the men seem more interested in posing and being admired than having fun."

"Well, it's early yet. No one wants to come too soon." His smile reveals yellow smoker's teeth. "As for me, I find it too confining. Almost claustrophobic."

"But it takes up nearly the entire block!"

"I prefer the great outdoors. Griffith Park." He crosses his legs. His toes are very long. "You ever been there?"

"Just to the Hollywood Bowl."

"God, you *are* naïve! I meant the trails. I love driving around the curves in my convertible, seeing a hot guy leaning against a tree, and then wandering off with him into the bushes. You ought to try it." He gives detailed directions on how to find the gay cruising spots. "But, unfortunately, the park isn't open at night."

"Were you there today?"

"Oh sure. For three hours. And I'll probably be there tomorrow, too." He put his hand on my leg and slides it under my towel. "You're cute."

"I don't want to be cute." I stand. "I think I'll get lost in the maze."

Only a few naked red bulbs light the maze. Strategically placed wall mirrors not only make the space appear bigger but complicate the labyrinth, suggesting false openings where there are none. I pursue a man with a dark mustache through the right-angle turns, and it isn't until I smack into him that I realize it's my reflection.

After an hour of roaming the halls and exploring the various playrooms, I'm bored. I hear guys moaning, groaning, slapping and whispering behind the doors to the cubicle-sized rooms, but so far the only men who have shown interest in me don't arouse me.

I enter a large room with only one red bulb hanging from the ceiling. At one end there are two tiered platforms, as in the steam room at the gym. It's too dark to see more than shadows, but the slurping sounds like feeding time on a farm.

A circular mattress fills the center of the room. Entwined shadows. And a fetid smell. I back against the wall.

I've been to other baths before and had good times, but it was a mistake to come tonight. I'm still too angry about being stood up by the guy from the gym, even if he was practically a stranger. I cross my arms, lean my head back and shut my eyes.

For what seems a long while, I'm lost in the music and don't even look down when someone removes my towel and swallows my penis. Maybe it's best not to know what he looks like; it could be the redhead with the yellow teeth and long bony toes. Whoever it is, he has a wonderful mouth. I never want him to stop.

It isn't until the man stands up that I recognize him.

"Now we can be sisters," Timmy whispers in my ear.

MAY 3, 1977

"**W**hat're you doing?"

I jump, not expecting anyone else to be at the magazine at seven-thirty in the morning. Or to find me in Leaf's office.

"Oh, hi, Timmy. You startled me. I'm just putting a birthday present on Leaf's desk."

"She said she didn't want us to give her anything."

"And you believed her? Didn't you ever see that *I Love Lucy* episode where Lucy tells everyone not to bother with her birthday, and when they don't she thinks no one loves her and ends up with the Friends of the Friendless band?"

"Somehow I can't picture Leaf marching in a band."

"That's not the point, Timmy. Aren't you going to have a cake or anything?"

"No, Anthony. We don't celebrate birthdays around here."

"By the way," I ask, "how old is Leaf?"

"She told Jake White she's 38. He said he'd accept 42." Timmy holds up five fingers then two. *Fifty-two.* Then he points to the gift-wrapped package on Leaf's desk. "So what did you get her?"

"I don't really know her at all, and I can't afford to buy anything that would be as tasteful as the things shown in the magazine, so I played it safe and went with gourmet cookies. I hope she'll like them."

"Oh, she'll love them. Especially if they're chocolate."

"Chocolate chocolate chip."

As others arrive, I ask if they bought Leaf a present. Larry, Walter, Tom, Jane and Mrs. Wright didn't even buy her a card. I knock on the managing editor's door. "Ivory, did you get anything for Leaf for her birthday?"

"Yes. Why?"

"You and I seem to be the only ones who have. Everyone else took her at her word when she said she didn't want any gifts."

"They're nuts. Of course you have to buy her something."

JUNE 1, 1977

Jake White wants new headshots of Leaf. I wonder if she asked me to be at the photo shoot because I gave her makeup brushes for her birthday.

Jake smells like an ashtray. Even when he's not holding a cigarette between his skeletal fingers, the stale smoke is oppressive. His teeth are the color of cold tea. I've never seen a man this thin outside of a photograph of a prisoner of war. The sides of his forehead are concave, as if he'd been pulled out of the womb with forceps. A few wisps of gray hair accent his baldness. For a press agent, he is not a pretty picture.

Timmy has arranged for two men he knows to bring out the best of Leaf's features. A hairdresser has made her freshly blond and bouffant without being a caricature. A makeup artist applied cosmetics to make Leaf's round face appear more angular. A perfectly applied smudge of slate gray eye shadow brings out the blue in her hazel eyes. Her glasses are banned.

Leaf goes behind a folding screen and emerges in an olive green blouse with a big bow at the neck. The hairstylist and the makeup man look at Timmy, who looks at me. No one can be more critical than a gay man, and we have four.

"Ready?" The photographer is straight, so he doesn't see the problem.

"Leaf," I say when no one else speaks up, "that color isn't the best for your skin tone. Did you bring anything else?"

"Oh, sure. I brought several things." She heads back behind the screen.

A white blouse is too frilly. A pink angora sweater is too youthful and too tight. A black turtleneck only works if the photographer is Victor Srebneski. We're stuck with a photographer Jake recommended, probably because he smokes just as much as Jake does.

Finally Leaf dons a blue blazer with a Gucci scarf tied around her neck in place of a blouse. Everyone is pleased. Everyone but me.

Leaf can tell something is bothering me. "Go on, Anthony. Don't be shy. Just say it. I'm a big girl. I can take it."

"You don't have much of a neck and that scarf hides whatever you do have."

"I didn't bring anything else."

I walk toward her. "May I?" I untie the scarf and tuck it in so it borders the jacket's lapel. "Exposing more of your chest makes your neck look longer."

Leaf walks over to a full-length mirror. "You're right. Everyone okay with this?"

She sits on a stool centered on a roll of white seamless paper.

The first few poses are stiff, and even allowing time for her to grow comfortable with the camera, I'm afraid we're not going to get even one good image. I head to the prop room.

When I first saw Leaf, I didn't think she was pretty. But when she smiles, she is. She looks alive when she spontaneously laughs. So I stand behind the photographer and don outrageous wigs and prance around with a feathery boa.

We get at least four great shots.

JUNE 12, 1977

My mother frustrates me. I phoned her today, since it's her wedding anniversary and tomorrow's her birthday. Every good thing I tell her she has to turn into a negative or offer advice. When I say how well the photo shoot went with Leaf, Mom seems unable to be glad for me. Instead she says, "Don't get too close to the people in charge. Things have a way of backfiring." And when I mention that Leaf liked my Geraldo Cortez layout, Mom says, "Be careful, Anthony. You don't want to annoy Larry. He can fire you."

She never asks me if I'm dating anyone, but she's quick to tell me if one of my married cousins has another child. All the while I'm on the phone, I have to struggle not to shout at her. Before we hang up, she says how much she enjoyed talking with me and that she'd enjoy seeing me in person even more. Fat chance.

I want to stand in the middle of my apartment and scream. Instead I decide to explore Griffith Park. I avoid the grassy areas where families picnic, zip past the golf course and turn at a "Mountain Roads Closed at Sunset" sign.

Almost immediately I spot a handsome man sitting on a large rock by a curve in the road. He must be about thirty-five, has brown curly hair and a full mustache. A tight red t-shirt outlines his muscles. The top button of his faded jeans is unfastened. Tennis shoes; no socks.

I like that casual *I-just-threw-these-things-on* look. It reminds me of the boys in my old neighborhood who ran around together—but not with me—in blue jeans and white t-shirts. I always wore shirts with collars, buttoned up to my neck. Why hadn't I seen what a dork I was?

I guess I'll never have that casual look. Today it took me a half hour to decide what to wear to the park: gray athletic shorts, black tank top and tan Top Siders.

I drive higher up the hill. A half-dozen cars cluster between two "No Parking" signs. There may be action there, but not for me. Having sex in a park with a stranger may not be the height of intimacy, but I don't want to share it with other peering eyes and reaching hands.

I drive on, eager to see what other teases the park offers. Some men pose by their cars. They know a black Jeep or an old rusted truck adds to their sex appeal. I have a truck too; but a turquoise Toyota is not sexy. One sandy blond sits inside his 1959 Seminole red Cadillac Coupe de Ville. In the connotation of Griffith Park the pointy, tapered taillights in the soaring fins make their own special statement.

Around a curve, a young man with black construction boots and baggy white socks walks beside the road. He's barely wearing a skimpy white Speedo, which contrasts with his dark skin. The swimsuit is so low on his hips the top of his ass crack is visible. I slow down, and when I'm beside him, he pinches a nipple. His chest is very hairy. His Speedo is bursting.

He smiles, lowers his swimsuit and lets a thick uncut penis pop out.

A brown Mercedes I didn't know was behind me toots its horn and I speed up. I pull over at the first inlet where I can park and watch for Mr. Speedo in my rearview mirror. When he's about fifty feet away, he removes the swimsuit completely and walks with his erection pointing straight toward me.

I think he'll come up to my window, but instead he hops into the truck bed. I join him. As I pull my tank top over my head, he lowers my shorts. And we attack each other. He removes a small bottle labeled Bolt from his sock, opens it and inhales. He offers me a hit, but I decline. Instead, I caress his wonderfully hairy ass, and, without a word, he invites me inside.

One part of me hopes the sides of the truck are high enough to hide us from the people in passing cars, but another side wishes they could see me fucking this oh-so-hot reckless young man. It isn't until later that I consider we could have been arrested.

Often when I have anonymous sex, I fantasize my partner is a grease-smeared mechanic or a construction worker or a sooty fireman or a gruff cop. I'm usually disappointed when the man turns out to be a florist or an airline steward or a bank teller or, God forbid, an interior designer. I have no idea about Mr. Speedo's job. We do not say one word to each other.

JUNE 24, 1977

The buzzer on my phone goes off. It's Timmy. "Leaf wants to see you in her office."

I crunch a Certs and head down the hall. Squinting into a compact mirror, Leaf applies pale pink lipstick.

"Want to see Carol Burnett's house?"

"Sure!" I can't contain my smile.

"Then let's go."

Leaf can barely see over the steering wheel of her silver 1976 Cadillac Seville. As we head toward Beverly Hills, she says, "There are certain things I've learned when scouting a house. Never accept any refreshment. They'll think you owe them something—even if all they give you is a glass of water. Never sit down. Once you do that, you're trapped. Always keep moving." She drives over the curb while making a right-hand turn. "The most important thing is never say a word about what you think of a house, not even a whisper, until you're back in the car, because you never know if they've bugged the place. People will go to any length."

She stops in front of an ornate iron gate and announces herself through an intercom. At the top of a curving driveway, a pseudo-German Tudor house is too perfect to be authentic. The interior designer greets us at the front door. He's lanky with straight hair sharply parted in the middle. I'm sure he doesn't even hear my name. All his attention is geared toward Leaf.

I guess we're not going to meet Carol.

In the living room, oversize floral-print sofas seem arranged not for conversation but for viewing a movie screen that descends from behind a foot-wide beam. The designer points with pride to the ceiling. "Four men beat that wood with chains and hammers to create a centuries-old look."

We move on. A narrow, wood-paneled dining room looks like an afterthought. It's more suited for a conference than a family meal.

The staircase is monstrous, perfect for Carol to descend as Scarlett O'Hara dressed "in something I just found in the window." I smile as I remember the skit from her television show.

The only room of interest is Carol's closet. As large as a boutique shop, it's filled with Bob Mackie creations.

On the way out, Leaf comments about a police car parked in the driveway. "It's to deter tourists and fans from snooping around," says the decorator. "There's no engine. It's a prop."

Once we're driving back to the office, Leaf asks my opinion of the house.

"I think the fake police car says it all: It's a movie set. Nothing's real."

"Well, of course you're right. But that doesn't mean we shouldn't publish it. It will be perfect for our 'At Home with...' series. People love spying on celebrities."

JUNE 30, 1977

"Come on, Anthony," Timmy calls from my office doorway. "We're meeting Leaf on the thirtieth floor."

"What's up there?"

Timmy winks instead of answering.

As we exit the elevator, we face a very pulled together woman. Emphasis on pulled: It's a really good facelift. Her short, combed-back hair is the color of a ripe apricot. The makeup looks professionally applied: russet lipstick outlined with a thin brown line; shadow accents make her eyes appear bigger. She's tall, toothpick-thin. Her Aegean green silk blouse is free of frills and a tan skirt is severely tailored. Her tan-and-black shoes are chic yet understated.

Next to her, Leaf, in four-inch heels and a black nylon jumpsuit with an exposed zipper, is a fashion disaster. She makes a terse introduction. "Sarah Cohen. Anthony Dimora. You know Timmy."

Sarah's handshake is firmer than mine. I'll have to work on that.

She turns to Leaf. "Now will you tell me why I'm here?" Her voice is brittle.

"Jack White, our press agent, said that if reporters are going to interview me, *Inside*'s offices have to be as beautiful as the homes we publish. It's taken a while, but Claret's managed to get this entire floor for the magazine." Leaf seems like a child eager to tell a secret. "And I want you, Sarah, to decorate the reception area and my new office."

Sarah doesn't smile. "I'm flattered, but I'm not an interior designer."

Leaf ignores this. "Come on. Wait until you see the view." She opens one side of a double door and heads toward the southwest corner.

As we follow behind Sarah, Timmy whispers, "Mrs. Cohen owns Selection, the best to-the-trade shop in the city—maybe in all of California."

Two walls of Leaf's new corner office have floor-to-ceiling glass. The blinds are missing a few slats; the carpet is stained.

"You can have complete *carte blanche*, Sarah." Leaf spreads her arms to encompass the space. "Within the budget, of course."

"Leaf, I run a showroom," Sarah says. "Sure, I've designed a few pieces of furniture and a line of fabrics, but only to fill in the gaps of what's missing in the lines we carry."

"Who sets up the room displays in your showroom?"

"I do."

"And who decorated your home?"

"I did."

"Then you're an interior designer."

Sarah walks to the window and looks out. Los Angeles stretches to infinity.

"I can't wait to see the faces of all those snooty decorators who shop at Selection when they find out Leaf wants Sarah to do her office." Timmy whispers to me, but deliberately loud enough for Sarah to hear.

Sarah turns toward Leaf. "I would love to do your office."

"And the reception area," Leaf says.

"And the reception area. But I'm curious. Why do you want me to design it?"

"Because I admire your style. Because I know we can work well together. And really, Sarah, how could I pick a *real* interior designer? If I chose one of the top ten decorators, the other nine would be furious—and probably not let me publish any more of their work. I can't afford to risk that. The fact that you're not a professional designer makes you the perfect choice."

Sarah's eyebrows rise, but she quickly forces a smile.

In the elevator, Leaf says, "Oh, Anthony. We lost Carol Burnett. She insisted on the title being 'At Home with Mr. and Mrs. Joe Hamilton.' Sure, people in the industry know he's a TV producer, but no one east of Hollywood does, and that title wouldn't sell a single magazine. Anyway, as you said, it's not a great home. And I'm not going to have a television comic tell me what I can and cannot do in my own magazine! We don't need Carol Burnett."

JULY 1, 1977

Sensing someone watching me, I look up from my drawing board to see Cole Bruin in the doorway drinking from a can of 7UP.

"So why haven't you called me?" He's angelic. White-blond curls brush across his eyebrows. The ends of his pouty lips turn down, as if he's about to cry.

"I don't have your number."

"That's what I thought." He hands me a folded piece of paper: His number and "Cole" with the "o" replaced with a heart.

"Did you take the bus here?"

"No, I got a ride with my mom."

He's wearing a white t-shirt and ripped Levi's. When he sits down, I stare at his hairy knees. I nearly say, "You have the same carelessness of Bud Anderson on *Father Knows Best,*" but then I realize he wasn't even born when the show was on television.

"Why is your mom here?"

"To cause trouble." He tilts back his head to take a swig of his soda, and I watch his Adam's apple dance. "She's meeting with her decorator about her new office. She let me select the decorator. Guess who I picked?"

"*Whom.* Sorry, I know that's annoying." I make a gun with

my fingers and shoot myself in the temple. "Did you pick Jason Hunt?"

"Oh God no." Cole waves a hand as if shooing a fly. "He's boring—as a person and as a decorator. No, I picked Geraldo Cortez. He has style."

"I did a layout for one of his projects. It'll be in the next issue."

"Have you met him?"

I shake my head.

"Remember I told you about my fascination with Peter Pan?"

"Of course." I remember every word he said, every gesture.

"Well, Geraldo's like one of the pirates come to life."

"Only Cuban."

"Yes! So dark and—I can never pronounce the word."

"*Swarthy*? So where did you meet Mr. Cortez?"

"At the urinals at the Pacific Design Center."

I try not to look shocked. "Aren't these designers afraid of being arrested for corrupting a minor?"

"I was the one with the woody." A mischievous smile spreads across his face.

My mind flashes back to the steam room at the gym and Cole's pink nipples. I start applying wax to the back of a Photostat so I'll think of something else.

"Why does your mom want an office at the magazine?"

"For Inside Choices."

"What's that?"

"Her latest brainstorm. A couple of months ago during one of their regular arguments, Dad told her that all she knows how to do is shop. Well, it took her a while, but she finally figured out a way to turn that comment against him. Mom came up with Inside Choices—a mail-order company like Horchow."

"Horchow advertises in the magazine." I position the Photostat as a two-page spread on a layout board and trim off the excess edges.

"According to my mom, they make a fortune selling over-priced items to *Inside*'s readers. So Mom thinks we should beat Horchow at its own game. She'll pick out the objects and run an ad in the magazine."

"What was your Dad's reaction?"

"He said, 'It's certainly something we can think about,' which Mom and I know means 'no,' but she just ignored him. She has the money to do whatever she wants, whether Dad approves or not."

"Does Leaf know about this?"

"Of course not. I told you my mom was here to cause trouble." There's that mischievous smile again. "I've learned a lot from her."

JULY 5, 1977

Sitting on the white-tiled platform above me in the steam room, Timmy straddles my arms.

"You have quite a knot here." He applies pressure on my right shoulder just under my neck. "What have you got to be so tense about?"

"The magazine."

"I thought you liked your job."

"Oh, I do. But the editors were way behind with the copy for the next issue, so I had to work overtime to catch up so we can meet the print schedule. Everyone left at two on Friday for the long weekend, but I was there until ten. Then I worked nine more hours on Saturday." I yelp as Timmy pushes too hard with his thumb.

"Sorry!" He gently makes circles over the spot. "Did you hear Judy Berlin's going to start writing for the magazine?"

"The gossip columnist at the *L.A. Times*? What's she going to write about?"

"She's doing the interview with Andy Williams."

"I wonder if she knows anything about interior design. Not that it matters if she's writing about Andy Williams' home." With his thumb and index finger, Timmy squeezes the nape of my neck. "That feels good, Timmy."

"Did you read Judy's column today?"

"I usually just scan the bold-faced names to see if there's anyone interesting. I like to know what movie stars are doing, but I'm not interested in the Beverly Hills society ladies."

"She wrote about a charity banquet at Harold Sloan's. Leaf was furious."

"Why should she care about a film producer's party?"

"Because she was there." Timmy makes a dramatic pause. *"And Judy Berlin didn't mention her."*

"Oh. But really, Timmy, did Leaf actually expect to be listed with Loretta Young and Charleton Heston? Or even Farrah Fawcett?"

"Well, she had me get Jake White on the phone at once, and did she let him have it!" Timmy imitates Leaf's throaty voice. *"How is the magazine supposed to get national coverage if you can't even get me mentioned in the local paper? What sort of a press agent are you?"*

"So let me guess." I turn my head and face Timmy. "Jake White said if Leaf wanted to be mentioned in Judy Berlin's column to assign her a story for *Inside*."

Timmy taps my temple. "Bingo! And that's not all. Leaf said to tell you that she wants to expand her editorial from two-thirds of a page to a full page. And to run her photograph next to it."

JULY 19, 1977

At two, Timmy calls saying Leaf isn't back from lunch so Picture Selection for the next issue is delayed. She returns at three but meets with the circulation director, then with Jake White. Larry seems to take this as a personal slight and leaves the office promptly at five, followed by Ivory, who has a yoga class.

I walk down the hall to ask Timmy when the meeting will be rescheduled but he's also gone. Leaf's at her desk reading the latest issue of *People*.

"Let's do it now," she says. "Without the others."

About a month earlier, I'd asked Larry if we could order high stools for the production room, so now Leaf and I sit side-by-side in front of the light table.

"I've already gone ahead and removed all the duplicates." I lay out twelve four-by-five transparencies in a horizontal row. "These are the best exposures of the Lloyd-Paxton design in Dallas."

"Oh, that's great, Anthony. It'll save so much time." Leaf pushes her glasses up to her forehead and practically puts her nose on the photos. She must be as near-sighted as I am. "These boys are so over the top they almost give opulence a bad name."

"Why do you publish it if you don't like it?"

"If I only published the homes I liked, we wouldn't be able to fill six issues a year. Besides, the magazine isn't for me. It's really a record of what's happening in the design world. Designers tell me they see it as a *bible*."

"If that's true, it seems it's even more important to show only good projects."

"Again, we wouldn't have enough to fill an issue. Besides, this Lloyd-Paxton job isn't bad. It may not be to your taste, but for those who do like extravagance—and a lot of people do—they do a very good job." She points to a large wood console with carved filigree in one of the photos. "For example, that's a very good piece. Yes, it's ornate, but I imagine several museums wouldn't mind owning it."

"I think it would be better if it were the only antique in the room. If everything else were simple, you could really appreciate the piece. But I understand: We can't show the same type of residence over and over. We have to have a variety. But wouldn't it have been great if the photographer had taken a close-up shot of just a detail of the carving? Then I could have made that a full page so it could be appreciated, and put a small overall room shot on the facing page."

"That's a great idea, Anthony. Can't you crop into the photo?"

I grab a Loupe to magnify the image. "I'm afraid it's not in sharp enough focus to blow up that large."

"Too bad."

"Could we send the photographer back?"

"We don't have a budget for that. Especially not for this home. Maybe for a home that was going to be on the cover. But remember that idea and tell one of the photographers to do something similar in another residence." She squints at the pictures. "So what else are we going to show of this residence?"

I move two pictures to the side. "I'd start by eliminating

the guest bedrooms. There's nothing unique about them, and there are plenty of other rooms to show."

"I agree, but I'm not crazy about the master bedroom. I hate all those ditzy pillows on the bed."

"What if we don't show the bed at all, just the chaise with the Art Deco screen behind it?" With an orange grease pencil, I draw a rectangle around the chaise and screen then cross the bed with an X.

Leaf smiles.

"What so amusing?"

"Nothing. I just remember when I used big orange grease-marker Xes to make a point."

During the next half hour we go through nine residences selected for the next issue. Occasionally Leaf points to a garden in bloom or a rustic dining room and says, "That's a pretty shot." But mainly she lets me choose which pictures to publish.

Instead of arranging the next set a photos on the light table, I put out two homes. "Don't you think that these two residences are too similar to run in the same issue? They both have a neutral color scheme and transitional furnishings."

Leaf gives them a closer look. "You're right." She points to one of the homes and pushes the other photos aside. "Let's keep this one. Go through the files and see what you can find to replace the other one. Something with color." She pats my hand. "Good catch, Anthony. Why don't you attend the next Issue Planning meeting?"

"Thank you. That'd be great." I quickly decide that now is the time to mention something I've been thinking about. "Leaf, may I make another suggestion?"

"Sure."

"I think we should improve the paper stock. It should be thicker and whiter, with more sheen. I read in one of your interviews that you're not afraid to take on 'the fat cat.' Well, if

Inside's paper stock were better than *House & Garden*'s, I think people would notice."

"Have the production director give me some samples and costs for an upgrade. Our advertising pages have doubled from last year, so maybe I can use that as leverage to convince Claret it's worth the additional cost."

We've selected all the photos, but Leaf stays on her stool. "You've probably heard about Inside Choices?" When I nod, she continues. "I want to tell you something before you hear any rumors and get the wrong idea. Claret wanted you to design the ad. I said *no*."

I wish I could control my reaction, but I'm sure my face shows first surprise and then disappointment.

"I want you to concentrate on the magazine, to do more layouts. Larry can do the ads and brochure for Inside Choices. The magazine's much more important than those stupid doo-dads Colette will hawk. I've seen their house. She has horrible taste. I told Claret that if it uses *Inside*'s name, I must have final approval over the items for Inside Choices. He was reluctant, at first. I can't blame him. Colette can be a real bitch. But Jake White agreed with me, so Claret went along."

Leaf reviews the folders of the residences we've just gone through. She puts three of them in a pile. "Larry can lay out these and the Antiques feature." She hands me the other seven folders. "You do these layouts. And once you have a colorful residence to replace the beige one, let me see your picture selections, then you can do that one too."

"What should I tell Larry?"

"Nothing. I'll speak to him."

Later, in the elevator to the garage, Leaf asks, "Do you have a boyfriend?"

At first I'm surprised. Did Timmy tell her I'm gay? Does the rest of the staff know? Then I worry: *Am I too obvious, even ef-*

feminate? "No, I don't have a boyfriend. Right now, I'm not even looking for one."

"Well, when you do start looking, my advice is to stay away from interior designers. You'll never be sure if they like you or just want to be published."

When the elevator stops, Leaf opens her purse. "Do you realize that I haven't had one cigarette the entire time we were working?" She lights one. "I actually enjoyed working for a change. It was fun. Have a nice night." Her shoulders drooping, she walks to her Seville. "I'm going home to my cat and a microwave dinner."

JULY 20, 1977

The next morning Leaf waves at me as she walks by and enters Larry's office.

"I've decided to put Anthony in charge of the photographers." She seems to deliberately speak loud enough for me to hear. "We need one person to act as liaison, to follow their schedules and make sure that there's always someone available when we need a home shot right away. I know you don't have the time to be bothered with this. Besides, it's really rather clerical."

"Okay, Leaf." Larry practically whispers. "I'll tell Anthony."

"I've already told him."

AUGUST 4, 1977

This is the fourth day Leaf has been out of the office with a sore throat. To stay on schedule, we should have shown her the layouts for the November/December issue last week. The editors are always late in giving me the text, and I don't want them to have another excuse, so I ask Timmy to let Leaf know the layouts are ready. She suggests I bring them to her house.

Larry thinks he should take them, but Timmy grins. "She said Anthony." He hands me a large brown bag. "I picked up lunch for her from the café downstairs."

Leaf lives in a one-story stucco box cantilevered over a canyon in Bel Air. Timmy told me to just walk in, that Leaf didn't want to get out of bed.

At first I think the entrance—a sliding-glass door—is strange, but this is Los Angeles, and most of the architecture is bizarre. In this neighborhood, a Japanese-inspired cottage can stand between a Greek-columned mansion and a Swiss chalet.

Leaf's foyer is a large square with absolutely nothing in it. On either side is a bedroom and bath. In the exact center of the house is the kitchen, surrounded on three sides by living and dining areas. All the outside walls in this space are floor-to-ceiling glass. The view is impressive: The ocean sparkles in the west, downtown towers in the east, and the smog meets

Disneyland in the south.

I expect Leaf's décor to be right out of *Inside*. Am I disappointed!

The living area is completely empty. Actually that's not true. There's a tall ficus tree in a ceramic pot; most of the leaves are on the marble floor. A dining space is defined by a parson's table with six mismatched chairs. In another living area—the den, I guess—a nubby brown tweed sofa and a pair of club chairs in an orange, green and brown stripe face an empty wall with a dusty television cable box on the floor.

The bedroom suite is pseudo-Arts-and-Crafts. The bedspread is pink and purple paisley. A stack of magazines leans against a nightstand. A portable television on a rolling stand, which must have been opposite the sofa, is next to the bed.

I smell cough medicine and unwashed hair. Leaf looks exhausted but when I ask if she's too tired to review the layouts, she cries, "God, no! It's the only thing I've looked forward to all day. Push the TV out of the way and bring in one of the chairs from the dining room."

I put the layouts on the queen-size bed and hold out the paper bag. "Timmy gave me your lunch."

"Oh good! I never remember if it's 'Feed a cold, starve a fever' or the other way round, but I *am* starving. There's a tray in the kitchen. Would you mind setting it out with real silverware? I can't stand plastic utensils."

Also in the kitchen is a kitty litter box—one that hasn't been changed in quite a while. Timmy's provided enough food for lunch *and* dinner. I pour chicken soup into a bowl, add a spoon and napkin, and return to the bedroom.

"There's also a sandwich, a pot pie, a salad and some cookies. Do you want orange juice or hot tea?"

"Tea, please. What kind of cookies?"

"They look like peanut butter."

"Oh goodie! We'll have those later. Would you mind putting the rest in the refrigerator? Unless you want the sandwich or pot pie."

"I've already had lunch, thanks."

The refrigerator has a pizza box on the bottom shelf. Nothing else.

I pour the tea out of the plastic cup into a ceramic mug and put it on the nightstand. Then I move the television and bring in the lightest chair from the dining table. "This is quite a house. The view is unbelievable."

"The architect, Ted Powell, positioned the house to maximize the view. I never tire of looking at it. What's amazing to me is the house is almost all glass, but I don't see any of my neighbors because of the landscaping."

Leaf has moved the layouts next to her but concentrates on the soup.

"Do you have any siblings, Anthony?"

"A brother." I wonder why she wants to know—and how much I should say. "He's ten years younger than I am, so we aren't close. I went away to college when he started first grade."

"So at least for a while you were an only child. So was I. Well, actually I was adopted."

Why is she's telling me this?

She points her chin toward the television. "I had to disconnect the cable box because the wires wouldn't stretch all the way to the bedroom, so I can only get a few channels. But I watched *Auntie Mame* this morning."

"That's a great movie. I love when the sofas go up and down."

"That little boy was so lucky to be raised by Mame. My adoptive parents were very boring."

"They're not still alive?"

"Oh, they're probably still breathing. I don't stay in touch."

"Where were you born?"

"Cedar Rapids, Iowa. It may be the geographic center of America but it's also the center of nothing. It's a place to leave."

"When did you find out you were adopted? Do you mind my asking these personal questions?"

"Ask away. My adoptive parents told me when I turned fifteen. Happy birthday and we're not your parents! I always knew there was something different about me. I'd go into a store and some old biddies would look at me and whisper behind their hands. I was probably the only person in town who didn't know I was adopted."

"Are you curious about your real parents?"

"Oh I know who they are. Well, I know who my mother is. I thought she was my aunt—my adoptive mother's sister. I guess I should have suspected something because 'Aunt Lacey' was always around, especially on Sundays when we'd have to play cards. One time I suggested we play Old Maid, and you should have seen the look she gave me! She was very clingy and would join us for dinner at least twice a week, and when she'd leave she'd practically smoother me. She always smelled like dead roses."

Leaf finishes the soup, opens the cellophane-wrapped crackers and eats them.

It hits me why she's telling me personal things. She wants to see if she can trust me with information. She doesn't need another tell-all Timmy.

I take the tray back to the kitchen, and when I come back with the cookies she's sipping the tea. I have one more question.

"Do you know why you were called 'Leaf'?"

"Oh, yes. They told me that on my fifteenth birthday, too. My mother discovered she was pregnant when the leaves were changing color, and she said I was a leaf that had fallen into her life. Makes you want to puke, doesn't it?"

"I'm surprised Hallmark hasn't used it on a greeting card."

Leaf points a finger at me. "I knew you'd understand. You know, for a long time I was upset and angry about the whole adoption thing—my mother giving me up, not being told sooner, then being told—all of it. But I'm glad it happened, because otherwise I probably would have ended up marrying Steve Padino and still be in Cedar Rapids with six screaming kids." She dusts cookie crumbs off her nightgown. "Shall we look at the layouts?"

She examines them without saying a word, but she separates them into two piles. When she's through, she hands me one of the piles. "I know I told you to do the layouts on these homes, but I would have recognized your work regardless. I don't know what makes them different, but I can tell which ones you design."

"I learned layout from Beethoven."

"The composer? What did he ever design?"

"Symphonies. Each of his compositions has a theme, and from that he creates variations. That's what I do in my layouts." I pick up a layout of a house in Montana. "This cattle ranch is huge, and I wanted to convey that in my layout, so I made all the pictures bleed only on the sides, not at the top and bottom of the page. That makes the photos long and wide, like CinemaScope."

"That's very clever. Show me another."

I select a layout of a high-rise apartment in Manhattan. "In this one, the photos bleed only on the top."

"Okay, height—that's the theme. What's the variation?"

"On this spread, the picture goes across two pages, but it still only bleeds at the top, not at the sides or bottom. On the next page, the picture, still bleeding only at the top, is only two columns wide with a caption next to it."

"It's practically subliminal." Leaf coughs several times and reaches out her arm.

I hand her a glass of water from the nightstand. Once she's settled down again, I say, "Larry seems to simply position a picture on a page. Have you noticed how he never crops a photo?" I point to one of his layouts. "Who needs to see all those boring white ceilings?"

"You're absolutely right." She looks through Larry's layouts. "Jesus, I give him three little layouts and he can't even do those right." She hands them to me. "Redo them."

"That would be awkward, Leaf. Larry is, after all, my boss."

"No, he's not. *I'm* your boss. Fix the layouts."

AUGUST 24, 1977

Timmy rushes into my office practically panting. "You've got to see who Burton Fisher brought with him. He's adorable! He's short maybe your height and has dark Italian skin with a thick mustache and the most angelic eyes I've ever seen. Let me tell you my heart is not the only thing in this body pumping blood! He's in Leaf's office. Come on, bring some papers. We'll pretend we're talking about them and you can take a peek."

"Oh, Anthony," Leaf calls as Timmy and I stand in the corridor outside her office. "I'm glad you're here. Would you come in a minute?"

I smile at Timmy and go in. Burton Fisher is massive. At least six-feet-two, broad-shouldered and five pounds short of being overweight, he looks just under fifty. His salt-and-pepper hair is carefully, and probably expensively, styled to minimize a receding hairline. He's handsome in a burly way. He may be polite enough to rise when Leaf introduces him, but the feeling I get, as he squeezes my hand too tightly, is that he's not a nice person.

Timmy is right about the younger man: Mark Romano is cherubic. His straight black hair falls over his forehead and tickles his ears; his mustache is equally dark and as manicured as his nails. His eyes are the color of olives, topped by two perfectly horizontal eyebrows. His upper lip is as fleshy as the bottom. He looks barely twenty-one. Can he be as innocent as he appears?

"Mark took some shots of a house Burton designed in Monterey," Leaf tells me. "Naturally, the décor is wonderful. Why don't you go over the pictures with Mark? The color looks a bit off. See what you think. I want to talk with Burton about when his Russian River home is going to be finished."

I bring Mark to the production room. He spreads his transparencies on the light table and I lean in next to him to get a close look. He smells natural. No cologne to hide his essence. I inhale and find it difficult to concentrate on the photos.

I exhale. There are several beautiful compositions, but most of the photos are too green. "Do you use filters?"

"You mean for making coffee?"

I laugh. "I'm sorry, I'm not laughing at you. But that's very funny." And I laugh again. "I meant do you use colored filters to balance the color in your photos?"

"I don't know what those are."

"They're round disks of transparent plastic that you place in front of the lens." I point to a photo of a two-story living room. "With the floor-to-ceiling glass, this room gets a lot of outdoor light, and all those trees outside bring a green cast inside. If you had used a magenta filter, it would have counter-balanced the green and made the colors more natural. The filters come in various intensities, so you'll have to take several shots with different filters until you get the hang of it."

"Does that mean these shots are unusable?" He seems as if he's going to cry.

"No, we can apply filters when we do the color separations, but it adds another expense that could have been avoided."

"I'm sorry." He pouts his lower lip, and in one brief flash, I wonder if his angelic innocence is an act.

"You may already know this, but the colors of light are different than the color-wheel we all learned in school. In that chart, the opposite of red is green, the opposite of yellow is purple, and the opposite of blue is orange." I wonder if I'm boring him. "Yellow is also one of the primary colors of light. The others are magenta, which is a strong pink, and cyan, a sort of blue-green. And in light the opposites are yellow and blue, cyan and red, and as I said, magenta and green."

"Sounds complicated."

"Only at first." I point to another photo. "You can avoid dark corners like this by using carefully placed strobe lights."

"I know about strobes." Mark looks puzzled, his eyebrows slanting twenty-five degrees. "But I thought the magazine preferred natural light. You're always publishing Derry Moore's pictures."

"Sometimes an artificial light source is made to look natural. Don't forget we're in Hollywood!"

Mark doesn't seem amused. "All this equipment sounds like it's going to be expensive. I'm not sure what I'm getting myself into. This is only the second house I've photographed."

"Did you select the angles of the shots or did Burton?"

"I did. But he stood over my shoulder, and when he didn't like something, he let me know it."

"Well, you have a good eye. And if you enjoy it, you should do more. You just need to improve your technique. Why don't you see if you can be a photographer's assistant? He'll have all the equipment, so you won't have to make an investment while you see if photography is something you really want to pursue."

"Lesson's over." Burton fills the doorway. "We've got a plane to catch. We're going to Hawaii for a few days."

Are that gruff bear and sweet boy lovers? Timmy will know.

SEPTEMBER 3, 1977

Yesterday everyone packed their possessions into Bekins boxes, and now Timmy and I are here to see that the movers take everything to the correct office on the thirtieth floor. Promptly at nine o'clock six men with dollies get off one elevator, while directly across the hall Sarah Cohen and her crew emerge from another elevator.

Timmy eyes the young Hispanic men in their white jumpsuits. "I'll work with these guys," he whispers. "You take care of Mrs. Cohen."

"I can't believe this building doesn't have a freight elevator," Sarah Cohen says.

"No, but there are six elevators," I respond. "And since it's Saturday, you should have no trouble getting as many as you need. Do you think it would be possible to do Leaf's office before installing the reception area? Movers will be coming and going, and I know you don't want anything damaged."

Sarah, in sleek black pants and turtleneck, doesn't acknowledge my comments. "David, go back downstairs and supervise the unloading of the truck. Make sure they bring up only the pieces for Leaf's office. I'll meet you on the thirtieth floor."

Earlier in the week Sarah had the walls in Leaf's new office covered in fawn-colored grass cloth. With the mushroom-hued carpet the room is a subtle study in beige. A gauzy ecru textile curtains the windows. Leaf's oval desk is veneered with oatmeal parchment. There's only one center drawer for pens and paper, but behind the desk is a wall-to-wall console with the same finish; no handles or hinges are visible. Leaf's chair is covered in aqua Ultrasuede. Two guest chairs, with waterfall Lucite arms, are upholstered in sand suede. Wrapping one corner, a banquette of cream, taupe and aqua stripes holds three oversize pale aqua raw silk pillows. A khaki ostrich-skin table rests in front of it. Before a pillar between two windows stands a copper pedestal holding a larger-than-life bronze head of Buddha.

As I stand admiring the statue, Sarah Cohen enters. "That's one of the two accents in the room."

I look around. The only other accent I see is a handmade ceramic ashtray in coffee and cream.

"Not that," Sarah says. "The other accent is Leaf."

SEPTEMBER 4, 1977

Yesterday, after working with Timmy and the movers, I straightened my own office. Allowed to select one new piece of furniture, I chose a sleek white Italian drawing table. Larry's office is on one side of mine, and our assistant shares the space on the other side with someone from production.

With the magazine taking up the entire thirtieth floor, there are four corner offices. Mr. Bruin, Leaf and the circulation director each have one. The remaining office is for Colette Bruin.

While I work on setting up the new Viewing Room, Geraldo Coretz and his crew install Colette's furnishings on the other side of the building. I'm eager to see her office, but Cole Bruin asks me to wait until it's complete.

"I was right in suggesting Geraldo to my mother," he says. "She wants her office to astound and Geraldo's not afraid to go to the limit, like most designers are."

"I suppose you've 'gone to the limit' with him in other ways, too?"

Cole Bruin smiles and flops down on a chair. He's wearing the jeans with the ripped knees. "Guess who asked me to pose for one of his sculptures?"

"Robert Graham."

"Never heard of him."

"He recently had a show at the Nicholas Wilder Gallery on La Cienega."

"Guess again!"

I'm tempted to name Michelangelo or Rodin, even though they're long dead, just to see if Cole's heard of them, but I guess that's rude. I compromise and pick the most famous living sculptor of the human form. "Henry Moore."

"Never heard of him either. You're taking all the fun out of this."

"Sorry." I offer him a Bordeaux cookie from a Pepperidge Farm bag. "So who asked you to pose?"

"Christopher Richter."

"Where'd you meet him? And don't tell me in a bathroom at the art museum."

"Very funny." Cole gives me the finger. "I met him at my house. Mom invited a bunch of artists to a fund-raiser. She wouldn't let me attend unless I wore a tux."

"I bet you looked adorable."

"Let's just say I got a lot of attention."

"From Christopher Richter."

"Among others."

"Does your mom know you're posing for him?"

"Sure."

I sense he's lying. "And does she know he only does nudes?"

"Sure."

He's definitely lying.

He taps my drawing board. "I'll come get you when everything's set up in my mom's office." He takes another cookie. "Don't say anything about me posing, okay?"

"Sure."

Cole gives me the finger again.

Several hours later, the unveiling is ready.

Colette's office glistens. The walls are covered in shimmering silver lame. Windows are screened with acrylic louvers embedded with silver dust. Colette's desk is a thick plate of glass perched on two slabs of ragged black marble. Facing it are two Louis XVI-style armchairs, but instead of being carved of wood, they are reproduced in acrylic with black leather upholstery. A loveseat, also in black leather, stands behind a coffee table featuring shattered glass. The carpet and Colette's chair are vibrant red.

"Anthony," Cole says, "do you know Geraldo?"

A man arranging red accessories on a black lacquered console turns around. All in black, he has slicked-back hair and a well-trimmed mustache. He looks vaguely familiar. His smile exposes very white teeth, and his eyes sparkle mischievously. "I believe we've met before."

And it hits me. Mr. Speedo from Griffith Park.

Before I can say anything, a tall slender woman enters. She obviously belongs in this office: black slacks, silk red blouse and a necklace made of hunks of black stone.

"Mom," Cole says. "This is Anthony Dimora. He's the assistant art director."

She barely smiles. "I just had a look at Leaf's office. It's tasteful, but utterly dull."

"I think it's refined and understated," I say.

"You sound like a caption." Colette sweeps her blond shoulder-length hair behind one ear. It's clear that Cole inherited his beauty from her. "I'll admit it's well done for what it is. Certainly no critical comment can be made of its style. In fact, I doubt anyone will comment about it *at all*."

"Well, they'll certainly comment about your office." A bead of sweat trails down my side. I can't believe I'm being sassy to the owner of the company.

Cole interjects, "Geraldo's given my mom exactly what she wants."

"And what's that?"

"She wants people to walk into her office and be dazzled."

"That," I say, "they will be."

"But not you?" For the first time Colette Bruin really looks at me. I sense she'd like to grind her red high heel into my face.

"I think it's brilliant. In more ways than one."

"But you don't like it."

"Really, Mrs. Bruin, does it matter if I don't like it?"

"Not one bit."

SEPTEMBER 6, 1977

I've worked the entire Labor Day weekend and am exhausted, but I'm ready for the January/February Issue Planning meeting.

When the thirtieth floor plan was being configured, I requested the new Viewing Room be directly opposite my office. Since it's a windowless room, no one was interested in it, so it worked out. We now have three stand-alone light tables and enough file cabinets to hold all the photography folders of homes awaiting publication. I also ordered three large bulletin boards for the Issue Planning cards. There used to be just one board in Ivory's office, but I convinced her it would be better to have the boards with the photography in the viewing room for easy reference. She reluctantly agreed.

In the past we had a three-by-five white index card for every photographed residence that is still to be published. Ivory had them arranged on the bulletin board by geographic location.

I've spent hours making all new cards.

At eleven o'clock I move folding chairs into the Viewing Room, positioning them to face the bulletin boards. After Ivory and Larry arrive, I buzz Timmy that we're ready for Leaf. She walks in wearing a huge black poncho over gray slacks and munching on a handful of M&Ms.

She scans the room. "It looks good, Anthony."

"Before we begin," I say, "I'd like to take a few minutes to explain how I've reconfigured the cards. We still have columns for the geographic locations, but now we have more room so everything isn't crowded together." I point to the first bulletin board. "We also now have a column for each issue. We'll be able to see what was in the previous issue"—I point to the first column—"and schedule in advance any home that can only run in one or two issues. For example, under January/February I put the Bruce residence in Vail because there's snow in the exterior shots. But, of course, Leaf, if you don't want to keep it there, I'll move it."

"No, that's great," she says. "Leave it there."

Ivory offers Leaf a cigarette and lights it, then her own. Larry pulls out his tobacco pouch and stuffs his pipe.

"After the issue columns," I continue, "the next one contains all the homes that Leaf said might have a cover shot. I figure you'd want to plan an issue around what home is on the cover."

Larry looks as if this never occurred to him. I'm sure he'd rather be unpacking his things for his new office than be in this meeting.

"Why are there different colored cards?" Ivory blows smoke toward the ceiling.

"I'm coming to that." I indicate a card. "The white cards are for contemporary interiors; the tan ones are for traditional designs; and the cream are for transitional. Antiques features are on blue cards, and the Art features are on green."

"Does that mean," Larry says with his pipe in his mouth, "that you went through all the folders to see what style the décor was?"

I nod.

"That must have taken hours."

I shrug. "I misunderstood Labor Day. I thought it meant you

had to work." No one laughs. No one even smiles. "And besides, I wanted to become familiar with what homes we had in the files."

"This is wonderful, Anthony." Leaf points to a card in the covers column. "Shall we begin? Move the Angelo Donghia residence to Jan/Feb. So we've got our cover story and Los Angeles as well as Bruce in Colorado." She squints. "What's that Brown residence under New York? I don't remember it."

I pull the folder from a file cabinet and spread several transparencies on a light table. Leaf gets up to look at them.

"Oh, yeah. Now I know why I couldn't remember it. I don't know why I accepted it in the first place."

"At the time, we were low on New York residences," Ivory says.

"Well, we'll have to be low again before we run this." She pushes the pictures into a pile.

I scoop them up, return them to the folder and file it.

Leaf takes a tan card from the New York column and moves in under Jan/Feb. "This apartment by Robin Rainbow will be a nice contrast to the Donghia. What celebrities do we have ready?"

Ivory flips pages in a small notebook. "Walter said Judy Berlin turned in the Burt Reynolds text, and Reynolds' agent called last week and asked when it was going to published."

"Tell him it will be in the same issue as the Brown residence."

"Are you considering Herbert Ross for 'At Home with…'?" Ivory snuffs out her cigarette in a small beanbag ashtray she brings to meetings.

"Probably, depends on how desperate we are." Leaf looks at me. "Has the Robert Redford residence been shot?"

"He doesn't want it photographed until he returns from location at the end of the month."

Leaf hands Ivory her cigarette to put out. "Anthony, you

have to get some ashtrays in here."

"Okay. The Lee Radziwill pictures arrived this morning. I haven't even made a folder yet."

"How's it look?" Leaf asks.

"Fabulous." I walk across the hall and take an envelope off my desk. "Here it is." I lay the photos on the light table. "She's already phoned and asked us not to publish Jaime's portrait of her." I point to one of the shots.

"I can see why not. What was she thinking? It doesn't even look like she washed her hair." Leaf massages her temples. "Well, let's put it in this issue as the 'At Home' feature. Maybe Jaime can take a portrait of her at her office. I'm sure she doesn't look like this when she's meeting her clients."

"Leaf," Ivory interjects, "if we include Lee Radziwill we'll have two New York residences in the same issue."

"Well, Lee's place is in Southampton, so I think we can get away with it." Leaf counts off on her fingers. "So we have Radziwill, L.A., New York and Vail. Jan/Feb's a small issue but we need at least two more—maybe three."

"What about the Bruce Gregga project in Chicago?" I suggest. "That pale pink he uses in the living room would make a nice contrast to the bold colors of Donghia and the transitional design contrasts with the traditional décor of Robin Rainbow."

Leaf moves the Gregga card under Jan/Feb and points to a tan card. "What about this Ron Pearl house in San Francisco? It can be a small feature."

"We need something historic," Ivory says. "If we do that British manor house Derry shot a while ago, it will take care of international, too."

Leaf agrees, and I move the appropriate card.

Leaf asks, "What's the Antiques feature?"

Ivory consults her notebook again. "Murano glass. And we just got in the Art feature on Hudson River School landscapes."

"I love Murano glass," Leaf says, "but who decided on Hudson River paintings? They're so gloomy. We can't run them in January. People will commit suicide in droves. See if Tom can find something else. And if he can't, tell him we want only bright paintings. No Frederic Church icebergs."

She stands up, ready to leave, but squints again at the bulletin boards.

"Anthony, take down that Geraldo Cortez project." She points to a white card in the California column. "I looked at the photos again and decided it's not really right for the magazine. Put it in the *Kill* file."

I remove the card. No one says anything, but I know we're all thinking the same thing: *Leaf killed the story because Geraldo designed Colette's office.*

Ivory waits for Leaf and Larry to leave. She picks up her ashtray, and while I collapse the folding chairs, she stands so close I have to look directly in her eyes. She says, "I don't give a fuck if you go after Larry's job but don't you dare try for mine."

SEPTEMBER 9, 1977

Ivory's comment gives me pause. I *do* want Larry's job, but I reorganized the Issue Planning cards to make the magazine run more smoothly. I certainly don't want Ivory's job. What does she do anyway? She's a traffic cop, routing the text from one editor to the next. And she always turns the copy in late. Most of the time she doesn't give it to me to get typeset until I ask for it.

I brace myself for her to be upset at the Picture Selection meeting today. Once again I've done something to make the magazine run smoother. Ivory or Larry could have done the same thing if they'd thought about it.

When Leaf, Larry and Ivory are ready to begin, I indicate the transparencies for the Donghia cover story on the first light table. I've already selected the best exposures. But I've also pre-edited the pictures. There are two rows of images.

"The bottom row has the shots I think we should show." I've selected fewer images then we usually publish for a feature, figuring if a picture is worth including, we should show it big. "On the top row are the pictures I'd eliminate."

Leaf pushes her glasses to her forehead and examines the shots. "Okay. Anthony, show me alternate layouts depending on which shot goes on the cover."

Larry and Ivory glare at me, but Leaf seems pleased with my initiative. She moves down the light table, where I've set up the Lee Radziwill transparencies.

"Jaime shot her portrait yesterday," I say. "It will be here on Friday."

"Show it to me as soon as it arrives. If it's good, let's make it a full page." Leaf slides one of the top row shots down to the lower row then slides it back. "Okay. Anthony, why don't you do this layout too?"

Ivory studies the Donghia pictures. Larry doesn't even bother.

Leaf admires the eight shots of the Robin Rainbow design. "Jaime's photos are always so beautiful. I see why you didn't eliminate any. You might as well do this layout, too. You can give it ten pages."

"Next is the Ron Pearl apartment in San Francisco." I've selected only five shots.

"All you've picked are vignettes, Anthony," Leaf says. "Don't you think we should show at least one overall room shot of the living room?"

"They all show that horrible sculpted carpet."

Leaf examines the pictures with a Loupe. "It *is* ghastly."

"If we have a title like 'Polished Details' and just show huge close-ups it would be a nice change-of-pace for us."

"Okay. Ron will be furious, but that's too bad."

She moves on to the Vail cabin. "I love all these outdoor shots with the snow." I've selected two exterior shots, but she moves two more to the lower row. "You can make this eight pages." She bends closer to pictures. "Don't you think these interior shots are a bit orange?"

"Actually, the transparencies for the last couple of homes David shot have been too orange," I say. "I don't know what he's doing different, but his exposures are way off."

"Well, call him and tell him I'm not pleased. Better yet, why don't you fly up to San Francisco and discuss his photography with him directly? It will be my treat."

Ivory leaves the room.

Leaf pats my hand and looks at the Bruce Gregga project. "Oh, I love his work! The colors are always so soothing. Make this one ten pages, too, Anthony."

Larry fills his pipe.

Ivory returns smoking a cigarette and carrying her beanbag ashtray. I guess she didn't notice the glass ashtray I put on top of the file cabinet.

Leaf doesn't show much interest in the English manor house. "We'll put this at the end. Just seven pages. Larry, you do this one—and the Art and Antiques layouts as well."

For the January/February issue I'm designing twice as many layouts as Larry.

OCTOBER 3, 1977

Timmy brings in a portable television so the staff can watch Leaf on *Dinah!*

Earlier in the week, Leaf had asked the editors to come up with interesting or amusing incidents about the designers and homes *Inside* had published that she could use on the program. I thought they'd all participate, but Timmy said only Ivory and I presented a couple of ideas.

At first Leaf seems frightened to be on the air, but when the audience laughs at one of her witty comments, she visibly relaxes. And Dinah Shore is so easygoing anyone would feel comfortable; she shows pictures of her own home from when it was published in *Inside*.

During a commercial break, Ivory says, "Leaf hasn't mentioned Inside Choices. I thought that was the whole purpose of being on the show."

"Not to Leaf," Timmy says. "She rejected almost all of Mrs. Bruin's selections."

"Yeah, but Colette reinstated some of them." Larry looks smug. "I'm designing the ad, and Colette said Leaf wouldn't remember what she'd rejected, that Leaf was just doing it to show that she could."

"Network Battle of the Super Egos," Walter whispers to me,

but everyone hears.

"They're not the only ones with big egos around here." Larry looks right at me. Since he hadn't said anything when I redesigned his layouts, I figured he didn't care; but obviously he does.

Everyone but Timmy looks at me with puzzled expressions. That man knows more secrets than J. Edgar Hover. I shrug, raise my eyebrows and smile. I'm surprised that Larry would say anything disparaging about Leaf in front of Timmy, even if Mrs. Bruin were the source. Timmy winks at me.

When the program resumes, I'm shocked that Leaf says something I had told her as a joke. The incident hadn't happened; I had just made it up because I thought it was esoteric and funny.

Dinah asks, "Do you think homeowners appreciate fine furnishings as much as their decorator does?"

"Well," Leaf says, "One homeowner thought Le Corbusier was a spa south of San Diego."

NOVEMBER 28, 1977

"Smile, Anthony." Timmy puts his head in my office on his way back from the break room. "Didn't you have a good Thanksgiving?"

"It was fine. I'm just concerned about whether Larry's done his layouts for tomorrow's meeting with Leaf."

"How many did he have to do this time?"

"Only two. Art and Antiques. He's had two-and-a-half weeks; you'd think he could get them done. I've done seven layouts." I tap my pencil frantically against my drawing board. "What does he do all day? His door's always closed."

"Why don't we have a look? What time did he leave for lunch?"

"About ten minutes ago."

"So he won't be back for at least a half hour, probably longer." Timmy motions with his hand. "Come on!"

We don't open any of Larry's drawers. We don't have to. The answer is right there on his drawing board. "Look, he's doing a layout of vintage airplanes."

Timmy rifles through a stack of layout boards on the credenza. "These are all layouts of airplanes." He moves to a bookcase and picks a miniature bi-plane. "I wondered why he has all these models everywhere. He must have at least a dozen.

What is he, fourteen?"

I hold up one of the layouts. "Here's the title page. *Winging It: A Pictorial History of World War I Aircraft* by Larry Stein. No wonder he doesn't have time to do any layouts for the magazine. This book must be at least one hundred pages. I wonder if he has a publisher."

"And I wonder if Leaf knows he's doing this." Timmy replaces the model plane. "Do you want me to postpone the meeting with her tomorrow?"

I take the Art and Antiques folders from the corner of Larry's desk. "No. If necessary, I'll work late tonight to finish the layouts." I make sure Larry's papers are just as we found them. "Do you realize, Timmy, this means I'll have designed the entire March/April issue?"

DECEMBER 12, 1977

"I can not believe," Burton Fisher booms, "that the American Society of Interior Designers named Leaf Wyks Woman of the Year."

"Not so loud, Burton." Mark Romano waves his hands as if he's quieting an orchestra. "Or do you *want* her to hear you?"

"I don't care if she hears me or not."

"She could decide not to publish any more of your work," I say.

"She won't do that." Burton shakes his head. "Believe me, she needs me more than I need her. She knows *House & Garden* would *kill* to have one of my projects. And so would she."

"I think it was a bit much for the ASID to call Leaf the 'Arbiter of Taste,'" Jason Hunt interjects, but in a much softer voice than Burton.

"Judging from that in/out list she gave in the *Los Angeles Times*, I'd say she was the *Albatross* of Taste." Burton asks me, "Who's paying for this shindig? I thought the award banquet was Saturday."

"Which *you* didn't attend!" Jason smirks. "Lucky you! It was *so boring*! I never saw so many wannabe designers—most of them housewives who just want a discount on to-the-trade merchandise."

"Saturday's event was for the industry," I say, "and the magazine staff wasn't invited, so Mr. Bruin decided to use the company Christmas party to honor Leaf, and she decided to invite a few of her special designers."

Burton looks bored, as if I gave the wrong answer. He hands his glass to Mark.

"Can I get anyone else another glass of Champagne?" Mark asks Jason and me.

"You won't be able to carry them all," I say. "I'll come help you."

As we make our way across the Wilshire Country Club ballroom to the bar, I overhear Sarah Cohen congratulate Leaf. "What an honor!" Sarah's dressed in tailored neutral tones. Her meticulously applied make-up is equally monochromatic. Except for her lips. They are painted a brilliant tulip red, the upper one shaped into two distinct points. "You must be very excited."

"I'm bursting!" Leaf is squeezed into a frilly peacock blue dress displaying an abundance of cleavage. "I can hardly believe out of all the women in the world of interior design they chose me. It's such a privilege."

"Well, hang on to it for dear life. Fame passes fast."

"Oh, do you really think I'm going to be famous?"

"You already are."

Leaf takes a spring roll from a passing waiter. "You know what's so funny about my in/out list, Sarah? People will *believe* it. If I'd said wallpaper is unsophisticated, I could have destroyed an entire industry, the way Clark Gable upset the undershirt manufacturers by not wearing one in *It Happened One Night*."

I glance over my shoulder to see if Sarah is too courteous to roll her eyes to the ceiling. She is.

While the bartender pours Champagne, Mark says, "You

look so cute in your tuxedo. Burton thinks you and I could be twins."

I think he's the one who looks cute. "I'm going to San Francisco in about two weeks. Maybe we could have dinner." I deliberately leave it vague: *We* could mean just Mark and me or include Burton.

Before Mark can reply, Timmy puts a hand on my shoulder. "What are you two dolls plotting?" He doesn't expect an answer. "Anthony, Robin Rainbow spotted you across the room and wants to meet you."

"Go on, Anthony. I can manage these." Mark positions three Champagne flutes between his hands. "But be careful. I heard Robin's got a tongue sharper than cheddar cheese."

"Oh, it's not Robin's tongue Anthony has to worry about. Wait, it is, but not the way you mean." And Timmy leads me toward the New York designer.

I wonder if Robin Rainbow was ever attractive. He must be nearing sixty. His facial features—eyes, nose, mouth—are disproportionately small to his large pink head, which seems too heavy for his delicate body. His thinning hair is dyed an unnatural shade of red. A sedate charcoal gray suit is offset by a long magenta scarf cascading nearly to his knees. Instead of shaking my hand, he holds his out like a dog offering a paw. "I saw you standing there with your *mauve* bowtie and I just had to find out *all* about you." I'm sure he deliberately exaggerates his Southern accent.

"I hate that the women get to wear all different kinds of gowns," I say, "and we men are stuck looking alike, so this color is my little gesture of independence."

"Ooh, I *like* a man who's independent."

"You like any man who breathes." Geraldo Coretz approaches and flutters the ruffles on my shirt.

"He doesn't even have to be breathing for *you* to like him," says Timmy.

"That's not true and you know it. That's why I've never made it with you." Geraldo slips a finger between the studs of my shirt trying to reach a nipple. "I have very particular tastes, don't I, Anthony?"

"Anthony, just how *well* do you know this infamous *inferior* designer?" Robin flecks his shoulder twice as if he could brush Geraldo away.

"Let's just say we've met before."

"In a pickup truck," adds Geraldo.

"My oh my oh my!" Robin fans his face with a flittering hand.

"My oh my oh my, indeed." Timmy's antenna rises to attention. "Anthony, we *will* talk."

"I don't usually *settle* for sloppy seconds, *my dear*," Robin adds, "but in your case I'll make an exception."

"Watch out, Anthony, Gums might attack you behind that fake potted palm." But Geraldo does the attacking, rubbing my crotch.

A gray-haired dowager stares at us as if we've eternally offended her. I remove Geraldo's hand. Robin bestows the woman an insincere smile.

"That, my friends," whispers Timmy, "is Colette Bruin's mother."

"And that gown is right out of a 1950s Modess ad," says Robin, "although you boys are probably too young to remember."

"Oh, I remember those ads," I say. "When I was a kid I'd see them in *Life* magazine and my mom would never tell me what they were selling."

"What *were* they selling?" Timmy asks.

"Sanitary napkins," Robin says without moving his lips.

"That old cow has probably had one stuck in her twat for sixty years." Geraldo smirks. "I wouldn't let her intimidate us."

The woman moves away with what I am sure she thinks is regal dignity.

"Geraldo wouldn't let *anything* intimidate him," Robin says. "He steals all my best ideas."

"Like you ever had an idea."

Robin lifts his Champagne flute as if giving him the finger. "Have you seen the January/February issue? The apartment I designed was given *ten* pages."

"Anthony did the layout," Timmy says.

"You mean you're the *art* director?"

"Not quite yet," Timmy says before I can respond. "Give him another week."

"I'm the *assistant* art director."

"But he does *all* the layouts," Timmy adds.

"My dear boy! That layout was *fabulous*!" Robin dramatically clutches his chest as if he's going to have a heart attack. "When I saw Jaime's photos, I thought, 'Well, they'll spread the living room across two pages, but when I got the issue, you had made the *pillows* two pages. Brilliant, *absolutely* brilliant."

"They were beautiful pillows," I say.

"*Hand*-dyed to my *exact* specifications in a tiny village in Thailand. I sent over the tiniest samples of the colors I wanted—a *dried* petal of a rose, a piece of *bark* from a tree, a *shard* from an old broken plate, oh, I can't remember what else. But, my dear, for my next project—this *fabulous* apartment in the Dakota—you simply must be *sure* to give me the cover." Robin giggles.

"Leaf says if anyone *asks* for the cover, he's *sure* not to get it." Timmy rubs his fingers and thumb together. "Shall I tell her what you just said?"

"My dear *darling* boy!" Robin caresses Timmy's sleeve. "What would you like Santa to bring you for Christmas this year?"

When Geraldo spins around to find a waiter to bring more Champagne, the balloon sleeves of his black silk shirt billow. He is sealed in tight black leather pants tucked into knee-high black boots with six buckles parading up the side.

"You look as if you're ready to burst into a song from *The Pirates of Penzance*," Robin says.

"And you look ready to sing 'Poor Wand'ring One!'" When Robin seems surprised, Geraldo adds, "Just because I ride a motorcycle, Gums, doesn't mean I don't know Gilbert and Sullivan."

"Why does Geraldo keep calling you 'Gums'?" I ask Robin.

"Well, if you're a *very* good boy, I might show you."

Geraldo isn't as evasive. "Robin removes his teeth when he blows someone."

"It's a sensation, I *assure* you, Geraldo, you will *never* experience." Robin turns to me. "Have you been at the magazine very long? Why have *I* never heard of you?"

"I've been there for almost exactly one year."

"I've been a decorator for a lot longer than that. In fact, the first job I ever had was decorating my mother's womb in moire silk." Robin tosses one strand of his scarf over his shoulder. "Before I was a decorator I was a *whore*. It always helps to have *something* to fall back on."

"Usually you fall on your face." Geraldo pretends to whisper in my ear, but he wants everyone to hear. "Robin's had at least two facelifts. He's over sixty but pretends he's only forty."

"At least *I'm* not pretending to be *butch*," Robin says and prances away.

"I guess I should go say 'hello' to Larry's wife," I tell Timmy.

"God, whatever for? She's as mousey as her husband. *No one* wears the pants in that family. Say, Geraldo, did you bring any snow? Oh, Anthony, don't look so naïve! Figure it out."

Oh. Cocaine.

"I think the weatherman predicted snow flurries in the men's room in five minutes." Geraldo pats his back pocket. "I'll meet you there."

At first I decide not to join them. Then I think: *I've never had cocaine. And this is free.* I come out of the bathroom soaring. "That made me so horny I could hump a fire hydrant."

"You dog!" Timmy nods his head toward a young waiter. "I'm sure that one would welcome a blowjob in the stairwell."

"Not my type."

"Oh, right. No mustache. Well, if you're not interested…" Timmy floats toward the waiter.

I'm left alone for a moment, but I'm afraid to talk to anyone when I'm this high. So I meander through the room eavesdropping on conversations.

"I'm surprised Geraldo Cortez was invited," Walter says to Ivory. "I'm even more surprised he came."

"Of course Leaf invited him. She's not going to tell him she's not publishing his project. It's simply never going to appear in the magazine."

I'm suddenly famished and head to the dessert table. Munching on miniature fruit tarts, I overhear Colette Bruin talking to columnist Judy Berlin.

"Did you notice who *wasn't* invited to this little soiree? Jake White. No one wants to be reminded that our press agent might have purchased this honor for our elite editor-in-chief."

Suddenly Claret Bruin is tapping a microphone with his scotch glass until he gets everyone's attention. Obviously drunk, he rambles on about how pleased he is with the magazine, what a wonderful group of people work for him, and finally gets around to congratulating Leaf on her award.

Leaf teeters to the microphone in stiletto heels. After saying what an honor it is to be named Woman of the Year, she adds, "Since I became editor, *Inside* has not only doubled its subscriptions, it's doubled its ad pages. But as everyone knows, no single person is responsible for our tremendous growth and national recognition. And I'm truly indebted to the little people who help make *Inside* such a good publication."

"So that's what we are," Walter whispers behind me. "*Little people.*"

And Burton Fisher adds, "Leaf Wyks wouldn't know the difference between Louis XIV and Louis Armstrong."

PART TWO
THE ART DIRECTOR

DECEMBER 27, 1977

"When the walls are white we want them to come out white in the photograph," I tell David Ellis over lunch at a tiny restaurant he chose in Chinatown. In September, Leaf offered me a trip to San Francisco to discuss the poor quality of David's shots, but I haven't been able to get away before now.

"You don't have to tell me what to do." The photographer is wearing a loose sweater, but it doesn't hide a thick waistline. He's had a permanent in an attempt to cover his bald spots, but it isn't working. He's not approaching fifty very well. "I've been at this a lot longer than you have."

"I'm sure you have." I'm tired of being diplomatic. David is defensive about everything I suggest. "But as I said earlier, lately the pictures you send us have been too orange."

"Leaf likes my photos. She's told me so a hundred times." When David speaks, he barely opens his mouth, maybe to obscure a bottom row of overlapping teeth. "She said they look like they're lit by candlelight."

"You can have *some* of the pictures glow, especially in a night shoot, but you still need highlights, to see details in the shadows. You have to use the right exposure."

"I know damn well what's the right exposure, Anthony!" A Chinese couple at the next table looks over. David frowns at them. "Listen, kid, if Leaf's happy, I'm happy. I'll just keep doing what I've always done, okay?" He signals to the waiter to bring him another Tsingtao beer. His third.

"Do what you want, David." I've no patience left. "But think about this: When was the last time one of your photos was on the cover of *Inside*?"

David doesn't meet my eyes. We barely talk as we finish the meal, neither one of us mentioning photography again. Outside the restaurant, David says, "Listen, my assistant, who's been with me for years, moved to New York a couple of months ago. I haven't been able to find another one I can work with, but I'll get it together. I mean it." And he walks away.

I'm not interested in seeing Burton Fisher while I'm in San Francisco, even if he is the best designer on the West Coast, but Leaf said he's being evasive about giving *Inside* his Russian River getaway and I should see what I could do. The person I *am* interested in seeing again is Mark Romano. Burton has dinner plans every night I'm here, so he suggests we meet for drinks at Lion Pub, a gay bar in Pacific Heights.

Burton commands a space by the fireplace. Some of the men at the bar take notice of him, not because they're attracted, but because of his booming voice. Everyone ogles Mark. The well-dressed crowd is mainly older, so youthful Mark stands out. I sense he's aware of this. No one gives me a second look. I must give off don't-approach-me vibes. I don't care; Mark's the only one who appeals to me.

"When I was in L.A. I had a meeting with Sarah Cohen about carrying my furniture designs in her showroom," Burton says. "I'm tough but that woman is unbending."

"Do you know what Jason Hunt calls her?" I figure I might as well share some of Timmy's gossip. "'Sarah Serpent.'"

"Fitting."

"So is she going to carry your line?"

"Of course! Selection is the best to-the-trade showroom in L.A., and I want my work seen—and bought."

"How's the photographing going?" I ask Mark.

"I've been taking a class. There's a lot to learn but I'm enjoying it."

"David Ellis is looking for a new assistant."

"He's an old friend," Burton says.

"Emphasis on *old*." Mark grins.

"Why don't you call him, Mark? He has all the photo equipment, even if he doesn't always use it properly—maybe I shouldn't have said that." I raise my eyebrows.

"I'll call him myself." Burton pinches Mark's cheek. "It's about time you start earning money of your own."

Mark glowers and turns red. "Excuse me, I have to use the facilities." He walks to the back of the bar.

"He's so sensitive," Burton says. "What's a little teasing among friends?"

I'm not sure I want Mr. Fisher as a friend but I must be polite. "What made you interested in interior design, Burton?"

"Latino workmen." He roars as if he's said the funniest thing ever. "Whenever those hot young men painted our living room, I'd sit there and drool. One guy never wore the regulation white jumpsuit. He always had on a thin tank top. He noticed me staring at his nipples and suggested I follow him into the bathroom. The other workers must have thought he had the smallest bladder in the world, because he spent more time in the john with me than he did painting." Once again he laughs too loudly. "My mother was one of those women who redecorated wherever she got bored. Some women buy hats. My mother bought pillows. One year when she decided to redo the living room, I suggested a color scheme, so she took me shopping with her, and I ended up selecting all the furniture. After her bridge club ladies saw what I'd done, they wanted me to do their homes too."

"Did they pay you?"

"Of course they paid me! The more I charged the more they wanted me. Believe me, over the years I've encountered several husbands who would have liked to kill me. But they signed the checks." He lights a slender brown cigarette. "You know what I hate about all my rich lady clients? Their voices. Whenever they run into each other, their voices go up an octave as they squeal their false delight in seeing one another. I want to slap them."

Mark returns from the restroom.

"Meet anyone interesting?" Burton asks. Mark's smile is sad. "You two have a chat. I'm going to talk with Hutch."

"Robert Hutchinson," Mark tells me as Burton crosses the bar. "He did a fabulous design for Wilkes Bashford's men's shop. Of course, Burton claims Hutch learned everything from him but he's actually very jealous."

"How did you and Burton meet?"

"He used to go to the 'Y' to watch the young guys swim. He probably still does." Mark finishes his drink. "I stayed at the 'Y' when I first moved here."

"From where?"

"Idaho. Anyway, Burton was very obvious. He didn't get in the pool. He sat in the stands fully dressed and *stared*. One day he asked me to dinner. I hadn't had a decent meal in two weeks, so I accepted. Three weeks later I moved into his house."

"How long ago was this?"

"About a year and a half." He follows my gaze. "Who are you looking at?"

"The strawberry blond. He has beautiful hair."

"And the rest of him ain't bad either! His name's 'Dallas.' He works for Hutch. Do you want to meet him?"

"No, I'd rather just watch."

"Like Burton," Mark says softly. "Is Dallas your type?"

"I don't think I have a type. As long as he has a moustache, I think he's gorgeous. Is Burton your type?"

"You're my type." Mark leans forward, his lips grazing my ear. "You have a really hairy chest."

Even though I'm wearing a winter coat, two buttons of my shirt are unfastened. Unlike half the men here, I'm not adorned with six chains: just one gold choker. "You're Italian. Don't you have a hairy chest, too?"

"Not like you." Mark slips a hand inside my shirt and caresses my chest. "Do you mind if I touch you?"

"Not at all. But it seems risky."

"Life's risky, Anthony. That's what makes it endurable." His smile is bitter.

Burton returns and we have another round of drinks. I ask him about his home on the Russian River.

"Oh, don't worry about it. Of course I'm giving it to Leaf. *Inside*'s got all the other magazines beat. I just wanted to watch her squirm." He wraps his chenille scarf around his throat. "Listen, I'll call Dave Ellis tomorrow and ask if Mark can borrow his equipment, then the three of us can drive out to the River and shoot my place. What do you say?"

He doesn't wait for an answer. As soon as we exit the bar, Burton's sexy young chauffer pulls up in a Bentley.

DECEMBER 28, 1977

Early the next morning Burton sits next to the chauffer in the Bentley while Mark and I ride in the back. Burton has the car heater on full, and our coats—and a picnic basket packed by his butler—are in the trunk. As we approach the Golden Gate Bridge, it's a calendar picture with fog as dense as clouds. Once we're on the other side, I stare out the back window for one more look.

Mark takes a sip of coffee. "What were you planning to do today before Burton high-jacked you?"

"Visit the de Young Museum."

"You can visit the museum any day," Burton says over his shoulder.

"No, *you* can the museum any day." I tell him. "*I* live in Los Angeles."

"Art is boring. Tell us about the first time you had sex."

"I haven't. I'm a virgin."

Mark pinches my thigh. He seems to enjoy my sassing Burton.

"Well, then, Mark, you'll have to tell him about the first time *you* had sex." Burton lights one of his brown cigarettes and lowers his window half an inch so the smoke escapes.

Mark twists so he's facing me. "Do you want to hear?"

"Every detail."

"Give him the flashback, first," Burton commands.

I get a strange feeling that this has all been rehearsed; that there's a set up. And I'm the mark.

"The Flashback," Mark announces. "When I was fifteen my older brother Tony found my so-called 'collection of fag porn.'" Mark makes quote marks with his fingers. "It consisted of exactly two rather tame magazines of men posing in g-strings against rock formations or romping with horses. Tony brought 'the filth' to our father, who thought he could beat 'the evil' out of me with his belt." His dark eyes mist over.

"This was in Idaho?"

"Yeah, Burley—dead center in the middle of nowhere between Boise and Salt Lake City. After Tony spread the word, you can be sure my last two years at high school were not pleasant. I don't know what I would have done if it hadn't been for my mother. She convinced me that there was a better world out there and I just had to hang on until I could leave. The day after graduation she handed me $300 and I left for San Francisco.

"I took a Greyhound bus, and not realizing how far it was, I walked from the terminal to the Embarcadero 'Y,' dragging my suitcase. I arrived soaked in sweat. As soon as I got my room, I headed for the showers. Within less than a minute, a young man swaggered in and turned on the faucet next to me. He was immediately erect and just stood under the spray soaping his genitals. He was very thin and so white it looked like he'd never once been in the sun. He had bright red pubes, almost orange. He also had about a dozen pimples on his face."

"About how old was he?"

"Eighteen? Nineteen? Anyway, he wasn't attractive at *all*. But I got erect. I mean there was a guy in a public shower with a hard-on standing right next to me! Of course, I got hard. So he reaches over and puts his hand on my head. And at first I thought he was going to kiss me, but he just kept pushing on the back of my head until it dawned on me. So I knelt down in front of him, and for the first time in my life I had another man's penis in his mouth. It tasted like Ivory soap."

I don't say anything.

"Did that story gross you out?" Mark puts a hand on my knee. "You're so quiet."

"I thought it was touching." We ride in silence for a while.

Burton lowers his window and Mark shouts, "Don't you dare toss out that cigarette! You know there's a drought and a fire hazard."

Burton holds up his middle finger—I notice he's wearing diamond cufflinks—but he puts the butt in the ashtray and raises the window. He tunes the radio to a classical station. Mark falls asleep before we reach San Rafael, and I look at the landscape as we zoom along Redwood Highway. Burton also dozes.

The chauffer smiles at me in the rearview mirror. He's probably not yet thirty. Under a black motorcycle cap, straight greasy black hair covers the back of his neck. Black wool pants are teamed with a long-sleeve black cotton shirt with double pockets. His skin is dark—maybe he's Greek or Latin—and acne-scarred. His black eyes are under the shadow of a single thick brow, not usually appealing but on him it's sexy. "My name's Paul," he says in a soft deep voice. "Sometimes Mr. Fisher forgets the introductions."

"I'm Anthony."

"Yes, I know. You need *anything* this weekend, you let me know."

Past Guerneville, Paul turns onto a narrow twisting road. The trees are so dense little sun gets through. I wonder how dark the rooms will be at Burton's house and if he's borrowed enough lighting equipment from David.

As we spiral up, we pass pseudo-cabins with vertical wood panels painted red or white or blue. Most of them don't have much style although a couple could be described as "cute." Paul turns onto a gravel drive. "We're here," he announces, and Burton and Mark stir.

Of course, Burton's house isn't "cute." It's not even a cabin.

If Frank Lloyd Wright had designed vertical homes instead of long horizontal structures with extended eaves, this is what he would have built. In fact, it looks like a Wright home placed on its side. Thick square wood columns soar skyward, echoing the Redwoods surrounding the property. Most of the house is red-stained wood, but one tall, windowless wall presents a façade of rough bark.

The interiors are equally breathtaking. The main room soars three stories; the tallest wall is all glass so that we seem to be in the midst of the giant trees. A fireplace is composed of irregular stones. An oversized U-shaped banquette is upholstered in creamy leather; large pillows are made of woven strips of brown leather. The coffee table is a flat-topped boulder—a miniature mesa. The dining area features round plate glass supported by half a dozen rough-hewn tree stumps. Upstairs, the master bedroom looks toward a cantilevered terrace with a Redwood rising through a hole in the middle. *Majestic* doesn't begin to describe it.

While Mark and Paul unload the photo equipment Burton makes a pot of coffee.

"There's a slight chance of rain this afternoon," he says, "so we should probably shoot the exterior first. Let's look at angles while the coffee's brewing."

He suggests a shot looking directly toward the front door, but I think it's uninteresting. While Mark assembles the tripod and camera, I walk around looking for other views. At the side of the driveway, I shout, "I think we should take it from here.

Is there a wide-angle lens?"

Burton doesn't even bother coming over. "You can't see the front door from there."

"The front door is a boring piece of planed wood. From here you not only get the soaring height of the house, you see the bedroom terrace jutting into the trees. Mark, please bring the camera here so Burton can look through the lens to see what I mean."

As he positions the camera, Mark whispers, "Nobody talks to Burton like that."

"Well, maybe they should. Look, I just want to get the best shots."

"Burton, you really should see it from here," Mark calls. "It's like the house is a rocket ship ready to blast off."

Burton ambles over and stands behind Mark. Then he walks away. "I'll ask Paul to put out the deck chairs since the terrace will be in the shot."

"Mark, turn the camera." I motion ninety degrees with my hand.

"But you said to use a wide-angle."

"Yes, but not horizontally. Vertically."

By the time Burton returns, I'm examining a black-and-white Polaroid under a Loupe. I hand it to Burton then remove a fallen branch that's cluttering the yard.

"The architect will be pleased," Burton says.

"Who's the architect?" I ask.

"Me." Burton's laugh shatters the stillness.

"Okay, Mark. I think we're ready for film. After you shoot this, please do a close-up of the rough bark on that wall. Don't include any of the structure, just a detail of the bark. I want it to be all texture, very sharp focus, almost three-dimensional. I'll be inside."

I don't tell them that I plan to make this detail shot a full page with just the title of the article dropped out in white.

Because no lights are needed, the exterior shots go quickly. When Burton and Mark come inside, they find me kneeling in the great room.

"I hope to God," Burton says, "you're praying for forgiveness."

"I'm considering camera angles. Come sit down for a minute."

Burton gets his cigarettes from the kitchen counter. He lights one, then sits as far away from me as the banquette allows. Mark plops down between us.

"For some reason," I begin, "all the interior photographers shoot looking down on a room. I don't know if it's because they're taller than I am, but I find their shots uninviting. It's as if they're making a record of the room."

"Isn't that what we're supposed to do?" Mark asks.

"I don't think it is. I find it distancing. I want the reader to *experience* the room. I want him to feel he's *sitting* in the room. I want *intimate* shots."

"And how do you propose doing this?" This time it's Burton with the question.

"By positioning the camera lower. By focusing closer into the room." I get on my knees again, beside the banquette, facing the coffee table and the large window. I frame my eyes with my hands. "If this is the entire shot, you're *part* of the room."

Mark kneels beside me, making a frame with his hands. "Wow! It's incredible!"

Burton frowns. "But how much of the room do you see? You're just getting a sliver."

"I'm getting the *feel* of the room. Mark, take a Polaroid to show him. Don't worry about the lights right now. Just do a quick vertical shot to show him the angle."

"You're very excited about this, aren't you?" Burton actually smiles at me.

"I love doing this." I don't tell him this is the first time I've art directed a photo shoot of a home. I've been thinking about this for a long time, about how I can make *Inside*'s photography different from the other shelter magazines. I hardly slept last night I was so excited about this opportunity.

And there's another advantage to me being on the shoot: I can do the layout on the spot and take only the pictures I need. "We can do two shots in here: this vertical one to show the height. Then with the wide-angle lens we can do a horizontal, getting in the whole living room with the dining table in the background. We can also do a close-up of the table's tree stumps. The whole story will be about texture and height."

It takes more than an hour to get the lighting right on the first shot, but it's as beautiful an image as I saw in my mind.

"Anyone know what time the sun sets?" I ask. "Not that it matters much with all these trees."

"Just before five," Burton says.

"Mark, we have to get the next two shots done before then so the lighting will be consistent. We can do the master bedroom at night. There are lights on the terrace, aren't there, Burton?"

"There are lights in the trees, as well."

The accessories are few but perfectly chosen, so we don't have to do much fiddling. Once we have the best angle we merely make slight adjustments to make everything look right from the eye of the camera. Lighting takes the most time, flooding the interior for balance so that the view through the windows won't wash out but keeping the shadows realistic and eliminating glares and reflections.

Mark and I do all the work. Paul hovers in the background, refilling our glasses with water. Burton paces and smokes, occasionally tossing out a comment or asking me a question.

"You're a little dictator, aren't you? I bet you even bossed your parents around."

"They're both Gemini. They can't make a decision."

"You probably drove your teachers mad too, telling them how to run the class. What was your major?"

"I split it between graphic design and photography."

When we finish the two living room shots, we take a short break to eat the sandwiches from the picnic basket. Then we move on to the next shot. And the next. And two more. Around midnight, Mark exposes the last sheet of film and we're done. He falls flat on his back.

"These low angles are murder on my knees!"

While I help Mark pack the photo equipment, Burton uncorks a bottle of wine.

"This *vino* is from right around here." He sounds as proud as a vintner.

"Did you stomp the grapes yourself?" I think I might have gone too far so try to turn it into a joke. "Like on *I Love Lucy* when they went to Italy."

"You're relentless, you know that?" Burton looks again at the Polaroids laid out on the dining table. "But you're good. Thank you."

"Thank you for letting me do it."

"I think you have some ice cream in the freezer." Paul goes into the kitchen.

"I told the IRS my San Francisco house is my showroom and therefore tax deductible," Burton says. "They actually bought it. But it didn't work on this house. The taxes are outrageous."

"Is the magazine going to pay me for these photos?" Mark asks.

"Absolutely. And you deserves every penny."

"It better be more substantial than a few cents," Burton says

Paul brings back four bowls of vanilla ice cream drizzled with red syrup.

"What's that on top?" I ask.

"Raspberry liqueur," Paul says.

"Framboise," Burton says.

"It's awful to drink," adds Paul, "but great on ice cream."

After practically licking his bowl, Burton gets up. "I don't want to go back to the city tonight. Let's spend the night here."

"I didn't pack my toothbrush." I wonder if this is an effort by Burton to exert control.

"There's everything you need in the guest bedroom." Burton starts up the stairs. He adds only one word, but it's charged with meaning. "Mark."

I think Burton wants Mark to join him upstairs, but Mark flips a switch to ignite the logs in the fireplace then turns off the lights so the room glows.

Paul takes the bowls into the kitchen.

I examine the Polaroids on the dining table. Mark stands besides me, massaging my back.

Paul returns with another bottle of wine and refills the glasses, then picks up his own. "I'll say goodnight." He disappears into a room off the kitchen.

"Come on," Mark says, "Let's go into the living room and relax."

I sit in the middle of the banquette, hoping Mark will sit beside me, but he settles on the floor at my feet.

Burton returns in a black silk kimono with a dragon embroidered in gold on the back. He sits next to me. "Shall I tell you about the first boy I had a crush on?"

I'm afraid my voice will display too much feeling—surprise, discomfort, anxiety, maybe even panic. I nod.

"I was just an average student," Burton begins, "but I was great at tennis. My biggest rival on the court was Roberto Marino. We went to different schools but would play against each other at the country club."

"They were both fifteen," Mark whispers. "Sophomores."

"I knew from an early age that I didn't like girls. For one thing, I couldn't stand their shrill squeals and giggling. I didn't want to be around them. And I hated it when they hung around Roberto. The girls called him *Bobby*, but I think he liked it that I called him *Roberto*.

"At the country club, the swimming pool was separated from the tennis court by the long low building. On the pool side were complete changing rooms for both sexes, but on the court side there was just a cabana with a few lockers and a vending machine. One day after a game of tennis Roberto went into the cabana and got us both a Coke.

"'It's so hot!' he said and took off his shirt. For a teenager he already had more chest hair than most grown men. He dropped down into a bamboo chair and stretched out his legs, his toes pointing toward me. He tapped his heel. I just stood there staring at him. And he kept tapping his heel. He seemed to be getting really impatient. Tap, tap, tap. Finally I understood. I got down on my knees, loosened the laces and removed his shoe."

Mark slowly takes off my shoes.

"I took a deep breath as I held his foot to my nose," Burton continues. "When I took off his sock, he thrust his foot toward my mouth and I sucked his big toe."

Burton tilts his head back, shuts his eyes and inhales as if he's recalling the aroma of Roberto's sweaty feet. And Mark nibbles my toes.

"I did the same thing with Roberto's other foot. I licked the dark hairs on his toes. I made love to his feet—kissing and sucking them. Devouring them."

Mark runs his tongue along my instep.

I long to put a hand on Mark's head and caress his soft hair, but he's too far away. I look at Burton. His kimono is open and his stubby penis erect. He takes a long swallow of wine.

"Roberto drank his Coke. Then he unfastened his belt buckle and lowered his zipper. He was wearing an old jockstrap; the mesh was so worn public hair poked through and I could see the dark skin underneath. 'This was my father's jockstrap,' Roberto said. 'Now it smells like both of us.' He raised his hips and I pulled down his shorts then buried my nose in his crotch. I love the smell of male sweat."

Mark unfastens my belt buckle, lowers my zipper, and I raise my hips so he can pull down my jeans. Only I'm not wearing underwear, and my penis springs straight up.

"Ah, you cheated." Burton stretches his arm and curls the hair at the nape of my neck. "Your cock is the same size as Roberto's. I knew it would be. You look so much like him. You could be his brother. I bet you have just as much chest hair."

Mark lifts my polo shirt over my head.

"Hard pink nipples just like Roberto's. I loved sucking his nipples."

And Mark sucks one of mine and pinches the other.

"I found it erotic that Roberto was completely naked and I was fully clothed. I opened my mouth and Roberto watched me swallow his entire erection."

Mark takes good direction.

"Roberto taught me how to suck cock. I learned from his breathing what he merely enjoyed and what drove him wild. I stuck the tip of my tongue into his piss hole, and I bit the frenum. I slowly swallowed the whole shaft then I went up and down on it so fast it was just a blur."

Mark does everything he's told.

"I knew I was doing a good job when I saw tears in Roberto's eyes. That first time I watched his cum gush forth and land on that hairy chest. It smelled even better than the jockstrap. Essence of male. And then I licked up every drop."

Mark does that too.

"That whole time I never touched myself, but when I stood up, my shorts were stained. I had come too."

"That I *can't* do." Mark lowers his jeans and boxers, stands on the banquette straddling my legs, and I open my mouth.

Burton gently twists the hair above my neck. "Roberto and I played tennis at least three days a week until we graduated. I never did it with any other boy. Later, when I was in the Navy, I serviced several Italians on my ship. Excuse the deliberate pun. I never expected them to reciprocate. And they never did."

Mark climaxes. I lean back. Burton's come too, without touching himself.

Paul hands me a warm cloth and small towel. Was he behind us, watching the entire time?

DECEMBER 29, 1977

The next morning I come downstairs barefoot in jeans.

"I know you don't drink coffee, but there's orange juice." Mark piles plates on two trays. "Help me carry this upstairs, okay? It's freezing, but Burton wants to eat on the terrace."

We place the trays on a round teak table. Burton's smoking and nods in greeting. Even in a sunny spot it's too cold for me, and I put on my shoes and coat.

'The bacon is raw!" Burton holds a strip of bacon between his thumb and index finger. "You know I like it crispy."

"If it were any more crisp," Mark says, "it'd be burnt."

"Where'd you get these eggs?" Burton's voice is huskier than usual.

"They were in the refrigerator."

"They smell rotten."

I consume my breakfast, which tastes just fine.

Then Burton yells, "The toast is buttered! You know I hate it soggy!" He picks up his plate and flings it across the terrace like a Frisbee into the trees. Then he goes into the bedroom, and we soon hear the shower.

"Is he often like this?"

"No, usually he's worse."

The drive back to San Francisco is silent.

FEBRUARY 8, 1978

I stick my head in Leaf's office. "Do you want to ride together or take separate cars?"

"Where are we going?" Leaf looks up from a copy of *W*.

"To Christopher Richter's opening at the Frampton Gallery. It's just five blocks down the street. We could walk."

"I can barely walk to the ladies room in these heels. Let's take my car. I hope they have good hors d'oeuvres."

As soon as we enter the gallery, Christopher Richter rushes up to Leaf and kisses her on both cheeks. "I'm so glad you could come." His voice is hoarse and scratchy with a resolute accent, probably German.

"Do you know Anthony Dimora?" We shake hands.

Unlike many other artists, Christopher Richter is dressed impeccably. A gray pin-stripe suit enhances his tall, slender frame. I recognize a Ferragamo necktie from a recent ad in *Gentlemen's Quarterly*. I imagine he's approaching fifty. With short dark eyebrows pointing toward his completely shaved head, Richter looks somewhat satanic. I get the feeling it's a look he cultivates.

I'm uncomfortable under his gaze and want to move away. Besides, I'm eager to see his sculpture of Cole Bruin.

"Let me get you something to drink," Christopher tells Leaf. "We're serving three different German beers." He leads her to a bar.

I spot Cole standing by one of the life-size bronze torsos.

"I'm looking forward to seeing the sculpture of you. Which one is it?"

"It's not here. Christopher sold it to one of Geraldo's clients." He looks bored.

And I'm disappointed I won't get to see it. I wonder if the sculptor captured Cole's long eyelashes.

"Anyway," Cole adds, "it wouldn't have fit in with these pieces."

"Why not?"

"Well, for one thing, these are all torsos and mine wasn't. Mine is full body—from head to foot. And another difference is all the models in this show are assistants." He opens his palm like a magician and points to the torso's penis. "Don't you recognize Timmy? It's an exact replica. Down to the inch."

"Amazing. I'm surprised Timmy isn't here. You'd think he'd be basking in all the attention."

"Which is exactly why Christopher told the assistants they couldn't attend the opening. Herr Richter wants all the attention tonight. There's another party tomorrow night for the models and their guests."

"The invitation said the name of this show is—I can't pronounce it." I take a card out of my jacket pocket and point to the word: *entwurfsassistenten*. "Do you know what that means?"

"*Design assistant*. Not only are all the models assistants, they're all connected to the world of design."

"Do you know who they are?"

"Most of them. Shall I give you a tour?" Cole walks to a nearby sculpture and reads the label. "'Jimmy' is Sarah Cohen's secretary."

"Do you think she knows this? She's so refined, I'd think she'd be horrified."

"Christopher said she was going to buy this sculpture until he told her who it is." Cole moves to another work. "Sarah's the only one who has two assistants in the show. 'David' is my favorite. Doesn't he have a beautiful navel?"

"It's remarkable how each piece has its own individual characteristics. Does Richter make a plaster cast?"

"No, he sculpts from clay, then casts it in bronze. When I posed for him, it took nearly a month."

Geraldo Cortez joins us. Once again, he's all in black. He gets right to the point. "Do you know when the home I designed is going to be published? It's been nearly a year."

I can't tell Geraldo Leaf dropped the residence he designed because he decorated Colette's office. "Leaf makes the decision about when a home will be published."

"Well, she better get it in soon, or she won't get my latest project. It's nearly ready to photograph, but she has to run the one she has before I give her the new one. It's *fabuloso*, isn't it, Cole?"

"*Impresionante*." Cole smiles.

"I'd love to see it." Even though I know Leaf won't publish Geraldo's work, I'm interested in seeing what he's done. Some of his designs may be over-the-top, but at least he's creative and unique.

"Hello, boys," Colette Bruin says as she sweeps by. She's wearing pistachio green and too much perfume.

A waiter presents a tray. "*Gefüllte Eier*."

We look puzzled.

"Stuffed eggs."

Jason Hunt, in his usual blazer and chinos, comes over with Aiko Shimizu, who owns a very expensive flower shop. "Do you know one of my *assistants* posed for Christopher?" A vein throbs on Jason's forehead. "The nerve!"

"Which one is it?" I ask.

"Follow me."

We stop at a slim torso with an arched back so that the penis is thrust forward.

"I never realized how 'qualified' Terry is," Jason says. "Do you believe the size of that slong?"

Aiko has flawless skin. Not a blemish. Not a wrinkle. He's delicate and favors rather feminine clothes. This evening it's a mauve see-thru shirt. He's so slender I can see his ribs. His nipples are tiny buttons.

"I'm sure Christopher didn't ask your assistant to pose," Geraldo says.

"Of course not." Aiko smiles. "My assistant is female."

I watch Judy Berlin approach Leaf and Colette with a photographer from the *Los Angeles Times*. Leaf and Collette pose on either side of Christopher Richter. The two women beam that dazzling smile that only the insincere can master.

"Do you think," Aiko says in a whisper, "that Richter is really into all that S&M stuff like everyone says?"

"Whatever you heard is probably a lie: It's not sick enough." Jason sounds like an elderly spinster casting judgment. "A lot of gay men are into S&M, but it's only a game, a costume. Christopher takes it seriously. Too seriously."

"Are you speaking from experience?" I want to know.

"God, no!" Jason looks horrified. "Even raw silk is too rough for me!"

A waiter approaches. "Sauerkraut Balls."

"That sounds both disgusting and enticing." Geraldo takes one on a napkin.

I decline. "I wonder if they're going to serve anything sweet?"

Cole wanders away.

"Do you see who just went up to Leaf?" Jason quickly adds, "Don't everyone turn at once!"

The skinny man has a pointed nose, a receding chin and thinning hair. "Who is he?" I ask.

"Ted Powell," Jason answers. "An *alleged* architect."

The name sounds familiar.

Cole returns. "Try this." He holds a miniature pastry to my lips. "*Kleine Kraeple*. Little Doughnut."

I love the intimacy of the gesture and take a bite. Cole swallows the rest.

"That's what I'm going to call you from now on." Geraldo puts a possessive arm around Cole. "*Kleine Kraeple*. You have such a delicious hole."

"Oh, I remember now," I say. "Ted Powell is the architect of Leaf's house."

"Well," Jason says, "he's as boring as beige."

"Anthony, could you drive my car back to the office garage?" Leaf hands me the key to her Seville. "Ted Powell is going to take me to dinner."

FEBRUARY 11, 1978

Mr. Bruin enters my office just after five. I stand up, but he motions me to sit back down. "I just saw the advance copy of the May/June issue and wanted to tell you how good it looks."

"Thank you."

"I think the layouts are irreproachable, but some of the homes tend to be heavy and stilted. For the life of me, I can't figure out the criteria Leaf uses in selecting homes. Maybe she doesn't have any."

I don't know what to say, and perhaps he doesn't expect a response.

"I'm very pleased with you," he continues. "I was glad when you first came to me with your mock-up, but I'm afraid you'll get bored and want to leave."

"Why do you think I'd get bored?"

"Because the graphics may not be as challenging as at a magazine such as *Esquire*. The art director at *Esquire* has to come up with the graphic element to illustrate a story, but at *Inside*, you're presented with the images, and except for the art and antiques features, they're always homes. It must get repetitious."

"Not for me. I find it a challenge. How can I show a home to its best advantage? What subtle thing can I do to make the layout augment the home? How can I make each layout different so that it helps separate one home from another? I have lots of ideas before I get bored." I decide to plant a seed. "And if in the future I can go on photo shoots, I'd have another creative opportunity to select what to show and what to avoid in the interiors. I went on a photo shoot last year and did the layout right on the spot. It saved a lot of time, as well as money, since we only shot the pictures we needed."

Mr. Bruin's brow crinkles. "You don't usually go on photo shoots?

"I've only been on that one. If Leaf doesn't see a home in person we usually look at scouting shots and decide what to shoot that way. If there's an interior designer he or she is always at the shoot. Otherwise the photographer goes by himself."

"I'll have to talk with Leaf about that. She told me you're the best art director she's worked with, and coming from Leaf that means a lot."

"Thank you for telling me."

"If there's anything you ever want or if Leaf gives you any trouble, you come to me. My door's always open." He taps my drawing table three times and leaves.

APRIL 12, 1978

When I finished decorating my new apartment, I invited Leaf over for lunch, assuring her I don't think my place is even remotely suitable for the magazine. She accepted then canceled—twice—Timmy relaying flimsy excuses. I haven't pursued it. Now he's just told me she can come over today. In two hours!

I rush home and set my Cuisinart on puree. Leaf arrives as I'm setting the table.

"That's a beautiful mantel. Is it original to the building?"

"Actually, it's older. The building is from the fifties, and in the other apartments all the other surrounds are mid-century modern. The landlord told me the previous tenant bought this at an auction. She actually wanted to take it with her when she moved, but he wouldn't let her. I like that it's the only old piece in the room and that everything else is more contemporary."

The space is not large—there's a loveseat rather than a sofa— with the dining area at one end, but Leaf strolls around. "I like the hunter green walls above the white wainscoting. Most people are afraid to use strong colors."

"I read that people who like gray are depressed, but it's my favorite color, so I used it in the bedroom." I lead the way.

"Is most of the furniture from Harrison-Van Horn?"

"Yes. Not that I can afford it, but when I was freelancing, I did their brochures and they paid me in furniture." I point to a window. "I want to show you the curtain rod. It's just a dowel from an art supply shop, but I twisted twine around it."

Leaf looks up. "That must have taken *weeks* to do it for all the windows."

"I watched a lot of movies on the Z Channel while I did it."

"I know you said you're place is not for the magazine—and you're right, it's not—but it's nicely done and presentable. Have you seen Ivory's place?"

I shake my head.

"She stacked Knudsen milk crates for a bookcase. The coffee table is a cardboard box with a shawl thrown over it. Everything's a mishmash. There's a butterfly chair and a beanbag. She even has a waterbed. It's like she's still in college."

You should talk, I think, remembering the unfinished condition of her house.

"I should talk. I'm actually embarrassed to have people over. Well, you saw it, that time you brought over the layouts. Believe me, not much as improved. I really should fix it up, but I wouldn't know where to begin. So I do nothing."

"Sarah Cohen did such a good job on your office and the reception area, why don't you ask her to decorate your home too?"

"That's not a bad idea, Anthony. She told me that she expected to get some design projects after she did my office, and she did, but nothing she wanted. They were all offices, and she wants to do residential; so maybe I will ask her."

"Are you ready for lunch?"

I begin with crème of almond soup. Leaf doesn't say she likes it but finishes all in her bowl. Then she lights a cigarette.

"Do you have any idea what's wrong with Ivory?" She shouts to me as I work in the kitchen. "I walked by her office and she was sitting at her desk crying."

"She went through est last weekend, and it brought up disturbing memories."

"She's always latching on to the latest fad therapy. I don't understand why she just doesn't *live*." Leaf butters a roll. "You'd think at least if she was going to cry she'd close her door."

"Maybe she wants the attention."

"I wonder what her daughter thinks of all the therapies Ivory experiments with."

I stop in the doorway with a dish of sliced tomatoes in my hands. "Ivory has a daughter?"

"She's about thirteen and chubby. I have a feeling Ivory thinks chubby girls shouldn't be seen in public."

"Or mentioned. It's the first I've heard of her."

"You know what's wrong with Ivory?" Leaf stabs a tomato slice with her fork. "She's too good with the little things. She simply cannot grasp the overall picture."

I'm pleased at how high my spinach soufflé rose and cut a large wedge for Leaf.

"I went to the King Tut exhibit," I say. "Have you been?"

"I went to the members opening, but I really should go back. There were too many people to see any of the objects up close."

"I was surprised at how awed I was. It was very moving. I know the dramatic lighting had a lot to do with it, but still. The detail and workmanship on all the pieces, not just the Golden Mask, are exquisite. And all of it was crafted so long ago. We don't have anything in our culture to compare with it."

Leaf finishes her soufflé and I'm afraid she'll light another cigarette before I finish mine, but instead she serves herself a second helping.

"I want you to have Ted Powell's home photographed while I'm in Texas next week. He's an architect and I want to start featuring more architecture in the magazine. We can fly Mark

Romano down from San Francisco. But you art direct the shoot. The two of you did such a good job on Burton Fisher's Russian River house, I'm going to send you on more photo shoots." Before I can say how pleased I am, she continues. "You might have to do a bit of editing at Ted's place. Take a few things out. It might be best to shoot it at night."

"Isn't Ted Powell the architect who designed your house?"

"Yes."

She doesn't add more, but I know from Timmy that Leaf and Ted have been seeing each other ever since they met at Christopher Richter's art exhibit a few months ago. Then she says something that makes me forget she's being less than candid.

"I have a little announcement I think you'll like, Anthony. I've spoken with Larry, and from now on, you'll design *all* of the stories in the well—even the art and antique features."

"Thank you, Leaf. I'm thrilled! I won't let you down." I nearly kiss her check, but realize just in time she'd not like the gesture. "This may not be the right time to ask for it, but if I'm going to design the magazine, I have to have the title of art director."

"You're right. This is not the time. And you should have the title. It will happen. But not right now."

This is better than the dessert—homemade strawberry Italian ice.

At the door as she's ready to leave, Leaf says, "Be careful of Claret Bruin, Anthony. He's really not the nice man he pretends to be."

APRIL 18-19, 1978

"**W**as David Ellis upset," I ask, "when he didn't get the assignment?" My truck is filled with photo equipment as Mark Romano and I head toward the Los Feliz district to photograph Ted Powell's house.

"I don't know if he knows," Mark replies. "I haven't seen him in a while."

"How'd you borrow his equipment?"

"I didn't. Burton was so pleased with what I'd done with his Russian River house he bought all new equipment for me—more than I'll ever need."

I pull up next to a brown Mercedes. Ted Powell opens his front door in baggy sweat pants and a tank top. He has the thinnest, whitest arms I've ever seen. A large anchor is tattooed in blue under a smallpox vaccination scar. Maybe Ted was in the Navy. As he gives us a tour of the house, Mark and I keep glancing at each other with shocked expressions.

When we're back outside to unload the truck, Mark says, "Do we have the right house? Why would Leaf want this dump for the magazine?"

"She and Ted having been dating."

"What does she see in him? I don't think he's the least bit attractive, do you?"

"His nose his too big, he has a receding hairline and a receding chin, practically no lips, and big ears. No, I wouldn't say he's attractive." I grunt. The equipment is heavy, but fortunately most of boxes are on wheels. "In profile he's almost like a Dürer drawing, and a lot of people find them appealing."

"They admire the *artist*, Anthony, not the grotesque he's drawn. This one's the heaviest, so we'll have to lift it out of the truck together." When the metal box is on the driveway, Mark adds, "Of course, Ted Powell may have other qualities. Like a big dick! Did you notice it bouncing around in those baggy sweat pants?"

I lift out a duffle bag filled with tripods for the lights. "When Leaf told me about this place, she said I'd have to do 'a bit of editing. Take a few things out.' Hell, we need a Dumpster."

"Even shooting it at night, we're going to see too much."

We stack the equipment in the kitchen since we won't be shooting that room. I wish we weren't shooting any of the rooms. I'm sure Leaf will want to give her "friend" eight pages, which means I have to come up with at least six shots—if I can find one to make a two-page spread.

"Ted, did you get any flowers?" I stand in the dining room wishing I could just wave a wand or wiggle my nose and make everything disappear.

"No. Was I supposed to?"

"We usually like a bouquet on the dining table, something smaller in the living room and maybe an orchid or other specimen in the bedroom."

"Sorry. No one told me."

Don't you look at the magazine? "The Farmers Market is open until nine. Would you mind going there? It's not that far away. Third and Fairfax."

"I know where the Farmers Market is, Anthony."

As soon as he's out the door, I tell Paul, "I want to set up the first shot before he gets back. I don't want him interfering. We've got a lot of stuff to move. I like that screen in the living room. I don't know if it's authentic Deco, but it's graphically interesting. The sofa can stay, but I hate the coffee table. The one in the den is better, and we're not going to shoot the den, so let's move that one in here."

But first I have to dust. And when we move the coffee table and two chairs, I have to vacuum. "While I'm doing this, would you take a vertical detail shot of the screen? That section in the corner where the scrolls look like waves is nice."

At least Ted has a large collection of architecture books. I pick two with attractive covers for the repositioned coffee table. I don't like the side tables in any of the rooms. They don't have to be designer pieces, but these look like yard sale rejects. In lieu of a table, I stack several armloads of the architecture books next to the sofa. The living room lamps are worse than the tables; the shades are out of scale and the ceramic bases are chipped—and ugly with poorly rendered leaves. So on the other side of the sofa I position a contemporary floor lamp I find in the den.

"Wow!" Ted's back from the market. "It doesn't even look like my place."

"Which is a good thing," Mark whispers.

"Don't worry," I tell Ted. "We'll put everything back." I look at the flowers he's holding. Pathetic. Besides having poor taste, he's cheap. He's purchased barely enough to make one decent bouquet. White hydrangeas, which I can use in the dining room, are already wilting. I take them into the kitchen and fill the sink with water. "Let's see your vases."

Nothing good. Most are generic glass containers that florists use. I select a round vase. At least it will echo the circles on the screen. Roses would be nice in the living room, but Ted's purchased daisies. Almost the cheapest flower one can buy. I guess I should be thankful they aren't dyed carnations. I just can't use the daisies in the living room; maybe they'll work on the nightstand in the bedroom. I break off all the hydrangea leaves and arrange just the greenery in the round vase. That ought to give florists pause. I place the vase on the stack of books.

"Okay, Mark, I'm ready. It's a horizontal shot. Take a Polaroid first before you do the lights so I can study the composition." He gives me a look. *"Please."*

Mark positions the camera low like I want it.

Ted hovers too close—and doesn't stop talking. "I see you found my architecture books. I decided to be an architect when I was nine and my parents took me and my brother to Greece. Of course, everyone raved about the Acropolis, but what interested me was how the columns had collapsed and were lying in ruin all over the site. I became fascinated with why a wall or a column would stand."

Mark hands me a Polaroid. "I want it tighter. I want to see just a sliver of these chairs in the foreground. No backs."

Ted doesn't even glance at the Polaroid but continues his monolog as if there hadn't been an interruption. "I went to Yale. Not that my grades merited it, but my father had gone there and had a lot of money, so I got in. And I must say, I excelled at structural engineering. What I lacked was creativity."

Mark and I can't resist exchanging looks, our eyebrows high in our foreheads.

"The buildings I design will stand a lot longer than the Acropolis. But I'm the first to admit my designs are derivative. Take Leaf's house, for example. I modeled it after Richard Neutra's Singleton house."

Mark hands me another Polaroid. "Perfect. Let me just rearrange this stack of books so it looks more structurally sound."

Mark covers his mouth to hide his smile.

"Is there something I can do?" Ted wonders.

"Clean off the dining room table. Remove *everything*. I'll be in there in a minute to help you."

Mark sets up the lights. Since it's a night shoot, we don't have to be concerned with the light appearing as if it's coming from a single, natural source, but I don't want hard, crisscrossing shadows.

We finish with the living room shot at 11:30. With the close-up of the screen, we have two images. I know I can get one each in the dining room and the master bedroom. That's only four. Not enough.

A simple china cabinet in the dining room is filled with high school field-and-track trophies, model cars, an abandoned saxophone and a pile of comic books. But this isn't a teenager's bedroom. I remove it all.

Ted continues to chatter as if someone were interested. "I got married right after graduation. She was a drama student but later admitted she had gone to college not to study acting by to find a husband. Well, she found one. We were together for four years, but it probably wouldn't have lasted that long if I hadn't been stationed in Korea for two of them. We have a daughter, Jenny. She's married with two kids of her own, but she lives in Germany, so I hardly ever see her."

"Do you have any furniture polish?"

Ted gets an old t-shirt and a can of Pledge. He wipes the table and the cabinet while I look through kitchen cupboards. A least the dishes are white, and there are a lot of them. I carry handfuls into the dining room.

"I don't want to set the table. Let's do a grouping of a stack of dishes, glasses and silverware at this end of the table, as if it's just before the table is set. I'll use the larger pieces on the shelves. We'll make them blurry and have just the foreground in focus." I begin arranging serving platters in the cabinet.

"All that belonged to my mother," Ted says.

"She must have had large dinner parties."

"She liked to entertain." Ted points to a small tureen. "You can use that for the flowers. I think I bought enough daises to fill it."

"Too expected," I say. "Do you have a plain white tea towel?"

"I think so." He brings a waffle-weave cloth from the kitchen. "Will this do?"

"Perfect." I place it beside the plates on the table. "Just before Mark snaps the shot, I'll place the hydrangeas on the towel. Everything will look spontaneous. But you'll have to shoot the exposures right away, Mark, because hydrangeas wilt fast."

"Maybe," he says, "you can wrap the stems in wet paper towels and cover them with a corner of the cloth."

"Great idea. Ted, you can start on the bedroom. Do you have fresh linen?"

"Yes."

"Iron the pillowcases. I don't want to see a single crease."

"He's a real dictator, isn't he, Mark?"

"He's heard that before, but he knows what he's doing."

The dining room is finished by 1:30 in the morning.

"I don't know what to do with the window above the nightstand in the bedroom," I say.

"What's wrong with it?" Ted asks.

"Since we're shooting at night it's going to be a black hole."

"Well, I don't have any curtains because the neighbors can't see in because of the hedge."

"Maybe we can light the shrubbery. Do you have electricity outside?"

"No. It's an old house."

"I guess we could run an extension cord."

Mark goes to the other bedroom window. "I think I can point a light out this window. Shall I try it?"

It works. I array a few items on the nightstand, fluff the duvet and arrange the pillows with their freshly ironed crease-
less linen. The daises don't look right, so I use one hydrangea
in a small tortoiseshell cup—Ted's toothbrush glass. A framed
family picture would make the setting more personal, but
there isn't one personal photograph in the entire house—not
even one of his daughter and grandchildren. Makes me wonder if they really exist.

Mark adjusts his lights, takes the shot.

Two fifty-five.

"Let's take a break while I think what else to shoot."

Ted asks, "Do you guys want any coffee?"

Mark does. I have juice.

I walk around looking for angles. Ted watches an old movie
on the television in the den. Mark unloads the exposed film in
the holders and reloads fresh sheets.

If he can fit his camera in the cramped space of the entry, I
can do a vignette of a red lacquered chest. On top I place the
most visually interesting trophy —a runner in full stride. I add
a woven reed box, a trio of small books—and the daises. I prop
the saxophone against the chest. On the other side, I place a
Charles Rennie Mackintosh chair I find in the guest bedroom.
It's probably the most valuable thing in the house. What's it doing hiding? Maybe it's fake. Well, the camera won't know. All
the while I'm thinking, *I need one more shot. I need one more shot.*

Mark's asleep on the sofa, his coffee cold and untouched.
Ted's snoring.

The foyer vignette, with the title, credits and a caption, can
open the left-hand page. The screen detail will look good as a
full page on the right. Then the two-page spread of the living
room. The dining shot will be a page and a quarter with two
columns left for the text. The bedroom shot can end the feature, but what to place opposite it?

I walk through the rooms for the sixteenth time. I even open all the closets.

And there they are. On the closet shelf in the den. Three architectural models.

I drag a chair away from the wall and position a small table in its place. I don't care what it looks like; I need only the flat surface and nothing on the wall. I gather more architecture books and arrange two piles, one higher than the other, and top them each with a model. The third model goes on the table.

Time to wake up Mark.

We finish shooting at 5:17. I still have to put everything back they way I found it while Mark packs up the photo equipment. I don't worry about making noise, hoping Ted will wake up and help me, but he keeps snoring.

We load the truck.

"Let's just go." I shut the front door. "I don't want to say goodbye to him. I don't want to see him ever again."

The sun has barely risen.

"Isn't Griffith Park around here?" Mark asks as I start the engine.

"It's right behind us. The entrance is just a few streets over."

"Can we go? I read about it in *Numbers* and would love to see the trails where the gays play."

"It's locked from sunset to sunrise. We can see if anyone's opened the gate."

A park ranger is unlocking the gate as we approach. He waves us through.

I drive to a spot high up with a view of downtown. The skyscrapers are golden with sunlight. We get out and lean against the truck.

"I'm so tired I could cry." I shut my eyes.

"And I was going to give you a blowjob."

"I'm all sweaty."

"I know. That's why I want to do it."

I'm not as attracted to Mark as I was before our adventure at Burton's Russian River house. That was sexually exciting, but I wanted more intimacy from him. Now he's offering another impersonal encounter. Don't I get a kiss? "We can't go into the trails and leave your new photo equipment in the truck."

"So let's do it right here. No one's around." He unzips my jeans.

"If that park ranger arrests us, you're calling Burton to bail us out." Then I shut up and let Mark perform his magic.

As we're driving down to the exit, Mark's head whips around as a car goes past heading up the road.

"Wasn't that Ted Powell's brown Mercedes?"

APRIL 21, 1978

Is it just coincidence that while Leaf is out of town scouting homes Colette Bruin asks to see me in her office?

I can smell her perfume in the corridor. Yves Saint Laurent Opium. I like the spicy scent but not in this quantity.

"The figures are awful." She waves a couple of sheets of paper as if I'm supposed to know what she's talking about. "Inside Choices is failing. I don't blame myself. The products I've selected are winners, but Leaf continues to veto all the interesting items, leaving only objects found in other catalogues. At the last minute, I added a hand-painted cachepot without showing it to Leaf. It's the only item that sold well."

She picks up the latest issue of *Inside* and opens to a two-page spread she's dog-eared. It's a photograph of a geranium red bedroom with a Jacuzzi, large enough for four, at the foot of the bed.

"Was it your decision to make this picture this large?"

"Yes." I sniffle then blow my nose.

"Do you have a cold?"

"It's your perfume."

"No one could possibly be allergic to a perfume this expensive." She shuffles through papers on her desk then hands me a mock-up for the next Inside Choices ad. "What do you think of this?"

"The pictures are too small," I blurt out before realizing that Larry probably designed it. And maybe I should have said something positive first. But I don't see anything positive.

"Don't stop. What else is wrong with it?"

"Well, the headline has too many words—no one's going to read it—and there's too much merchandise—it's chaotic."

Colette grabs the ad back, crosses out four of the objects with a black Sharpie marker. She marks through five words in the headline. Then she hands it back to me. "I need a new ad by Monday noon. And don't show it to anyone."

I know she means *don't show it to Leaf.*

APRIL 25, 1978

"There are some really awful homes out there," Leaf says when she returns from Texas. "The sad part is the homeowners don't know it."

"I know you've just seen a lot of homes, but Timmy said he has two boxes of submissions for you to review."

"They can wait until I get back from Europe."

"When are you leaving?"

"Sunday." She lights a cigarette. "With all the publicity the magazine's been getting, it's a good time to lock up some important homes. Derry is going to show me some of the great British manor houses. I'll also see some historic homes in France. But what I really want to concentrate on are some of the newer designers. We need a few really shocking interiors— lots of color and modern art. It's time to give our readers a jolt."

"That's great, Leaf. The readers shouldn't come to expect anything. Keep them surprised. How exciting!"

"I detest traveling—especially to foreign countries. I hate not knowing how much to tip or what the people are talking about. I always imagine they're talking about *me*."

"Well, if they're French, they're probably talking about their next great meal or tryst."

"Oh, I especially despise the snooty French women who

think they're better than everyone just because they're thin and have fabulous clothes." She stubs out her cigarette. "But I do enjoy room service. And I have a new Dick Francis mystery to read on the plane."

"Sometimes the flight's the best part of a trip."

"Listen, I need you to do something for me. Claret's secretary has been pestering me to see the house of a friend of hers, who, Maxine says, is 'a big movie star.' She isn't. She's a small-time actress who will never amount to anything. Her name is Joan Collins, and her only claim to notoriety is that she was once married to Anthony Newley, a fate I wouldn't wish on anyone. I'm sure the house is terrible, but you go. If you like it, we'll discuss it. Also Jake White has a client whose house he wants me to see. Another actress. She's married to Carl Reiner's son."

"Penny Marshall. She's one of the stars of *Laverne & Shirley*. It's the number one show on television, Leaf."

She waves her arm dismissively. "That doesn't mean it will be a good house, but we must be fair. There is one house that holds promise. George Burns. He had a decorator so it might pass. Timmy's set up the appointments while I was in Texas. But I've seen all the homes I care to see for a while. And I want to be fresh for Europe. So I want you to go. Timmy called, so they'll be expecting you."

"You mean you want me to go today?"

"Yes. Timmy has the addresses." As I turn to leave she adds, "Oh, by the way, Anthony, I think since you'll be scouting homes and going on photo shoots as well as doing all the layouts that you'll be too busy to design ads. *For anyone.*"

When I return from seeing the homes, Leaf isn't interested in hearing the details, just *yes* or *no*. I tell her, "We can get a small feature with George Burns, especially if it's 'At Home with…'"

"Okay, set it up."

By the time Timmy and I get to the gym I'm bursting to share all the details.

"This is the first time Leaf has asked me to scout homes on my own."

"She just wanted to get out of obligations she found tedious."

"I also think it was a perk so I wouldn't design any more ads for Inside Choices."

"Yeah, why did you do that? You must have known Leaf wouldn't like it."

"I was in a bind. Leaf is my boss but Colette owns the company."

"That's what I told Leaf. She understood."

"Thanks for sticking up for me."

"You ready to work on our biceps?"

We take turns on an incline bench doing curls. Timmy counts the reps.

"Eight. Nine. Ten. So what was Penny Marshall's house like?"

"Well you know she and Rob Reiner live in Encino, and not in the hills but in the flats, which is not very picturesque. I really don't understand why someone with money who lives in Los Angeles, where there's the ocean and the hills and the canyons, would pick an area that looks exactly like any town in the Mid-West."

"Nine. Ten. Maybe they're from the Mid-West and feel comfortable there."

"Rob's the son of Carl Reiner. He grew up in Hollywood. He conducted the tour. He's very glib. 'This is a chair. This is a window. If you stand in front of it, you can see the backyard. Not a pretty sight, is it?'"

"Seven. What was the house like?"

"Pleasant but not publishable."

"Nine. Was Penny there?"

"She arrived as I was about to leave. She didn't say hello to me, didn't acknowledge I was even in the room. She just collapsed at the kitchen table holding her head in her hands. A man who came in with her said she had to leave the set because she felt sick. 'I hate it, Rob. I just hate it,' she whined. I waved goodbye but no one waved back."

"Six. Did you meet George Burns? Seven."

"No, he wasn't there—just the designer. The living room gives new meaning to 'eclectic,' but I know what to shoot. There are two chairs covered in deep blue chintz with gold stars that will make a pretty composition around the fireplace. The dining room has foil Chinese wallpaper and an Edward Field carpet."

"Four. Leaf won't like that. Five."

"I know, but I envision a tight shot of the table set for dinner. He has good china. The designer said George's favorite room is the den. It's casual and comfortable, with floral chintz on the sofa and sunshine streaming through shutters."

We shake our arms and take a brief rest.

"To me the best part of George Burns' house is the bedroom, but Leaf would probably hate it. It's exactly as Gracie Allen left it—dusty blue with 1940s Moderne furniture. The time lapse doesn't function with the rest of the house, but I'm thinking a close-up of George's desk with a photo of Gracie on it. Pose George at the piano and we have a charming six-page feature."

We move on to side arm raises. I can finally lift as much weight as Timmy. But I can't do this exercise and talk at the same time, so I wait until we do the first rep.

"Joan Collins opened the door herself. Her lips were so thick and red they looked like Halloween candy. She wore a white tunic made of gauze. No slip. No bra. No panties. Timmy, I could see her pubic hair."

"Yuk!"

"Wait until I tell you about the décor. It was mainly white: shag carpet, low sofas, cotton drapes. There was some yellow, but those were urine stains. I hope they were from her dogs and not her."

"Oh my god!"

"It gets worse. The house had an open floor plan. Separating the living and dining areas was a small pond. The water was dark and stagnant. It probably hadn't been cleaned in years."

"What did you tell her?"

"That we'd be in touch. What I wanted to tell her was that her home isn't right for *Inside*. It isn't right for *House & Garden*. It isn't right for *Field & Stream*. But close."

MAY 12, 1978

Munching M&Ms, Leaf walks into my office. She extends the bag, and when I hold out my palm she lets two candies tumble into it.

"Well," she begins, "I've finally given Larry something he *can* do: nothing. Claret has agreed to make him corporate art director. His main responsibility will be designing the company Christmas card." She pours more M&Ms into her hand and shoves them in her mouth. "Now that you're art director, I want you to really concentrate on the covers. It looks like the November/December issue is going to be our biggest one ever with nearly double the ads we had last year. It's going to get a lot of attention, Anthony, and I want the cover to be special."

Before I can thank her, she tosses the M&M bag at me and leaves. There's exactly one piece left.

MAY 19, 1978

"Can you come pick me up?" Cole sounds upset.

"Where are you?"

"Beverly Hills High. Do you know where it is?"

"Yes. Where will you be?"

"I'll walk over to Lasky Drive, near the Moreno corner. It'll be easier for you to pull over there. Thanks, Anthony."

I tell Timmy I'm leaving the office early and won't be joining him at the gym.

"Is everything okay? You look worried."

"I'm fine. See you tomorrow, okay?"

Timmy lets it go. He knows he'll find out soon enough.

Sucking a Tootsie Pop, Cole hops in my truck. He's wearing gray slacks, a white button-down shirt and saddle shoes.

"I like you're shoes," I say. "I haven't seen a pair since I was in school."

"I'm bringing them back in fashion."

"You don't have any books or anything?"

"They're in my locker."

"No homework, huh?"

"I'll do it tomorrow in homeroom."

"Don't you have finals coming up soon?"

He shoots me an annoyed look.

"Sorry. If you wanted to have your parents quiz you, you would have called them instead of me." I squeeze his knee. "What's up? You sounded upset."

"I'm okay now. Some jerk was spreading a rumor about me. It didn't bother me, but then my closest friend asked me about it, and when I told her the truth, she spit in my face and walked away."

"I'm sorry." I sense he doesn't want to tell me the rumor.

"I don't have a lot of friends at school—I don't have a lot of friends period. But that doesn't bother me because most of the kids my age are stupid. Hey, I don't want to go home right now," he says as I approach Canon Drive. "Let's go to Hollywood."

"I'm surprised you don't attend a private school."

"My mom said she wasn't going to waste the money if I didn't have the grades."

"What'd your dad say?"

"Dad pretty much goes along with whatever Mom wants. He used to argue but realized there was no point."

"Don't most of the students in your grade have cars?"

"Yeah. I had one too. An old Karmann Ghia. But I got drunk and crashed it. My folks said I have to buy my next car myself." He pokes a finger into my side. "I understand congratulations are in order."

"What do you mean?"

"You're officially the art director."

"Yeah, it's great to have the title. But I didn't realize until three days later that Leaf didn't give me a raise."

"I've learned that if you don't ask for something you won't get it."

I turn onto Melrose Avenue and head east. Cole leans his head back and shuts his eyes. I decide to distract him from his problems by talking about myself.

"The very first night I arrived in Los Angeles, I went to Dude City."

Cole keeps his eyes closed but says, "On Highland Avenue."

"Right. I figured from the name that it was a Western bar, so I wore an unbuttoned denim jacket with no shirt."

"You must have looked hot."

"Well, some guy with a Dutch Boy haircut came up to me and said 'smile.' I replied that whenever someone says that to me I want to frown even more. Then he asked me if I wanted to go to his place and I said *yes*."

"Just like that? I'm surprised, Anthony."

"I have sex, Cole. Just not with guys who are underage. Anyway, I didn't have a place to stay and figured this would be cheaper than a hotel. Dan had a waterbed, and at first I thought I was going to be seasick, but it was great for sex. The next morning he told me I was glib and a little too rough."

Cole glances at me then shuts his eyes again.

"So I asked Dan if I could stay with him for a while. He said okay; I asked how long, and he said, 'Until it's time for you to go,' which is a song by Buffy Sainte-Marie."

"Never heard of her."

"Dan worked for *Billboard* magazine. He knew all the songs. Anyway, I stayed with Dan for two years."

"That's a long time. The sex *must* have been good."

"Actually, the best time was probably that first night. Dan's idea of a relationship was for him to go to the baths then come home and cuddle with me. He was also very cheap. He'd say, 'Let's go to the movies,' and when we'd get to the box office he'd announce he had a pass but I'd have to pay. Or he'd say, 'Let's go have ice cream,' and after he'd order he'd say he forgot his wallet. He would get free albums because of his job, and once he gave me one for my birthday. I could tell because it had a notch cut in the corner, which is how they mark promo copies."

"He sounds like a winner."

"It was Diana Ross' latest album, so at least I appreciated that. I was a big fan and told Dan that Diana was singing at Caesar's Palace in Las Vegas and I wanted to see her. Of course, he was too cheap to go until I said I'd pay for the hotel and tickets and the gas if he would drive. So we got there and I couldn't figure out why there weren't any tickets. All you did was make reservations. The night of the concert, I handed Dan five dollars and said, 'Give this to the man who seats us and maybe we won't be put at the *very* back.' Well, the man just kept walking and walking. There was one long table that butted up perpendicular to the stage, and this is where he sat us. I was the third seat from the stage. I said to Dan, 'Maybe if we had given him a twenty we could've sat in her dressing room.'"

Cole smiles but keeps his eyes closed.

"A frantic waitress came over and said it was a four drink minimum, so Dan and I each ordered two Black Russians and two White Russians. When she brought the drinks she was even more frazzled and said she'd collect the money later, that she had to get everyone's order because 'Miss Ross' wouldn't allow anyone to serve during her performance.

"So the show starts, and at one point Diana comes out into the audience singing 'Reach Out and Touch (Somebody's Hand)' and I put up my hand and she holds it. She stood right there singing to me and I tried to figure out how many layers of false eyelashes she had on." I turn on Highland and drive past Dude City, but Cole's eyes are still shut, so I don't point it out. "Well, after the show, I was a good boy and waited for the waitress to come collect the tab but she never did. The entire show cost me five dollars. And here's the kicker: Dan was furious that I got something for practically nothing."

"What a jerk! Why'd you stay with him for two years?"

"I didn't know any better. I thought I could get him to love me. He did love me, but not the way I wanted." I turn right on Franklin. "One night we got into an argument and I said, 'You remind me of my father,' and he shouted back, 'You remind me of my mother.' We both looked at each other and knew it was time to part. A few days later he put a record on the turntable and said, 'This is our song.' It was Gladys Knight singing, 'Neither One of Us (Wants to Be the First to Say Goodbye).'" I turn left on Grace Avenue, and halfway up the hill I nudge Cole and slow down. "This is the apartment building where Dan and I lived. Second floor."

Cole looks out the window. "Where's Dan now?"

"In the Valley."

I drive up the hill, and when I stop at the intersection, Cole says, "Let's go look at the hustlers on Selma Avenue."

I make a U-turn and head back down to Franklin. I want to ask Cole how he knows about the hustlers on Selma, but I'm afraid of the answer.

"That was the rumor the guy was spreading at school." Cole's voice is barely a whisper. "That I'm a hustler."

I don't have to ask if it's true.

"I just did it once. Or twice." Cole turns toward me and shouts, "Okay, six times!" He sits back. "It's a good way to make money."

"Don't your parents give you an allowance?"

"It's not the same. It hadn't even occurred to me to do it until one day I was hitchhiking and a guy stopped and asked if I was working. At first I didn't understand, and he said, 'Come on, kid. I'm not a cop. How much do you want for letting me suck your cock?' Of course, I had no idea, but I wasn't going to come cheap—unintentional pun—so I said fifty bucks. He said it was a bit steep but I was worth it. Then he saw my dick and said he'd give me twenty."

"That must have been upsetting."

"I was just glad he didn't kick me out of the car. Besides, I got twenty bucks and a blow job."

I turn left on Las Palmas, and just before we reach Selma Avenue, Cole says, "Drop me off at this corner and circle around the block a couple of times cruising me. It'll be fun."

He jumps out of the truck before I come to a complete stop. As I pull away a frightening question pops in my head. *How do I know you won't go with someone else?*

I quickly make four left-hand turns, and when I'm on Las Palmas again, I don't see Cole on the corner. When I'm back on Selma, I spot him leaning against tree. A Mercedes slows down followed by a Chevy El Camino. Cole is a forbidden fantasy: an innocent-looking schoolboy who wants to play.

I drive down a long block so when I double back this time I'll be on the same side of the street as Cole. It takes longer than I imagined, and I spot Cole bending into the window of white Lincoln Mark V. A guy with money. Will Cole get in? I slow to a crawl. Cole doesn't even look at me as I inch past.

I'm tempted to leave him and drive off but I circle the block again. When I'm back on Selma, the Mark V is gone. I stop in front of Cole and roll down the window.

"That guy only wanted to give me twenty. I told him it would be twice that." Cole flashes a teasing smile. "How much are you offering?"

"Cole." I hope he hears the sadness in my voice.

"Go around one more time. *Please!* Then park in that spot over there and I'll get in."

I don't want to but I do. I barely stop at the intersections and am parked in less than five minutes. I open the passenger door and Cole gets in.

"I know you're annoyed, but just sit here a minute, okay?"

Cole yanks his pants and boxers below his knees.

His three-inch penis looks like a mushroom poking out of thick blond pubic hair. I think it will be longer when he's hard, then I realize he *is* hard. I don't care that his cock is smaller than average—I'm not a size queen—and I have to force myself to not reach over and touch him.

I'm grateful there are no passing cars and no one on foot.

Cole pulls up his shirt. In ten quick pulls he squirts cum on his chest. Lots of it.

He breathes deeply. Then he wipes his chest with his undershirt.

"You can take me home now."

JUNE 1, 1978

"The submissions have really piled up," I tell Leaf. Timmy has twice set a meeting for her to review the pictures of residences designers and homeowners hope will be selected for publication. Twice Leaf has canceled. "We're up to three boxes."

"I know, but I hate going through all those photos," she says. "The homes are always so awful, it depresses me."

"It won't be so bad this time. I've gone through everything and weeded out the really terrible ones."

"Oh, but I have to see every one!" Leaf grabs my wrist. "I don't want you to reject anything without my seeing it."

I'm hurt by her reaction. "All I meant was that I've sorted through the submissions, putting the homes I think you'll like first and the bad ones last. It will go much faster this way."

"Good. Have you got the first batch out on the light tables?"

"Yes. It's all set up."

"Okay, let's do it."

"I'll tell Ivory we're ready."

"Let's do it without her." Leaf grabs a handful of M&Ms from a bowl on Timmy's desk.

I flick the switch for the first table lighting up six four-by-five transparencies.

"Whose house is this?"

"Ted Powell's."

Leaf leans in closer. "You're kidding! You did a great job."

"Thank you."

"When did you photograph this?"

"While you were in Europe."

"I've seen Ted twice since then, and he never mentioned it."

"Maybe he was waiting for you to say something."

"Let's publish it right away."

"The next issue's November/December."

"Perfect. Don't forget I want a special cover."

"I'm working on it." I indicate the next series of shots. "This is Princess Margaret's home in Mustique."

"There are only five shots. Why didn't Derry photograph the bedroom?"

"He said it looked like a hotel room. One you'd want to check out of."

"There's no picture of the Princess!"

"He said she was always in a swimsuit."

"Well, maybe we can get a PR shot. We can make this work."

Leaf quickly approves the photography of the next five residences then moves on to the next group of pictures, Joan Fontaine's New York apartment.

"I really love these shots," I say. They're moody and effused with a rosy glow, as if a setting sun were the only light filtering into the rooms. "There might even be a cover shot." I point to one of the images.

"Joan *hates* these photos. She said the photographer moved the furniture all around."

The photographer already alerted me. "He did move things a bit, to make the right compositions. He said a table might have been positioned *two* inches closer to the sofa and the dining chairs not rigidly lined up so that in the photographs everything appeared balanced. He said Miss Fontaine was furious and that he should merely aim his camera and shoot."

"Joan's invited me to weekend with her in Pebble Beach." Leaf pushes the transparencies aside. "We'll discuss the photos then."

While I clear the tables and put out pictures of more homes Leaf gets another handful of M&Ms. She points to a series of slides. "What's this?"

"It's a house in Santa Barbara designed by John Green."

Leaf doesn't look at the images. "Ever since I published that one project of his, he's been impossible. I see him at parties and all he talks about is himself. He thinks he's the biggest thing to have happened to decorating since chintz." She lights a cigarette. "He expected me to drive to Santa Barbara to see this house. And when I told him to take scouting shots, he said he didn't work that way." She blows out so much smoke Bette Davis would be envious. "I reminded him that I was the one who gave him his big break, but if he didn't want to submit scouting shots, I fully understood."

"Well, I guess he reconsidered, because here are the shots. I like that it's contemporary but has a few Spanish colonial pieces—it fits in perfectly with the area's heritage."

Leaf still doesn't look at the pictures. "Reject it. These designers have to learn a sense of loyalty." She squashes her cigarette in an ashtray.

Ivory walks by the open doorway.

I indicate the next set of transparencies. "This is a condo Teri Watson designed in Santa Monica. She had Chuck White photograph it on spec."

"I've seen this place before. Teri showed it to me a couple of months ago. I didn't like it then, and I don't like it now. Reject it."

"This is a house in Seattle." I indicate the next array. "We published a home by this same designer two years ago."

"We must have been desperate. Wait, what's this?"

"Tear sheets from a local Seattle magazine."

"Good, it's already been published. Explain to the designer that we don't publish homes that have already been shown. Let him think that's why we're rejecting this one. No use hurting his feelings. But don't encourage him to submit anything else. Maybe he'll just disappear."

Ivory walks by more slowly, her tense neck projecting her head like a driver stretching closer to the windshield when it rains.

"This apartment was designed by Joseph Little," I tell Leaf, who deliberately doesn't look toward the doorway. "Last year we published a loft he did in Brooklyn. This one's in Manhattan."

"Are those medical supplies?"

"All the accessories are. The vase is a specimen bottle."

"He's flipped out."

"Look at the bathroom. The towel racks are metal bars used in rest rooms for the handicapped. Even the bed is hospital issue."

"Maybe the person who lives there is disabled."

"No, she's a healthy young woman. I asked."

"Well, reject it. I think high tech has reached a new low."

The next house is in Arizona. "The architect studied under Frank Lloyd Wright."

"He didn't study long enough." Leaf moves on. "Oh, this is nice."

"I thought so, too, but it's been published. It was in *Ambiente* three years ago."

"That's all right. It's charming. Besides, no one ever reads that magazine. Let's do it. And get lots of shots of the horses."

"These are record shots of a house Pat James designed. Remember we showed his own place last year? It's hard to believe the same man who lives with minimal Shaker furniture could have decorated a place with all this clutter."

"You're so naive, Anthony. He had to pay for his own furniture, so naturally he only had a few choice pieces, but here he gets a commission on each piece of furniture he uses. It's a shame he's so greedy, because there are some nice things here. That painted cabinet in the dining room is to die for. But he ruined the effect with the Rococo mirror and heavy sideboard. Reject it. I'll be right back."

Leaf returns smelling of M&Ms.

"The next one is the New York apartment of the president of ASID."

"I didn't expect to like it," Leaf says, "but this is terrible. But make sure he gets the V.I.P. reject letter."

"Here's a strange one. These people are building a French château in the middle of the desert."

"They're spending a fortune and they will never understand why it's so awful. They should be arrested." Leaf shoves the pictures aside and picks up several snapshots. "Oh, Anthony, this one is pretty."

"It's a model."

"Too bad. Explain about our policy of not showing model homes, but tell the designer that if the place is sold intact, we'll reconsider. She'll probably buy it herself just to get in the magazine."

Leaf examines the next set of photos. "Didn't we publish this house?"

"It only looks familiar. The bedroom is almost identical to one we had on the cover for May/June 1977. It's the same fabric."

"I remember that cover! It was one of our most popular. Did the designer think we wouldn't remember one of our own covers? Reject it. And be sure to say why."

"This one's in Santa Fe."

"I love Santa Fe." Leaf flips through the snapshots. "Pretty views. Pretty exteriors. Oh, too bad. They ruined it with the furniture."

Next are two Polaroids. "How do they expect me to decide if I want to publish their home if they only send two snapshots of the exterior? But I don't think this one's worth pursuing, do you?"

She picks up an envelope and reads the return address. "Detroit. You know this isn't going to be any good. Nothing's any good in Detroit. But I must be fair and take a look. I was right. Reject."

Leaf glances at another residence. "Don't these people ever look at the magazine? Reject this. And this one, too."

Leaf looks through the pictures as fast as I can put them on the light tables. "This is the worse house I've ever seen. No, I take that back. Rock Hudson's place is the worst house I've ever seen. But this is next. Reject it. How many more have we got?"

"About a dozen."

All are rejected.

I laugh.

"What's so funny?"

"I just thought of a commercial for American Express. You're standing in a living room that has been obviously over-decorated. The camera pans in for a close-up and you say, 'Do you know me? I just rejected your home.'"

JULY 6, 1978

"Leaf, I have a cover proposal for the November/December issue."

She rises from her desk and sits on the corner banquette. She lights a cigarette, inhales deeply then slowly releases the smoke. "Okay, I'm ready."

I hand her a photographic mock-up.

Her eyes widen. "That's really daring."

"My mother would refer to it as a 'nudie.'"

"It's not that. Well, it is a nude, but it's a sculpture, so that's okay. What's so shocking is the cover's simplicity. It's a Christopher Richter bronze, isn't it?"

"Yes."

Standing in front of a dark gray wall is a rear view of a life-size bronze statue of a young man, his hands on his hips drawing attention to his well-rounded ass. A sofa is cropped so tightly that only a curved arm is in the picture.

"We've never had a cover like this before. I don't think *any* shelter magazine has." Leaf holds the image at arm's length. "There's no room. There's no interior."

"That's the point. I think it will immediately grab people's attention."

"It will stun our readers—but we can't not do it." She inhales more smoke. "I don't recognize this shot. What home is this?"

"Ah, that's the problem. We didn't commission this photography. Chuck White shot it on spec."

"That's okay. Then we don't have to pay for the pictures. But what does the rest of the home look like?" She balances her cigarette on the ashtray.

One by one I hand her a four-by-five transparency, which she holds up to the light.

"It looks good," she says. "But put them out on the light table so I can be sure."

"There's a bit of a complication."

"Yes?" She makes the word five syllables.

I'm tempted to take a drag on her cigarette. "The house was designed by Geraldo Cortez."

She doesn't do anything. She doesn't pick up her cigarette. She doesn't throw the transparencies in my face. She doesn't rip the cover in half.

She sits. I wait.

"Fine. I can be impartial." She looks at the cover again. "Tell Walter to make the text about the homeowner and to mention Cortez's name only once." She hands me the mock-up and picks up her cigarette. "Is there something else?"

"I've been thinking a lot about the covers, and I wouldn't like this cover to be a one-time event. I think we should have a new format that would be our signature."

"I don't think we should change our logo, if that's where you're heading. We've finally gotten national recognition, and it would be confusing."

"Oh no, I'm not thinking of that." I point to the mock-up. "This photo is shot straight on with a one-point perspective. That's what I think we should do from now on. Straight-on, tight shots in one-point perspective."

"Well, if you think you can get the right shots, let's do."

"Oh, I can get the shots. Especially if I go on more photo shoots." I pick up a set of layout boards from by my feet. "I have one more thing to show you. It's the layout for the Luis Barragán project in Mexico."

She quickly glances at the first spread but stops when she comes to the second. There's a three-page foldout. It's a picture of pink stucco courtyard with a trough waterfall cascading into a long narrow pool, and when the foldout is opened there's a man on horseback.

"It's stunning! But won't this be awfully expensive to produce?"

"Production got an estimate from the printer. A fold-out would cost six to seven thousand dollars."

"Claret can certainly afford that. Let's do it!"

There's still one more thing. But I don't tell Leaf.

The boy in the Christopher Richter statue is Cole Bruin.

JULY 21, 1978

"Oh my god, Anthony!" Timmy rushes into my office. "Have you heard?"

"Heard what?"

"Geraldo Cortez is dead!" Timmy sits down, picks up a sheet of paper and fans his face. "I have to cool down. I feel I'm on fire."

I pour a glass of water, which he drinks in one swoop.

"Okay. Okay." He exhales a deep breath. "There's more." He fans himself, takes another breath. "It was Cole Bruin who found the body!"

"Is Cole okay?"

"Would you be okay if you found the man you were sleeping with dead?"

"Jesus."

"Can I have some more water?"

I refill his glass. "How did Geraldo die?"

"Probably a drug overdose. You know Jason Hunt referred to him as 'the decorators' dealer.'"

As soon as Timmy leaves my office I phone Cole.

"Are you okay?"

"Can you come to the house and get me? Take me to Malibu?"

Cole is standing outside the gate as I pull up. He's wearing cut-off jeans, a black tank top and sneakers. Under a L.A. Dodgers baseball hat, messy curls straggle over his ears. He doesn't say anything as he hops into my truck. He smells of sweat. It's not unpleasant.

"I'm so sorry, Cole." I turn west onto Sunset Boulevard. "I don't know what else to say. And you don't have to say anything if you don't want to."

"Thank you for coming to get me." He squeezes my hand once then looks out the side window. Maybe he doesn't want me to see how red his eyes are.

We ride in silence until the ocean is visible as we descend Chautauqua.

"It's not like Geraldo was my boyfriend. We just fooled around." Cole stares straight ahead at the water. "I hadn't heard from him in a while and thought I'd bicycle over to his place to see if he was there."

"Where does—where did he live?"

"Hancock Park."

"And you bicycled all the way from Beverly Hills?"

"I've done it before. It's only about five miles." He drums his knee with his fingers. "The front door was unlocked so I walked in. Geraldo was lying naked on the bed." His fingers beat faster. "I thought he was asleep, but when I touched his ass, it was—" His fingers freeze. He takes several deep breaths. "I told myself that maybe he was just in a coma from too many drugs, but I knew. I couldn't breathe. I opened my mouth but I just couldn't get enough air, so I ran outside." His fingers resume the frantic tempo. "I thought of just getting on my bike and leaving. But I went inside and called 9-1-1."

Traffic slows on Pacific Coast Highway. Friday afternoon and people are getting a jump on the weekend.

"While I was waiting for the paramedics, I looked around.

On the coffee table, there was a mirror and a razorblade, and from the traces of coke, I could tell that two people had used it. I bent over Geraldo to see if there was any coke residue on his nose. I thought I'd rub it off before the paramedics arrived, but then I was afraid I'd get into trouble. And that's when I noticed he smelled like raspberries and I thought maybe he had a bad reaction because he's allergic to them. I looked around but I didn't see any, not in the refrigerator or even an empty packet in the trash. When I turned on the tap to get a drink of water, I noticed there were two glasses on the drain board. Then the paramedics showed up and as soon as they looked at him they called the police."

"Did you tell the police all this?"

"Some of it, but they seemed more interested in whether I was the one snorting coke with Geraldo." He rubs his nose— a subconscious gesture? "The doctor said Geraldo had been dead at least eighteen hours. The police were way too interested in my relationship with him. I'm sure they assumed Geraldo was gay because of all the male nude photographs hanging on his walls." He lifts his hat and scratches his messy hair. "One of the cops remembered Geraldo had been arrested about a year ago for dealing drugs and that a lawyer had gotten him off on a technicality."

"Did they take you to the police station?"

"No. They told me to call my parents. And when Dad arrived, the police made me go over everything again."

So that's how Timmy knew: one secretary to another. "Did your Dad know about you and Geraldo?"

He shrugs. "I think Mom suspected when I recommended Geraldo to do her office. I think Dad is deliberately oblivious."

"Your mom didn't come with your dad after you phoned him?"

"I told him not to bring her. She'd call her lawyer and make everything worse. She wouldn't be concerned about Geraldo—or even me. It'd be all about keeping the family's name out of the papers."

"You didn't think about calling your parents until the police suggested it?"

"I didn't think about much of anything. I kept feeling like I was going to vomit."

I squeeze his hand. "Do the police think there's anything suspicious about Geraldo death?"

"The medical examiner seemed pretty sure it was an overdose."

"I imagine they'll do an autopsy to be sure."

"Geraldo doesn't have any relatives here. His mother's dead and his father lives in Mexico. He kicked Geraldo out when he found him having sex with another guy. Geraldo hasn't seen any of his family for years."

"So there's no one to push the police for the truth."

"Right. Besides, the police don't care. To them Geraldo was a faggot and a drug dealer and they can't decide which is worse."

We drive miles in silence.

"It's just up ahead," Cole says. "Turn left at Escondido Beach Road."

It may be Malibu but this isn't the plush area. Here the homes are very close together. I guess with oceanfront property this valuable they'd have to be.

"Just past the curve."

I slow, he points, and I pull into a narrow carport. He unlocks the front door, kicks off his sneakers, and as he crosses the living room, throws off his clothes. He has a yellow Speedo on underneath. He removes a security board from a sliding glass door, dashes across the sand and into the ocean. His hat floats away but he doesn't seem to care—or even notice.

I put his clothes on a chair then find a bathroom and look for fresh towels. I grab a large blue one. I stand on the deck and watch Cole repeatedly smack himself into the waves. I slip off my shoes and socks and roll up my pants above my ankles. In the distance a woman is running with a dog. Otherwise it's absolutely quiet—just the barrage of waves.

Cole punishes his body until he's exhausted. When he finally staggers toward the shore, I meet him on the sand and wrap him in the towel. He leans against me and cries.

I hold him. I think how my clothes are getting wet, and I try not to think how his body is pressed against me. I brush his golden curls off his forehead. I take his hand and lead him toward the house.

We rinse the sand from our feet under a spigot next to the deck steps then wipe them on the same blue towel, and I love the intimacy. He takes out two canvas chairs from a cupboard at the end of the deck.

"Can you see if there's anything to drink in the fridge?"

I bring him a 7UP and a Coke for myself.

"How'd you know that's what I like?"

"It's what you were drinking the first time you came to my office."

"And you remembered."

"You're unforgettable, Cole."

"Like Nat King Cole."

"You're too young to know who he is."

"My dad sang me that song when I was a little boy and he put me to bed."

He takes a long swig of his soda then pulls down his Speedo and hangs it on the deck rail. He walks into the house naked. In a moment he comes back in a red Speedo. He hands me a blue one.

"Let's go for a walk."

I change in the living room, piling my office clothes next to his. I grab a plastic bottle of Coppertone from the kitchen counter.

"Do you want some suntan lotion?"

"Maybe on my nose."

His skin is rich amber. He's lucky he tans so well, not the blistering pink of many blonds and redheads. He probably built it up slowly during the last two months.

When I hold out the bottle of lotion, he says, "You do it."

He's almost half a foot taller than I am, and I reach up to gently dab his nose. He closes his eyes and I smooth more lotion on his face.

I want to cry. Not because someone has died, but because Cole Bruin is so utterly beautiful and I am overwhelmed.

I quickly hop behind him and squeeze a line of lotion across his shoulders. I don't want him to see my face, to read my emotions.

After I cover his back, he twirls round and presents his chest like a proud turkey.

"You're such a tease," I say, and toss him the bottle.

"Shall I put some one you? Although with all that hair…"

"Do my face."

I stare into his eyes as he applies the lotion and wonder if he knows how I feel about him. Then I think how callous I am for not showing more concern about what he's been through.

The sand is too hot so we walk in the wet edge of the ocean.

"Geraldo's the first person I've ever seen dead."

"When I was about twelve, I went to the funeral home when my grandfather died. I told myself I'd never do that again."

"I wonder if there'll be a funeral for Geraldo."

If he doesn't have any relatives here, maybe no one will claim the body, but I don't mention this to Cole.

"When my dad was driving me home from Geraldo's," Cole

says after we've been silent for a while, "he took Hollywood Boulevard and we passed Musso & Frank. Have you ever been there?"

"No, but I heard they have great steaks."

"Well, when I was younger, about twice a year Dad would take me there for dinner, just the two of us. I thought it was very grown-up. He'd have a steak and I'd have Chicken Pot Pie.

"Dad had a bright red convertible—a Chrysler New Yorker. My Mom hated it and she'd make Dad put the top up so it didn't mess up her hair, but when it was just Dad and me, the top would be down and I'd get to sit up front.

"One evening we stopped at a traffic light on Hollywood Boulevard, and there was a woman waiting for a bus. She had long blonde hair, a bright pink miniskirt and knee-high boots with fringe."

"How old was she?"

"I don't know. I was eleven. She looked old, but she was probably twenty, twenty-two. So Dad looks at her and she looks at the car, and he tells me to hop in the back seat and she gets in. I see Dad rub her naked thigh. They don't say anything. She just tells him where to turn. He pulls up in front of a small apartment building and says he'll be right out. But he was gone a long time. Or so it seemed.

"When he came back he said she was one of the secretaries at the magazine who needed a ride home. I remember exactly what he said. 'Don't tell your mom I gave her a ride. She wouldn't understand.' But *I* did.

Cole kicks a large shell. "We didn't go to Musso & Frank that night. He bought me hot dogs at some dirty street stand. I was furious and wouldn't sit in the front seat. It still smelled like her perfume.

"A few months later when he suggested we go to Musso &

Frank I said I didn't want to. We never went again. In fact, we've never had dinner alone again."

I tousle the curls covering the nape of his neck. "Do you like being an only child?"

"I'm not. I have a sister. She's mentally handicapped from some drug my mom took when she was pregnant."

"I'm sorry. No one's ever mentioned her."

"A lot of people don't know. I think Mom's embarrassed."

"Does your sister live at home?"

"You obviously don't know my mom."

"You mean she put her in an institution?"

"That's what Mom wanted. But Dad wouldn't hear of it. So my grandmother takes care of her in Pasadena."

"What's her name?"

"Claudette."

My mind shoots out questions. *How capable is she? Does she go to school? How often do you see her?* But I ask: "Have you and your parents talked about you being gay?"

"Why should they? It's not about them."

"Earlier you said you thought your mom had suspicions about you and Geraldo. You don't think that concerns her?"

"I think she be a lot more upset if I got some girl pregnant."

"Do you and your parents have dinner together?"

"Rarely. Of course, Mom's never cooked a day in her life. Inez does all the cooking, and she always has something ready, so we each eat when we want. They only time we ever eat as a family is when we visit my grandmother in Pasadena."

More questions race through my mind, but before I can bombard him, he takes my hand. "I'm seventeen now."

"That's still underage."

"Not in Malibu. In Malibu *fifteen* is considered middle-aged."

"When did you turn seventeen?"

"On the seventeenth."

"And I didn't give you a present."

"This is my present. When you were silent on the drive here, that was my present. When you held me in the sand and let me cry, that was my present."

I kiss his forehead. Salty.

We approach a pier where people are fishing.

"Let's turn back." He runs in the water, jumping, kicking, splashing.

He falls and screams and I run to him. I bend down. "Are you hurt?"

He splatters me with water and jumps up laughing. "If I had twisted my ankle, would you have carried me home?"

"Right now I want to carry you into the ocean and dump you." I pelt him with wet sand. "I think you father should have spanked you—frequently."

"You can do it now if you like."

He takes off and we race back to the house.

"The best shower is in my parents' bath."

After I clean up and head back to the living room, I hear another shower running. I look around the room: a mismatched collection of hand-me-down pieces, probably furniture passed on from the homestead in Pasadena.

"I ordered pizza." Cole has on his cut-off jeans, nothing else. "I hope you like sausage and black olives."

"An unusual combination, but I do like them both."

We sit on the deck watching the sun set while we eat.

"So you're going to be a senior. Have you picked a college?"

"I don't know if I want to go to college. Although it might be fun to join a frat house—all those horny boys getting drunk."

"What do you want to do? I mean as a career."

"Something with films."

"Sounds vague. Do you have a goal or a dream?"

"What's the difference?"

"A goal is something you take steps to achieve. A dream is something you just fantasize about."

"You're tough."

"My goal was to be art director. I got it in eighteen months."

"I'm just a kid."

"Only when you want to be. Most kids don't aggressively pursue men."

He stands up. "I told Inez we were going to spend the night here, but I don't want to anymore. Will you drive me home?"

"Of course."

His moods switch so quickly. He thinks his parents are self-centered, and they probably are, but as I watch him put on his sneakers, I realize he is equally self-involved, wanting everything to go his way. And yet all I want to do is take him in my arms and kiss him.

Driving back I don't turn on the radio but deliberately let the silence dominate. It's probably arrogant of me to think I can influence Cole's life.

In his driveway, I expect him to slam the truck door shut, but he leaves it open and walks up the steps.

"Cole!"

He stops but doesn't turn around.

"You *are* unforgettable."

He gives me the finger and goes inside.

AUGUST 14, 1978

"I called Claudette Colbert in Barbados on Friday like you asked me to," I tell Leaf on Monday.

"And she said *no*."

"She was very sweet and charming. She said her place simply wasn't up to what we showed in the magazine. I told her it was she we were interested in, that we could show a table with some personal items on it and a just part of a chair or sofa, concentrating on the view."

"And she still said *no*."

I nod. "It seems like we're always scrambling to get a celebrity feature, so I prepared a list of names." I hand her several sheets of paper stapled together. I thought you could cross off those you aren't interested in and the rest we can pursue."

"Why don't you read off the names?" Leaf lights a cigarette. "If you leave it, it will just get buried with all the other papers."

"Okay. It doesn't include anyone we're already working on or people I know you want such as Katharine Hepburn and Elizabeth Taylor." I hold a pencil beside the first name. "Alan Alda."

"I asked him. He said *no*."

"Dame Judith Anderson."

"Is she still alive?"

"Yes."

"She's a maybe."

"Isaac Asimov."

"No."

"Richard Avedon."

"It's been shown."

"Charles Aznavour."

"If the interiors are good. Ask for scouting shots."

"Lauren Bacall."

"Her New York apartment's been shown. Try for the South-ampton house. We don't need scouting shots. I don't care what it looks like, we'll run it. But I'm sure it will be nice."

"George Balanchine."

"Yes, if not shown and the interiors are good."

"Warren Beatty."

"Maybe."

"Harry Belafonte."

"No."

"Wait a minute. I'm still stuck on saying *no* to Warren Beatty."

"We're talking about publishing his house, Anthony, not ending up in his bed."

"Tony Bennett."

"Is it in San Francisco?"

"I don't know."

"No, even if it is."

"Milton Berle."

"We could never work with his wife. She'd drive us all crazy."

"Igmar Bergman."

"Get scouting shots."

"Ingrid Bergman."

"I hear she's very ill. But yes."

"Leonard Bernstein."

"If the interiors are good, but I think it's been shown."

"Yul Brynner."

"No."

"Anthony Burgess."

"Yes, the one in Monaco. If we can get it."

"Richard Burton."

"Does he have a house he *lives* in? He's a maybe."

"Michael Caine."

"It's been shown."

"Kitty Carlisle."

"No."

"She's always been one of my favorites."

"Too bad."

"Leslie Caron."

"I'd be interested in seeing it, but probably we wouldn't run it as a celebrity feature."

"Marc Chagall."

"Is he alive? Yes, if he is."

"Carol Channing."

"Shown, I think."

"Alistair Cooke."

"He said *no*."

"Walter Cronkite."

"Yes! We don't need scouting shots."

"Hume Cronyn and Jessica Tandy."

"No. She's okay but I can't stand him."

"Agnes de Mille."

"Isn't she dead?"

"I don't think so, Leaf."

"Check it out."

"Bette Davis."

"She says *yes* then backs out. Says she's too busy. I think she's afraid her place isn't all that great. I don't care if it's a *dump*!"

"Robert De Niro."

"In a few years, if he's still hot. But I bet it's a mess."

"Marlene Dietrich."

"Yes." Leaf stubs out her cigarette.

"John Denver."

"Oh, God, no."

"Very funny. Coleen Dewhurst."

"No."

"Faye Dunaway."

"She said yes, but it will never happen."

"Douglas Fairbanks Jr."

"Check if it's been shown. If it hasn't, get scouting shots."

"Federico Fellini."

"Yes!"

"Ella Fitzgerald."

"No."

"Henry Fonda."

"Shown."

"Jane Fonda."

"Yes, but she'll probably want her husband in it."

"Margot Fontaine."

"No."

"Bob Fosse."

"He said *no.*"

"Buckminster Fuller."

"If the interiors are good."

"John Gielgud."

"He said *no.*"

"Ruth Gordon."

"Okay for scouting shots, but make sure we include Garson Kanin in the letter or we'll lose it."

"Cary Grant."

"He said *no.*"

"Alec Guinness."

"Yes."

"Armand Hammer."

"The houses are *all* awful. There is no art. Surprising but true. We would have to be very desperate."

"Valerie Harper."

"She said *no*. I don't understand these people. They have a big hit show, and then they say they are 'private people.' You can't be a celebrity and be private."

"Helen Hayes."

"No. Well, maybe."

"Jascha Heifetz."

"Yes."

"Audrey Hepburn."

"She said *no* once, but let's try again."

"Bob Hope."

"His wife's worse than Milton Berle's."

"Vladimir Horowitz."

"Maybe."

"Christopher Isherwood."

"No."

"Eugene Ionesco."

"I never know whether these people are alive."

"I'll check. Mick Jagger."

"Yes. Surprised?" Leaf lights another cigarette.

"I had him on the list. Glenda Jackson."

"Said *no*."

"Lady Bird Johnson."

"No."

"Elia Kazan."

"No."

"Gene Kelly."

"Yes, but check that he didn't already say *no*."

"Angela Lansbury."

"Maybe."

"John Le Carre."

"Yes."

"Jack Lemmon."

"No."

"Myrna Loy."

"Oh, yes."

"Mary Martin."

"Shown."

"Walter Matthau."

"Maybe."

"Why would you say 'maybe' to Matthau and 'no' to Jack Lemmon? They both seem to be in the same league."

"Because Matthau seems like such a lovable puppy and Lemmon appears to take himself too seriously."

"Paul McCartney."

"Yes. I hear he has a great art collection."

"Melina Mercouri."

"Sure. Why not be controversial?"

"Robert Motherwell."

"Yes."

"Rudolph Nureyev."

"If the interiors are good."

"Laurence Olivier."

"Shown."

"Peter O'Toole."

"Yes."

"Luciano Pavarotti."

"Shown."

"Harold Prince."

"Wouldn't that be interesting? Yes."

"Donna Reed."

"No. And not Jane Wyman or Harriet Nelson or *Leave It to Beaver*'s mother."

"Barbara Billingsley. What about Barbara Stanwyck or Loretta Young? All these women were on TV when I was growing up."

"At least Stanwyck and Young didn't always play mothers. We could do them."

"Okay. Ginger Rogers."

"She hasn't done anything for years. No."

"Arthur Rubenstein."

"He's pretty much out of it now."

"Jonas Salk."

"Been shown."

"Gloria Swanson."

"Shown."

"François Truffaut."

"Maybe."

"Orson Welles."

"Said *no*."

"Tennessee Williams."

"We've tried."

"Tom Wolf."

"Yes."

"Franco Zeffirelli."

"Shown."

"That's it."

"Okay, have Ivory draft a letter—to come from me—to the 'yeses.' We'll see how many we get. Of course, not all of them will have good interiors. We'll have to wait and see."

"Maybe we should include tear sheets from past celebrity articles so they can see what type of coverage we're talking about."

"No, if they haven't seen the magazine, it's their loss. Let them buy a copy. They can afford it."

SEPTEMBER 5, 1978

"Leaf went to lunch with Ted Powell." Timmy collapses on the guest chair in my office as if Atlas had just lifted the world off his shoulders. "I *hate* when he comes to the office. Leaf is a completely different person when he's around."

"What do you mean?" I offer him a carrot stick from a paper plate on the edge of my drawing board even though I know he'll make too much noise chewing it. Fortunately, he declines.

"I can deal with Leaf when she's in a snit and demands everything be done *this instant!* I know how to get her to sign off on paperwork someone needs when she has absolutely no interest in seeing it. I understand *all* her non-verbal gestures when someone calls and she doesn't want to talk with them. I can even calm Leaf down when Colette starts pushing her buttons. But for the life of me, I have *no* idea where Leaf Wyks goes when Ted Powell calls her." He grabs a carrot and chomps on it like Bugs Bunny.

"You mean she won't take his call and hides in the restroom or something?"

"No, I mean she becomes a completely different person! It's like she's back in high school and the quarterback asked her out. Her voice goes all gooey and she moves around like a kitten about to leap on his lap."

"Maybe she's in love."

"With Ted Powell? You've met him, Anthony. He's more boring than this carrot! What can she possibly see in him?"

"Mark Romano said maybe Ted has other qualities."

"Believe me, there isn't a dick big enough to make that man interesting. Is this all you're having for lunch? Carrot sticks?"

"I had a tuna sandwich. This is dessert."

"What we don't sacrifice to get another man to think we're hot! But listen, Leaf wants to know if you did the layout for Ted Powell's home."

"I did it months ago. I've just been waiting for her to schedule it before showing it to her."

"Oh, she's not going to *schedule* it—at least not anytime soon. The longer she doesn't publish his house the longer he hangs around." He reaches for another carrot. "She'll dangle publishing his house like a carrot in front of a donkey. But I guess he's getting impatient, because she told him if you've done the layout he can see it when they get back." Timmy stands up. "So I'll call you when they return from lunch and you can bring it to her office, okay?"

It's nearly three hours before Timmy calls to say Leaf and Ted are back. "I think they stopped off for a 'matinee.'"

The upholstered banquette Sarah Cohen designed for Leaf's office is so plump and soft that whenever I sit on it, I want to curl up and take a nap, but Ted Powell is so stiff it's as if he's sitting in a straight-back wooden chair. His tie is knotted tightly at his throat and his black wing-tip shoes are planted squarely in front of him.

Leaf's stocking feet are in Ted's lap, and he mechanically massages her toes, his eyes focused out the window. Leaf takes a drag on a cigarette then bends forward and holds it out for Ted, who inhales deeply. So many buttons of her navy blue blouse are unfastened I can see the top of her black lacy bra.

"Is that the layout, Anthony?" Her voice is softer than Marilyn Monroe's. She swings her feet to the floor, squashes out the cigarette in the ashtray, scoots next to Ted and reaches out for the layout boards. Timmy's right: Who *is* this woman?

"This, of course, isn't the real type," she tells Ted, pointing to the dummy text on the first board. "It's just to indicate how long Anthony wants the title to be."

"You get to make that decision?" Ted asks me.

Before I can respond, Leaf says, "Oh, Anthony makes all the decisions around here." She turns to the next board, the two-page spread of the living room. "Oh, this looks nice, doesn't it, Teddy?"

"Better than my place." He turns to me. "I should have never let you put everything back. I should have left it just the way you arranged it."

Leaf and Ted study the two remaining boards. "Eight pages." She sounds surprised. She probably thought I could get only six out of that disaster of a home.

"What issue is it going to be in?" Ted wants to know.

"We work so far in advance, I can never keep track," Leaf says in an innocent little girl voice. "But we'll put it in the next available issue."

I know she's deliberately being vague. Maybe she expected more than a matinee. Maybe she wanted a double feature.

But Ted is persistent. "What is the next available issue?"

We have a meeting scheduled for tomorrow to plan January/February, but that's a small issue because there aren't many ads, and Ted's place would stand out. It would be better to bury it in a thicker issue when we show more homes. I glance at Leaf and sense she'd welcome a lie. "As you said, Leaf, we work quite far in advance, so the next available issue would be March/April."

OCTOBER 10, 1978

"Why didn't you tell me?" Cole calls me at home.

I know exactly what he's talking about but feign ignorance. "Tell you what?"

"That my sculpture's on the cover of the new issue!"

"I wanted it to be a surprise."

"Surprise? I didn't even know Leaf was publishing that home. I was lying on my bed listening to *Evita* and Dad tossed the magazine at me."

"I didn't know you liked *Evita*. You know, it's supposed to open here next year."

"I have both albums: the original concept album and the London cast."

"What's your favorite song? Wait! Don't tell me. I bet it's 'High Flying, Adored.'"

"Why, because you think everyone adores me? They don't, Anthony."

"Well they will once they see your cute ass on the cover." I may refuse to have sex with Cole because he's underage, but that doesn't mean when I'm alone in my room and he's on the phone, my hand doesn't unzip my jeans.

"So you think my ass is cute?"

If he saw my instant erection he'd know just how cute I think he is. "Quit fishing for compliments. What's your favorite song from *Evita*?

"'Another Suitcase in Another Hall.'"

"That's sad."

"It's realistic."

"Next time you play 'Don't Cry for Me, Argentina,' think of Leaf singing it and substitute '*Inside* readers' for 'Argentina.' It's fascinating, especially if you know she grew up 'a poor orphan' in Iowa. She just 'had to let it happen.'"

"That's hysterical! I can hear it in my head now, but I'll play it as soon as we get off the phone."

"What did your dad say about the cover? He knew you posed for Christopher Richter, didn't he?"

"Of course, he knew. I think he was pleased. Although he did say something about you."

"What?"

"That if the issue doesn't sell he's going to have *your* ass."

"Did your Mom say anything?"

"I don't think she's formed an opinion. If the snooty ladies of Pasadena find it distasteful, then Mom won't like it. But if they congratulate her for having a son who has not only posed for a famous artist but also gets on the cover of a national magazine, then she'll love it."

"I'm surprised she'd be swayed by other people's opinions. She always comes across as so dogmatic."

"When it concerns her work, yes, but not when it concerns society—or what she considers society. Anyway, thank you for putting me on the cover. Do you think you can get a big blow up of it for my room?"

"So you can stare at your own ass? That's a bit narcissistic, but yes, I can have an enlargement made." Maybe I'll get one for me as well. *I am so hard.*

"The only sad part is Geraldo isn't here to see his last project published."

"Walter did a wonderful tribute in the text."

"Oh, I haven't read it yet." He muffles the receiver but I can still hear him shout, "I'm on the phone. I'll be down in a minute." Then he's back to me. "I noticed you cropped the inside picture so the penis doesn't show."

"Well, as Leaf said, we can put a nude on the cover because it's a sculpture. But I thought it would be pushing it to show the penis. Besides, it isn't your penis, is it?"

"No, Christopher added a few inches."

"How did that make you feel?"

"Christopher said if he sculpted a small penis people would see it as a prepubescent boy and think he's a pedophile—which he may be. He wanted me to shave my pubes so I'd look ten years old."

I wonder if Cole had sex with Richter.

"I told him I waited a long time to grow pubic hair and I wasn't shaving it. He said my cock would look bigger if it wasn't buried in my pubes, but I still wouldn't do it."

I close my eyes and picture Cole pulling down his pants and jacking off in my truck on Selma Avenue. His thick blond bush. His precious penis.

"Anthony, are you there?"

"Yeah, I just dropped the phone. Sorry. After we got the first proof of the cover, I began to worry that if your classmates saw it they might give you a hard time."

"I don't care what those jerks think. Besides, it might actually help. I mean, most of them want to be famous and now I will be." He shouts again. "Okay! I'm coming! I gotta go, Anthony. We're going to my grandmother's for dinner. Shall I show her the cover?"

He hangs up before I respond, which is just as well, since it's difficult for me to control my breathing at the moment.

NOVEMBER 21, 1978

"We've just received the preliminary figures for newsstand sales." Leaf trails her index finger down a sheet of paper. "In New York, Los Angeles, San Francisco, Chicago and Washington, D.C., the issue has sold out and more than half the retailers ordered additional copies. Boston, Houston, Dallas, Miami and Las Vegas have sold at least eighty percent. Detroit, Atlanta and New Orleans are at sixty percent. The rest of the South, as expected, is underselling."

"Herb Caen mentioned it in today's San Francisco *Chronicle*." I quote from his column, which I've cut out. "'*Inside* magazine is creating quite a stir with its male nude cover. Seems the boys in the Castro all want a copy.'"

"Where did you get that? Did someone send it to you?"

"I have a subscription. I'm hooked on 'Tales of the City,' a serial about—"

Leaf's phone buzzes and Timmy announces, "It's Ted Powell," over the intercom.

I rise to leave but Leaf signals me to stay seated.

"Hello, Teddy." There's that little girl voice again. Does she seriously think that sounds sexy? While she listens to him, she twists an enormous yellow/orange gemstone hanging around her neck from a gold chain. "That's wonderful, Ted! I knew you'd get the project."

She slides her chair toward the window, parts the gauzy curtains and holds the gem in the brilliant sunlight; it blazes as if it's on fire. I've not seen it before and wonder if it's a gift from Ted. Leaf abruptly lets go of the curtain and the jewel, stands and turns her back to me.

"But, Teddy, I thought we were going to spend Thanksgiving weekend together." After his response there's no sweetness in her voice. "But they can't expect you to work on Thanksgiving!"

Ted also raises his voice and I hear undecipherable words.

"No, I understand. It's best to have them sign the contract before they leave for Hong Kong; that way you can work on the plans while they're gone. It's just that I was really counting on us being together. Now I'm going to spend Thanksgiving all alone. Eating a peanut butter sandwich."

And she hangs up.

I leave her office before she turns around.

Timmy waves me into his office. "I overheard," he whispers. "I hope she just goes home. The rest of the day will be unbearable if she stays around."

"That's quite a gem she has hanging into her cleavage."

"Christopher Richter gave it to her for putting his sculpture on the cover."

I think, *that cover was my idea*, but don't say anything.

Timmy's phone buzzes long and loud: Leaf wants him. He picks up a steno pad and pencil. "And we're off."

NOVEMBER 23, 1978

"Shit! I forgot you don't have reclining bucket seats." Cole climbs into my pickup.

"It's a truck. What do you want?"

"I want to go to sleep!"

"That's not part of the deal," I remind him. "You said if I drove I could ask you anything I want—and that you'd tell me the truth. So don't even think about taking a nap."

We're on our way to the desert, to have Thanksgiving dinner at Jason Hunt's Rancho Mirage home. I'm wearing chinos, a blue button-down shirt and loafers, but Cole's more relaxed in faded jeans, a pink t-shirt and his dirty sneakers.

"I don't know why you don't want to go. Fun in the sun with horny gay men—what could be better?" He gulps from a can of Coke.

"And I don't see how you can drink that so early in the morning. Besides, I thought you liked 7UP."

"Some people drink coffee in the morning. I have a Coke— same jolt of caffeine. I do like 7UP but it doesn't have caffeine. Don't you drink coffee in the morning?"

"I don't drink coffee at any time. I don't like the taste."

"How do you wake up in the morning?"

"With an alarm clock."

"Very funny."

"Once I'm up, I'm up. I don't know, I just wake up and am ready to go."

"Lucky you." He takes another swallow. "So what did you want to ask me?"

"Oh, I have a litany of questions."

"How long does it take to get there?"

"Two-and-a-half hours."

"Are we going to stop for breakfast?"

"I thought we could stop at an old-fashioned pancake house near Ontario. So. First question: When you were a kid did you fool around with other boys?"

"Not with boys my own age. We had a Hispanic gardener, Carlos, and whenever I was outside he'd take his shirt off. He had incredible muscles and a beautiful chest, and he saw me watching him."

"How old were you?"

"Eleven."

"And?"

"And one time Carlos went behind a bush and motioned for me to follow him. He had his dick out, and he took my hand and showed me how to masturbate him."

"What did you think when he came?"

"That he was peeing."

"Did it excite you?"

"Did it excite you?" He grabs my crotch. "I guess not." He folds his arms across his chest.

"Were you telling me the truth about the gardener?"

"Of course I was. I won't lie to you, Anthony."

"Is that the only time you and the gardener played around?"

"I wanted to do it again, but the next couple of times he was there someone was always about—the maid or the cook. Then a couple of weeks later I was in the pool, and I wasn't expecting him because it was a Tuesday and he came on Wednesdays. As soon as he took off his shirt, I got out of the pool and went behind that bush. This time when he came, I caught it in my hand—and I tasted it."

"Did he seem surprised?"

"He just patted my head. We only did it those two times, because he never came back. I don't know if he was fired or moved away or what, but the next week we had a Japanese gardener who was about a hundred years old." Cole crushes his empty soda can. "Do you want to hear something kinky?"

"An eleven-year-old boy tasting a Hispanic gardener's cum isn't kinky? You know it wasn't that long ago that *Lady Chatterley's Lover* was banned. But tell me."

"One time I made Geraldo stand in the bushes in his back yard and I jacked him off and pretended he was that gardener."

"So the gardener was the first person you had sex with?"

"If you consider masturbating sex."

"Don't you?"

"I guess, but it's more like you said—fooling around."

"And when was the next time you 'fooled around'?"

"Are we going to spend the entire drive discussing my sex life?"

"Do we have enough time?"

"Very funny. Why do you want to know all this stuff?" He rubs my crotch again. "Especially if it doesn't make you hard."

"People's sex lives interest me—well, gay men's sex lives. Answer the question."

"The next time I fooled around. That would be when I was thirteen."

"Wait! Between eleven and thirteen did you masturbate?"

"I tried. I got hard but nothing came out. Then I tried it again when I turned twelve. And there was a gusher. After that, I did it almost everyday—sometimes twice a day."

"What did you think about when you jacked off?"

"I wonder why some people say 'jack off' and others say 'jerk off.'"

"It's probably regional. So what did you think about?"

"The gardener or other men I had seen—guys in the neighborhood with their shirts off."

"No one your own age?"

"God no! I imagined the boys my age all had puny dicks like I did. Later I realized Carlos' cock wasn't all that big, but at the time it seemed huge."

"So at thirteen—?"

"My Dad took me on my first trip to New York—and to my first Broadway musical. We were supposed to see *The Magic Show*, only at the last minute Dad said he couldn't go because an important business meeting had come up, so he dropped me off at the theater." Cole slips off his sneakers and props his bare feet on the dashboard. His toes are very hairy. "I had a seat on the aisle in the mezzanine, and the seat next to me was taken, so I knew Dad was lying, that he never even got a ticket for himself, that he was probably back at the hotel fucking the maid or somebody. Anyway, it was a good show, but not so engrossing that I didn't notice the cute usher walking down the aisle and that when he headed *up* the aisle he was staring at me. So after the third time he did this, I followed him. He headed right for the men's room and went into a stall and I went in right after him—even though my heart was beating so fast I thought it was going to explode. He unzipped his pants and pulled out this huge uncut cock—"

"You're making this up."

"I am not! He had a huge uncut cock—at least to me, who had only seen my own and the gardener's. So I immediately start stroking it, but he whispers, 'Suck it,' but I don't know what he means, so he says, 'Put it in your mouth.' And I think,

'How am I going to get that big thing in my mouth?' And, 'What if he pisses in my mouth?' But he pushes down on my shoulders and I open my mouth. And, of course, I don't know what to do. I mean, I'd never sucked a cock before; so then he starts fucking my face, and at first I'm panicked that I'm going to choke but he slows down, and I start to really enjoy it. And just when I'm thinking, 'This is better than the magic on stage,' he pulls out and shoots against the stall wall. It was really thick, and I took a bit on my finger and put it on my tongue, because I wanted to see if it tasted different than the gardener's."

"And did it?"

"Yeah, it was sweeter. And he patted me on the head just like the gardener did, zipped up and left. I noticed there was a drop of his cum on my shirt and I worried everyone would know what I'd done."

"So when you saw how big this guy's dick was, did you wonder about yours?"

"No, I didn't, because I was still growing and thought it would grow too."

"Did you know what your mom was talking about when she called your father 'Tinkerbell'?"

"Not at the time. It wasn't until I joined the high school swim team that I noticed all the other guys had a bigger cock than me."

Than I, I think, but I don't say it. "Do you think hustling and being promiscuous is your way of acting out your anger at having a small penis?"

"Do you think I'm promiscuous?"

"Do you?"

"I think I'm a teenager. All the straight teenage guys are either terrified of getting a girl pregnant or can't get a girl to have sex with them, but I can do whatever I want and with anyone

I want." He squeezes my crotch again. "Well, almost anyone."

"And you're not attracted to guys your own age?"

"I wouldn't say that. It's just that the few guys my age that I've been with are, I don't know, inexperienced, I guess. Older men know what they want. And older guys don't tease me about my dick." Cole's stomach makes a loud noise. "I don't think I can last all the way to Ontario."

"Well, let's get past downtown, and then we can stop."

"So can I ask *you* a question?"

"You just did, but go ahead."

"Do you realize how annoying you can be sometimes?"

"Is that the question?"

"No, that was one of those non-questions."

"Rhetorical."

"Right." He looks out the side widow for a while.

I can't imagine why he's suddenly so annoyed. He's done this before. The simplest thing seems to make him angry. As we drive in silence, I think maybe it has something to do with intelligence. I'll have to notice if he gets upset if he thinks someone's making fun of his lack of knowledge. I ask a different kind of question.

"Do you want to eat at a sit-down restaurant or a drive-thru?"

"Go to McDonald's. I like the Egg McMuffin."

There's one in a couple of miles, and he's pissed when they won't make a milkshake because it's not on the breakfast menu. He settles for chocolate milk.

After we eat, he lets out a long sigh and I figure the annoyance has passed. Before I can ask him another question, he takes the initiative.

"What kind of men are you attracted to? I mean physically."

"I don't think I have a type," I respond. "I like redheads, blonds, brunets. I like them tall, short and in between. I *don't* like guys who are overweight. I usually like them my age or younger, at the most up to five years older."

"But not seventeen."

I ignore the implication. "The one thing I've noticed is I am unreasonably attracted to mustaches. A guy can be practically ugly, but if he's got a mustache, I think he's hot. One time I dated a man with a thick mustache, and when he shaved it off I stopped seeing him."

"You must be in Heaven, with almost every gay man having a mustache."

"Yeah, it's a wonderful time. It's funny because the time period I find most attractive is Edwardian—1901-1910—when almost all the men had mustaches. Now they've caught on again, but as soon as too many straight men start sporting them, gays will move on to something else—maybe goatees. We seem determined to have signals to spot each other. Like Oscar Wilde and green carnations, or different color hankies worn in the right or left rear pocket."

"Do you think gays set trends?"

"Absolutely. Most of the fashion designers are gay. So are most hairdressers and florists—and, of course, interior designers. Gay men tell people how to dress, comb their hair, and decorate their homes. We determine what's in and what's out."

"Listen, Anthony, this is not a come-on, but I'm *really* sleepy. Can I put my head on your lap?"

I pat my leg. Cole curls his long body as much as he can in the tight confines of the truck and rests his head on my right leg. He's lightly snoring in five minutes.

Thinking about our conversation, I realize Cole hasn't asked me any questions about my early sex life. Is he not interested? Is he too self-involved? Does he want to be the center of attention? He only asked me what attracts me physically because he wanted to see where he fit in. It frightens me how fascinated I am with this boy.

He sleeps for about an hour, and when he lifts his head, there's a wet spot on my pants where he drooled.

"Did I make you come?" His eyes are still sleepy and his curls are flattened against his head.

"You're the one who came. You drool like a St. Bernard."

"Where are we?"

"We passed Redlands a while ago. We have less than an hour to go."

"Can we stop and get something to drink?"

"Sure. I'll turn off at the next exit."

Cole picks up a McDonald's napkin from the floor and dabs at the wet spot on my pants. "I'm sorry."

"Don't worry about it. It'll dry."

I pull into another fast food franchise, and Cole finally gets his milkshake. I have a root beer. When we're back on I-10 again, I ask him if he's ready for another question.

"I'm not going to answer any more of your questions unless I can see your cock."

"That wasn't the deal. I drive. You talk. I already let you sleep for an hour."

He feigns zippering his mouth and folds his arms.

"Cole, I'm driving. I can't take my dick out."

He reaches for my zipper. "I'll take it out."

"Cole!"

"I just want to see it."

"Not while I'm driving."

"Why don't you want me to see it? Is it really huge and you think I'll be envious? Or is just average and you think I'll be disappointed?"

"Is that why you want to see it—to satisfy your curiosity?"

"Partly."

"And why else?"

"I'm not going to tell you."

"That's okay. I know the answer." At least I think I do.

"Sometimes you can be so smug, you know that?" There's that quick anger again. "But you don't know everything. You don't know how to live."

"So now you're Mame and I'm Miss Gooch?"

"Fuck you and your fucking references that only old gay queens know—or care about!"

I don't say anything, not because I'm hurt, but because all I want to say is: *You're afraid of the truth.* But I know Cole doesn't want to hear that.

We ride in silence, and Cole again falls asleep—or pretends to. This time he doesn't put his head on my lap.

Jason Hunt opens the door wearing a short, frilly French maid's apron—and nothing else. Gray chest hair adds fringe to the bib. Not appealing. "Everyone's by the pool. There're Mimosas in the cabana. I'll be in the kitchen basting the turkey."

I think of offering to help but don't really want to so follow Cole out the sliding glass doors.

"My appetite has plummeted," I whisper in his ear. "I don't fancy picking chest hair out of the gravy. What did you ever see in him?"

"He was very generous. And I don't just mean the size of his cock."

There's a white whale beached on a chaise. Oh, it's Burton Fisher. Mark Romano is in the pool talking with a man with a tight Afro, a bushy mustache and eyebrows that nearly meet above his nose. They're not wearing swimsuits. Aiko Shimizu, in a pink Speedo, sits on a pink towel lathering lotion on his legs. Cole strips to his yellow Speedo and cannonballs into the pool. Aiko squeals like a teenage girl when he's splashed.

The black man lifts himself out of the pool—his biceps are huge—and extends a hand toward me. "Hi. I'm Raymond."

When I introduce myself I try to look into his eyes but I'm distracted by what's hanging between his legs.

"That's Ray Junior." A smile dimples across his acne-scarred face. "He's such a cliché. Take your clothes off and come get acquainted in the pool."

I pick up Cole's discarded clothes and carry them toward the cabana. "I think I'll get a Mimosa first. The drive from L.A. was a little stressful."

"I'll join you." He leads the way, I'm sure so I can admire the perfectly round contours of his ebony ass.

I wiggle my fingers at Burton as I pass and he looks up from the book he's reading—*Mommie Dearest*. Aiko and I wave to each other.

Raymond hands me a Champagne flute.

"Are you a dancer?" I ask.

"I was when I was younger." He looks well under forty. "I'm the manager of Selection."

"Sarah Cohen's showroom."

"Right."

"I don't recognize your accent. Where are you from?"

"New Orleans by way of Jamaica." He looks at the pool. "Is that cute blond your boyfriend?"

"Not yet."

Raymond raises his eyebrows, downs his Mimosa and dives into the water. He yanks down Cole's Speedo, exposing his hairy ass. Cole quickly hitches up his swimsuit, turns around and smiles at Raymond.

I notice a basket of towels and suntan products. I strip and stack my clothes on a chair, grab a bottle of Bain de Soleil and walk down the steps into the pool toward Cole. The water is bathtub warm. "Let me put some lotion on your shoulders so you don't burn."

"Put some on my face, too." Then Cole whispers in my ear,

"You showed me your cock."

"You and everyone else."

"It's perfect." He takes my penis in his hand. "Now I have to see it hard."

"Look who just arrived—or should I say *what* just arrived?"

Cole follows my gaze to the sliding glass doors. Christopher Richter, in full leather, holds a hand above his eyes to shield the sun as he scans the pool.

"Wait until you see his 'jewelry.'" Cole pinches my nipple.

Christopher strolls to the cabana, not greeting anyone, and quickly consumes two Mimosas. He takes off his black bomber jacket then he slowly unbuttons his crisp white shirt as if all eyes are on him—and they are. Two silver rings pierce his nipples. I thought I was a neatnik but he's a fanatic, precisely folding the shirt as if he worked at a men's store. He sits down to unlace his highly polished knee-high boots. Looking straight ahead and not at us—but I'm sure he knows we're watching—he stands, unzips his black leather pants and slides them down his hips. No underwear, so we see it immediately: a large circle of silver pierces his glans.

"It's called a Prince Albert," Cole whispers.

Mark swims toward us. "You could chip a tooth on that thing."

"Imagine it up your ass." Raymond grimaces.

Cole squeezes my hand, and I wonder if that's what happened while he was posing for the artist.

Christopher's skin is darkly tanned—all over. He tosses a plastic air mattress in the water then mounts it, lying on his back, his silver ornaments glittering.

The sliding door opens again. And Ted Powell steps out.

"Everything is delicious," I tell Jason, who is sitting next to me at the head of the table. He's changed into a pale green linen shirt and very tight white pants—without underwear; he's circumcised. "Thanks for going to so much trouble."

"Trouble?" Terry, Jason's assistant, looks as if he's sucked a lemon. "All he did was hand me the phone." The young freckled redhead holds up his hands for quiet. "Before anyone else thinks Jason slaved over a hot stove all day, let me inform you that I ordered this entire feast from Divine Catering."

"You're fired!" Jason shouts at his assistant.

"That's the third time this week. One day I'm going to believe you and start collecting unemployment."

"But what were you two doing in the kitchen all that time?" Raymond points a finger at Jason. "Or maybe I shouldn't ask."

"We were playing Gin Rummy." Terry must be quite hairy; red tufts poke out all around his white t-shirt; and where there's no hair there are freckles. "Jason's completely addicted. Not that he's given up any of his other addictions. Gin and coke—it's the latest combination." Terry sneers at his boss. "Jason is determined to beat me, but I win nearly every game."

"We'll have to start calling you 'Fonsia,'" says Burton.

"Who's that?" asks Aiko.

"The name of Jessica Tandy's character in *The Gin Game*," Mark answers. "We saw it on Broadway."

Cole says, "Miss Tandy won the Tony."

I'm surprised he knows that.

"That's a really cute shirt you're wearing, " Terry tells Aiko.

"It's actually the top of a woman's pajama set." Aiko fingers the flimsy fabric.

"I used to sleep in the nude," says Burton, "until I realized I was ruining the décor."

"I saw Suzanne Somers interviewed on TV the other day," says Mark, "and I couldn't believe how articulate she was."

"Was it dubbed?" I ask.

"Anthony, the cover of the last issue is very daring." Mark

raises his eyebrows. "I can't believe Leaf let you show a *male* nude!"

"*That's* not the shocking part. There's no room!" Jason glares at me. "What do you want to do, put us designers out of work?"

"Don't be silly, Jason," Aiko says. "Everyone who comes into my shop is talking about the cover. People who would never think of looking at *Inside* have bought it. So designers are getting a lot more exposure with this issue than they ever had."

Terry smiles at me. "The fold-out with the man on the horse was spectacular!"

"Thank you," I respond. "Expect more surprises."

"You've changed the margins, haven't you?" Burton asks.

"Thanks for noticing. Yes, there's now an inch of white, double what it was."

"So tell me, *mein liebluch,*" Christopher turns to Cole, "have you been getting a lot of attention from being on the cover?"

Before Cole can respond, Raymond says, "That sculpture was you? How absolutely wonderful!"

"Exquisite," adds Aiko.

"Christopher's best sculpture," says Burton. "Don't you think, Mark?"

"Perfect," Mark agrees.

"*Ruhig*! Let the boy speak," demands Christopher. "Cole, what did the students at your school think?"

"Some of the boys asked if you would pay them to model."

"Depends on their—shall we say—'qualifications.' But by all means, give them my number and I will...interview...them."

"Did you get any negative comments?" Mark asks Cole.

"Well, she didn't say anything to *me*, but I heard my grandmother was not pleased." Cole flutters his long blond lashes. "But the best news is that the May Company asked me to model clothes for its summer catalog."

"Lots of skimpy swimsuits, I hope." Burton's expression

borders on obscene.

Suddenly I can't hold back any longer. Or maybe it's the third glass of wine talking. "You haven't said a word, Ted. Are you thinking about your project in Atlanta?"

Ted doesn't answer the question. "I didn't know you would be here."

"I could say the same about you. So could Leaf."

"If she weren't at home eating a peanut butter sandwich." Ted laugh is so callous I want to slap him.

"Do you even have a project in Atlanta?"

"Of course I do. Only, contrary to what I told Leaf, the contract was signed last week."

The other guests are suddenly quiet. Then Christopher asks Ted, "Is it true you're fucking Leaf Wyks?"

"I managed to avoid the act for the first two months we dated." Ted seems to relish the attention. "She took me to Chasen's and a movie premiere. I took her to Dar Maghreb, where we reclined on pillows and ate couscous with our hands. She took me to Mr. Chow's. I took her to lunch at Le Restaurant. She took me to a party at Harold Robbins' house. I took her to The Magic Castle. For two months I took her everywhere but the one place she wanted to go: to my bed."

"Why did you finally 'surrender'?" Aiko asks.

Jason shouts, "Because he wanted to be published!"

"Yes," Ted admits, "I prostituted myself in order to get my house published. Jason said he gets at least one new job every time one of his projects is shown in *Inside*. And I need the work. But wouldn't you know it, as soon as I had screwed Madame Editor I got a new project—and I haven't even been published yet."

"Maybe Leaf's a witch," says Terry. "A designer doesn't have to wait to be published, he just has to screw her—and presto! He gets another job."

"Timmy told me," Jason says, "that you and Leaf are going to Rio for the holidays."

"Which means I'll need to get my 'courage' up at least one more time."

"What you need, Ted Powell, is talent. A little integrity wouldn't hurt either." Everyone stares at me—some with their mouths open, others with their eyes wide.

Jason stands up. "Terry, shall we bring the dessert?"

Raymond, Aiko and Mark carry their plates into the kitchen. Terry clears away the rest.

"So what was it like burying your *schwanz* in Frau Editor?" Christopher curls his lips in distaste.

Before Ted can reply, I say, "I'm sure he's as good a lover as he is an architect."

"You've obviously never read the Kinsey report," Ted says to me. "There are a lot more bisexuals than most people realize."

"Just because you have sex with a woman doesn't make you bisexual, Ted," says Burton. "You're gayer than Liberace."

"Oh, that reminds me, Burton." Mark enters with a pumpkin pie. "You promised to show me Liberace's house."

Terry carries a large tray loaded with silver serving pieces. "Who wants coffee?"

Jason brings in an apple pie and vanilla ice cream. "There's also after dinner liqueurs, if anyone wants them. I have Armagnac, Drambuie and Benedictine."

"Jason, there's also that bottle of raspberry liqueur that someone brought," Terry says. "It's on the table in the foyer."

"*Framboise?*" Christopher sneers. "What a sissy drink!"

No one admits to having brought it.

After dessert Christopher announces, "I shall now don my leather and make an appearance at the bars in Cathedral City."

Ted says, "I might as well go have a drink at Dave's Villa

Capri."

"Who are you kidding, Ted?" Jason shoots him a look of disbelief. "You're going to cruise the bushes *outside* Dave's Villa Capri."

"You're the one who showed me where to find them."

Cole asks me if I want to go dancing at the local gay bar.

"Don't you need I.D. to get in?" As soon as the words are out of my mouth, I realize it's a silly question.

"I've had a fake I.D. for two years. To get one, all you need is $5 and someone who knows a studio prop man. Believe me, at Beverly Hills High, that's not a problem."

"Can we go a little later? I know you should walk—or go dancing—after a heavy meal, but I feel more stuffed than the turkey. And I've had too much to drink. If I don't lie down for a few minutes, I'm going to *fall* down."

I collapse on a chaise by the pool.

I wake up to a hand inside my shirt pinching a nipple.

"It's funny how we don't know how long we sleep," I say. "It could be a minute or an hour or a day, and we have know idea until we look at a clock."

"If you're asking me what time it is," Raymond says, "it's 9:35."

I look around.

"Your blond friend's not here. He's with Mark and Burton."

"Did they go dancing?"

"No, they went to the guest bedroom."

Of course.

"The trouble with twinkies," Raymond says, "is that they can only grow up to be cupcakes. Forget him. Ray Junior has something he wants to say to you."

"Your penis talks?"

"Not out loud. He's learned sign language." He presses my hand against his erection. "That means, 'I want to play.' Does your penis know sign language?" He rubs my pants. "Oh, I think someone's lonely and needs a friend." He bends forward and kisses my lips. "There's a sofa in the cabana. Why don't we go there?"

He takes my hand, helps me up, and I follow him. And learn a few more words.

I dive naked into the pool thinking I'll swim laps, but I'm only good for one circuit: I'm reduced to the dog paddle. I sit on the steps at the shallow end. Just my head is exposed since the night air is cooler than the water.

Cole drops the towel wrapped around his waist and swims toward me. "At the risk of sounding like your ex-boyfriend, would you mind just holding me?"

He sits between my legs on the step below and I fold my arms around him.

"So," I ask, "did Burton tell you all about Roberto?"

"Who's Roberto?"

"A sexy Italian that Burton played tennis with in high school."

"He told me about Sven. A sexy Swede he played tennis with in high school."

Ah, so Burton changes the details depending on the boy. And Mark goes along.

Cole leans back, resting his head against my shoulder. "You know, Anthony. I think we're very compatible. I like having sex and you like hearing about it."

He seems uncurious, not asking how I knew about the tennis player or what I did while he was with Burton and Mark. I bite his ear. "I had sex too."

He whips his head around. "With *whom*?" He punches my chest. "I bet you're surprised I got that right."

"Not really. I'm a good teacher." I nibble his ear again. "With

Raymond."

"Raymond! What did you do with that monster?"

"It's not what *I* did. It's what *he* did."

"Jesus that must have hurt. Is that why you're soaking in the pool?"

"Actually, the only painful part was when the suntan lotion we used as a lubricant started to sting."

"Well, now I'm jealous. All I got was a lot of talk and a mediocre blowjob."

I pull him in tighter. "I'm always amazed when I see how hairy your legs are."

"Your satyr."

I love holding him. I love the closeness.

But the air gets colder. "Do you want to head back to L.A.?" I ask.

"Not really. It's so quiet here. The chaise in the TV room is big enough for two. I'll find a blanket and we can crash there."

On the chaise, I lie on my stomach so Cole doesn't know I have an erection. He wraps an arm around me and rests his head on my back.

He falls asleep much faster than I do.

DECEMBER 6, 1978

"Order anything you want," Timmy tells me. "The magazine is paying for it."

"I can't believe this is Ma Maison! I've heard so much about it, and *this* is what it looks like? The floor is Astroturf, the ceiling is corrugated plastic, and this chair is decidedly uncomfortable."

"It's Leaf's favorite restaurant. She comes here all the time."

"I thought it was going to be chic and French, but it looks like a middle-class patio in the Midwest."

"Well, Leaf is from Iowa." He lowers his voice and discretely points to the left of me. "All the celebrities come here. There's Valerie Harper."

I turn and Valerie waves at me. I smile and wave back.

Timmy looks astounded. "Do you know Valerie Harper?"

"I've been to a couple of *Rhoda* tapings."

"And she recognizes you from the audience? That's amazing!"

"Actually, I met her in her dressing room. I know her hairdresser, Mack Eden, and he took me backstage."

"How many times did this happen?"

"Just twice."

"But she seems to know who you are."

"Well, we talked while Mack did her hair. She's very nice."

"I can't believe you've never told me this."

"The main thing I dislike about Los Angeles is the way so-called status revolves around celebrities. If someone knows the friend of a friend who knows someone on a movie or television crew, they boast about their closeness to a star. I can't stand it."

"So are you and Mack Eden friends?"

"I wouldn't say that. We went out a couple of times."

"You mean you were fuck buddies."

"You get right to the point, don't you, Timmy?"

"I believe in calling a spade a spade." He smiles. "And speaking of spades, I hear you and Raymond Washington did the deed at Jason Hunt's."

Before I can suggest his comment might be a bit racist as well as none of his business, a waiter brings a bottle of Champagne. "Compliments of Leaf Wyks."

After he fills our glass flutes, I ask Timmy, "Are we celebrating something?"

"Sarah Cohen finished decorating Leaf's home."

"I would think Leaf and Sarah would be the ones drinking Champagne."

"Their relationship is a little strained right now. I'll tell you all about it, but let's look at the menu first." Timmy drinks half his glass of Champagne. And smacks his lips.

We order appetizers and entrees. "We'll have dessert too," Timmy says when the waiter leaves. "Might as well have it all if we're not paying." He frowns and clears his throat. "Now, Anthony, I don't want you to get upset, but—"

"I knew the Champagne had an ulterior motive."

"Mr. Bruin asked Larry to design a book featuring all the celebrity homes we've published in At Home with…"

"Why should I be upset about that? Oh sure, it'd be nice to have designing a book on my résumé, but it's just going to be a rehash. I'd rather concentrate on the magazine."

"I'm glad you see it that way." He's smiling again.

"I hope Mr. Bruin isn't expecting too much from Larry. The Christmas card he designed was uninspired. A metallic red 'B' on a green background? Boring!" I sip Champagne. "So what happened to cause a strain between Leaf and Sarah?"

"The usual: money. When Sarah started the project, Leaf gave her $50,000. Now that it's finished, Sarah presented her with a bill for $120,000."

"How many rooms did Sarah do in Leaf's house?"

"Well, that big center room—which really is a living room, dining area and a den—as well as the entrance hall and the master and guest bedrooms."

"So Sarah didn't redo the kitchen or bathrooms?"

"No. She wanted to but Leaf thought they were fine as is."

"One designer told me it usually costs $50,000 to decorate a room if everything is to-the-trade. He usually gets a quarter of a million dollars to do a house, but that includes the kitchen and baths; and Burton Fisher said he gets even more than that." I add figures in my mind. "So $170,000 doesn't seem unreasonable."

"Sarah told Leaf she was going to give her a break, since most of the furniture would come from her own showroom."

"Did Leaf sign a contract with Sarah?"

"Of course. Sarah insisted, but I'm sure Leaf never read it. But you know how clever she is. She told Sarah that designers always get new projects after their work appears in the magazine, so Sarah agreed to reduce the final invoice to $90,000 if Leaf publishes her home." Timmy's smile is mischievous. "That's where *you* come in. Leaf said you have to art direct the photography it like your job depended on it. You can fly down Mark Romano, since you two seem to work really well together."

"When does she want us to shoot?"

"After the holidays."

"Is Leaf going to say it's her house in the article?"

"No, she'll run it anonymously. At first Sarah wouldn't go along with that. She said if people knew she designed the home of the editor-in-chief of *Inside*, that would have a big impact on her career, but an anonymous house would mean nothing. But Leaf said she'd make sure the right people know it's her house."

"So, if Sarah doesn't get another project after Leaf's home is published, I'm the one who gets the blame. And what do I get if she does get a project?"

"Leaf said you'd ask that. She also said that she was negligent in not giving you a raise when you became art director, so as of today you'll be getting $10,000 more a year. *And*, if Sarah gets a new project after publication, you get another ten thousand as a bonus. Isn't that great?"

"Yeah, it's great."

"You don't sound very enthusiastic."

"That's because there's one more thing, isn't there, Timmy?"

"If you're so smart, what is it?"

"I have to come up with a shot for the cover."

DECEMBER 30, 1978

"Anthony, I'm sorry to bother you at home, especially during the holidays." Leaf sounds artificial. "I'm at the Rio airport. It's very noisy. Can you hear me alright?"

"Yes," I shout.

"Is it too late to pull Ted Powell's house?"

"The color separations are still being worked on, but the text has been edited." I haven't told Leaf Ted was at Jason Hunt's for Thanksgiving. I'm afraid instead of her being upset with Ted, she'll take out her anger on me. And what exactly am I supposed to say—*By the way, your boyfriend's gay?* But if she's at the Rio airport two days early, maybe she's found out on her own. "It's possible to reschedule Ted's house for a later issue, but we'll have to find a home to replace it in March/April."

"Great! We'll go through the files on Tuesday and find a replacement." Leaf is silent until a loud announcement in Portuguese is complete. "And, Anthony, we're not going to reschedule Ted's place. We're not going to publish it. *Ever.*"

PART THREE

THE MOST BEAUTIFUL
MAGAZINE IN AMERICA

JANUARY 9, 1979

I'm supposed to meet Sarah Cohen at Leaf's house to make sure everything's ready for the photo shoot tomorrow, so I'm surprised when Raymond Washington greets me at the front door. He looks sexy in a gray suit and a striped tie.

"Mrs. Cohen is inside," he whispers. "And she's a nervous wreck. I think she's already had two Valiums."

This is my first view of Sarah's design for the interiors. Floor-to-ceiling black glass mirrors the walls of the square foyer. Two four-foot-tall ceramic figures face each other across the room. "These are grotesque," I whisper.

"They're Chinese burial guards."

A black lacquered console disappears against the back wall so that the three red ceramic vases resting on it seem to float. They're filled with gnarly twigs that nearly touch the ceiling.

Sarah, in a mid-calf black skirt and a gray wool turtleneck, stands in the living area clutching a Chanel handbag. There's not a relaxed bone in her body. No *hello*. No *nice-to-see-you-again*. Right to the point: "It's ready, but let me know if you want anything adjusted."

An armless chaise covered in a tapestry of verdant vines and a reproduction Louis-XV chair with black leather make an intimate seating area in front of the fireplace with a surround of black glass echoing the foyer. An *L*-shaped banquette uphol-stered in raw ecru silk takes up most of the living area, but the dominant piece is a five-panel Coromandel screen depicting swooping cranes in gold detail.

Bamboo blinds hang at the floor-to-ceiling windows defus-ing the light and view. A large area rug is sisal.

In the dining area, the table is a square slab of parchment-colored marble resting on an onyx cylinder. A black glass vase holds a dozen vanilla tulips. Four armchairs are upholstered in inky cotton.

In another sitting area, twin oak chaises are nearly overpow-ered with oversize black and puce pillows, each indented with a deep karate chop. A rugged stone table, designed I believe by Burton Fisher, stands between the chaises. Floor lamps are understated and gold-plated.

Sarah remains by the fireplace but Raymond follows me around.

The four-poster in Leaf's bedroom is draped in misty pink silk. The same textile is used for the duvet and to cover the walls.

"I've never really seen one, thank God," Raymond whispers, "but this room looks like the inside of a vagina."

A mirrored Art Deco nightstand holds a lamp from the same period. This is the only room without a plant. Giant fishtail palms are sprinkled throughout the rest of the house. Another bedroom has a daybed, bamboo side chairs and a desk so Leaf can use it as an office.

I pick up a silver frame displaying a small photograph. "This is the only personal item in the whole house. Do you know who this man is?"

Raymond shakes his head.

"It's Leaf's father," Sarah says when I'm back in the living area.

"I thought she was adopted and didn't know her father."

"That's true. But her real mother recently found that photo tucked in an old book. She sent it to Leaf, saying she wondered all these years where she had put it, and she wanted Leaf to have it." Sarah whispers, "You know, Leaf's father abandoned her mother before Leaf was born."

I shake my head. "I didn't know. I think Leaf's mentioned her family to me only once."

Sarah continues, "She hasn't talked to her mother or her adoptive parents in years. But both her real mother and her adoptive mother continued to send Leaf birthday and Christmas cards every year."

"Maybe one day," I say, "someone will find one of them tucked in an old book."

"I think not. Leaf said she tosses them in the trash."

"Thank God," says Raymond, "Leaf Wyks never had children."

Sarah glares at him as if he's spoken out of turn.

"It seems odd," I say, "that Leaf would keep a picture of a man who abandoned her but she ignores her mother and adoptive parents, who want to be in contact with her."

"Enough about Leaf." Sarah makes a gesture encompassing the large room. "What do you think?"

"You've done a beautiful job, Sarah, but we can't photograph it like it is now."

Before I can explain, she snaps, "What do you mean? We have to!"

"There are no accessories. It looks unfinished. Your showroom looks more like a home than this does."

Again she interrupts. "Leaf doesn't have *anything* good. And what she does have I wouldn't have in this house."

Behind her, Raymond rolls his eyes.

"The solution is simple," I tell them. "You'll simply have

to bring in some of your accessories from Selection. Designers do it all the time. Let's go through the rooms again, and I'll tell you what I think we need." I point to a low vase filled with a mound of moss on the coffee table. "I'm tired of seeing mounds of moss. All the designers are doing it. Can you find something else? I'm sure Aiko Shimizu could provide something tasteful."

"Are you writing this down?" Sarah asks Raymond.

"I'll remember."

She rifles through her Chanel bag and hands him a small Louis Vuitton notepad and a Monte Blanc pen.

"We have plenty of large picture books at the office," I continue. "Tomorrow I'll bring over a half-dozen, and we can see what works. We need some objects on this console. They have to be tall enough so they'll be seen over the banquette."

"The eighteenth-century celadon charger would work," Raymond tells Sarah.

"And those three square ceramic Chinese vases," she adds. "The pale celadon ones, not the yellow."

I move to the dining table. "We certainly need more than a dozen limp tulips."

"Those were especially imported from Holland!" Sarah's indignant.

"I can get more," Raymond says.

They trail me as I head to the kitchen and open a cupboard.

"If you're looking for fine china, you won't find it," says Sarah. "No good stemware or flatware either."

"Well, we either need a bigger vase with a *lot* more flowers or we have to set the table," I tell her.

"Raymond, go to Bullock's-Wilshire and buy a set of black stemware. I saw some there last week that will be perfect." She turns to me. "You aren't going to put any liquid in the glasses are you?"

"No, that's not necessary."

"Good. We can return the glassware after the shoot. I have striking black plates, half matte, half glossy. I'll bring those. And, Raymond, you might as well get some flatware while you're at Bullock's. You know what I like: stark and heavy. Anything else, Anthony?"

"Napkins."

"I'll bring my black linen, but, Raymond, see if there are any deep red or puce."

I indicate the wall behind the dining area. "Is it possible to hang a painting here?"

"Do you give galleries credit in the captions?" Raymond asks.

"No. We name the artist. But if a gallery has an exclusive with an artist…"

"Right. I'll go to the Frampton Gallery and see what's there."

"While you're at it," I say, "see if they have a small sculpture to put on the low dresser opposite Leaf's bed."

"Get something pre-Columbian," Sarah instructs. "None of those Christopher Richter nudes. So are we finished?"

"Maybe you could bring up an assortment of small items—something for the table between the oak chaises and for the nightstand."

"I'll arrange it," Raymond says. "Do you think you and I could go to Bullock's and the gallery in your car? That way you can be sure to get exactly what you want."

"I have a truck, so there's no trunk to hold the merchandise we pick up."

"Well, then would you mind following Sarah to the showroom? You can leave your truck there, and we'll use my car."

"Don't forget the tulips," Sarah says.

Raymond pulls into a West Hollywood parking lot. "One last

stop."

We've already loaded the trunk of his car with an array of accessories from Selection. He's bought Georg Jenson flatware, black glasses and rusty red napkins at Bullock's-Wilshire. The Frampton Gallery has promised to deliver a Jasper Johns painting and a pre-Columbian reclining figure first thing in the morning. Aiko Shimizu is providing an exotic orchid for the bedroom and a lush succulent for the coffee table.

I wait in the car while Raymond dashes into the Safeway grocery store. In ten minutes he returns carrying three-dozen cream-colored tulips. He hands them to me to hold. "Sarah's precious tulips were imported all right. From a local hothouse."

I manage a weak smile.

"What's wrong? You look worried."

"I'm just thinking about what to shoot for the cover."

"Why don't you come over to my apartment for a drink? I make a mean martini." He puts his hand on my thigh. "And I give good massage."

"Will Ray Junior be there?"

"Oh, I'm pretty sure we'll get a rise out of him."

We get more than that.

JANUARY 15, 1979

"Excuse me for interrupting," I tell Leaf as I knock on the doorframe of her office.

"That's okay, Anthony. You're one of two people who can come into my office anytime."

I wonder if the other person is Mr. Bruin then realize it must be Timmy.

"I have Mark's transparencies of your house out on the light table."

"Oh, I can't wait! Are they good? No, don't tell me!" She scampers on her too-high heels to the viewing room.

"Wow! They're fabulous, aren't they?" Leaf removes her eyeglasses and bends over the light table so she's only three inches away from the pictures. "My bedroom looks so cozy. Tell Mark I love the shots!"

"We took three verticals for possible covers." There's a view toward the fireplace, a tight shot of the twin oak chaises and a close-up of the dining table. "I prefer the shot of the table with the Jasper Johns in the background."

"Oh, I do too. The tulips look practically wistful. Sarah said they were flown over from Holland just for the shoot." Leaf steps out into the corridor. "Timmy!" She shouts. "Come see the pictures!"

After Timmy has *oohed* and *aahed*, Leaf asks me, "How many pages are you thinking?"

"We shot enough to give it ten pages."

"Good." She looks at the bulletin boards. "What's the last issue we planned?"

"May/June." I indicate the column of index cards.

"Let's take another look at it. Do we have time to make any changes?" Leaf has no concept of—or interest in—deadlines.

"We're still missing a couple of the transparencies for the Art feature," I say.

Timmy adds, "There's a meeting scheduled a week from to-day for Anthony to show you the layouts."

Leaf runs a finger down the index cards. "The issue needs a strong contemporary, don't you think? Maybe we should put in my house. Sarah did such a good job. It will make the whole issue better."

"We don't have enough pages to add another story," I tell her. "We could take out the Burton Fisher feature. That way we would be replacing one contemporary California residence with another. He was going to be on the cover, so this would also replace one cover story with another."

"Okay. Take out Burton."

JANUARY 19, 1979

"**Y**ou know I have been dying to find out what happened between Leaf and Ted, but Leaf changes the subject every time I bring up Rio." Timmy smirks. "So I finally went to the only other person who knows what occurred."

"You asked Ted Powell?" I can't believe Timmy would have such gall. "What did he say?"

"He hasn't told me—yet. Whatever you have planned, cancel it, because you and I are going to lunch with Ted and he's going to tell all!" Timmy pokes my chest with his index finger. "You'll never guess what restaurant he picked."

"The Carriage Trade."

"How did you know that?" Timmy's crushed.

"It's the gayest restaurant in town."

"The trip started off just fine," Ted said once we were settled in a booth. "We actually had fun. We rode the funicular railway up to Sugar Loaf and toured the Botanical Gardens. Leaf's not pretentious, so she didn't fake interest in the art at the national museum. We ran out of there the second we got bored. And, of course, we ate in fabulous restaurants."

I guess Ted's still in a Latin mood, because he orders a pitcher of Margaritas from the waiter, who looks as if he just got out of bed; probably not his own.

"Did you go to Ipanema?" Timmy wants to know.

"Fortunately, Leaf did not want to go to the beach," Ted says. "I don't think I could have looked at her in a swimsuit."

"No," I say, "you would have been too busy eyeing the boys in bikinis."

"You know, Anthony, sometimes I enjoy being with a woman." Ted gives me what he probably thinks is a condescending look, but with his pinched features he looks constipated. "We danced in the moonlight. We even made love. Once."

"How romantic."

"Of course, it was very humid, and Leaf went to the beauty salon in the hotel every morning to have her hair styled. I think she just enjoyed the luxury of having someone wash it for her."

Timmy drums his fingers on the table, but Ted seems to enjoy dragging out the tale with minute details.

"I usually had a cup of coffee and read the newspaper in our room while I waited, then we'd go out for breakfast. Well, one day the newspaper wasn't delivered and I called down to the front desk. And the most beautiful boy brought it up. Of course he was gorgeous! He was Brazilian. Just dark enough to look ethnic, with thick brows and the darkest eyes I've ever seen. And, of course, the smile was perfect. And, of course, he knew just how to use it."

"He probably practiced in front of a mirror."

Ted continues as if I hadn't interrupted. "I was only wearing the hotel robe, and I guess I forgot to tie it—"

"*Of course*," I say. This time it's Timmy who gives me a look.

"And when I reached for my wallet to tip the dear boy, my dick popped out. Well, I saw where those gorgeous eyes went, so instead of handing him a couple of pesos, I offered him a U.S. twenty. Well, to make a long story short—"

"Please don't," Timmy pleads.

"Well, he sucked my cock for a bit, but I wasn't really interested in that. So I soon had his zipper down. His trousers dropped around his ankles and he crunched his shirt above his waist, and I soon had that delicious uncut prick in my mouth. Some men don't like a ripe cock, but frankly, the smell of smegma turns me on."

"Is this enough detail for you, Timmy?" I ask.

"It suddenly started to rain—a real downpour and very loud. I had my back to the door, so I didn't see or hear Leaf open it. What gave it away was the smell of hairspray."

"I'm surprised you could get a whiff with that smelly cock in your mouth."

Timmy puckers his lips but the twinkle in his eyes says he liked my comment.

"Well, when I looked around Leaf wasn't there. But I knew she had seen me on my knees in front of the bellhop."

"I bet that image is etched on her retina." This time it's Timmy who interrupts.

And the waiter does too, bringing the pitcher of Margaritas. "Are you gentlemen ready to order?"

"We haven't had time to look at the menu yet," Ted says. "But bring us the appetizer platter to start, please."

"So what did you do?" Timmy asks Ted.

"What could I do? I finished blowing the bellhop!"

"But what happened about Leaf?" Timmy doesn't seem to realize that Ted has a captive audience, and he's going to tell his story in his own too-detailed way.

"Well, the boy left, and I showered and got dressed. The rain had stopped, and I stood on the balcony—we were on the fifteenth floor—and admired the rainbow. I smoked a cigarette, and it finally dawned on me that Leaf wasn't going to come back to the room. So I went to breakfast alone."

"You didn't really expect her to eat with you after what she'd seen, did you?" I can't believe Ted would be that unaffected.

"No, but I did expect her to scream and maybe hit me. I sort of got off on it when my wife would strike me." Ted lowers his voice. "Sometimes I think I deliberately provoked her. Anyway, I decided to walk around town for a while and when I returned the room was a wreck. My clothes were tossed everywhere. And Leaf's suitcases were gone. And across the bathroom mirror she had written *FAGGOT!* in bright red lipstick."

"Just like a *telenovela*." Timmy loves this. "So did you leave?"

"God no! I wasn't about to pass up New Year's Eve in Rio. I had a blast!"

"It took Leaf two planes and four stops before she got back to Los Angeles." Timmy at last shows some sympathy for his boss. "I saw the ticket with her expense report. It took her twenty-two hours, counting all the layovers."

"What can I say?" Ted shrugs. "I'm sorry."

"You mean you're sorry you got caught." I refill our glasses.

"That too." Ted takes a big swallow. "You know, I'd really rather not be homosexual. Sure, you can have a lot of fun, especially in places like Rio de Janeiro on New Year's Eve, but most of the time it's a burden I'd rather not have. If I'm involved with a woman I love, I can go for months without the desire for a man. Then suddenly something stirs—maybe I get a glance out of the car window of a shirtless guy mowing a lawn—and I'm unable to erase the image from my mind. It's like it haunts me. I keep seeing the flash of taut skin, the sweat, and the urge, the need just keeps growing until I seek release."

"Do you ever get these feelings about women?" I ask.

"What feelings?"

"Where you see maybe a bit of her breast, and it 'haunts' you for days?"

"Well, now that you mention it, I don't think I have."

"Then stop kidding yourself, Ted."

"Yeah, you're as queer as everyone in this restaurant," Timmy adds.

The waiter places a large plate of appetizers in the center of the table.

After we've tasted the samples, I say to Ted, "You do realize that Leaf isn't going to publish your home?"

"Yeah, I figured. Do you think I could buy the pictures? You and that kid did such a great job with the pictures."

"I think you can count on Leaf letting you have the photography when Rio freezes over."

JANUARY 22, 1979

Timmy storms into my office. "Leaf just came back from a meeting with Mr. Bruin. She wants to see us right away. And she's not in a happy mood."

We don't sit down when we enter Leaf's office. We stand before her like naughty boys facing the principal.

"Which one of you told Claret I was publishing my own home?"

"Not me!" Timmy blurts out. I shake my head and lift my shoulders.

"Well somebody told him and he threatened to not let me publish it."

"Leaf, everyone in editorial knows your home is scheduled for May/June," I say. "It's been up on the bulletin board in the viewing room for a week."

"But it's supposed to be anonymous!"

"And it will be in the issue, but on the index card it has your name in parentheses," I explain. "We run so many anonymous homes that if he didn't put the homeowners names on the cards we wouldn't know which home was which."

"Is he making you pull the story?" Timmy asks.

"No." Leaf calms down enough to light a cigarette. "I convinced him that Sarah did such a good job that she should get the recognition. I asked him if he'd rather have it published in *House & Garden* or *Town & Country*. He agreed we could run it but said it couldn't be on the cover."

"You promised Sarah," Timmy says.

"I know damn well what I promised!" Leaf blows smoke at Timmy and turns to me. "I told Claret I'll hang the two possible covers for this issue on a wall and let the editorial staff vote on which they think is the better. And that I'll go along with the one they choose."

So I pushpin two covers on the wall. Leaf's shows a close-up of the dining table—with the borrowed place settings and the supermarket tulips—with the Jasper Johns painting in the background. The other cover is a tight shot of a Picasso mural behind a travertine console in a New York apartment.

I pass out ballots to everyone in editorial, editors as well as secretaries.

My eyes widen as I tally the ballots. "I can't believe it, Leaf! The staff didn't pick your home for the cover. They chose the Picasso!"

"You're kidding. I'll fire them all! They *knew* it was my home." She gets up from behind her desk and grabs the ballots out of my hands. "Wait! It was a secret ballot, wasn't it? So no one knows I've lost." She starts tearing the ballots into tiny pieces. "Destroy the ballots and put my home on the cover. Even if some of them discuss it, they won't be able to figure out the exact count. This will be our little secret."

"I wonder," I say, "if this is how Rosemary Woods felt."

JANUARY 27, 1979

Cole looks different when I pick him up in front of his house. "What's this?" I rub a finger across his upper lip.

"A mustache."

"For me?"

"You said you liked them."

I have to admit it's enticing. There are flecks of red among the gold. I lean over and kiss him on the lips.

"You mean all I had to do to get you to kiss me was grow a mustache?"

"I've kissed you before." I wait for the security gate to swing open.

"Not on the lips."

"I didn't realize you were so romantic."

"I'm not. Just with you." He pinches my side. "The mustache is only temporary. I have to shave it off next week. I have another photo shoot for May's, and the art director thinks it makes me look too old. It's underwear, and I think what he really wants is child porn."

"I saw your photos in Sunday's supplement. You looked cute."

"Just what I always wanted to be. Cute."

"There's nothing wrong with cute."

"Do you like when people say you're cute?"

"No."

"So there."

"Okay, you looked—angelic."

"I've been looking forward to this all week."

"Me too." We head north to Magic Mountain. "I love roller coasters."

"I meant showing you my mustache."

I pat the space next to me, and Cole slides closer.

"Are you enjoying modeling?"

"Not really. Everyone's a prima donna. There are three stylists: clothes, hair and makeup, and they each think they're the most important person on the shoot."

"Not realizing that it's *you*."

"Exactly. Then there's the photographer, who's always disagreeing with the art director. And they each have an assistant, who think they know better than anyone. And besides, it's rather tedious. Setting up the lights takes forever. I can't see why they can't set up the lights and everything before I get there."

"Maybe have a stand-in like on a movie set?"

"Right! The worst part is I'm not allowed to *do* anything. Or say anything. Nobody wants my opinion. The art director's an old queen with attitude and a big diamond ring on his pinkie. He wants absolutely no emotion from the models. If I smile he tells me to stop. I can't look puzzled or interested or *anything*. Just blank. At first I didn't know how to do that. How do you look blank? Then I realized when I was totally bored *that* was the look he wanted."

"I'm sorry you're not enjoying it."

"The photographer's the nicest. He said I should take acting lessons. He's going to introduce me to a teacher."

"And what does the photographer expect in return?"

"You're so cynical." Cole punches my leg. "He doesn't expect anything. He's just being a nice guy. Besides, he's straight."

When we arrive at the amusement park, we immediately get in line to ride Colossus. It's fun with its two steep drops, but I'm eager to ride Revolution, which has a vertical loop so that at one point we're completely upside down.

"You scream like a girl," Cole says when we're back on solid ground.

"That's what my father said."

Cole wants to ride Colossus again, but the queue of people waiting to get on is quite long, so I suggest Enterprise.

"It must not be very exciting since there's no line," Cole says.

But he's wrong. The reason there's no line is the ride is terrifying. It's similar to a Ferris wheel on its side except instead of bucket cars bullet-shaped closed-glass two-person capsules hang from the outer end of the wheel's radial axles. Since he's several inches taller than I am, Cole gets in the back of a capsule, spreading his legs so I nestle against his torso. As the wheel spins faster and faster the capsules swing out and soon we're not perpendicular to the ground but parallel. Then the wheel begins lifting off the horizontal until it is completely vertical, all while still spinning. We get flashes of the fairgrounds at disorienting angles crossed with glimpses of the blue sky. Then the entire procedure is reversed until we're totally dizzy when the capsule is once more perpendicular and we've stopped.

"That was the most exhilarating ride I've ever been on." Cole's face glows.

Without another word, we get right back on. Then we go a third time. When we emerge from the capsule, we can barely walk in a straight line. We collapse on a bench.

"I am so glad I didn't eat anything this morning." I hold my head in my hands.

Suddenly Cole grabs my shoulders and kisses me as if he

needs my air. A woman rapidly pushes a stroller past us as if her baby might be contaminated. Her husband sneers. But one of two nearby young men gives me a thumbs-up.

"What brought that on?" I ask Cole.

"I don't know. I suddenly felt so *alive!*"

None of the other rides compare to the excitement of Enterprise. We spend the entire day at the park, eating cotton candy as if we were ten years old and having our picture taken with King Troll, one of the roaming mascots.

On the way back to Los Angeles, Cole says, "Can I spend the night with you?"

"What would your parents say?"

"I could tell them we were tired and decided to spend the night at our Malibu house. In fact, why don't we do that?"

"I don't think it's a good idea, Cole."

He slides away from me and toward the passenger window. "You know what hurts me the most about you not wanting to have sex with me? That you don't trust me."

"I do trust you, Cole. And it's not that I don't want to. It's that I won't. At first it was because you're a minor and it's illegal, but now I realize you're a mature young man and probably more sexually experienced than I am. So now it's become more of a matter of principle. I said I wouldn't have sex with a minor and I won't."

"But that's just silly!"

"I know a guy in San Francisco who was dating someone in the Police Academy. Peter would go on and on about how hot the guy was, how he was 'the one.' And I said that as soon as the guy got his uniform and they had sex with him wearing it, the relationship would be over."

"And was it?"

"Within a month."

"Did you tell me that story because you think that as soon as we have sex—if we ever do—that I won't be interested in you anymore?"

"Yes."

"Maybe that was true at one time but it changed that day you took me to Malibu after Geraldo died. No one ever made me feel so protected. No one has ever just let me be who I am as you did that day. And that's the way I felt today. That I could be me and you would like me."

"I like you very much. I think you're wonderful. I realize that in several countries someone your age could legally have sex, so the number is arbitrary. But, Cole, I don't think you know the difference between sex and love."

I look straight ahead, but my eyes are wet and the road turns bleary.

Cole moves back next to me. He kisses my cheek. "That's why I need you, Anthony. To show me the difference."

I wipe my eyes. "Cole, I wonder if I could schedule a date with you a bit in advance."

"Sure. When?"

"July 16, 1979."

"That's my birthday."

"You'll be eighteen."

MARCH 7, 1979

"I'm driving to Covina to see a psychic," Leaf says. "Do you want to come?"

Maybe I'm being skeptical, but I wonder if she wants me to join her or just doesn't want to make the trip by herself, but I don't have anything to do today that can't wait until tomorrow, so I go.

"How'd you hear about this psychic?" I ask when we're heading east on I-10.

"Judy Berlin recommended her. She said several people at the *Times* had gone and everything she predicted came true. Of course people exaggerate, and a lot of psychics phrase things in generalities that can fit many events, but Judy thinks this one is authentic." Leaf pushes in the car lighter. "Would you get me a cigarette from my bag?"

On the back seat is a large black nylon tote containing Leaf's purse, a small tape recorder, a yellow legal pad, a couple of ballpoint pens and two packs of Virginia Slims Lights.

"Have you ever gone to a psychic, Anthony?" Leaf lowers her window an inch to let out the smoke.

"No, but I've had my astrological chart done."

"I did that too a few years ago. The woman nailed my personality, but I should really listen to that tape again to see if what she predicted came true."

"I see you brought a tape recorder with you."

"When I made the appointment, the psychic said she didn't permit recordings, but I brought it along just in case."

"I guess she doesn't want people to play it later and see how often she was wrong in her predictions."

"Oh, she said it wasn't that. She's afraid of the law. Supposedly there's a local ordinance against fortune-tellers who do it as a business, so she's very careful to not charge anyone, but she made it clear that a $100 tip would be appreciated."

"Do you know what she does? I mean, does she read Tarot cards or tea leaves?"

"Judy said there isn't anything like that."

"I had my Tarot cards read, but it was a friend who simply consulted a book. He didn't claim to be a psychic. I was supposed to think of a question and the cards would give the answer. Are you going to see this woman for a particular question you want answered?"

Maybe my inquiry is too personal, because Leaf doesn't say anything. She deeply inhales several times in succession then puts the cigarette out in the ashtray.

"I'm going about Ted. I can't seem to get over the whole thing, and I thought maybe if I had something in the future to look forward to I could move on."

"I'm sorry, Leaf. I knew from the night Mark and I photographed his home that he was totally self-centered."

"Did you suspect he was gay?"

"I didn't really think about it."

Leaf lights another cigarette. "Ted wasn't, I must admit, the most romantic of men, but I thought that was just his way, that like a lot of men he just wasn't real affectionate. Oh, he *did* perform. Occasionally." She talks rapidly, as if she's had her feelings bottled up for a long time but now that she's removed the cork, it just pours out. "The important thing to me was that he was fun and intelligent. We had good times together. I finally had someone to go to the movies with, and Ted seemed to enjoy talking about them afterward. One time we even read the same murder mystery so we could talk about who we thought had done it."

I sense that I shouldn't say anything, just let the silence be. Leaf smokes and I look out the windshield.

"Then after a while," she continues, "I started getting anonymous phone calls. Someone would call, always late at night, and say that Ted was gay. Of course, the caller didn't put it that nicely—*much* more descriptive. The first time I ignored it. There are always rumors, especially in this industry, but the calls persisted. Once I even thought the caller sounded like Ted trying to disguise his voice.

"Eventually, I confronted him with it. He admitted he had had a male lover, but that it had been years ago. He said he hadn't the slightest inclination toward men since that one time. I believed him. I *wanted* to."

She smashes her cigarette in the ashtray.

"So we kept seeing each other. But I should have known. Of course, as soon as it was over, one of those bitchy decorators couldn't wait to tell that he had seen Ted at the baths almost every week. It hasn't been easy. It's taken me a long time to get to the point where I can even think about it without wanting to throw up.

"I still feel so used. Oh, I know people use me to a certain extent, inviting me to parties and dinners just so that they get me to see their homes. I understand that. It comes with the job. I know I wouldn't get ninety percent of the invitations I do if I weren't editor-in-chief. But I cannot accept what Ted did. It was a terrible violation."

Leaf pushes in the lighter and I hand her another cigarette.

"But here's the awful part. *I miss him.* We used to talk on the phone every day. I miss his sense of humor, his polite manners. Even his recessed chin. And I don't want to miss him, so I'm going to this damn psychic, who better tell me something good about my future."

The psychic's house is on a dead-end street in a neighborhood that appears to have died a couple of decades ago. The cottage-size house is wrapped in pale blue aluminum siding. Several of the slats by the porch are dented, as if a car had pulled up too close.

An obese woman with fraudulent red hair opens the front door before we knock. "Hi! You must be Leaf." She takes a cigarette out of her orange lipstick-smeared mouth and smiles broadly. I bet she's never seen a dentist. "I'm Cora."

"This is Anthony," Leaf says.

I smile and clutch her tote bag close to my chest.

Cora has on a bright purple cardigan sweater over a wrinkled pink and orange floral muumuu short enough to expose blotchy fat ankles. She shuffles into the living room in once-white fake-fur slippers.

I doubt if the avocado green shag carpet has ever been vacuumed. Who knows what's crawling in it? I wish I had worn boots instead of loafers.

Brown draperies, one slipping off its rod, flank two dirty windows. A tripod table in front of one of the windows holds a dying philodendron in an orange plastic pot. It's hard to kill a philodendron but I bet it hasn't been watered this year. A television console faces a maroon velvet sofa dense with cat hair; four fat white cats don't bother to look up as we enter.

In one corner a square table is draped with a yellow and green paisley shawl. Behind it is a gray four-drawer file cabinet. Beside it is an executive-style chair; the red vinyl is supposed to resemble tufted leather; it doesn't. Another fat white cat sleeps on a smaller chair that looks as if it's wearing its original black horsehair. A third chair—wooden and straight-backed—is stacked with old magazines and tabloids and topped with a dish encrusted with dried egg yolk. At least five mismatched tables are scattered about, all littered with what can only be described as dime-store junk. Wallpaper with large red roses makes the cluttered room appear even more chaotic. Pervading the air is the sour smell of cat piss and body odor.

Cora pushes the cat off the horsehair chair; it joins its companions on the sofa and immediately falls back to sleep. The other cats don't even stir.

"Sit here," she commands Leaf.

Leaf practically cowers in this woman's presence. Gone is the strong woman who runs a prominent national magazine. She seems too intimidated to ask Cora if she can record the session. "Is it alright if Anthony writes down what you say?"

Now I know why she brought the legal pad and pens—and me.

"Sure, but I talk fast and won't stop so he can catch up."

"I'll do the best I can."

"You do that." Cora leaves the room and returns with another straight-backed wooden chair that she places in the doorway. "Sit here so you don't distract me."

I'm glad to be practically out of the room since I'm allergic to cats.

Cora squeezes her bulky body into the executive chair. She places her flabby forearms on the table, palms up, fingers slightly curved. The remains of purple polish dot her broken nails. "Put your hands on top of mine."

Cora clasps her fingers around Leaf's then she shuts her eyes. Smears of aqua cover her eyelids. Her hampered breathing fills the room. When Cora opens her eyes they are unfocused mirrors. She doesn't say anything for nearly a full minute—just the strained breathing fills the room.

"I don't know whether you have always been alone or whether you simply think of yourself as being alone." Cora's voice is lower than when she spoke before. "We make our own destiny, you know? We're given the tools, the material, the know-how; but it's up to us how we use them, you know? I see you going it alone. This doesn't mean that there aren't other people around you. You're around a lot of people. But you don't depend on them. You only depend on yourself, you know? You think you can't count on anyone but yourself. And maybe you can't.

"I see three people around you when you were a child. Did your grandmother or another relative have a big influence on you?"

"I was adopted."

"Yes." Cora nods. "Two mothers. But you didn't like them. Not the one who adopted you and not your real mother. You don't like many people, do you? Why do you make it so hard on yourself? Maybe someone you shut out could help you, you know? But I see you shutting out a lot of people. No one can make a mistake with you. They make one mistake and you shut the door. I can't tell you what to do. You know? I can only tell you what I see and you must decide. But I see you shutting many doors. I don't know why you do this. You want people around you, but, honey, you do not make it easy."

I scribble as fast as I can, hoping to get it all down. I wonder if I'll be able to decipher my abbreviations later. My eyes are beginning to itch from the cat dander.

"There're more men in your life than women. You don't think you're pretty, but many men find you appealing. You're not a delicate little flower that a lot of women pretend to be when they first meet a man. You fight back and a lot of men like to be put in their place.

"Most of the men will not be right for you. But I can't tell you who to choose, you know? You may need to be with a person in order to learn a lesson for this lifetime. But you should be careful. Not so careful that you don't open a door, because you already close many doors, you know? But a man is going to betray you."

"Do I already know him?"

"Do not interrupt!" Cora grips Leaf's fingers tighter for a moment. "A man with dark hair will betray you. I don't know how. I see you sad and alone—more alone than you usually are. You have very few people to talk to. You don't share secrets, do you? But you should try to—there is another man, younger."

I sneeze.

Cora glances at me. "Maybe. I don't know. It's not clear. I see the young man listening to you. He's not the man who will betray you, but there's betrayal all around you, you know? Everywhere.

"There's also much success. Lots of money. Lots of prestige. You have a lot now, but you'll have more, you know? You're going to the White House. But the president isn't there. I don't see Jimmy Carter. You'll take many trips. Some across water. But you don't like to travel.

"Now I see lace. Lots and lots of lace. It's everywhere, you know? And there's a woman standing in the middle of it— she's wearing lace. Her arms are outstretched. She's calling to you. Don't shut another door, you know?"

Leaf looks shocked. She gasps.

Cora's eyes suddenly snap shut. She lets go of Leaf's hands. "There is nothing else."

"But I have lots of questions." Leaf whines like a little girl.

"I said there's nothing more. You must go now."

"You saw something, didn't you?" Forceful Leaf has returned. "I want to know what it is! I don't care how terrible it is, you must tell me."

"There's nothing else."

"I won't pay you unless you tell me."

The psychic looks directly into Leaf's eyes. "You are not as strong as you think you are, my dear. Remember you insisted I tell you. It's only what I see. I'm not responsible for the pictures that come."

"Tell me!"

"I see—you're going to die under bizarre circumstances."

"What do you mean 'bizarre'?"

"You won't die of natural causes. I see many people but you're again alone."

"When is this going to happen?"

"When it's time."

Leaf is silent most of the drive back to Los Angeles. She smokes cigarette after cigarette. I sneeze. I blow my nose.

Finally she says, "The woman in the lace is my real mother. Her name is Lacey. About a week ago my adoptive mother called me—we haven't spoken in years—and said Lacey is dying and asking for me."

"Is this in Iowa?"

"Yes." She pushes in the cigarette lighter and raises yet another Virginia Slims to her lips, which have lost all traces of her usual bright red lipstick.

"Why don't you go." It's not a question. It's a plea. "Maybe it will complete something for you."

"I completed that life years ago. It's over. I can't go back." She stubs out the barely smoked cigarette. "I won't!"

APRIL 24, 1979

Mr. Bruin has a twenty-five-inch television placed in the break room so the staff can watch Leaf on *The Mike Douglas Show*. But Timmy still brings in his smaller set, and he and I watch the program with Walter in Leaf's office.

"I've never seen this show." Walter arranges a pillow behind his back on the banquette. "Is it on one of the three networks?"

"It's syndicated," Timmy says. "It used to be filmed in Philadelphia but moved to Los Angeles last year."

"It also won an Emmy last year," I add.

Mike Douglas starts the show with a song then introduces this week's co-host, Joan Rivers, who does a very funny monolog.

During a commercial Walter says, "I think Douglas is wearing a wig."

"And a dark suit to hide his fat," says Timmy.

"It's really a dull set, isn't it?" I turn down the sound as the commercials continue. "I guess it's beige so it won't conflict with anything the guests wear, but it's just wallpaper and two office chairs. There's not even a table for a glass of water or a bouquet. Very cheap."

Della Reese sings a song, then she and Mike duet. Just before another round of commercials, he announces Leaf will be his next guest. Timmy phones Ivory on the intercom, and I scoot over so she can sit next to me. She immediately lights a cigarette, which makes Walter light one.

"You two sit next to each other so you can share the ashtray." I don't like being sandwiched between the smokestacks and switch places with Ivory.

"Oh God!" Timmy says when Leaf appears. "What did they do to her hair?"

It's been teased into a full bouffant and sprayed so much it looks lacquered.

"Too much makeup, too," I add. "It's one thing to try to give her cheekbones, but that just looks like she has a dirty face."

"Shush!" Ivory waves her hand and ash lands on her skirt.

A third chair has been added, and when Leaf sits between Mike and Joan her shoes don't touch the floor. Mike asks boring questions about the history of the magazine. It sounds too rehearsed and Leaf shows no animation.

The camera jumps to Joan when she suddenly interjects, "Leaf, what do you think of High Tech?"

"The fifteen minutes it lasted were about fourteen too long." The audience laughs and Leaf looks relieved. "Those high-tech lofts have no originality. They all have stark white walls, uncomfortable black furniture and one red flower."

"I hate that rubber flooring with the little bumps," Joan says. "Have you ever tried walking on it with bare feet? At first I thought, 'Oh this will be great! I'll get a foot massage.' But my feet kept sticking to it. Awful!"

"It's worse in heels," Leaf says. "You land on one of those bumps the wrong way and you nearly tip over."

Joan points to Leaf's bosom. "No wonder you nearly tip over. You have knockers!" She touches her own flat chest. "I have a doorbell."

The audience roars.

Mike points the conversation back to decorating. "Tell me,

Leaf, what do you think is the next trend?"

"I don't think people should follow trends," she responds. "They should decorate their home in a way that's comfortable for them. I know interior designers are going to hate me, but I don't think someone should hire a decorator just because he's the latest one getting all the attention. They should find one who understands what they want and how they live."

The audience applauds.

"That can't be spontaneous," Walter says. "I bet there's an 'Applause' sign that lights up."

"Well, not counting trends," Mike pursues, "do you see any major changes on the horizon?"

"I think the dining room is going to become obsolete. With everyone having outside activities, there aren't a lot of family meals. The room is pretty much wasted—sometimes not even used every day. All the home computers that are springing up have got to go someplace, and I think that place is going to be the dining room."

Joan asks, "Are there any decorating ideas that you personally hate?"

"Joan's questions are more interesting than Mike's," Timmy whispers.

"Almost anything can work if it's done well and with an air of confidence." Leaf doesn't seem nervous but I wish she'd stop swinging her feet. Then as if she telegraphically read my mind, she crosses her ankles. "What I hate is when everyone does the same thing. For a while all the designers were putting beds on the diagonal. It was amusing once, maybe twice, but when everyone does the same thing, it loses its charm."

"You're certainly not shy about saying what you dislike," Joan says.

"I'm more afraid to say I like something for fear everyone will start doing it."

"Leaf, you see thousands of homes," Mike says, looking at the camera instead of his guest, "but can only publish about sixty a year. I'm sure you have tactful ways of telling people you don't want to show their homes. But how do you tell a *celebrity* his or her home isn't good enough to be published?"

Joan leans toward Mike. "What did she tell *you*?"

After the audience stops laughing, Leaf says, "I usually try to visit homes when the owners are away. But if they are there, I just walk through saying 'charming' a lot. Then when I get back to the office, I have my secretary send a polite 'no, thank you' letter. I don't treat celebrities any different from everyone else. But one time a certain actor—"

Joan grabs Leaf's arm. "Who?"

"I can't say, Joan, but his TV series had just been cancelled. It was on Friday night. At nine o'clock. On NBC. But I can't say who, so don't ask."

"Where's my stack of old *TV Guides*?" Joan looks as if she's searching.

"Anyway," Leaf continues, looking at Mike, "this actor was there when I went to see his house and insisted I give him an answer right then—he probably sensed I didn't like it. I tried to be polite and say his privacy was too important to invade by publishing his home. He didn't buy *that*. He was *starved* for publicity. So I said it wouldn't photograph well—and ran for the door!"

The audience again applauds. "Got to be a sign," Timmy says.

"*Inside* is the most beautiful magazine in America, Leaf," Mike says.

"Because of *you*." Timmy rubs my calf.

"You publish only the very best homes," Mike continues. "But what is your own home like?"

"Here it comes," says Walter.

"It was decorated by Sarah Cohen," Leaf says. "It's very understated and monochromatic—lots of khaki. I see so many homes every day, that when I go home, I don't want to see any color."

"Would you consider publishing it in the magazine?"

The four of us simultaneously lean toward the screen.

"I have! When Sarah was finished, it was so fabulous I thought it would be unfair to her not to publish it just because it was my home. So I ran it anonymously."

Joan grabs Leaf's wrist. "Well, just between you and me, what issue was it in?"

"You can't expect me to tell you that in front of all the viewers, now can you?"

"They won't tell," Mike says, as the audience applauds once more. "See, they promise."

"Well, all right. It's in the latest issue." Leaf pauses. "It's the cover story."

Mike Douglas holds up *Inside* as a camera zooms in for a close-up.

Then Mike introduces someone named *Edward*, and a chimpanzee in a business suit walks out and shakes his hand.

"We'll be right back," Mike announces.

Leaf isn't there when the show resumes.

APRIL 24, 1979

"It's nice to finally have a gay bar on Santa Monica Boulevard with a picture window." I hand Timmy a Budweiser. "No more hiding." I leave a generous tip for the cute bartender. "Let's go stand over there so we can watch everyone come in."

It's only five-thirty but the place is already packed, and I have to be careful not to spill my salty dog as we cross the floor.

"Did Leaf come into the office today? I haven't seen her all week."

"She thought Mr. Bruin was going to be furious she showed her home on Mike Douglas." Timmy unconsciously starts peeling the label off the beer bottle. "That's why she hasn't been in. She was giving him time to cool down. And he did call her several times. She finally came in for an hour today to meet with him. And guess what he's doing?"

"I have no idea."

"He's restructuring the company and going to become Chairman of the Board—and he's naming Leaf president!"

"I didn't know the company had a board."

"It doesn't. And that's the catch. Leaf will get a bigger title but now she'll have to answer to the board."

"Who else is going to be on the board?"

"Mr. B. Mrs. B, of course, Brian Willoughby and Larry Stein."

I throw my hands up. "I can understand the circulation director being on the board, but how does Larry get away with it? He does *nothing* right and keeps getting promoted. Have you seen his layouts for the celebrities' home book?"

Timmy shakes his head.

"They're terrible! You'd think he'd have the sense to just copy the layouts from when the homes ran in the magazine, which would save the company a lot of money by not having to make new color separations, but, no, Larry has to redesign them. And, of course, he doesn't do it right, making the wrong picture a full page and the best pictures too small. I can't believe Leaf and Mr. Bruin let him get away with it."

"I don't think Leaf's really interested in the book."

"Her name is going on the cover! She's the one who's going to get all the publicity. You'd think she'd show *some* interest." I swallow the rest of my drink. "I can't believe Larry Stein is on the board."

"I think Mr. B selected Larry because he knows he can control him. Willoughby is also under Mr. B's thumb, so if it comes down to a battle, he's got three votes to fight Leaf and Mrs. B." Timmy takes a wrinkled envelope out of his back pocket. "Here. This ought to calm you down."

"What is it?"

"You'll see."

It's a check for $10,000.

"Leaf said it's your bonus."

"This certainly takes the sting out of Larry being on the board." I fold the envelop in thirds and put it in my wallet. "Does this mean Sarah Cohen's gotten a new project already?"

"Yep. A big tycoon wants her to design his new home in Maui."

"Oh look." I point my chin toward the door. "Jason's assistant Terry just came in. Shall we invite him over?"

"Only if you want to piss on him."

"What do you mean?"

"Terry's into water sports big time."

"Well, I still think he's sexy. What's a little pee among friends?"

Timmy raises his eyebrows. "You never cease to surprise me, Anthony."

"What can I say? Besides, I like red hair."

"He's got enough of it. I don't think there's an inch of his body not covered in hair. And when someone's peed on him, he smells worse than a wet poodle."

"So how many times have you done it with him?"

"As Miss Susann would say, 'Once is enough.'"

"Actually, Timmy, the title is *Once Is Not Enough*."

He dismisses the correction with a flick of his wrist. "Terry told me that Jason's getting worse and worse with coke. He's even supplying some of his Hollywood clients—taking over Geraldo's gig as 'the decorator's dealer.' And Terry also said Jason's getting into younger and younger guys. He said Jason tries to pick them up in his new Porsche at Hollywood High, but if that doesn't work he drives over to Selma Avenue for some trade. Terry's actually thinking of finding another job."

"Maybe he should work at Sherle Wagner."

"Why would he want to do that?"

"It was supposed to be funny. You know Sherle Wagner makes sinks and tubs and other bathroom fixtures, and you said Terry's into water sports."

"Try again, honey. And speaking of redheads, what's the story on that Irish doll you hired as your assistant?"

"Sean O'Brien. It took me forever to fill that position. I saw several qualified applicants, but what they really wanted was *my* job. When I explained there would be no design work at all—that I design not only the well but also the departments—

they all backed away. Oh, some said the pay was too low, but they were just looking for an out. Then Sean O'Brien came in and said he'd be perfectly happy doing only paste-up."

"And you believe him?"

"I do. He said he wants a mindless job so he could think about his real love. He's in a band and writes songs."

"What kind of job did he have before?"

"He worked at his father's ad agency in the Valley. He did paste-up and said he enjoyed the precision of it—he's a Virgo like me—but that after a while it just got too complicated working for his dad."

"Well, I guess you better hope he doesn't write a hit record." Timmy tilts his head back to get the last drop of beer. "If his fellow band members are as cute as Sean, I'd buy their record."

"Well, keep your dick in your pants. Sean's straight."

"How do you know?"

"Does he have a mustache?"

"No."

"Does he wear polo shirts with a crocodile nipping his left nipple?"

"No."

"Does he have a colored handkerchief in his back pocket telling the world what he likes to do in bed?"

"No."

"Then he's straight. Besides, he told me."

"He just blurted it out?"

"I told him I wanted to hire him and that I'm gay and if that's a problem for him, he shouldn't accept the job. He said he was straight and there'd be no problem; he said the drummer in the band is gay."

"What's the band's name?"

"'Ginger Boys.' It seems they're all redheads."

Timmy hands me his bottle, now stripped of its label. "You're the one who just got a big bonus. How about buying me another beer?"

When I return with two fresh drinks, Timmy is talking with Aiko Shimizu.

"Oh, hi, Aiko. If I had seen you earlier I would have bought you a drink too."

"Don't worry about it, Anthony. I was just telling Timmy that this has been the shop's biggest month ever. We had a lot of orders for Oscar parties, and then the next day everyone was sending flowers to the winners. But what surprised me was how many people sent flowers to the *losers*."

"I'm not surprised," I say. "I gave Diana Ross gardenias when she lost for *Lady Sings the Blues*."

"Oh, that was the year Liza won for *Cabaret*."

"Do you know Diana Ross?" Timmy asks.

"No, but I knew where she lived—a fortress of a house with hardly any windows facing the street. The door was opened by a white butler."

"Well, nice seeing you two," Aiko says. "Time for my *first* martini of the night."

As soon as the florist is out of earshot, Timmy asks, "Guess what that delicate little flower is into?"

"Since you bring it up, it must be something bizarre. Please don't say scat."

"Fist fucking."

"Giving or receiving?"

"Receiving."

"Someone should write a book about the sexual practices of interior designers."

"It would be a best seller." Timmy tilts his head toward the entrance. "Ted Powell just walked in."

"Is he coming over?"

"No, he's going up to Terry."

"Good. Maybe they can piss on each other."

"God this place is turning into an interior design convention. Raymond Washington just entered."

"I hear he has a prick bigger than John Holmes."

"Maybe not *that* big, but at least Raymond's gets hard." Timmy's eyebrows shoot up again, but I pretend not to notice. "Have you ever seen a John Holmes film? It may be huge but it just hangs there."

"Anthony, did you go to town with Mr. Washington?"

I'm saved from answering by Raymond's approach. He kisses my lips and Timmy's cheek. "So what are the boys from *Inside* up to?"

"Not nearly enough," Timmy responds.

"Timmy said Sarah got a project in Hawaii." I hope my voice doesn't betray the quiver running through my body. Raymond Washington is very sexy. He's the only man in the bar wearing a tie. Everyone else, even those still in their office clothes, are dressed more casually; if they did have on a tie, it's in their pocket now. And Raymond is standing very close to me. I sniff Geoffrey Beene's Gray Flannel.

"Mrs. Cohen is elated! I mean, the magazine's only been out less than a week."

"Subscribers get it earlier," Timmy says.

"She's flying to Maui on Monday to meet the new client."

"Is it someone connected to Dole Pineapple?" Timmy asks.

"No. He's Greek. His name is Kikonos. This is going to be *one* of his vacation homes. He's supposedly richer than Niarchos."

"If I lived in Greece," I say, "I don't think I'd need a vacation home in Maui."

"You know what they say: The rich are different. They get bored *very* easily." Raymond's smile dazzles. "Hey, what am I doing standing here? Let me get you guys a drink."

"I don't think I should have another."

"Sure you should," Timmy and Raymond say simultaneously.

While Raymond's at the bar, Timmy asks, "So tell me, Anthony, is Raymond big enough for two?"

"What do you mean?"

"He's obviously interested in you. Why don't you get him to invite *both* of us over to his place?"

And I do.

APRIL 26, 1979

"**W**hat does Leaf want to see me about?" I ask while I wait in Timmy's office.

"Mrs. Bruin has a brochure for *Celebrities at Home* that she wants to show Leaf, and Leaf wants you to be there."

"Where is Leaf?"

"She said she was going to the ladies, but she probably went down to the newsstand to buy M&Ms." He opens a drawer in his desk with half a dozen bags of the candy. "She should have simply asked me and quit playing—" Timmy suddenly looks indignant. "The nerve of some people!"

I turn around to look out his door. "What?"

"Mrs. Bruin walked right into Leaf's office without asking if Leaf was ready to see her."

Timmy storms off but when he addresses Colette there's no hint of anger in his voice—just a slight tone of condescension. "May I get you a cup of coffee or a glass of water, Mrs. Bruin?"

"No, thank you. Where's Leaf?"

"She'll be right in."

"Now I know why Mrs. B has been out of the office for over a month," Timmy whispers when he returns to his office. "I'm sure she's had her eyes done. And maybe her neck too."

"Isn't she a little young for a facelift?"

"Oh, none of the really rich women have complete facelifts anymore. They just get a little tuck here, a little nip there every other year, so that nothing's extreme. But I can always spot them."

Leaf enters munching M&Ms.

"She's already in your office," Timmy says.

"Yeah, I could smell the trail of Opium down the hall." She tosses the bag of candy on Timmy's desk. "Come on, Anthony. Let's get this over with."

Colette, a red folder on her lap, is sitting on the long branch of the banquette. She's wearing a wrap-around black leather skirt with a large silver pin, a simple white blouse and a necklace made of chunks of turquoise. Her black pumps are lined up squarely in front of her. Black nylons are dotted with tiny bumblebees.

Leaf chooses the short side of the banquette, as far away from Colette as possible, so I settle into the corner between them.

"We received nearly three hundred orders for the book from the quarter-page ad I ran in the March/April issue," Mrs. Bruin begins, "and I expect to do even better with the half-page in the current issue. By the time the full-page appears in July/August, we may have already made a profit on the book before it even comes out."

Leaf gets up, walks across the room and picks up a pack of Virginia Slims from her desk. Colette waits until Leaf is sitting down again and has lighted her cigarette before continuing. I wonder why these two women are such adversaries.

"I thought that since the magazine appeals to such a sophisticated group of people, it would be best to—"

"Forget the sales pitch, Colette," Leaf interrupts. "We know the magazine's market. Let's just see the brochure."

"You have to realize this is a rough." Colette opens the folder and hands Leaf a full-color mock-up as if it were a religious icon. "But it was done by Curtis Singer, so it's quite detailed. He's the best in the business."

"Here, Anthony, you look at it first." Leaf passes the brochure to me without a glance. "What do you think?"

I unfold the five-by-eight-inch document to eight-by-ten then to ten-by-sixteen and finally to sixteen-by-twenty. "Well, I understand it's a brochure and for a book and not the magazine," I say, "but it isn't *Inside*'s style of graphics. We never use overlapping pictures or drop shadows and most of the photos are too small. This is extremely cluttered. *Inside* is very clean."

"I *appreciate* your comments, Anthony," Colette says, "but as you said, a brochure is not the magazine. It's a sales tool. Curtis has been designing circulation brochures for years and has had tremendous success in adding new subscribers."

"For what magazines?"

Colette looks at me as if I don't have the right to speak let alone question.

"In case you didn't understand," Leaf says, blowing out smoke, "Anthony wants to know what magazines Singer—"

"I heard what he said." Colette's coral red lips are pulled tighter than her neck. "Curtis has had great success with *House Beautiful*, *Good Housekeeping* and *McCall's*, to name just a few."

"I think it's important for the brochure to convey the style of the magazine," I say. "This flyer would be fine for *Good Housekeeping*. It might even do for *House Beautiful*. Of course, those magazines do not have the elegance of *Inside*. And neither does this brochure."

Colette yanks the brochure out of my hands and refolds it as I continue speaking.

"But it's not just the *look* of this brochure that's disturbing. The headlines make it seem as if *Inside* is a how-to magazine and this book is going to tell people how to decorate their homes like celebrities. You may get a lot of people ordering the book, but once they see it, they'll realize it's not what they expected. I imagine some of them may even ask for their money back."

"Anthony's right," Leaf says. "I hope you haven't paid Singer a lot of money, Colette, because the brochure is not useable. I don't think it's even salvageable."

Colette puts the brochure in her folder and walks out.

I sneeze. "*Way* too much perfume."

"Sometimes I wonder if we shouldn't just tell Colette everything looks wonderful and let her fall flat on her smug plastic face." Leaf stubs out her cigarette. "Thank you, Anthony. That was perfect."

"I only said what I thought." What I *didn't* say is that the book, with Larry's dull, repetitive layouts, will probably also be a disappointment to *Inside* readers.

Leaf pats my arm. "I can always rely on you to tell the truth."

APRIL 29, 1979

I ask Cole if we can drive out to his family's Malibu house. "I have something to show you."

"I've already seen your cock," he whispers over the phone.

"This is somewhat bigger."

"Oh wow!" he exclaims when I pull up to the Bruin front door. "A Fiat Spider."

It's dusty blue, and the convertible top is down. "Hop in."

Cole runs his hand along the dashboard. "When did you get it?"

"Tuesday."

"Dad said if I graduate with nothing lower than a C, he'd get me a new car—well, not 'new' but new to me."

"Do you think you'll make it?"

"Yeah, the only class I'm having a problem with is Chemistry, but if I get a C on the final, I'll be okay."

"What kind of car do you think he'll give you?"

"I tried talking my mom into getting a new car for herself and giving me her XK-E, but it's a '75, and since that's the last year Jaguar made that style she wants to hang on to it." He kicks off his sneakers and wiggles his toes. "I want a Camaro or Mustang, but they'll probably give me a huge ten-year-old Buick that one of Mom's Pasadena friends no longer wants."

He lifts his t-shirt over his head.

I take my eyes off the road to glance at his trim body clad only in old jeans cut off so short his balls nearly hang out. "There's a tube of suntan lotion in the glove compartment."

He lathers his chest and shoulders then leans in close to me to look in the rear-view mirror as he rubs lotion on his face. "Your turn." He tugs my polo shirt out of khaki shorts, and I raise one arm then the other as he pulls it over my head.

"I like the bucket seats, but now I can't sit next to you." He applies lotion to my torso, tweaking my nipples.

"Don't bother about my face," I say. "I put some on before I left my apartment. And would you fasten your seat belt? I don't want you flying over the windshield if I have to make a sudden stop."

"Yes, Mother." Cole buckles up but twists to face me. "And speaking of Mom, what did you say to her last week? Usually she just bitches about Leaf, but she really tore into you."

"I just told her what I thought of the brochure to promote *Inside*'s first book."

"Well she ranted for about ten minutes then said the worst part was that you were right."

"And I was!" I pull hairs on his leg. "That meeting was very uncomfortable. Why are Leaf and your mom such rivals?"

"Mom thinks Leaf became editor by sleeping with Dad."

"That would explain a lot. Do you think it's true?"

"Leaf is older than his usual bimbos, but who knows?" He twists his mouth. "Well I guess only two people know."

"This is really none of my business, but your father has a reputation for—for"

"Fucking a lot of women?"

"Yet you said he has a really small dick and I wonder—"

"He primes them with his tongue, then he uses his hand. He says women tell him they have orgasms with him more than other men."

"He told you that?"

"Yeah, when we had the birds-and-bees talk. I guess he fig-ured I was small like him and he wanted to help me out."

"One happy family." It's difficult for me not to caress his hairy leg, so I distract myself with another personal question. "Have you had sex with a girl?"

"No, and I don't want to. Not even with effeminate boys. Have *you* had sex with a woman?"

"No, and I don't want to either. When I worked at *Motor Trend* the publisher asked me that same question: *Have I ever had sex with a woman?* And I said, 'No, have you ever had sex with a man?'"

"I bet that shut him up."

"Actually what he said was, 'No, but I've thought about it once or twice.'"

We're silent for a while, than Cole says, "Are you close to Leaf?"

"Walter says I'm closer to her than anyone on the staff is. Why?"

"If I tell you something, do you promise not to say anything to her?"

"Depends on what it is."

"Well she's going to find out soon enough anyway. Mom and Dad are reorganizing the company. There's going to be a Board of Directors, and Dad's going to be Chairman."

"I hate to disappoint you, but I already know this."

"Do you know who's going to be president?"

Before I can say "Leaf," Cole says, "My Mom."

I could mention that Timmy said Leaf was going to be named president, but perhaps this is one time Timmy is wrong; Cole would be in a better position to know. All I say is, "There are going to be fireworks."

"Dad likes fireworks." Cole pinches my nipple again. "He said you were the hit of the sales retreat."

"What exactly did he say?"

"That all the sales reps were practically asleep as Larry droned on, but then you came on and saved the day."

"Larry *was* boring, but the fact is the sales reps aren't interested in *Inside*'s book. And why should they be? There are no ads in it. They have nothing to sell. I don't know why Larry was even asked to speak at the retreat."

"Dad said you were very funny."

"I started out filled with excitement—with good gestures and voice inflection. I had practiced in front of a mirror. But when I saw everyone looking at me—your dad and mom, all the reps, Leaf and the editors, I suddenly panicked, so I said, 'I have to consult my notes.' I had brought a folder up with me to the podium, so I opened it, and there was one piece of paper inside, and I held it up. It was a picture of Ruth Gordon. I said, 'These are my notes. If this woman can persevere until she won an Oscar at age seventy-two, I can give this speech.' That got a big laugh, and that was all I needed."

"I love *Harold and Maude*. All those fake suicides." He rubs my chest. "Dad said you gave the reps a challenge."

"I said that when we published the three-page foldout in November, everyone raved about it, but it ended up costing a lot more than the production manager estimated, so your dad said I couldn't do anymore. But if I did a foldout *cover*, we could get the advertiser on the other side to pay the full production cost. Then I said, 'Who's going to do that for me?' and five hands went up. So we'll see."

Cole turns on the radio, and we're silent until I turn onto Pacific Coast Highway, then he says, "I have some interesting news and wanted to wait until we get to Malibu to tell you, but I can't hold out any longer."

"You're pregnant."

"Very funny." Cole crosses his arms over his chest.

"I'm sorry. I really want to hear." I take the opportunity to stroke his leg again.

"Actually, I have two pieces of news. I'm taking acting lessons!"

"Where?"

"I'm in a small group—just ten people, five boys, five girls—with a private teacher—Boris Koslov. We meet every Saturday. Yesterday was the first class."

"How'd it go?"

"At first it was sort of boring, everyone introducing themselves and saying what they expect to get out of the class. Everyone wanted to be an *actor*, not a movie star, so when it was my turn, I said I didn't want to be a movie star either but I did want to shine. And Mr. Koslov said, 'You already do.'"

"And you do. What's Koslov's background?"

"You mean, *is he gay?* I don't think so. He looks about a hundred years old, and most of the actors he's worked with are long dead or haven't acted in years, but Mom made some inquiries, and he's got a good reputation."

"Is he Russian?"

"He said he was born in Moscow but became a U.S. citizen in 1939."

"Who was the Russian who developed the Method?"

"Stanislavski. Mr. Koslov says he uses his methods but adapted them especially for film rather than the stage."

"You might find acting just as tedious as modeling. I understand there's a lot of waiting around."

"Yes, but you eventually get to *do* something—not just stand there and look blank."

"I think you'll be a very good actor."

"Why do you say that?

"Don't take this the wrong way, Cole, but you're very good at being different people: the pouty little boy, the naive Peter Pan, the sexual predator."

"Is that how you see me—as a sexual predator?"

"Don't you think it's a part of who you are?"

"It sounds so calculating. I just like sex."

"You said you have two pieces of news. What's the other?"

"If I tell you now, we won't have anything to talk about at the beach."

"Oh, Cole. I think we'll always have things to talk about."

We stop at a deli to buy drinks and take-away sandwiches. Cole understands when I won't let him eat potato chips in my new car, "not this first week."

When we arrive at the house, Cole removes his cut-offs. "I like that I can walk around naked and know you won't attack me."

At least not until you're eighteen.

I strip down to a black Speedo and open the sliding-glass door to the deck. "Look at this, Cole." The deck is covered with a layer of gray ash from the recent fires in the hills.

After we hose it off—Cole puts on a red Speedo first—we run into the ocean and body surf. We exhaust ourselves and fall on the shore, the waves washing over our legs. I think I surprise him when I kiss his lips.

"Not as romantic as *From Here to Eternity*," I say, "but it's the best I can do."

"Is that another black-and-white movie?"

"Yes. I hope Mr. Koslov insists you watch some of the classics."

"He has! Class runs from one until four, but before that he'll show a film. Next week it's *A Streetcar Named Desire*."

"That's a good one to start with, since Marlon Brando studied Method acting. You said you had two pieces of news. What's the other thing?"

"I got a part-time job—at Selection. It's just for two hours a day after school, but after graduation, I can work full time."

"What are you doing?"

"Nothing interesting. I'm in the backroom filing fabric swatches. It's very tedious, and I'd rather be out front flirting with the decorators. Even though I'm in the back where no one can see me, Mrs. Cohen insists I wear a tie and absolutely forbids jeans. I only took the job to get some spending money. My parents may be rich but they sure are cheap."

"Maybe they're trying to teach you the value of earning a buck."

"I doubt it. Mom inherited hers and Dad married his."

"Isn't your senior prom coming up soon?"

"May 18th. But I'm not going."

"Why not?

"If I can't bring a guy, I don't want to go."

"I didn't go to my prom either—for the very same reason."

We lie on the beach holding hands, and Cole does not pressure me to do more. Maybe he's thinking about what I said about being a sexual predator.

All I feel is love.

MAY 15, 1979

"It's been two weeks since Leaf has been out of the office," Ivory says, "and Timmy has no idea when she'll be coming back, so I thought we should have a meeting."

I shake my head. "I still find it hard to believe Mr. Bruin would tell both his wife and Leaf he was naming her president and then appoint his attorney instead."

"I don't have any trouble believing it," Walter says. "Look at that interview he gave last month in *Ad Age*."

"You mean when the reporter asked about Mr. Bruin's management style?"

"And Claret replied, 'I like to put opponents in a room and let them fight it out.'"

"But I don't think Leaf is out of the office just because of what Mr. Bruin did. She went to San Francisco for several days." I don't mention the trip wasn't to scout homes but because she's seeing a man she met at a party. "But she's back now."

"And we can reach her by phone," adds Walter.

"Actually, we can't." Ivory lights a cigarette. "Every time I've called her machine picks up. Then she calls Timmy and *he* replies to my message."

"I think he's been to her house everyday," I say.

"To bring her the new issue of *Town & Country* or an invitation to a dinner party." Ivory sneers. "But nothing's being done about the next issue."

I don't know why Ivory is so upset. I've gotten a lot more accomplished with Leaf out of the office. "Timmy gave Leaf my suggestions for the homes to run in September/October and she approved it." I open a folder and give Ivory and Walter a list of the residences.

"You planned the issue by yourself? You had no right to do that without consulting me!" Ivory glares at me. "And when were you planning on showing me this list so I could assign the writers?"

"As soon as Leaf approved it. Timmy only brought it back from her house an hour ago."

"You have a lot of nerve—"

"All right. All right," Walter interjects. "We already have the Big Three at each other's throats. We don't need you two to go at it. If Leaf's approved the contents for the next issue, that's all we need to get back to work." He stands.

Ivory doesn't say anything further, so I walk out with Walter.

"Why didn't you involve Ivory in planning the issue?" Walter says when were back at his office. "You must have known she'd be furious when she found out."

"Because we'd still be planning it. Ivory is good at details but she can't see the overall picture. Literally." I sit down in front of Walter's desk. "One time Ivory wanted to see how the production director and I do color correcting, and she commented that a vase that took up less than an inch in the shot was too green. She failed to notice that the *entire* shot was too yellow."

"Sometimes she does the same thing with the text. She'll change three or four words and fail to notice the whole thing needs to be rewritten." Walter takes a package of Mallomars out of a drawer and passes it to me. "Ivory also takes things to extreme. In one of the articles, the writer had gone off on a tangent about the Vietnam War and Leaf deleted it saying she didn't think it was appropriate for the magazine to mention *war*. So now, even when an apartment is described as 'pre-war' Ivory crosses it out. That's going too far."

I finish eating a cookie before speaking. "Why do you think Mr. Bruin told both Leaf and his wife they would be president then named his attorney instead?"

"Because he's a sociopath."

"What exactly is that?"

"A person who has no conscience about anti-social behavior."

"You read about such people—see them in movies—but you never imagine you'll actually meet one, let alone work for one." I shake my head when Walter offers another cookie.

"Most of us assume the people we know are normal. And even if it's shown they aren't we find it hard to believe. Have you ever heard of a mother whose son is accused of a crime saying he's guilty? No, they all contend, to the day he's executed, that he's innocent." He takes another cookie but before biting into it puts it back in the package and shuts the drawer. "By the way, do you know what Colette is doing about this fiasco? I know she went to New York after it happened, but is she back?"

"She returned two days ago." Cole told me the details. "She asked Mr. Bruin to move out of the house, but she's not seeking a divorce, not with California's community property law. She's shutting down Inside Choices—"

"That venture never did make any money."

"And she's leaving the company and there won't be any more investments. It will have to survive on *Inside*'s profits. Fortunately, it's doing well, but I wouldn't count on any more bonuses."

"Any idea when Leaf will come back?" When I shake my head, Walter adds, "Well, she's not missed—or even needed."

"Mr. Bruin doesn't know that."

MAY 17, 1979

"Timmy!" Leaf scurries to her driveway in a pink coffee-stained sweat suit. "When you said you were coming over in a new car, I thought maybe you'd arrive in a Honda or one of those cute little Volkswagens. How can you afford a Mercedes on what I pay you?"

Leaf wiggles her fingers in greeting when I get out of the vehicle.

"I said I was bringing up a new car, but I didn't say it was *mine*." Timmy's eyes twinkle. "It's yours, Leaf! Mr. Bruin is giving you a brand new Mercedes-Benz 450 SLC! With power everything! Isn't the color to die? It's called 'Icon Gold.' Isn't it fabulous? And it's all paid for and registered in your name."

"Oh, I see." Leaf frowns. "Claret thinks he can buy my forgiveness with an expensive car. Well, I won't forgive him." She holds out her hand for the keys. "But I will accept the car."

"Mr. B said I wasn't to give you the keys unless you came back with us to the office." Like a petulant child, he holds the keys behind his back.

"You said the car is paid for and registered in my name, therefore it's legally mine. So give me the fucking keys." She stretches her arm out to his chest.

Timmy drops the keys in her hand.

"Now come inside. I had Carl's deliver groceries. I have Pecan Sandies!" At the sliding-glass door she abruptly turns around. "Did you bring the prescriptions?"

Timmy pats his tote.

As soon as we're seated in the living area, Leaf's cat pounces on my lap.

"I think cats know when a person is allergic and immediately head toward him Would you take him off me? If I get dander in my eye I'll tear the rest of the day."

"Come on, Alley. Let's go get a Pecan Sandie." Leaf takes it into the kitchen. "Do you want milk?" she shouts. "Or shall I make tea?"

Timmy goes to help her.

While they're in the kitchen, I walk around the large living area, which looks incomplete without all the borrowed art and accessories from the photo shoot. The television is on in the den area—*The Price Is Right*. There's an orange prescription pill vial on the coffee table: Valium.

Once the tea is poured, Timmy takes a handful of pink while-you-were-out telephone memos out of his bag and starts reading off the callers.

For three of the calls, Leaf says, "Give it to Ivory." Nine times she says, "Anthony, you handle it."

"And Jake White called."

"What'd he want?" Leaf bites into a cookie.

"He thought you had some reservations about an interview with the Des Moines *Register* and wanted to clarify it with you."

"I don't have any reservations about it. Just because I was born in Iowa doesn't mean I have to acknowledge it. I'm not doing the interview."

Timmy opens an appointment book. "You're scheduled to have lunch with Jason Hunt tomorrow at Chasen's."

"I don't want to have lunch with him. He never shuts up.

Who set this up?"

"You said Jason kept asking you to dinner and that you couldn't stand to spend an entire evening with him, so I should set up lunch. Don't you remember?"

"Vaguely. Call him and say I'm not feeling well."

"That's what we told him the last two times you cancelled."

"Three times a charm. I'm just not in the mood to hear one more decorator go on and on about how difficult his clients are." Leaf turns to me. "You go. Jason will forget all about having lunch with me if he can instead dine with an attractive man. Have you been to Chasen's?"

"No. Is the chili as good as Elizabeth Taylor claims?"

"Nothing's as good as Elizabeth Taylor claims. But have a bowl and decide for yourself. And make sure Jason pays for it."

Timmy consults his steno pad. "Your flight to San Francisco is confirmed for Saturday morning at 11:00. The travel agent will messenger over the ticket later this afternoon. I haven't booked the return trip because I thought you might want to fly directly from there to New York."

"Remind me what I'm supposed to do in New York."

Timmy flips to another page. "Mario Buatta, Mel Dwork and Michael de Santis all have new projects on the Upper East Side; Robin Rainbow has finished his own home on Fire Island; Alan Court has 'a cottage' in Southampton; Addison Saint James has done a penthouse on the West Side, and a new designer, Scott Riley, would like you to see his apartment in the Village."

"Every designer is the same person. I am so *bored* with them." Leaf suddenly points at me. "I'm going to put you in charge of them—just like you're in charge of the photographers. Keep in contact with all the designers we publish regularly to make sure they always show their work to us first. And *you* go to New York, Anthony. You look at the homes. I trust your judgment, and I'm sure all the gay designers would rather see you than me."

It's a great opportunity, but my immediate thought is: *Can I get tickets for* Sweeney Todd?

Timmy says, "Everyone's asking when you'll be back in the office. What shall I tell them?"

"I believe the standard reply is: *When I'm good and ready.*"

Since we arrived in the Mercedes, Leaf calls a taxi to take Timmy and me back to the office. Timmy whispers so the driver doesn't hear, but the man probably doesn't know much English. "I hope Leaf doesn't take that beautiful car out for a spin. I thought she was a little erratic, didn't you? Who knows how many of those pills she's taking: uppers in the morning and downers at night. Just like Judy Garland."

"That's such a cliché, Timmy."

"The thing about clichés, Mr. Smarty, is they're true. Only in this case Leaf can't click her heals and return home. Since she's an orphan, she doesn't have a home."

"I'm going to need a tissue if you keep this up. Or a basin to vomit in."

"Go on, make fun of me and I'll set up all your appointments in New York on the same day."

"You're too nice to do that."

"You're right. I'll arrange the schedule so you can go to Fire Island over the Memorial Day weekend. I live vicariously—so you have to tell me *all* the details."

MAY 17, 1979

"Now don't get mad." Timmy's smile is mischievous.

"About what?" I'm apprehensive.

"I've made all the arrangements for your trip to New York. You'll be staying at the Waldorf-Astoria. It's centrally located, so it will be easy to get to all the projects you have to see. Your flight will arrive in plenty of time for you to see *The Elephant Man* on Wednesday night like you wanted. The best I could do was twelfth row center. I had better luck with *Sweeney Todd* for Thursday—third row, but on the side. The tickets will be held at the box office."

"Why should I be upset about anything? It all sounds wonderful. Thank you very much."

"Here's the part you may not like. Since it's Memorial Day—the first big weekend of the season and all the gay boys will want to be there—I couldn't find a room in the Pines on Fire Island—and believe me, you want to stay there and not in tacky Cherry Grove—so I asked around and Robin Rainbow 'is thrilled' to have you stay at his place. I know he's older than God the Father, but you don't have to hang around with him— I mean just have dinner with him one night, then you can be on your own the rest of the time."

I twist my lips. "I don't know, Timmy. Won't it be awkward

for me to stay at his home since I have to decide whether to publish it or not?"

"Oh, even if his place is awful—which it won't be—you can make it work. Look what you did with Ted Powell's hovel. By the way, where'd you put those photos and layout of his place?"

"In the kill drawer."

"Such an apt name."

MAY 24-26, 1979

Timmy has arranged my schedule so that on Thursday morning I can easily make my way up the East side to see the Buatta, DeSantis and Dwork projects. I decide the magazine should publish all three and hope Leaf will let me fly back to art direct the photo shoots. Then I go across town to the Saint James penthouse, which I tell the designer "isn't quite right for us." He doesn't seem concerned—or surprised, since most of his past projects have been published in *House Beautiful*.

After a quick lunch, I taxi to Scott Riley's apartment in the Village: tiny with black walls and furnishings accented by bright pre-Raphaelite art. I've found my foldout cover.

Later I meet photographer Jaime Ardilles-Arce for drinks then dash to the Uris Theatre for *Sweeney Todd*. It's so good I want to see it again.

On Friday, Alan Court drives me to Southampton. It takes more than two hours, and the conversation dries up after forty minutes. I'm sure he's gay but oh-so straight-laced. He's not in the closet; he's in a vault. The interiors he designed are fine— all custom-made furniture and carpets—but they're as dull as he is. I snap a few photos to show Leaf. I'd pass on the project but will let her make the decision since she's published him at least twice before.

Alan gives me a tour of the area, pointing out who lives where. Many of the society names I don't recognize—or care about. He generously drives me to Sayville, and I catch the ferry to Fire Island.

Robin Rainbow meets me at the dock, drops my bag in a rusty red wagon and leads the way to the first boardwalk. Right on the ocean, his weathered gray "cottage" has five bedrooms, but I'm his only guest. After a light dinner, he suggests I nap then go dancing at midnight, but I'm exhausted and sleep until dawn.

At breakfast, I announce I'm going to lie on the beach and read *The World According to Garp*.

"No one *lies* on the beach," Robin says. "The *pretty* boys parade up and down in nylon Speedos, side by side like couples looking for an ark. No one would even *think* of reading. Except maybe *Blueboy* or some other rag with only photo captions. *Once* I did see an issue of *Inside* on a coffee table but it was merely used as *décor*. But I'll join you, if I may. Let me get my hat and basket."

The hat is woven, with a six-inch floppy brim and a fuchsia ribbon. Emerald green shorts expose skinny white legs dotted with freckles. A canary yellow t-shirt and tan espadrilles complete his ensemble. The basket he takes down from a hook hanging by the back door.

"Let me fill you in on Island life," Robin says once he's arranged a Bill Blass sheet on the sand. "'Are you going to tea?' is the *only* conversation heard from noon, when everyone *staggers* awake, until four, when tea dance begins at the Sandpiper. They pose, *rainbowed* in Lacoste shirts, on the bar's deck *à la* Greek statues, waiting to be admired, the 'men' gulping beer, the 'boys' sipping *greyhounds*, a subtle hint, no doubt, that they'd like to do it *doggie*-style. No one *dares* look back if he spots someone eyeing him. One must *never* display interest.

At the first *pounding* note of a Donna Summer song, they *whip* out poppers and *pounce* onto the dance floor like *savages* in a jungle. After an hour, *drenched* with sweat, they're ready for a nap with, they hope, an obliging boy and, *absolutely*, with a Quualude. It makes, they say, a nice *matinee*.

He removes his shoes and drenches his legs, feet and arms with suntan oil. "Not that it will do any good. I don't tan. I pink. Would you like me to do your back?"

I hand him a tube.

He squeezes a line of lotion across my shoulders. "To continue: Dinner is *never* served before *ten* and always at someone else's house *not* because no one wants to cook but because groceries are *so* expensive on the island and *no one* will be seen coming over on the ferry with a bag from the *A & P*. I have one large Vuitton satchel used *solely* for smuggling in food." He massages my back. "I do *all* the cooking and serving myself. I've had men I considered servants but, for *some* reason, they thought of themselves as *boyfriends*. Good help is *so* hard to find. But no one on the island is *really* interested in dining, unless, of course, it's on an eight-inch *tube* steak."

My eyes follow five men as they stroll past us.

"And which of those specimens is your *type*?" Robin wants to know.

"Is there a difference?"

"They are *rather* interchangeable, with their mustaches and pop-up nipples. Of course you have a mustache too."

"We all want to fit in, be part of the crowd."

"And you have pop-up nipples, too, although it's so *hard* to see with all that *masculine* chest hair."

I don't say anything.

"Shall I be quiet and let you read your *best-selling* novel?"

I squint at the ocean. "What do the guys in the water have around their necks?"

"Their Speedos. They think no one knows they're *fondling* each other under the water. They don't see themselves as *decadent* exhibitionists. But they *are*."

"You sounded just like Bette Davis."

"Oh dear. I'd much rather sound like Tallulah. *Darling*. You know, I'm *old* enough to have seen Tallulah on stage in *The Little Foxes*. She was *mesmerizing*. Do you *know* the play, darling?"

"I've seen the movie with Bette Davis."

"Not quite the same, my boy. Although I must admit I've watched it *at least* half a dozen times. You know what I admire about Regina Gibbens' character? Her capacity for revenge. So *luscious* as she simply stands there while her husband crawls up the steps to his death. For *years* I called myself 'Robin Regina.'"

"Is your real name 'Robin Rainbow'?"

"My, you *are* direct, aren't you?"

"I figure I can always ask. People have the right not to answer."

"My parents were not *clever* enough to give me this name. They selected something much more *mundane*—I shan't tell you. You know, my mother's *still* alive. I don't know how *much* longer I can wait to inherit her *jewels*. Although there may not be any left if she *keeps* hanging on." He whispers although no one is near us. "I go over to her *Park Avenue* apartment once a month for dried *meatloaf* and when I leave somehow a little *bon bijou* ends up in my pocket."

More tanned and toned men saunter by.

"That man practically *licked* you with his eyes. I do not think people should be so *blatant* in sunlight. But *traipse* after him if you want, like Marlene Dietrich *crawling* through the sand after Gary Cooper in *Morocco*. Or go splash in the ocean with your Speedo *necklace*. Don't worry about *me*."

"I love the water but I'm afraid of losing my contact lenses."

"So don't open your eyes underwater. Oh, but you'd want to *see* underwater, wouldn't you?"

"I'll go in later. To cool off."

Robin takes two tall cut-crystal glasses out of the basket and hands them to me. Then he pulls out a thermos and fills the cups. "*Water*, darling. Not vodka. Even *I* don't imbibe this early. And we mustn't get dehydrated. So bad for the skin. You have *lovely* skin. You don't have a *single* acne scar. You must have been the *envy* of all your classmates."

"Far from that. I think I have a good complexion because I never drank sodas when I was growing up. I still don't. I prefer milk."

A very tanned man walks by in a very tight very skimpy swimsuit displaying a near erection.

"Probably *Argentine*. Ignore him, Darling. He's just *pointing* the way to Cherry Grove. *Déclassé*." Robin finishes his water then holds out his hand waiting for me to drink mine and give him back the glass.

"Thank you for being so polite about not asking me what I think of your home. I know you wanted Leaf to considerate it for publication." I hold a hand above my eyebrows so I can see him in the glare of the sun and sand.

Robin reaches into his basket and puts a baseball cap on my head. "She'll come another time."

"Actually she sent me as her ambassador. I woke up rather early this morning and looked around. I love how everything—the walls, the floor, the fabrics—are all the exact shade of the sand. It's like being inside a dune. And painting that long wall that runs from the front door to the back deck the color of the ocean was brilliant. It leads the eye right outside to the view. And the ceilings! Such a subtle shade of blue, I bet a lot of people don't notice. What I'm trying to say is I'd like to publish it."

"*My dear boy!* For once this old queen is speechless." He pats my hand then sits very still, facing the ocean, for more than a minute. He lifts his t-shirt to dab his eyes and exhales deeply. "We're having *guests* for lunch. Not that we're *eating* them. Although Bobby's so cute you may want to. Control the urge."

"How many people did you invite?"

"Just two. Scott Riley and Bobby Mazzie. Scott is delighted you're going to publish his *pied-à-terre*. Bobby was so disappointed he couldn't be at Scott's when you saw it. He had a doctor's appointment he couldn't change. Probably being tested for gonorrhea—again. Anyway, he's *dying* to meet you."

"I'm sure he's dying to meet the art director of *Inside* and not me."

"But you *are* the art director."

"Is Bobby Scott's boyfriend?"

"At one time. I think it lasted all of a week. Now they have separate apartments in the Village but share a house out here with two other guys. Bobby's Scott's *assistant* and his biggest promoter. He *squealed* when I told him you were staying with me. He *begged* me not to ask their housemates to join us for lunch. Not that I *would* have. They're stockbrokers into bondage. It *amazes* me how some people can be kinky and boring at the same time. Bobby will probably talk your pants off at lunch. *Literally.*" He stands up. "We're having *lobster* salad."

"I'm allergic to shellfish."

"Oh dear. I'll see if I have any *baloney.*" He waves his hand toward the water. "Go for a *splash.* Let your *manhood* float free." He gathers his oil and basket. "I'll see you in an hour. There may be *peanut butter.*"

Scott Riley is slender and short, probably just past thirty. His Gucci loafers are worn without socks, a look I find pretentious. Khaki slacks. Only the two bottom buttons of his Lycra black shirt are fastened. I'm not sure if he wants us to applaud the thick black chest hair or the faux razor blade dangling from a silver chain. Probably both.

A blond, Bobby Mazzie is a few years younger and several inches taller. His black jeans are so tight he doesn't need a belt; the huge silver Hèrmes buckle is all for show. Black boots reach to his knees. His white tank top is deeply cut to display pink nipples. His chest, sans hair, is just short of being too muscled. His skin is not pale but golden; maybe it's an applied tan. Bobby's necklace is gold and the charm is a small arm with clenched fist. He has a Vassoon haircut, and his nails are polished.

They both have well-trimmed mustaches.

I'm in jeans, crocodile shirt and sandals. Robin's wearing something flowing that I suspect he stole from his mother's closet.

He offers a tray of mimosas. "We'll be lunching on the deck. Is anyone else allergic to lobster besides Anthony?"

"Oh, I love lobster!" Bobby's voice is falsetto high.

"Don't get too excited," Robin cautions. "It's not a *whole* lobster. Just salad."

While Robin's in the kitchen, Bobby gushes about how happy he is *Inside* is going to publish Scott's apartment. Then he asks all the typical questions: *How long have I been at the magazine? Do I like living in Los Angeles? When did I arrive on the island? How long am I staying?* Scott keeps mute.

"Everyone come in the kitchen and grab a tray," Robin announces. "Anthony, yours is the blue one. *Chicken* salad."

Robin and Scott sit on one side of a square table on the deck, with Bobby and I opposite.

"Have you seen *Big Wednesday*?" He asks me.

"Is that the surfer movie?"

"Oh, it's much more than that! There's Vietnam."

"Yeah, that's why you went." Scott finally speaks. "Because

of Vietnam."

"I'm not embarrassed to admit why I went. I can tell you why I went in three words. *Jan-Michael Vincent.*"

"I wonder," says Robin, "if *Jan-Michael* is considered one word?"

"I'd watch him in anything, and this one was especially enjoyable because he had his shirt off most of the time." Bobby's smile is as white as the movie star's. "And William Katt ain't bad either, although I don't usually go for skinny blonds. You could count his ribs. It's just a shame they didn't wear Speedos. Obviously the costume designer was not gay. But I'll tell you, Mr. Katt displayed a nice bulge. And Jan-Michael's jams were white, and when they got wet—yum!"

"It's really an awful movie," Scott says. "One reviewer said there was absolutely no chemistry between William Katt and Barbara Hale, who played his mother. And the thing is, Barbara Hale *is* his mother in real life." He sneers at Bobby. "Aren't you going to tell them what really turned you on?"

"Sure why not? I've nothing to hide."

"Not in *that* shirt," Robin interjects.

"I like feet. They really excite me. And in *Big Wednesday* there were lots of close-ups of Jan-Michael's feet when he was surfing." Bobby puts a hand on my arm. "When I walked in and saw you in sandals, I had to restrain myself from bending over and licking your toes."

"He bends over for a lot more than toes." Scott pours more wine into his glass.

Everything he says is a jab at Bobby, who doesn't seem to even notice the put-downs; maybe it's a common occurrence.

"I tell you what *really* gets me hot." Bobby moves his hand to my leg. "A man just has to pinch my nipple and I'm instantly hard."

I look across the table at Robin and raise my eyebrows.

"Gay men," he says, "seem to have *forgotten* the meaning of *'polite'* conversation. Now all they ever talk about is S-E-X. And I do *not* mean tantalizing gossip revealing who did it with *whom*. I mean *what* they did—and the raunchier the better. *Two* years ago it was piss. *Last* year it was fisting. This year it's *scat*. And I don't mean Ella Fitzgerald."

Bobby squeezes my thigh and whispers, "I still like fisting."

"Gay men seem *determined* to shove their sexuality down everyone's throats—pun *intended*." Robin puts down his fork and looks over my shoulder as if talking into a camera. "Homosexuals control *taste* and *style* in America—the way people decorate, dress, what music they listen to—they are the *first* to start the *latest* trend and the *quickest* to abandon it. They make *big* money. They finally get some *respect*, some recognition, and what do they *do*? They see how *degrading* they can become. It's not enough they do all this weird *stuff* to each other; they have to *flaunt* it. And they don't just tell each other. *They tell their Park Avenue clients!* I know for a *fact* that Addison Saint James described *'the delicate flavor'* of an uncircumcised cock to Bitsy Drake. Of course, she *acted* horrified, but she couldn't *wait* to call all her friends. So women are just as bad. *I* am the last *civilized* person in America."

After we finish our salads, Robin gathers our plates. "I shall prepare the dessert. Bobby, please have your clothes *on* when I return."

Bobby folds his hands on the table. "Gee, do you think I offended him?"

"Robin's a drama queen," Scott says. "I'm sure he welcomed the opportunity to recite one of his monologs."

"Oh good." Bobby puts his hand back on my leg and whispers. "Would you fuck my ass with your toes?"

I *think* he's joking.

Robin returns with a red tray. "I don't suppose *anyone* would believe me if I said I *churned* the ice cream myself and *trudged* to the country to pick the raspberries in a *coolie* hat." He passes around the bowls then holds up a liqueur bottle. "I'll let you add this yourself, *if* you want. It's framboise. A little too sweet for my taste, but, Bobby, you might like to put a *soupçon* on your *nipples*."

Robin suggests I accompany Scott and Bobby to tea dance at the Sandpiper.

As soon as we're on the boardwalk, Bobby wraps me in a hug. "You are so cute!" He nibbles an earlobe.

It's always nice to get attention, but Bobby is so forward it's unappealing.

Scott says, "I'm stopping at our place to change into something a little *less*."

"I'll change too." Bobby rubs my crotch. "If you come with me, we may never get to the dance."

I release myself from his grip. "What if I just meet you at the disco?"

I follow the thump of the music to the bar. Most of the dancers are shirtless, in gym shorts and sneakers with sagging socks. Now I know why Scott wanted to change. In a little while he waves to me from across the room before he's lost in the crush of dancers. I never see Bobby. Maybe he found someone along the boardwalk to ram a foot up his ass. Later Scott leaves with a boy with a face of pimples.

As soon as I return to Robin's house, he hands me a cocktail glass filled with blue liquid.

"What is this? Windex?"

"It's a Blue Glacier. Made with Curaçao and vodka. It's the *perfect* drink for a blue young man."

"What makes you think I'm blue?"

"Your eyes."

"They're brown."

"Only on the outside. I saw from the widow's walk that you split from Jekyll and Hyde. Bobby *can* be a bit *immodeste.* Come, sit down and tell Regina *all* about it."

I collapse in a club chair. "Not one of the gorgeous men asked me to dance."

"I don't mean to be *cruel*, but you probably stood there like a *bump* on a pickle—and looking *just* as sour. Did you ask any of *them* to dance?"

"Three. One merely shook his head. Another one accepted then walked away as soon as the song changed without saying a single word. The third man at least said 'thank you' before he turned back to his friends."

"I'm going to be blunt." Robin refills my glass. "I watched you at the beach today when the Adonises strolled by. You mentally reviewed, rated and *rejected* each one of them. You saw them for the *façades* they are. I have a feeling that's what you did at the Sandpiper. Those men may not *know* they're a façade but they *do* know when they're being judged. I know your type, Anthony, because I'm *exactly* like you. You have *all* the confidence in the world at work, but you're a *disaster* in your social life."

"What social life?"

"*Precisely.*" He claps his hands twice as if calling me to attention. "You'll do *much* better tonight at the Ice Palace. It's in Cherry Grove."

"I don't want to go."

"Of course you don't. You're *feeling* rejected. But I'll go with you. You'll take a little nap first, then we'll have a little soup, and then we'll take a water taxi."

"No one's going to even notice me." I hate when I whine.

"Not with what you're wearing." He reaches behind his chair and hands me a small shopping bag. "I went to the

Crow's Nest and bought you a little something. A *very* little something."

I pull out dark olive green shorts. "What's this material?"

"It's a nylon used to make parachutes. *So* clever. Now go try them on. I want to see. And don't wear a shirt!"

I change in my room. The shorts are briefer than boxers, the fabric practically sheer. When I return to the living room, Robin let's out a howl.

"*Not* with underwear!"

"Robin, you can see through them."

"I should hope so!" He points to the bedroom.

I can't believe I'm walking along the boardwalk at midnight in only tennis shoes and diaphanous shorts. I tell myself the dark fabric obscures detail but the outline of my penis is obvious. Robin, in contrast, is covered neck to foot in flowing silk pink-and-purple paisley pajamas.

The taxi driver helps me into his boat but doesn't give my shorts a second look; he's probably seen it all. Robin hands him some money. "He's going to Cherry Grove." Then he turns to me. "You'll have to find your own way home. If you *amble* through the Meat Rack—that bit of overgrown brush separating the Grove from the Pines, you'll find an array of *delights* that will happily *oblige* any urges."

"Aren't you coming?" There's that whine again.

"No, my dear. It's after midnight, and your *fairy* godmother has done all she could. Now you go to the ball and *find yourself a prince.* You may bring a *bon homme* back with you, but only if he doesn't say things like 'he don't.' I *detest* bad grammar and won't have it in my home."

My skin becomes goose flesh as the boat zips the few miles to the next conclave. I warm up as I follow the pervasive beat to the Ice Palace. *Here goes nothing.* And looking down once more at the barely there shorts, I mean *nothing*.

I fit right in. So many of the shirtless men are wearing tiny shorts, several of them leather. I recognize Victor Hugo from a photo I saw of him escorting Bianca on a white horse for her birthday party at Studio 54. The sexy mustached man is dancing alone on a platform in the middle of the vast room. He's wearing only a jockstrap, his hairy ass proudly on display.

Suddenly "Take Me Home" blares through the speakers, and without thinking, reviewing, rating or judging, I jump up on the platform next to Victor Hugo. As I dance I look below at all the beautiful sweaty men gyrating to Cher. I love the exuberance—and the smell.

Some of men are inhaling poppers; many are likely high from other drugs or alcohol. I've had nothing to drink and no drugs, but I soar. I am overwhelmed to be part of this orgy of shirtless men. No thinking. Just the feeling I belong. I beam joy.

A dancing man points up at me and shouts over the music to his partner, "I want to be *him*."

JUNE 18, 1979

Timmy continues his daily trips to Leaf's house; I bring her my layouts; Ivory sends her text, which Timmy says Leaf doesn't read. It's become routine to have her stay at home. She's out of the office for forty-eight days. What finally brings Leaf back is an inch-and-a-half write-up buried in the business section of the *Los Angeles Times*.

COLETTE BRUIN PLANS RIVAL MAGAZINE

Los Angeles. Colette Bruin plans to give her husband, Claret Bruin, publisher of tony *Inside*, competition with a magazine of her own, called *Luxe*. Like *Inside*, *Luxe* will focus on fine interior design, but according to Mrs. Bruin, it will also include features on luxury items such as jewelry and yachts. To be published bimonthly, the first issue of *Luxe* will be out in February 1980, with Mrs. Bruin as editor.

Leaf swoops into the office and calls an immediate meeting with Walter, Ivory, Timmy and me. She turns first to her assistant. "What have you found out?"

"You're not going to like it." Timmy consults his steno pad. "According to Maxine, Mr. Bruin knew Mrs. B was planning the magazine. He claims she'll lose interest when she realizes how hard it is to put out a magazine on a regular basis. He said she got bored with Inside Choices and she'll get bored with *Luxe*. He doesn't expect it to last more than six issues. He's unconcerned."

"Unconcerned? Colette has $70,000,000. Minimum. She can make that magazine last as long as she wants. Do we know who's in charge of advertising?"

"Some woman from Chicago. Mr. B said, 'The guys in the New York agencies will eat her alive.'"

"Has Colette hired an art director?"

"You won't believe this," I say, "but she's stolen my assistant, who swore, when I hired him *less than two months ago* that he was only interested in paste-up."

"Has she approached anyone else from our staff?"

"Not that I'm aware of," Ivory answers.

"Give me a list of everyone in editorial and we'll see who we want to keep and give them a raise." Leaf turns to Walter. "Draft a letter—over my signature—to all the designers we publish regularly. Make it non-threatening but clear that we expect *loyalty*, that they should show us their new projects before any other magazine." She looks at me. "Send out a similar letter to the photographers we use. Offer them a yearly fee and make them sign a contract that under no circumstances are they to shoot for our competitors. If they do, they're through with *Inside*. Don't either of you mention *Luxe* by name." She reaches for her cigarettes. "I wonder who came up with that name. It's not bad."

Timmy whispers, "Mr. Bruin."

"*WHAT!*" Leaf face flushes bright red. "Are you telling me that Claret gave his wife the name of a magazine that will likely be our biggest competitor?"

"Don't shoot the messenger, but that's what Maxine said."

"The man is certifiably insane." Leaf points a finger at me.

"Do you have all the submissions ready to review that have come in while I've been out?"

I nod. "Four boxes."

"Well, I can't face it today. We'll go over them tomorrow." She looks back at Timmy. "Does Maxine know who's doing Colette's PR?"

Timmy shakes his head.

"I wonder if Colette called the *Times* herself."

Timmy lowers his head and covers his eyes with his hand.

"Timmy," Leaf says in a deliberately calm voice, "please don't tell me it's who I'm thinking."

Timmy nods. "Mr. Bruin called the paper."

"Is he out of his fucking mind?" Leaf rams her cigarette into the ashtray.

Timmy softly says, "He claims it's wonderful publicity for us."

"Claret may delude himself, but Colette is not doing one of her stupid charity brochures." Leaf looks at each one of us. "She's starting a major magazine that will compete head-on with *Inside*. She'll do everything in her power to get the *same* homes we go after, the *same* advertisers and the *same* subscribers. Claret may not realize it, but we are at war. *At war!*"

JUNE 19, 1979

The light tables are covered with transparencies of seven residences Leaf wanted photographed. She approves five but decides she no longer likes the décor of two of them: an apartment in Phoenix and a condo in Atlanta.

"Do you want them reshot," I ask, "or should we tell the residents their homes did not photograph the way we anticipated and we won't be publishing them?"

"Don't say anything. If we tell them we're not going to use their homes, they might give them to Colette. Just put them in the files. If they call, tell them we haven't scheduled them yet, which is true. Maybe they'll just disappear."

Leaf heads to Timmy's office for M&Ms while I clear the light tables and put out scouting shots of celebrities' homes to consider for 'At Home with….' Leaf does not find the residences of Claire Bloom, Peggy Lee, Celeste Holm or Joseph Cotten fitting for the magazine. "These people are old. Can't we get anyone younger?"

"This next house is Olivia Newton-John's."

Leaf examines the pictures as she munches candy. "You can make this work, Anthony. You and Chuck White shoot it. Forget about the old-time actors. We need the new ones. See if you can get record shots of Jill Clayburgh's home—and Candice

Bergen's. Try Ryan O'Neal, too. We have to keep the magazine fresh."

I jot the names down on the back of an envelope. Then I show Leaf snapshots of the New York projects I saw. "I said okay to Michael de Santis, Mel Dwork, Scott Riley and Robin Rainbow."

"They're all good, aren't they?"

"Do you think I could go back to art direct the photo shoots?"

"I'm afraid not, Anthony. We had a board meeting this morning to go over the financial situation now that Colette's dissolving her interest in the company, and things are going to be tight for a while."

"But isn't the magazine making a profit?"

"Barely. The production costs are so high. They talked about going back to the lighter weight paper, but I said we can't risk looking cheaper than *Luxe*. I hadn't told you this, but Claret was thinking of doing nine issues next year, but now we're going to have to stick with six until we build up reserves." She smiles. "To cut expenses, Claret's agreed to let Larry go. But you mustn't say a word, because we aren't telling Larry until the *At Home* book goes to press sometime in August."

"Once Larry's gone will I have to design the press kit and things like that?"

"No, we'll use freelance." She pats my hand. "I know you're disappointed about not going back to New York, but have Jaime shoot them. I'm sure if you explain exactly what shots you want, he'll be glad to do it."

"Yes, he really is the best." I hand her snapshots of the Alan Court project in Southampton. "I'm not really enamored of this design. And since we're going to shoot four more New York homes, I think we can pass, but I haven't said anything to Alan."

Leaf barely looks at the pictures. "Yes, reject it. Use the V.I.P.

letter."

"There's one other New York project worth considering." I put out a dozen scouting shots. "I didn't see it while I was there because we weren't told it about. Bob Bray and Mike Schaible designed it. They always do innovative work, and with the right photography it could be a cover story."

"It's well done, but I can't publish this after what I said about High Tech on *The Mike Douglas Show*. I know it's not really High Tech, but it's too subtle for our readers to see the difference. I'll write the reject letter now."

I take down her dictation: *This one's not for us. But don't give it to anyone else. Button up your overcoat; you belong to me.*

I want to tell her that's not fair. I wonder if it could be considered "restraint of trade." But I keep quiet about it. I have something else on my mind.

She goes to Timmy's office for more M&Ms while I set out more submissions. I hope I sound casual when she returns. "Leaf, what's going to happen with Colette's office?"

"She's taking the furniture with her. No one else would want that glitz."

"Do you think I could move into her office?"

"It's on the other side of the building. I need you near me."

"What if the circulation director moves into Colette's office and I move into his?"

"Anthony, a corner office doesn't mean anything."

I look her right in the eye. "So can I have yours then?"

She stares right back. "If anyone from editorial is going to get a corner office, it probably should be Ivory. As managing editor, her name is above yours on the masthead."

"Why should it be? People are buying this magazine because of the way it looks, not because of the text. People tell me all the time they only read the captions. And even though you say a corner office doesn't mean anything, do you really want

Ivory to have one?"

"We can talk about this again when Larry's gone."

"It may be too late by then. No one is going to let Colette's office sit idle for long. I'm sure the production director will make a grab for it. Or maybe Mr. Bruin will decide that the company attorney should be on site now that he's president."

Leaf doesn't say a word, just eats one M&M after the other. When the bag is finished, she says, "Okay, I'll arrange it with Claret for you to have a corner office. And show me a mock-up of what you have in mind for the masthead."

What I have in mind is my name directly under Leaf's.

She points a finger at me. "You got the title. You got the raise. You got the bonus. Now you have a corner office and your name higher on the masthead. *Not one more thing*, Anthony."

"Thank you. I'm happy."

"But I have one more thing. The March/April issue has to be our best ever. It's what everyone will compare to the first issue of *Luxe*. It has to be stunning."

"When I saw Scott Riley's apartment, I immediately envisioned the foldout cover I spoke about at the sales meeting." I locate a snapshot of the living room and fold it in half so that only a black leather sofa and coffee table are visible; on the table is an onyx statue of naked wrestlers, and on a console behind the sofa is a terra-cotta mask, the only color in the shot. I hand the picture to Leaf, and when she unfolds the back half a brilliantly hued full-length pre-Raphaelite portrait is revealed. "What if we do that for March/April?"

"Fabulous. I'll tell Claret to line up the advertiser." Leaf glances at the light tables filled with photography. "Do we really have to look at the rest of these today?"

"I promise it will go fast. They're easy rejects."

I'm right. Leaf rejects all of the one hundred and forty-seven submissions. "Let Colette have them."

JULY 17, 1979

"It's so sweet of you to take me to Musso & Frank." Cole, sitting opposite me in a red leather booth, looks adorable in a coat and tie.

"Are you going to have the Chicken Pot Pie?"

"Oh, no. I'm all grown up now. I'm having a porterhouse steak." He smiles mischievously. "Tell me all the major things you're going to do to me now that I'm not a minor."

"I think I'll save that for dessert."

When an elderly waiter asks if I want a drink, Cole whips out his driver's license. "The real one!"

The waiter squints as he examines the identification. "Well, happy birthday, young man! What would you like to drink? On the house."

"A Bloody Mary, please."

"I'll have the same."

"I think," says Cole as the waiter shuffles to the bar, "that was the same man who waited on me when I was ten."

"So how's it going in acting class?"

"I love it, but something strange happened recently. We've been working on two-person scenes, and I was paired with Mike. He's about twenty-five, but seems older because he's married and already has a kid. Most of the people in class are just beginning like me, but Mike was an extra on *Starsky and Hutch*. So I told him he could pick the scene since he had more experience. He chose a scene from *Noon* by Terrence McNally."

"Oh, he wrote *The Ritz*."

"Right. Anyway, *Noon* is all about mistaken identities—I'll spare you the silly plot—but in the scene Mike picked, I had to pull down his pants."

"That's an interesting choice for a married man to select."

"And it got more interesting because the first time I did it, he had a woody. His boxer shorts pointed straight up! Naturally I forgot my line, and Mike apologized. The rest of the rehearsal went okay, and I thought that was it, we'd do the scene in class, but the next day Mike called and said we needed another rehearsal."

"Where did these rehearsals take place?"

"At his apartment in Hollywood."

"And where were the wife and kid?"

"At the first one, she was reading their daughter a bedtime story in her room and Mike and I were in the living room. But at the next rehearsal, they weren't around. Mike said that to get insight into our characters, we should do it once switching roles. So he pulled down my pants, and I don't know if he was disappointed, but I did not have a hard-on."

"Is he attractive?"

"Sort of, in an ethnic way. I think he's Greek. He's dark and has a big nose, but really nice eyes—like a puppy. So after we did the scene as each other's character, we did it again in our original roles, and when I pulled down his pants, he had another woody. *Only this time he wasn't wearing underwear.*"

"Should I ask what you did?"

"I asked him if this was how he was going to play the scene in front of the class. And he said, and I quote, 'Come on help me out. My wife doesn't like giving blow jobs.' And I said, 'Oh,

I do. But not to you.' And I walked out."

"Good for you. Have you done the scene in class yet?"

"On Saturday. It went fine. Mr. Koslov said Mike was a bit stiff and I could hardly contain my laughter."

"What did the teacher say about you?"

"He said when I forget I'm acting I'm good and that I have to forget more. But that's very hard to do."

The waiter brings our drinks and we order steaks.

"I got a promotion at Selection," Cole announces. "Now instead of just pulling and filing fabric swatches I'm actually on the showroom floor two days a week. Raymond said I sell more than the saleswoman who works the other three days."

"That's probably because all the gay designers adore you." I wonder if he's had sex with Raymond but am too afraid of the answer to ask.

"Mom's selling the house—it's in her name. She's buying a condo in Century City." Cole raises his eyebrows several times as if he's got more to tell.

"And?"

"And I said I wanted to get my own place in West Hollywood but she nixed that." Instead of an expected frown, he smiles broadly. "So she bought me my own condo in Century Towers! She bought a penthouse in the East building for herself, and I'm going to be on the sixth floor of the West building. We face opposite directions, so she can't even spy into my window."

"Congratulations. Are you going to hire a decorator?"

"Raymond said he'd help me. There're some furniture at Selection that for various reasons can't be sold—it's scratched or was upholstered wrong—so Mrs. Cohen will sell it to me at a big discount. Unlike my mom, I don't really care about the décor. I'm just thrilled I have my own place."

"Who's she hiring to decorate her place?"

"Waldo Fernandez."

"I wonder if she promised to publish it in *Luxe*. He's very talented."

Cole shrugs.

"Where's your father going to live?"

"He's been staying at the Beverly Wilshire Hotel—probably fucking his brains out. And speaking of fucking, guess who my mom has been 'dating.'"

"I have no idea."

"Sean O'Brien."

"*My former assistant?* No wonder she made him art director."

"I told her she should have hired you."

"Yeah, but I wouldn't fuck her." I smile. "Did you hear what Leaf said when a reporter asked what she thought of *Luxe* imitating *Inside*?

Cole shakes his head.

"'Butter's better.'"

"That's good. I bet my mom hated that. She's been having a lot of trouble lining up good homes. She already said she was going to show jewelry and yachts but now she's expanding the coverage to include watches, fashion, automobiles and travel in order to fill the pages. She might even do restaurants."

After dinner we drive to my apartment and devour each other.

As we snuggle together I worry Cole will think it was not worth the wait. Cole has his own concern.

"Do you mind that my dick is so small?"

"I'm sure your climax felt just as good as mine."

"Yeah, but do you mind?"

"I don't because it's a part of you. And, Cole, I have seen smaller. Stop worrying about it. I like you just the way you are. And I love every inch of your dick." I kiss it.

"Remember when we were driving to Jason's for Thanksgiving and I wanted you to show me your dick?" Cole rolls over onto his stomach. "You said you knew the reason why I wanted to see it. What did you think?"

"I can't tell you. You'll think I'm conceited."

He lifts my penis. "I wanted to see it because I wanted it to be perfect. And it is beautifully proportioned. So now you can be *really* conceited."

I kiss his lips. And we fall asleep.

At dawn, with the pale light seeping around the blinds, I twist Cole's golden curls around my fingers. I recall another blond, David, a straight student at college. I would lie alone in bed thinking about him, then one night I asked myself: *What do I want from David? What do I want to do with him?* And I realized I didn't want to *do* anything. I just wanted him to remove his clothes and let me stare at him. Now, I softly lower the sheet and stare at Cole's nakedness.

Instead of breakfast we feast on each other again.

"Last night we had sex," Cole says. "This morning we made love."

In the shower I enjoy the intimacy of Cole washing my hair. On my knees soaping his beautifully hairy satyr legs I unexpectedly cry. I gulp air hoping he won't notice but he sinks down beside me.

He puts his hands on my shoulders. "What's wrong?"

"Nothing. Nothing at all. I'm just so very happy."

JULY 28, 1979

"Thanks for offering to take Cole's headshots for free," I tell Mark Romano, "but I'll pay you."

"Really, Anthony, don't worry about it. Without you I wouldn't have a career, so consider this part of my payback. Besides, I'm thrilled to photograph Cole."

"He should be here soon. He's always late." I walk across the rented photo studio and look in the refrigerator: empty. I should have thought to bring coffee for Mark and 7UP for Cole. "Has Burton found a condo yet?"

"He made an offer on one in Westwood." Mark starts setting up his camera and a few lights.

"Why does he want a place in L.A.?"

"Because he's greedy. He already gets all the interesting design projects in San Francisco and the Bay Area, but he thinks he can get even more work down here."

Cole arrives without an apology for being late. I'm there to art direct, but he knows exactly what he wants, and Mark takes at least a dozen shots with Cole in various outfits from schoolboy to cowboy and from smiling to serious.

"Do you like acting?" Mark asks.

"I love it." Cole smiles at me. "Now I have a goal and not just a dream."

"What's your goal?"

"Promise not to laugh?"

"Cross my heart." And Mark does just that.

"I want to be on *All My Children*. My sister watches it every day."

After I lock up the studio, Cole and I head to his acting class. Today everyone has to sing an individual song, and the students are supposed to each bring a guest—I guess to make singing in front of an audience more intimidating.

There's a pianist for accompaniment, and most of the students select up-tempo numbers, two of them belting out "New York, New York."

When it's Cole's turn, he sits on a stool, looks right at me and sings "You Made Me Love You."

Everyone turns around and I wipe the tears running down my cheeks. I've got to stop crying like this.

Cole receives the loudest and longest applause.

AUGUST 31, 1979

The office is nearly empty by three on the Friday before Labor Day weekend, but I spot Timmy surrounded by books at the conference room table.

"Did Leaf go to San Francisco to see her 'beau'?"

"She broke it off," Timmy replies. "He's a cancer doctor and that's all he talked about. She said it was too depressing. She and Judy Berlin have gone to a spa in Ojai for the long weekend."

I pick up one of the books. *Celebrities at Home: From the Pages of* Inside. *Edited by Leaf Wyks.* "I like the leather cover with the intaglio lettering. I was afraid the title was going to be gold stamped."

"Not on the special edition. It is gold on the cloth-bound copies." He takes another book from a pile and opens it to the title page.

I flip through the pages determined not to say anything critical about Larry's layouts especially since it was his last day at the company. I look up and stare at Timmy in disbelief. "Are you doing what I think you're doing?"

He sets down a Montblanc fountain pen and shakes out his hand. "You can't expect Leaf to sign three hundred copies."

"Timmy, people have paid a hundred dollars for a numbered

edition signed by Leaf! This isn't right."

"Who's going to know?" He turns the last book he signed so I can see what he wrote. "Doesn't that look *exactly* like her signature?"

"Yes, but it still doesn't make it right."

"If it makes you any happier, she promised to sign the ones decorators ordered."

SEPTEMBER 19, 1979

I've brought a sketchpad and a large box of Prismacolor pencils over to Cole's condo. I have an idea for a line of wallpaper —diagonal stripes based on rep ties—and want to make illustrations to show Sarah Cohen. I sit on an iron stool at the counter separating the kitchen from the living area.

Cole moved into his new apartment at the beginning of the month but has shown zero interest in decorating it. Raymond got him a sofa and two chairs at a great discount from Selection, but they aren't even arranged to accommodate conversation. The dining area is empty; Cole usually eats in front of the television. In the bedroom, a mattress rests on the floor—no headboard. Raymond also supplied a slightly scratched nightstand but it's too high since the mattress is so low. Since there's no dresser, Cole's clothes are still in suitcases and boxes or tossed about the room. I've offered to go shopping with him at the design center, but he declined. Most showrooms will give me a discount—not that it matters since his mom will buy Cole anything he wants. I also suggested a trendy second-hand furniture shop, but he seems satisfied leaving his place as it is.

I line up the colored pencils and glance over at him. He's watching *Laverne & Shirley,* and I'm careful to talk only during the commercials. When I mention I've been reading *The*

Brethren he doesn't even know it's about the Supreme Court. "What's the last book you've read?"

"Don't ask me questions like that."

Okay. "I designed a layout today with eight consecutive pages with no text other than captions. Every issue I've made the text shorter and shorter. It used to be 1500 words, but I've gotten it down to 800. And yet most of the stories still say the same thing. 'My client gave me carte blanche.' Yeah, right."

Cole seems more interested in an ad for the new Sony Walkman. And maybe I shouldn't tell him what I'm doing at the magazine. He might pass it on to his mom, although he seems equally disinterested in *Luxe* as he is with *Inside*.

Cole showers then spends nearly an hour drying his curls so they twist the way he likes. He finally emerges in a thin white tank top, white gym shorts and white tennis shoes and socks.

"If you wear that people will expect you to bring them a drink." It's similar to the outfit waiters wear at Studio One.

"When I wore this last weekend Scott Forbes said I looked 'adorable.'"

"Did he ask you to bring him a vodka tonic?"

Cole sticks out his tongue and goes back to his bedroom to change. I think he'd be perfectly content to dance every night.

He returns in pink satin shorts, black fishnet t-shirt and construction boots with sagging gray socks. He's shaved off his mustache. "Are you ready?"

"I don't really want to go dancing tonight, Cole. I had enough last weekend. I want to work on my wallpaper designs."

He doesn't ask *what wallpaper designs?* "All right," he says. "I'll see you tomorrow."

I guess that means I'm not to be here when he returns. I gather up my pencils and pad so we can go down to the garage together. I hope he remembers tomorrow is my birthday.

SEPTEMBER 20, 1979

Mom calls to wish me a happy birthday, but I sense she really just wants to be acknowledged for sending me a hundred dollars. She urges me to "buy something special" to remember her, but I know the money will go toward groceries and other everyday expenses.

Cole gives me *The Board Game Book*. It's coffee-table size with reproductions of boards suitable for playing the games discussed. It's beautifully crafted and reading about the game's histories should be interesting. The ironic thing is Cole hates board games, refusing to play Scrabble or Cribbage with me.

He offers to take me to "a fancy dinner," but I want to have something quick and simple before going to a movie.

"I'd like to see Peter Weir's *The Last Wave*."

"Is it about surfing?"

"Hardly. An Australian aborigine is accused of murder."

"Wouldn't you rather see *The Concorde: Airport 79*?"

"Since I didn't like the original and refused to see the sequel, I don't think so, but if you don't want to see *The Last Wave*, I can go alone some other time. What about *North Dallas Forty*? Semi-naked football players in the locker room."

"No, it's your day, so it's your movie."

"You might actually enjoy *The Last Wave*. It's supposed to be 'eerie and chilling.'"

He falls asleep about halfway through.

Afterwards, on the drive to my apartment, he says, "I suppose you want to discuss the movie."

"How can we discuss it when you didn't see most of it?"

"I like to just sit back and *enjoy* a movie and when it's over I like to move on to the next thing. That's why I wanted to see *Concorde*. I don't see why you want to *discuss* everything."

"Well, what would you like to move on to next?"

He rubs my crotch.

It's always fun having birthday sex. But I want something more.

OCTOBER 23-24, 1979

When Leaf tells Sarah Cohen there's no budget for me to fly to Maui to art direct the photo shoot of the Kikinos house, the designer has her client foot the bill—first class, no less. And when Burton Fisher hears that, he pays to have Mark Romano's ticket upgraded. Mark wants to bring an assistant, but when no one agrees to pay *that* fare, he drops the idea. Colette Bruin, not to be outdone by Burton or Sarah, also provides a first class ticket for Cole, who's going along as one of Sarah's assistants. Raymond Washington, stuck in the back of the plane, smiles and says, "I won't turn this into a Rosa Parks incident," but I've a feeling he'd like to.

Soon after takeoff, Cole whispers, "I want to join the Mile High Club."

"It's too risky, especially with Sarah right across the aisle."

"We could go to the john when everyone's eating lunch."

"That's still too risky for me."

"What do you think would happen if we got caught? That prissy steward is not going to open the exit door and toss us out. He'd probably like to have a three-way."

"Life isn't just about sex, Cole."

"Maybe for me, it is."

I fall asleep during the movie, and when I wake up Cole's

seat is empty. I look behind me: Mark's seat is also vacant. The lavatory light is illuminated.

When Cole returns I pretend to be still asleep.

Although it's more than a five-hour flight, with the time change we can get in at least one shot at the Kikinos house. After seeing the grounds and the interiors, I suggest we set the dining room table and shoot looking out to the Majesty palms as the sun sets in the Pacific. There are low clouds that, if we're lucky, will glow pink and orange and lavender.

While Mark loads film into four-by-five holders, I mount lights on tripods. After Raymond wipes down the glass-topped table so there isn't a streak or a fingerprint, Cole, wearing white gloves, carefully positions glass placemats, each topped by more glass: a platter, a plate and a bowl. Then at Sarah's insistence, Raymond cleans the windows, although they already look spotless.

Opening a mound of blue Tiffany boxes, Sarah stacks gray flannel envelopes in neat piles on the kitchen counter. She dons her own pair of white gloves and removes glistening silver flatware, which she meticulously lines up in front of her.

Suddenly she rummages through the empty boxes and routs among the flannel. Her breathing becomes more frantic as she searches through everything twice, then a third time. Then she screams. "Where are the *fucking* fish forks?"

Raymond calmly goes to his briefcase, pulls out a folder and flips through pages of Tiffany invoices. "There are no fish forks listed on the inventory sheet."

Sarah paces the kitchen. "Where am I going to find Tiffany fish forks on this stupid island in the middle of the Pacific Ocean?"

Raymond stands perfectly still.

"Why am I surrounded by incompetence?" Sarah rips off the

white gloves and frantically opens and closes her hands as if releasing energy. "Do I have to do *everything* myself? Why do I even bother? Nobody ever appreciates my efforts!"

A buzzer sounds and Raymond speaks quietly into the intercom.

Cole continues to set the table as if a well-dressed woman with impeccable makeup were not continuing a tirade that must be heard across the island.

"The white orchids have arrived," Raymond announces.

"Wonderful," Sarah says in a normal tone. "Put five branches in each of the these four small vases. Cole, we'll set the table without fish forks. Who will notice?"

The next morning Sarah and I have breakfast together at the hotel; well, I have breakfast. Sarah has half of a half of a grapefruit and a soft-boiled egg.

"The house is beautiful," I tell her. "You did an exquisite job—such attention to detail. I noticed even the closet walls are upholstered in silk."

"Thank you. And this time not one thing is borrowed—like it was at Leaf's. The client paid for everything—including all the items we used to set the table yesterday."

"Well, I hope you'll order fish forks."

She does not smile.

Later, while Mark takes photos in the Kikinos gardens, with Cole assisting, Sarah and I discuss the interior shots.

"Maybe if there's still time after you finish the photography you need for the magazine Mark could take a few more shots—of the guests bedrooms and baths—for my portfolio." Sarah smiles. "Of course, I'll pay him extra." Then she dashes out of the living room.

"Diarrhetic's kicked in," Raymond says. When I look puzzled, he adds, "How do you think she stays so thin?"

Sarah returns as Raymond is accepting a large bouquet of gladioli from a florist.

"That's not what I ordered." She glares at the young delivery boy. "You would think for what I'm paying I could get what I ordered."

The blond boy, who looks as if he'd rather be surfing, pulls a receipt out of his pocket. "It says, 'three dozen red gladiolus.'"

"Are you color blind?" Sarah grabs the flowers from Raymond and thrusts them at the boy. "I ordered *coral*. These are vermillion."

"This is all we had in the shop, Ma'am." The boy looks defiant, as if he's used to standing up to rich demanding women. "In fact, we only had sixteen stems. The owner had to call two other shops to get the full three dozen. I overheard him say there wasn't a single gladiolus left in Maui."

Coles brings a tall clear-glass Baccarat vase. "That's such an intense color, Mrs. Cohen. It'll be a striking contrast to the painting. Don't you think you can get by with the vermillion?"

"Let me share a secret with you, young man." Sarah plants her feet wide and her hands on her hips just like Mama Rose ready to sing her big number in *Gypsy*. "I never 'get by.' That's why my shop is so successful and that's why this house looks so exceptional. I do not compromise. I do not *get by*."

The delivery boy speaks up. "There might be some *coral* ones in Kauai."

"Maybe we could charter a plane." Raymond manages to not smirk.

"Don't be ridiculous!" Sarah yanks back the flowers and takes them into the kitchen. "And don't you dare tip that brat!"

Raymond hands the blond a twenty.

"I don't know why she's always bitching about how much things cost," Cole says. "She marks up *everything* twenty percent and charges Kikinos."

"Cole!" Sarah shouts. "Bring me that vase."

As he walks by, I whisper to Cole, "How can you put up with her?"

"Oh, it reminds me of home."

I walk into the kitchen. "I can change the color to coral in retouching."

Sarah gives me an anemic smile.

There are no more bursts of temper, and we get all the shots we need, including the master bath with another striking sunset that looks as if a fiery *vermillion* ball is dipping into the tub.

As we're leaving the house, Sarah removes a large envelope from her Chanel bag. "I looked over your wallpaper designs, Anthony. They're unique. I don't think there's anything on the market like them. And that's the problem. I don't think they'd sell." Another insincere smile. "But thank you for letting me see them."

OCTOBER 25, 1979

Cole and I wake up before dawn so we can join a sunrise tour of Haleakala volcano. Of course, it's postcard perfect. When the clouds clear and we can see the other Hawaiian Islands and the vastness of the Pacific, I feel insignificant.

After lunch, I drop in at the Kikinos house to see if Mark needs me while he takes the additional shots for Sarah.

"She's enjoying being art director," he whispers. "Since she's paying me double what the magazine gives me, I just do as she says. Go have fun with Cole."

Cole is asleep on the beach, and I sit beside him thinking.

We've seen each other every weekend since his birthday and at least once during the week. From the first day I met him he has enchanted me. Now I'm bored. Was I merely infatuated by his beauty and youth? Once I would see Cole and ache with wanting to touch him. What caused that feeling? And why isn't it here anymore?

At first I trembled if he touched me. And later I loved kissing him. I wanted to continue kissing him long after he wanted to stop. Last night, lying on opposite sides of the bed, we didn't even kiss good night.

Just three months ago I told Cole I didn't think we'd ever run out of things to say. Now I can't think of a thing to talk about that might interest both of us. Sometimes I don't even want to hear his voice.

He never wants to go to an art museum or see a serious movie. He enjoys body surfing at the house in Malibu and dancing at Studio One. I think he's lost interest in being an actor; now he just wants to be a star. Perhaps that's all he ever wanted.

I love my job. I love talking about it. I'm fond of reading, especially biographies because I like to find out the why of a person. Every other book I read is an Agatha Christie mystery; I'm fascinated by the motives of the crimes, and how clever she is in concealing but still presenting the clues. I enjoy talking about this. But maybe I'm as boring as I think Cole is.

Maybe I'm as shallow as he is.

We may not have kissed last night, but we did have sex. Perhaps it's because I'm a Virgo, the virgin, but I see sex with a regular partner as making love, a way of expressing my affection for the person. Cole sees it as a form of entertainment. Sometimes I'd rather play Scrabble.

Many lovers and friends—even families—stay together because they fear the unknown "out there." They think it's better to endure the everyday monotony and the annoyances. They'd rather have the love-turned-to-hate than to be alone.

I'd rather be on my own.

An airplane is an odd place to break up: There's no walking out, no doors to slam, no shouting possible, and, one hopes, no tears.

How can we break up when we aren't really a couple? We never said we were in a relationship; we never referred to each other as a "boyfriend."

"You used to fall asleep in my arms. Now you drift off listening to a Barbra Streisand and Donna Summer duet on your Walkman. Enough is enough, Cole."

"What you're really telling me is *I'm* not enough."

"I'm not making myself clear."

"You're perfectly clear. You're an intellectual snob and I'm an ignorant nothing."

"Cole."

"Let's talk about the Concorde movie."

"How can we discuss a movie I haven't seen?"

"But you obviously have an opinion about it or else you wouldn't so readily dismiss it. So what do you think of *The Concorde: Airport 79?*"

I don't know what he's getting at, but I go along. "I think it would be worse than *Airport 2*, if that's possible."

"Which you also didn't see. And it's called *Airport 1975*."

"No matter what the title, it's a dumb movie."

"You don't think it's just the movie's dumb. You think *I'm* dumb, too."

"I don't think I'd say 'dumb.'"

"No, you'd analyze synonyms for ten minutes before finding the perfect word. You know what the biggest difference is between us, Anthony?" He doesn't wait for a response. "I want to live life and you want to analyze it. You think too much."

My mother often tells me this and it sets me off. I snap at Cole what I should say to her. "I'm surprised you thought of that since you don't think enough."

We don't talk much during the rest of the flight. He listens to his music, and I read Christie's *Death in the Clouds*.

I've left my car at the airport. When I drop Cole off at his building, he has the last word.

"I wish you had told me you loved me. No man has ever said that to me. I don't think anyone ever will."

NOVEMBER 14, 1979

Leaf is eager to see the photography of producer Harold Sloan's Palm Springs house, so as soon as Mark Romano's pictures arrive, I put them out on the light table. She enters the viewing room with a cigarette in one hand and M&Ms in the other. She crunches the candy and inhales the smoke; then she examines the photos.

"Harold Sloan is a friend of mine. I've been to his house many times, and Mark certainly didn't capture its charm. Everything looks so—wait a minute!" Squinting, she bends closer to one of the photos. "What are these books doing in the dining room hutch? I *told* Harold I didn't want them there. They're cheap novels and paperback Westerns. I wanted it plain with just those heavy earthenware plates. I removed the books myself. Look, they're not even neatly arranged. They're falling over! At least Mark could have straightened them up. And what are these two flower pots doing by the swimming pool?" Leaf points to another picture. "I *told* Harold to take them away. They're the wrong scale. Those huge rocks are so wonderful in the grass and now their impact is ruined by these stupid pots."

"Do you want Mark to reshoot, Leaf?"

"No." Leaf sighs. "We can get six pages out of this. If Harold were a big film producer, I'd consider rephotographing, but he just does TV movies."

Ten minutes later, Timmy buzzes me to say Leaf wants to see me right away.

She starts ranting even before I sit down. "I just got off the phone with Harold Sloan. He said Mark put the books back in the dining room hutch. *Mark* thought it looked too bare. We don't pay Mark to think. We pay him to point a camera and shoot! Harold also said that Mark decided the pool needed those two ditzy pots. Mark said, and I quote, 'Leaf doesn't know. She doesn't see with the eye of the camera. She doesn't know what would make the best shot.' Can you believe Mark was stupid enough to say something like that and not realize it would get back to me? How many homes has he photographed that we haven't published yet?"

"I can't be certain without looking through the files. There's the one in La Jolla that Steve Chase designed and one in Santa Fe; and at least two others in San Francisco. Maybe one or two more."

"Find out from our attorney if we have to give him photo credit when we run the pictures. If he says we *absolutely* have to, make the type as small as possible. Run it up the side of a picture or something. I don't ever want to see Mark Romano's name in the magazine again. After all I've done for that boy, I'll show him what 'Leaf doesn't know'!"

NOVEMBER 26, 1979

Timmy summons the editorial staff into Leaf's office as soon as she arrives after the long Thanksgiving weekend.

"It's that time of year again." Leaf's smile looks false, as if she can't wait to finish a task she doesn't want to do in the first place. "Timmy, do you want to explain to everyone how it works?"

"Every Christmas instead of everyone exchanging gifts, we play Silly Santa." He points to a round black vase on Leaf's desk. "I've put everyone's name on a slip of paper in here, and we'll each pick one, and that's who you'll buy a gift for."

Walter glances at Claire Winter, the proofreader, who mouths "whom."

"I see the grammar police is out in force today—as always." Timmy wags a finger at Mrs. Winter. "You better hope I don't draw your name." He picks up the vase and walks over to her. "Why don't you have first pick? But don't show it to anyone! Keeping it a secret is part of the fun."

"What's the dollar limit this year?" one of the secretaries asks.

"No more than $10." Timmy walks around the room extending the vase until everyone has chosen a name. "Now remember: It's called 'Silly Santa,' so use your imagination and have a sense of humor!"

Walter asks, "What days do we have off this year?"

"Christmas falls on a Tuesday this year," Timmy responds, "so we'll have that and the Monday before. The following week it will be the same: closed Monday the 31st and Tuesday the first of January."

I know what that means. Most of the staff will take vacation days Wednesday through Friday between the holidays so that essentially the editorial office will be shut down for ten days and I'll be the one to make up the lost time in order to get the next issue out.

"Are we going to do pot luck this year?" Ivory asks.

"Oh, thanks for reminding me," Timmy says. "Everyone should bring something on Friday, December 21st. We'll do Silly Santa and then have a buffet lunch. Please coordinate with me what you'll be bringing so we don't end up with six spinach dips like we did last year."

As we file out, Leaf stops me. "Whose name did you draw?" she asks.

"Joe."

"Joe who?"

"My new assistant, Joe Hill. I introduced you to him just before Thanksgiving."

"The mousey guy with the pointy chin?" She waves her slip of paper at me. "I got Claire Winter. Got any ideas what should I give her?"

"That's an easy one. Give her one of those little magnifying glasses she can wear on a chain around her neck."

"Maybe she'll strangle herself."

"Unless Timmy does it first."

DECEMBER 4, 1979

As soon as Leaf arrives, I dash into her office with a copy of the *San Francisco Chronicle*. "Listen to what Herb Caen wrote in his column: '*Inside*, the posh magazine, is planning to feature the posh apartment in the poshest building in town. The real inside story is that the owner, three months behind in the rent, is being evicted. It seems his dream of a "white" Christmas hasn't arrived from South America.'"

"I don't get it, Anthony. What's it mean?"

"You know that San Francisco apartment Mark shot month—with the fabulous view of the Golden Gate Bridge?"

"Donald Knight's place."

"Right. Well, Knight's 'white Christmas' was a shipment of cocaine that he was planning to sell to pay the rent. It hasn't arrived and he's being evicted."

"Timmy!"

He rushes in with his steno pad.

"Send a telegram immediately to Donald Knight in San Francisco—and copy Herb Caen at the *Chronicle*: WE DON'T PUBLISH 'WHITE' KNIGHTS."

DECEMBER 17, 1979

I push aside foam peanuts in a shipping carton and lift out a long box wrapped in gold metallic paper and tied with four-inch-wide red silk ribbon. Inside the box, under a layer of white tissue paper, is a Claude Montana leather jacket. It's butter soft and lined in silk. It's beautiful. It's expensive. It's my size.

I open a small envelope and read the note written on heavy paper: *Thank you for the exquisite cover and the breathtaking layout. You make Inside—and my interiors—delectable. Happy Holidays, Robin Rainbow.*

Other designers have sent cards and two have sent Champagne, but I'm astounded at Robin's generosity. I close my office door and don the jacket. The smell of the leather is intoxicating. I squint at my image in the chrome lamp on my desk.

Then it hits me: Maybe I'm not allowed to accept it.

I decide to ask Leaf. When I walk into her office I at once spot discarded gold metallic paper and red ribbon on the coffee table. A white box on the banquette is even larger than the one I received. And Leaf is modeling a full-length mink coat. She smiles. "I feel like a legend."

"What do we say when designers send us Christmas gifts?"

She caresses her face with the luxurious fur. "We say, 'Thank you.'"

JANUARY 16, 1980

Communication Arts magazine wants to know if they can reprint my Luis Barragán layout and the cover with Cole's statue. The editors plan on naming it one of the ten best visual presentations of 1979.

The American Society of Magazine Editors honors *Inside* for "overall excellence in magazine design."

Then the Columbia University Graduate School of Journal bestows not only its National Magazine Award for Visual Excellence to the March/April issue but also names *Inside* Magazine of the Year.

But we know *Inside* has officially arrived when *The New Yorker* features a full-page cartoon of a couple arguing in a beautiful room. The tagline: "You only married me because my apartment was published in *Inside*."

JANUARY 18, 1980

"Isn't that Tiffany?" I point to the brass lantern clock on Timmy's desk.

"Yes. It was a gift—twice."

"You lost me."

"A year ago I gave Leaf this clock for Christmas. This Christmas she gave it back to me."

"Are you sure it's the same one? Maybe she thought it was such a great gift she wanted you to have one too."

"It's the *exact* clock, Anthony." He turns it upside down. "See this tiny scratch? That how I was able to afford it. I'm sure Tiffany isn't in the business of scratching the bottom of all their clocks. So this *has* to be the same one."

"I bet she doesn't remember you gave it to her."

"If that's supposed to make me feel any better it doesn't help. Did you see the haul she got in this Christmas? Wait, I wrote everything down." He opens the file cabinet and takes out a folder. "There was enough swill to open a small boutique." He reads from a sheet of paper. "One mink coat. Six handbags—Hermès, Bottega Veneta, Chanel, Gucci and a Judith Leiber beaded clutch—a Paloma Picasso bracelet, a Cartier watch, a necklace made out of solid-gold paper clips, nine silk scarves and the largest box of Godiva chocolates I have ever seen—

and, of course, she didn't offer any of us a single piece. Then there were six magnums of Champagne and a bottle of framboise, whatever the hell that is. When I pointed out how generous most of the designers were, Leaf said they probably bill their clients for the gifts they give her, that they probably mark them up and make a profit. Even if they do, they still give her expensive things, and she's not the least bit grateful."

"I didn't know you and Leaf exchanged Christmas presents."

"Yeah, and this Christmas she *literally* exchanged presents."

"I thought the whole point of Silly Santa was to avoid everyone on staff having to buy each other gifts."

Timmy shakes his head. "The point of Silly Santa is so that *Leaf* doesn't have to buy everyone on staff a present."

"I see. Well, what did you get her this year?"

"Oh, it was the cutest thing! A handmade candy jar—it was ceramic but it looked like it was made out of M&M peanuts. Leaf said she 'adored' it, but I'll probably get it back next year. You didn't give her anything, did you?"

"No. I only give her a present on her birthday. Remember last year I gave her stationery I hand-embossed with her name? At least she can't pass that along to anyone else. Did you fill the candy jar with real M&M peanuts?"

"Of course I did!" Nobody's around but he lowers his voice. "And she probably devoured every last one of them in twenty minutes."

"What did Leaf do over the holidays?"

"I'm pretty sure she stayed home—alone with her cat. But don't feel sorry for her! It's her own fault if she's alone. She received stacks of invitations—skiing in Vail, a weekend in Palm Springs, dinners, lunches, parties. She said *no* to all of them. She got even more invitations for New Year's Eve. Turned them *all* down."

"It's almost as if Leaf wants to be unhappy, isn't it?"

JANUARY 24, 1980

"This is an incredible interview with you." Timmy waves *The Advocate*, a national gay newspaper as he enters my office. "Two full pages right in the center and a beautiful photo of you. Will you autograph my copy?"

"You're kidding. You don't really want me to sign it."

"Yes, I do!" He hands me a pen. "I'm proud of you for coming out. Things are slowly changing, but it still takes a lot of courage."

"Some people told me not to do it, but I have to be honest. Besides, I'm glad I'm gay." I write my name across the photo. "I imagine some of the male designers might be upset with me, since I said only one-and-a-half of them are straight."

"Oh, I don't think they'll be mad about *that*. But they *will* be furious you said all they're interested in is 'drugs, disco and dish.' But you left out one *d: dick*."

I smile. "The designers also probably won't like it that I said some of them decorate not for their clients but to impress each other."

"Jason Hunt does that, but he'll think you're talking about everyone but him. Scott Riley will be overjoyed you described his bedroom as 'masculine,' but I can't believe you said most designers are vain *and* insecure. "

"Well maybe Sarah Cohen will be pleased I said she's self-confident."

"I learned something reading the article." Timmy scans the text. "Here, where the interviewer says he never throws away any of the issues of *Inside*, and you say you hear that a lot, and the reason is because you design it as a book, not a magazine, and people don't throw out books. That's interesting."

"So in general, do you think it was okay? I didn't come across as a snob, did I?"

"Of course you did! And what's wrong with that?" Timmy laughs. "Are you going to send a copy to your parents?"

"No. And don't show it to Leaf, okay?"

But he does.

"If I didn't show her, at least a half dozen designers would have, and then she'd accuse me of trying to hide it from her," Timmy says at the gym.

"Did she say anything?"

"Well, I told her it was an article about you, and so, of course, the interviewer wanted to make you seem really important, so that's why he said you go on photo shoots, edit the pictures, do the layouts and select the order the homes will run in each issue."

"But I *do* all those things, Timmy! *And* I said Leaf selects the homes and makes the final decision on the cover."

"Know what she said about that? 'At least I do *something* at the magazine.' She also said, and I quote, 'Anthony's like a jungle: You have to cut him back every six months.'"

PART FOUR
COMPETITION

JANUARY 25, 1980

INTEROFFICE MEMO

DATE: January 25, 1980
TO: Inside staff
FROM: Leaf Wyks
RE: Interviews

We are contacted so frequently by media regarding comments, interviews, etc.—also by various organizations looking for a speaker—that I have asked Jake White to screen and handle all future requests.

If anyone contacts you, let Jake know right away and he will discuss with me.

Thanks for your cooperation.

FEBRUARY 6, 1980

At first I think it's generous of Leaf to invite me to dinner at the Polo Lounge, but when the mail arrives I receive an invitation to *Luxe*'s launch party for that same evening, so I assume Leaf's motive is to keep me from attending Colette's gathering, which is certain to attract the press.

Leaf arrives twenty minutes late, but I don't mind since I get to eavesdrop on the table next to me—Zsa Zsa Gabor celebrating her birthday. Of course, all her guests are too polite to ask which one. She's exquisitely dressed and coiffed, although the amount of makeup gives her a plastic appearance. I wonder if her husband—number seven?—is wearing a toupee.

When Leaf arrives, she orders Jack Daniels on the rocks and insists the waiter bring me another white wine spritzer.

She doesn't seem to notice Zsa Zsa but waves to a group several tables away. "The man in the blue shirt is Freddie Fields. He'll probably come over and ask when we're publishing his place."

"It's in May/June."

"How many pages?"

"Eight."

"He had the nerve to ask for text approval." Leaf stirs her ice with her finger. "I told him we didn't give text approval to

Barbra Streisand. We didn't give it to the Duchess of Alba. So why should we give it to him? He's lucky we're even publishing his house. He claims he did it himself and said he always wanted to be a decorator. So I said, 'Gee, that's funny, Freddie. All the really good decorators are gay. Are you trying to tell me something?' That shut him up!"

Leaf has another drink before we order dinner, but I decide to nurse my spritzer so I don't get drunk and say something I shouldn't.

"The real reason I went to New York," Leaf says, "was to talk to an editor at Doubleday about me doing a book for them."

My first thought is: *Won't Mr. Bruin be furious?*

"I know what you're thinking. Claret's been after us to do a follow-up to *Celebrities at Home*. I told him nothing sells like celebrities and we can't ever top that book, but his idea is to do an entire series of books that are simply reprints of the magazine. He wants to do one book on New York interiors, another on California interiors, one on historic houses, another on art collectors, etc." Leaf sucks an ice cube. "This time he doesn't want new layouts or text—he saw how much *that* cost. He wants to use the same color separations. And we can easily do that, Anthony. You can probably put together an entire book in a week. But you know he'll think it's part of your job and not give you any extra pay. And even though I'll be the editor and the one who has to go on book tours and TV to promote it, I won't get an extra cent either. But on the other hand, Doubleday is offering such a big advance it would be foolish of me not to accept it."

"What's the book about?"

"They want to call it *The Good Taste Book*."

"Sounds like a cookbook."

"That's what I said." She signals the waiter to bring another round. "I suggested *My Favorite Things*. The title's still up in the air, but anyway the idea for the book is I select the best of everything—ten beautiful sofas, six innovative dining tables, twelve great lamps, the finest linen—you get the idea."

"That should be the name: *The Best of Everything*.

"That's the title of Rona Jaffe's first book—and it was made into a movie."

"The Best of the Best?"

"That's pretty good. I'll tell them." She pats my hand. "Here's the thing, Anthony. Doubleday wants a mock-up—a table of contents and two or three sample chapters —before they make a final commitment. I can't offer you anything right now, but if Doubleday goes ahead with the book, I'll pay you $3000 to design it."

"Why wouldn't Doubleday pay me?"

"Their contracts aren't written that way. They pay the author an advance, and out of that the author has to pay any photographers and illustrators. They could have an in-house art director design the book, but I said I want to work with you and they agreed. It's a good opportunity, Anthony."

I want to say, "Aren't you afraid my jungle will have to be cut back if I start designing books?" Instead I smile. "I'm glad you want me to do it, Leaf, and of course I will."

Later, as we're gorging on dessert, Cole Bruin, in a tuxedo, walks into the restaurant and approaches our table. "I believe I have something you'd like to see." He hands Leaf the premiere issue of *Luxe*.

She passes the magazine to me as she pulls a small envelope out of her handbag and gives it to Cole. "Thank you. Will you join us for dessert or a drink?"

"No, I told the valet I was just dropping this off. Good night." He leaves without glancing at me.

I hold up the magazine so Leaf can see the cover—a photograph of Colette Bruin dramatically posed on a Recamier.

"That woman has some ego!" Leaf takes the issue from me. "Unbelievable! She put her own home on the cover!"

"Gee, didn't another editor I know do that?"

Leaf slaps my hand. "At least I didn't put my *face* on the cover."

"Colette's put more than her face. That dress is cut so low it could be on *Cosmo*."

"That photo's retouched. Colette's added a cup or two to her breasts."

I point to the gold *LUXE* logo. "I *knew* she'd use metallic ink."

Leaf pushes aside her dessert dish, scoots her chair next to mine and opens the magazine so we can both study it. The first twenty pages are mostly ads for high-end fashion—clothes, jewelry, perfume—as well as several luxury automobiles. "I heard Colette practically gave the ads away so the first issue would be plump."

Leaf studies Colette's editorial page with a portrait larger than Leaf's then she quickly passes by the various articles on watches, travel, shopping and fashion. She stops at the opening two-page spread of Colette's apartment. She continues through the feature then backtracks and counts. "She gave herself ten pages. I have to admit that Waldo did a good job. She was smart to hire him." She turns back to the title page. "Do you recognize the photographer?"

"Yes. I interviewed him about a year ago. I didn't care for his portfolio." I point to a photograph. "Look how flat the lighting is—there's no dimension. All the walls are the same value—no shadowing."

"You're right." Leaf moves on to an eight-page feature on a yacht. "Not bad. But not really good either."

Leaf flips by six pages on jewelry and looks at a feature on a Malibu home. "We rejected this house, so she's not getting homes we want."

When Leaf turns to the next home, I let out a yell. "Oh my God!"

"It can't be." Leaf whips past the six pages so fast they crackle. Then she goes back to opening to read the credits. "They're Mark's photos."

"It's my layout!"

"How in Hell did Colette get her hands on the photos and layout of Ted Powell's home?"

Neither one of us consider waiting until tomorrow. We race over to the office. I'm already in the viewing room when Leaf arrives.

I open a bottom file cabinet drawer labeled *KILLED* and lift out the Ted Powell folder. "The transparencies and my layout are gone."

"Who has access to that room?"

"Everyone. We lock it only at night."

"First thing tomorrow I'll have Timmy call a locksmith and change all the locks—not just on all the doors, but these file cabinets too. Keep them locked from now on and don't give anyone a key." Leaf kicks the drawer shut with her foot. "The big question remains: Who's the thief?"

"Do you think Colette could have taken the photos and layout before she left?"

"That would be the best scenario." She squeezes my wrist so tightly I wince. "Otherwise, Anthony, we have a mole."

MARCH 7, 1980

$\mathbf{M}$ark Romano never said a word to me when his photographs of Harold Sloan's residence appeared in *Inside* with his credit so small it was nearly unreadable. Nor has he said anything about not getting any new assignments in several months. But now Leaf has relented and said Mark can photograph Burton Fisher's new Los Angeles condo in Westwood.

"Has Leaf seen the apartment?" Mark asks as we take the elevator to the twentieth floor.

"No, she said she'd take anything Burton designed 'sight unseen,'" I respond, "but she especially wanted this one because it's his own place. She even promised him the cover."

"She may regret having said that."

"Why? Isn't it up to Burton's usual impeccable taste?"

"You'll see."

An area rug made of dense overlapping two-inch by three-inch brown leather strips defines the seating area. Two of Burton's signature banquettes face each other; their white cotton fabric is accented with basketball-size pillows covered in brilliant lime green silk. The coffee table—a thick oval of glass—seems as if it's floating above the rug until I spot two small chrome pyramids supporting it. The dining area repeats the illusion with another thick glass oval tabletop surrounded by six chairs, each with a single sleek swoop of chrome forming the base and arms; the lime green fabric covers the seats and backs. A monumental Louise Nevelson white wooden sculpture fills one wall.

Three pairs of glass doors lead to a large balcony. On the narrow walls between the doors, both in the living area and on the balcony, Burton has clustered bamboo trees so that the barrier of inside and outside disappears. The top of the balcony balustrade is hidden in a long row of cascading ferns.

The master bedroom displays a color scheme I've not seen in a room: three shades of gray and butter yellow. It's surprising yet serene.

Another bedroom is all white except for a Warhol *Campbell's Soup Can* painting between twin beds that sport two round tomato-red pillows.

Pleated matte silver wallpaper makes the powder room subtly shimmer.

"It's not Burton's usual all-white look, but it's chic."

Mark opens a drawer of a black waterfall console in the entry and takes out a newspaper clipping. "This is Leaf's in/out list that she gave the *Los Angeles Times* when it named her Woman of Year in '77. *Out: shag carpet, chrome and glass, bright colors, foil wallpaper, veined mirrors, tree-filled rooms and Boston ferns.*"

I raise my eyebrows. "Well, I guess that is a shag carpet, but it's leather and not the mop Leaf meant. The chrome dining chairs are a sleek variation on Mies van der Rohr's classic cantilever Brno chair. Did Burton design them?"

"Yes, and Sarah Cohen produced them."

"The chrome-and-glass coffee table is so understated it practically disappears, not at all like the clunky pieces from the past. As for bright color, the lime green comes from the bamboo; the tomato red comes from the Warhol, and the yellow is subdued by the gray. The foil wallpaper in the powder room is understated and not gaudy because it's matte. As for the ferns, I'm sure Leaf was referring to the single potted plant on a stand in the corner. And I don't see any veined mirrors."

"Even Burton couldn't go that far."

"So he did this on purpose."

"Absolutely."

"Maybe Leaf won't remember what she said was out. It was three years ago."

"Oh, Burton's considered that. He said if it isn't pointed out in the text, he's informing Herb Caen, who will certainly tell all in his column."

"Why would Burton do this?"

"Because he can."

"But Leaf has been very good to him. I think he's gotten more coverage in *Inside* than any other designer. Why would he mock her?"

Mark shrugs. "To get back at his mother? Who knows what warped psychological game he's playing? But he did it—with glee."

"He has to live here when he comes to L.A. I think it's very well done and chic, but does he like it?"

"Oh, he loves it. And he can't wait to see what you put on the cover."

MAY 12, 1980

I ask Walter to come to Ivory's office. "Timmy said Leaf picked up the stack of galleys from her inbox and handed them back without reading them."

"So she doesn't know Burton used her out list to decorate his L. A. apartment," Walter adds. "Although you'd think she'd remember her own list of don'ts."

"Maybe she does remember," I point out, "and thinks Burton did a good job."

"Since Leaf quit smoking her moods go up and down like an elevator. One minute she's perfectly reasonable and the next minute she lashes out at everyone and everything." Ivory looks at me. "You should have told her about Burton when you showed her the photos. And you had another opportunity when you showed her your layout."

"Maybe she'll never know," Walter says. "If she doesn't read the galleys, she probably doesn't read the magazine when it's printed either."

"The way you worded it in the text was clever," I tell him. "It *almost* makes it seem as if Leaf knew all about Burton's plan and wanted to show that anything can look good if it's done with style."

"Well, I hope she sees it that way, but as I say, maybe she

won't find out."

"Oh, I'm sure one of her friends will say something."

"What friends?" Ivory blows cigarette smoke toward the ceiling.

"One of the catty decorators is certain to say something snide to her." Walter lights his own cigarette.

"You have to tell her, Anthony," Ivory says. "You're the only one who ever says 'no' to her. She'd let you get away with murder."

"You should have told me sooner, Anthony." Leaf is surprisingly calm. "Before we spent money on color separations."

"Are you saying you're going to pull the story? I don't know if we have enough time to put in a different home. *And* it's the cover."

"Well, you'll have to make time. You'll have to find another cover."

"The text makes it seem—"

"I don't care what the text says. No one reads it anyway. They just look at the pictures. And I will not have everyone mocking me!" She picks up a pen, and for a moment I think she's going to fling it at me, but she holds it between her fingers as a substitute cigarette. "We'll let Burton think we're going to publish his condo, that everything is fine. We'll play along with his devious little game. But it will *never* be published. Not while I'm alive."

I take a deep breath. "Mark Romano said Burton would tell Herb Caen what happened if you didn't publish his place. You know the national media will pick up the story. Now that *Inside*'s considered the best, the press will look for anything to bring us down a peg or two." For a second I wonder how far I can go—and decide *all the way*. "If you run the story with Walter's text, it makes you look gracious and honorable. Caen will make you look like a spiteful bitch."

Leaf just stares at me. Maybe she's sharpening her machete. Finally she says, "Let me see the text." And I know Burton has triumphed. But not me: As I get up to leave, she commands, "Sit down. I don't know how to tell you this, so I'll just come right out with it. Doubleday rejected your layouts for my book."

"Did they say why?"

"They said the style is too 'classic.' They don't want the book to look like *Inside*. They want something livelier, more loose."

"I can do that."

"They're going to use one of the in-house designers."

"I'm not saying Doubleday didn't reject your layouts," Timmy informs me as we relax in the steam room after working out at the gym. "They may have, but Leaf didn't tell you the whole story."

"And what's the whole story?"

"They're not doing her book *at all*."

"Why not?"

"It turns out Leaf never had a contract in the first place. She came up with the concept for the book and used your layouts to submit the idea to Doubleday."

"So when Leaf took me to the Polo Lounge and told me about her contract, she hadn't even met with Doubleday?"

"Right. And when she did meet with them, no one there thought the book would sell. So they turned it down."

"When Leaf said Doubleday was using an in-house designer, it was to hurt me."

"You don't think she's going to admit her idea wasn't any good, do you?"

"Was Leaf always like this and I just didn't notice?"

"Perhaps you were flattered by her attention. But she's always lied to suit her purpose. I thought you knew that. But it's gotten worse since she found out about Ted. Then I noticed there was another shift after she saw that psychic. Leaf won't tell me what the psychic said, but it certainly shook her up."

"The woman said a man was going to betray Leaf."

"Well, we both know one who already has."

"The psychic made it clear it was in the future, not something in Leaf's past."

"So I guess now Leaf doesn't trust *any* man."

"Including me." I look in Timmy's eyes. "Or you."

"I've never seen her this erratic. She's taking more and more pills. She's gone to three different doctors to get prescriptions, and she makes me get them filled at three different drug stores so no one realizes just how much she's taking."

"What's she taking?"

"Valium to calm her, Benzedrine to perk her up, Seconal to make her sleep. Leaf's a pharmacy. The problem is she often takes more than the prescribed dose. And now that she's quit smoking and gaining more weight than Liz Taylor she's also taking Dexedrine as a diet pill. Not that it does any good since she's always stuffing her face with M&Ms and Pecan Sandies."

An older man enters the steam room and Timmy indicates with his head for us to leave. We shower in silence. Timmy broods. As we dry off, he lets it out.

"You saw how Leaf's office was filled last week with flowers and other gifts from designers for her birthday—*thousands* of dollars worth of presents. And who made sure all those designers remembered her special day? *Me!* And you know what she told me? That it was the unhappiest day of her life!"

"Maybe she realizes the designers only give her gifts because of her job, not because they like her."

"Well she doesn't have to take it out on me. I tell you, Anthony, lately she's been so mean to me sometimes I want to just walk away."

JUNE 10, 1980

"For the New York apartment in the November/December issue, I want to make this photograph the opening spread." I hold up a layout board for Walter to see. Across the two pages is a tight shot of a living room: a bit of a sofa and a chair, a floor lamp and covering the wall is a mural of a Hirschfeld drawing of a quartet playing musical instruments. "The homeowner is a composer, so I think this sets the scene perfectly."

"So do it. But why are you asking me?"

"There's barely any room for a title." I point to dummy type I've positioned at the bottom right corner. "In fact, there's room for only four letters."

Walter takes the layout and stares at it. "Let me see the other pages."

I hand him the rest of the layout. "And here are the photos I'm using."

He holds the transparencies up to the light. He opens a drawer and removes his bag of Mallomars. I sit down. He bites into a cookie. He walks over to the window and looks out for several minutes. He finishes the cookie. He sits down, stacks the photos into a pile and returns them and the layout to me. He says one word.

"*Jazz.*"

"It's perfect, Walter. I don't know how you do it, but it's perfect. Thank you."

"How he does what?" Leaf stands in the doorway.

I explain about the title.

"Very good, Walter." Leaf plops down in the chair next to me and reaches across Walter's desk for a Mallomar. "As you probably both know, I was in New York last week, and Sunday I went to the Tony Awards."

"That must have been fun," I interject, "seeing all the stars."

"You see more on television." Leaf brushes crumbs from her chest. "At one of the parties afterward I ran into Judy Berlin, and even though it wasn't the appropriate time or place, she asked me about several homes she suggested we publish. I told her I'd give her an answer when I got back to L.A. What are these homes she suggested?"

Walter rifles through a stack of papers and pulls one out. "Lynn Wyman's apartment in—"

"I've seen it and it's awful. Who else?"

"Richard Rockman. Judy said he has an extensive Fabergé collection."

"I'm sick of those stupid eggs, and if he collects all that ornate stuff, the house is probably overdone anyway."

Walter reads off another name. "Mr. and Mrs. Leonard Ahroni. They collect Marc Chagall drawings."

"Boring. I bet Judy tells everyone that she represents *Inside* so that she can get into their homes."

"As society columnist for the *Los Angeles Times*," Walter points out, "she has access to plenty of celebrity homes on her own."

"Whose side are you on?"

"I didn't know there were sides. I only meant—"

"Anyone else on that list?"

"Estelle Winwood."

"She'll probably die before we got a chance to publish it. Why is Judy giving you these suggestions instead of me?"

"I don't really know, Leaf." Walter sighs. "Maybe it's because I'm the one who goes over her text with her."

"I don't like it when people go behind my back. I don't understand why people can't be happy where they are. Why do they always have to grab, grab, grab?" Leaf takes another Mallomar. "How many stories has Judy been assigned to write?"

"She's only got one right now," Walter replies. "Ali Mac-Graw."

"Good. Let her write it. But, Walter, put her name at the end of the article, not on the title page like we usually do. She's getting too pushy. Anne Douglas told me how unprofessional Judy was when she interviewed Kirk. We really have to be more careful how we assign these stories. Some personalities are going to clash, and there's nothing we can do about it—except keep them apart."

"Yes, but Judy's text is always so good—she always comes up with a fresh slant, and I hardly have to edit it at all—I think she's worth a little aggravation."

"We can't afford to upset the homeowners, Walter, especially not celebrity wives. They're all prima donnas, but we have to live with that. We have to think of the magazine first. We can always get another writer, but you know how difficult it is to find a celebrity with a halfway decent home. We have to let Judy know she's made a mistake. She's starting to take herself too seriously. Tell her, 'No, thank you' to all the homes she's suggested. In fact, tell her, 'No scouting.' All she's to do is write what we assign her. Period. And let's cut back on the assignments we give her—say maybe one a year."

About an hour later Walter settles himself in my office guest chair with an extended wheeze. "When I called Judy Berlin to tell her our esteemed editor-in-chief wasn't interested in any of her suggestions, I found out why Leaf cut all her assignments. At the Tony Awards party Judy not only inappropriately asked La Wyks about the homes she suggested, the idiot also told Leaf she didn't know how to dress."

"You're kidding."

"As Jack Paar would say, 'I kid you not.' Judy said she told Leaf as a friend, and that all she said was Leaf's dress was 'less than flattering.'"

"What every friend wants to hear. Especially when she's gained thirty pounds."

"Forty. Judy said Leaf told her she didn't know where to shop, so Judy offered to take her to a few boutiques when they were both back in L.A."

"No one wants to hear criticism," I say, "but Judy seems to have been tactful."

"Not really. She finally told me that she might have used the word 'frumpy.'"

"Oops. So when you told Judy Leaf shot down all her suggestions do you think she understood the ramifications?"

"Judy's a smart cookie."

"Yeah, and we saw how Leaf chomped into those Mallomars. Judy should have known better than to say anything, but she's right. Leaf doesn't know how to dress. That pseudo-sailor outfit Leaf's wearing today looks ridiculous."

"She's not wearing a sailor outfit," Walter says. "She's got on the entire fleet."

As soon as Walter leaves, Timmy sits down. "What did Walter do to set Leaf off?"

"He wanted to keep giving Judy Berlin assignments when Leaf told him not to."

"Leaf asked if Walter had written her editorial yet. Before

I could find out, she said she didn't care if he wrote it or not. From now on she wants Tom to write it."

"Walter's been writing Leaf's column since she first became editor."

"Well, he's not anymore."

JULY 12, 1980

We stand in the sand for a full three minutes at Will Rogers State Beach while Timmy decides where we're going to bask.

"We don't want to be near a boom box, especially if it's blasting punk. Disco would be okay. And we don't want to be downwind of someone who smokes—unless it's pot. Also not by anyone old unless he's a sugar daddy."

"How would you know?"

"Big diamond ring. Cartier watch. Gucci bag." Timmy turns his back on a group of teenagers. "And we certainly don't want to be next to a gaggle of boys younger and cuter than us. We don't need the competition."

"We might as well go home. I've never seen so many cute boys in Speedos."

"Follow me. I see just the spot." Timmy heads to an open area near the edge of the crowd. "We want to leave enough room so that men who are attracted to us can find a spot close by and make obscene gestures with their tongues."

I carefully spread a king-size white sheet on the sand securing the corners with my tote bag, sneakers and Timmy's backpack. We place our towels on top. I remove my t-shirt.

"Slowly," Timmy says. "Every eye is always on the latest arrivals. We have to tease." He kicks off black flip-flops and unfastens the top button of his Levi's. He lifts his white tank top above his stomach but then lets it slide back down. He takes a circle of keys from a pocket and bends over, his ass pointing at the onlookers as he slips the keys into his backpack. The tank top finally comes off, and to make sure the gaping men notice his well-toned chest, he lightly brushes his palm across his left nipple. He unfastens the rest of buttons on his ripped jeans. "Don't just stand there, Anthony. Take something off."

"I wish I had a glove." He doesn't get the *Gypsy* reference. "Timmy, every eye is on you. No one would notice me even if I were completely naked. I bet you only stopped stripping because you want them to anticipate what's underneath your jeans."

"You got it. So take off your clothes and let me be the climax—so to speak."

There's not much left for me to remove. I step out of khaki shorts revealing a red Speedo. "I don't hear any applause."

Timmy drops his jeans. He's not wearing a Speedo. Barely covering his genitals is an extremely narrow strip of nylon. And it's white. The sun casts a dark shadow outlining his prominent penis.

"You're wearing a cock ring, aren't you?"

Timmy smiles. "Now we get to lather each other with suntan lotion making everyone wish *they* were touching us."

"They might think we're lovers and shy away."

"People *love* to break up lovers."

At last we lie on our backs, and I shut my eyes, tuning out the gay games of the beach. It's been a hectic week and I just want to fall asleep in the sun. Only Timmy doesn't shut up.

"Sarah Cohen's plastic surgeon refused to give Leaf a face-lift until she lost weight. He said her skin had stretched around the fat and was not strong enough to be pulled back. So she consulted another doctor, and that one informed her that he was unable to remove as much fat as she wanted: The body would go into trauma. A third surgeon said Leaf has an irregular heartbeat; he was afraid the adrenaline he'd have to inject to stop the bleeding would cause a heart attack on the operating table. But Leaf wouldn't give up. She believes a face-lift is going to change her whole life and that she'll magically become Jane Fonda."

"So that's where Leaf is—having her face lifted?"

"Actually, she's at Pritikin's for two weeks to lose weight. *Then* she gets a facelift. I finally found a doctor in San Diego who'll perform the operation."

"How long is she going to be out of the office?"

"Six weeks." Timmy whispers, "I thought that hunky guy with the thick chest hair was interested in me, but he obviously likes looking in the mirror. It's *you* he's after and I'm just blocking his view, so I think I'll take a stroll and see what else is on the menu." He adjusts his penis so it bulges even more and ambles away.

The man with the chest hair immediately comes over and sits facing me with his legs spread. He's wearing boxer shirts and I'm sure he's well aware the head of his dick is peaking out. "I'll get right to the point. I have a lover who's in D.C. for a week. I'm not interested in getting to know someone. I don't want to go to dinner and share life stories with a man I'll never see again. I just want to fool around with a hot stud in the ocean. And you're the hottest guy here."

"You don't even want to tell me your name?"

"Does it matter?"

I guess not, since I follow him into the Pacific.

AUGUST 25, 1980

"I planned the Jan/Feb issue while you were away." It's the last double issue before *Inside* goes monthly. I hand Leaf the layouts: a white-on-white beach house in Marina del Rey, a thatched-roof bungalow in Thailand, a chintz-filled New York apartment decorated by Mario Buatta, a Paris chateau filled with delicate French antiques and bold modern art, an eclectic town house in San Francisco, a Spanish castle romantically in ruin and a lush garden in North Carolina. The antiques article is on *pietra dura* furniture; the art story features Japanese watercolor landscapes on folding screens. I loved planning and designing an entire issue without any input, and wished Leaf had never returned. "I put Georgia O'Keeffe's Ghost Ranch on the cover."

"Oh, that's good." Leaf is wearing giant sunglasses and a synthetic blonde wig styled in a pageboy. She claims her hairdresser singed her hair, but the camouflage is to minimize the puffy scars around her ears and eyes. She doesn't look like she had a facelift. She's doesn't look like she lost any weight. Timmy said she spent $14,000 and she doesn't look any different.

She rapidly flips through the layouts. "They look good, as always." She hands them back to me. "Do you want to come with me to see Jason Hunt's latest design?" She's less than enthusiastic. "He claims it's the best work he's ever done."

"That's not much of a recommendation, is it?"

She slaps my hand. "You're terrible. But right." She grabs her purse and stops at Timmy's doorway. "Is there gas in my car?"

"Yes. I filled it up on my lunch hour."

As we head toward Beverly Hills, Leaf asks, "What did you think of the current issue of *Luxe*?" Before I can respond, she adds, "It's very thin, even for a summer issue; there aren't many ads, and I wonder how many were paid for."

"The problem with the magazine is no one knows who the audience is. I doubt if even Colette knows. What's an article about cigars doing in a magazine that features women's watches and jewelry?"

"She only ran two homes, and neither one was especially good."

"Actually they were both places we rejected."

Jason Hunt opens the front door of a Tudor-style house before I ring the doorbell. "Leaf! Your hair looks fabulous!" He doesn't acknowledge my presence. Doesn't he remember I attended his Thanksgiving dinner last year? "Well, this is the entrance hall. The floor is travertine, of course. The two chairs are covered in Brunschwig & Fils fabric, and the table is by Karl Springer. The chandelier—"

"You don't have to give me the captions, Jason," Leaf says. "Just lead the way."

"Well, let me just say the homeowners razed the house that was on this lot and built this one in the style of their English ancestry."

It's three stories with eight bedrooms and nine baths, but it takes Leaf only fifteen minutes to canvas it. When we're back in the foyer, Jason says, "I'll run around and make sure all the lights are off and meet you outside."

"What do you think, Anthony?" Leaf whispers as we wait

on the porch.

"This is not Jason's best work." My eyebrows rise. "This isn't *anyone's* best work. Sure, it's 'the largest living room in Beverly Hills,' but that does not make it 'grand' like Jason thinks. With all those different styles on each level, I thought it looked like a department store. And I can't believe he used a purple rug with pink wallpaper in the dining room."

"Shh, here he comes."

"Well, Leaf, how soon do you think you can publish it? Don't you think the dining room would look festive on the cover?"

"Jason, I have to be frank." Leaf looks directly into Jason's eyes. "I thought, for a minute in the living room, that we were in Bloomingdale's. There's too much going on. It will never photograph. But that's only my opinion. Maybe I'm too critical. What do you think, Anthony?"

Jason, for the first time that afternoon, looks at me.

"I don't understand why someone would deliberately build a fake-Tudor house and then not have even one piece of furniture from the period. Nothing gelled. Even the accessories are wrong."

Leaf smiles. "Jason, I think you can give this one to *Luxe*."

SEPTEMBER 11, 1980

"Trouble. Trouble. Trouble. With a capital *T*." Timmy enters my office waving sheets of paper. "Guess who gave an interview in the *New York Post* and didn't ask Leaf's permission?"

"Not me!"

"Ivory Cooke has cooked her goose."

"Where has she been for the past two weeks anyway?"

"In Boston, with, as my grandmother would demurely say, 'female problems.' Or to put it more bluntly, Ivory had a hysterectomy."

"She couldn't have done that here?"

"She wanted to be near her mother. She called me this morning—Ivory, not her mother—and was she in a state, wondering if Leaf had seen the article in the *Post*. Ivory said she stopped in New York on her way to Boston and had lunch with a college chum, Jane Kroft, who has the by-line on this damning article."

I'm tempted to snatch the paper out of Timmy's hands but it's best to let him proceed at his own meandering pace.

"It seems this Jane Kroft had recently been hired by the *Post* and asked her old college pal for an interview, saying it would help her standing at the paper. Well, like a good girl, Ivory said she called to ask Leaf—and she did call, but when I told her Leaf wasn't due back for another week, Ivory asked to be transferred to Jake White, who supposedly told her it was fine to proceed. I told Ivory I'd get someone in New York to fax me the article and call her back. After I did that, I called Jake and he denies giving Ivory the okay, but he always covers his ass, so it comes down to he-said she-said."

Timmy holds up one of the sheets of paper. There's a picture of Ivory and the current issue of *Inside* with the headline: *Inside Scoop on Inside.*

"Listen to this: *When told that the word in New York is that Leaf Wyks is a tyrant to work for, Cooke replied, 'Well, sometimes, but she doesn't run into your office screaming or anything like that. She rarely raises her voice. But she always gets her way. She's demanding only in the sense that when she wants something, she wants it immediately. She has her moods, but we all do, don't we?'* Can you believe Ivory would say that to a *reporter*? Of course Ivory said she was misquoted and that she had told her friend things 'off the record,' but I said when it comes to journalists, nothing is 'off the record' especially at the *Post*."

"Didn't Ivory know the *Post*'s a scandal rag? Leaf is going to be furious when she finds out."

"She probably knows by now. Robin Rainbow phoned her just after I got the fax." Timmy flips to another page. "You'll love this. *'Cooke said the art director selects the cover.'* Notice how she doesn't mention your name."

"Oh, Timmy, there you are." Leaf walks into my office. "I want you to send a telegram."

Timmy reaches out his hand and I pass him a pad and pencil.

"It's to go to Ivory—*immediately*." Leaf dictates: "*Glad you had such a great time in New York. Why don't you stay there? Permanently. Will no longer need you in Los Angeles. Or anywhere.*"

SEPTEMBER 17, 1980

"I should really make you managing editor." Leaf smiles at me. "You already run the magazine."

I don't mention that I'm not interested in the job. Maybe at other magazines the position is one of power, but at *Inside* it's just assigning text and making sure the copy flows from editor to editor.

Leaf picks up her phone when Timmy buzzes. "It's Claret," she tells me. "Stay. I'm sure this won't take long." She listens. She nods. She waves her hand in a sign for him to hurry even though he can't see her gesture. Finally she says, "I can't spare him, Claret. Anthony runs the magazine. I worry when he goes on vacation. You'll have to hire a freelancer." She hangs up. "He wanted you to design a new rate card for the press kit. I know you don't want to do that—just a bunch of numbers."

She's right, but she could have asked me.

"Where were we? Oh, yeah, managing editor. I've hired Leslie Manchester. He doesn't have experience in that position, but he seems bright and I'm sure he'll catch on quickly. He's only twenty-seven and eager."

"Where'd he work before?"

"He's the architecture editor at the L.A. *Times* and that's why I hired him. He has connections with all the important architects. I want their work in the magazine. He can't start until October first, but I asked him to come by this afternoon. I want you to show him around. Introduce him to everyone and go over the schedule and things with him. Show him what to do."

Leslie Manchester is beautiful. Not handsome: beautiful. Six-feet tall and in good shape, he could be a model in *Gentlemen's Quarterly*. Thick sandy-colored hair falls over his forehead. Green eyes look vulnerable and innocent, as if they have no idea how gorgeous he is. His eyelashes are so long they nearly brush against his wire-frame glasses. The nose is long and slender over lush lips—the top just as plump as the bottom, which turns down at the corners making him look appealingly sad. When he smiles a dimple dents his left cheek. His skin is unblemished. I see only two flaws: a tiny white scar bisecting his right eyebrow and a brown mole, about a quarter of inch round, between his right thumb and index finger.

He's wearing a navy blue sports coat, a blue Brooks Brothers button-down oxford cloth shirt with a striped tie, chinos, Bass oxblood penny loafers, grey socks. And a wedding ring.

"I went to Yale with every intention of being an architect." Of course his deep voice is as silky as a radio announcer on a classical music station. "But I couldn't hack the math, so I switched to journalism. I was so naïve I didn't realize architects don't have to worry how a building stands; that's up to the engineers. But in the end, I'm glad I made the switch."

"Do you like working at the *Times*?"

"I did for a while. For more than a year, I've tried to convince the editor that architecture belongs in the Sunday magazine with the other arts, but he insists on keeping it in the real estate section. So when Mrs. Wyks said I could bring architecture features to the magazine as well as being the managing editor, I jumped at the chance."

Leslie Manchester is so beautiful I think Leaf would have hired him even if he thought Frank Lloyd Wright had invented the airplane.

"The new issue of *Luxe* is here." Timmy rushes into my office. "And Burton Fisher's condo is on the cover!"

Instead of following him to Leaf's office, I stop at the viewing room and check the kill drawer. Our transparencies of Burton's Los Angeles home are missing as is my layout.

Even before I'm in her office, Leaf shouts, "How does this keep happening?"

"I don't know. The file cabinet is always locked and no one has a key but me."

Leaf throws the magazine at me. I quickly turn to the Burton Fisher feature. "Well, once again it's my layout. Can't we sue?"

"Timmy, ask our attorney."

Leaf searches through her console and finds a pack of Virginia Slims. Before she lights up, I grab them. "This incident is not worth starting to smoke again."

She snatches back the pack, takes a deep breath and tosses it on her desk.

I sit down and read the text accompanying Burton's condo. "Colette changed the story. Burton comes across as a genius who showed you that nothing is ever 'out' if it's done right."

"I wonder if Burton planned this all along. I don't want to speak to him. You call him. Tell him I'm furious. Tell him I'm so furious I can't even talk to him. Tell him he is not forgiven. Quote me."

As I leave her office, I hear her strike I match and I smell cigarette smoke.

When I telephone Burton, he laughs. "Not forgiven? Who does she think she is? God? How dare Leaf think I would be so unethical as to give another magazine my home when I had promised it to *Inside*. I'll tell you something, young man. I don't know how Colette Bruin got the transparencies. I certainly did not give her permission to publish my home. You think I want my work published in *Luxe*? No one will see it. That magazine is a disaster. When I saw my home in there I was outraged—a lot more 'furious' than Leaf, I assure you. I was ready to call her and see if she wanted to join me in suing Colette. But since I'm 'not forgiven,' I think I'll just keep laughing." And he hangs up.

OCTOBER 7, 1980

"Before we begin picture selection for the March/April issue," I tell Leaf in her office, "Leslie has a few scouting shots of architecture projects to show you."

When we enter the viewing room Leslie is waiting, but the light table arrayed with his transparencies is not illuminated.

"I have to start out by saying that in making many calls, I found a lot of architects are reluctant to give their designs to *Inside* on an exclusive basis like you want, Leaf." He flashes his dimple. "They're used to being published in *Architectural Record* and other trade publications."

"Don't they realize they'll get more coverage with us—and reach a wider audience. I'm sure *Inside* has a lot more readers than a trade journal."

"Of course you're right, Leaf. But most architects aren't interested in reaching a broad audience. They think most people wouldn't understand their work. Architects want to impress other architects." He turns on the light switch. "But I found three who are interested in having more exposure."

"You mean they're egotists."

"You said that not me. I have to work with them."

"So who are they?"

"Robert Venturi, Frank Gehry and Charles Gwathmey."

"Does Gehry have something other than his own home in Santa Monica?"

"I know that it's been shown before, but we can get different angles and he'll give us access to rooms that haven't been published."

"What else do you have?"

"This house is by Robert Venturi. It too has been shown, but it's been awhile and we can photograph it in a totally different way."

Leaf looks disappointed. "Let's see the Gwathmey. A while ago I wanted to publish an apartment he did in New York, but the homeowner gave it to another magazine."

"This is a house he just finished in Cincinnati. We'd get an exclusive if we do it right away."

Leaf examines the scouting shots then turns to me. "Have you looked at these, Anthony? What do you think?"

"I'm not fond of deconstructionism, but I'd pick Frank Gehry's house. It's nearly ten years old and still the most original thing out there. If we're going to run an architectural feature every issue, I think it's a good place to start. Shows we're serious. The Gwathmey is fine and contemporary but it's safe and the interiors are bland and typical of contemporary architecture. As for Venturi, Postmodernism doesn't seem very creative to me. The architects take a little from Internationalism, a bit from classicism, maybe throw in something else from Art & Crafts or regionalism and slap it all together."

"It's more complicated than that, Anthony," Leslie says.

"Maybe, but it doesn't look it. And Venturi actually talks about wit in architecture. Most buildings are rather permanent, and humor is fleeting. After awhile, Postmodern buildings simply look silly."

"Maybe Postmodern architects are saying buildings shouldn't be permanent."

"Really? Why don't you ask Robert Venturi which one of his buildings we can tear down and see what he says?"

"All right, boys," Leaf interrupts. "Let's not get into a pissing match. We'll do the Gwathmey. The interiors *aren't* stellar, but, Anthony, you could shoot around them. Just show an arm or a corner of a table like you do, and concentrate on the architecture. After all, it is an architecture feature. Shall we move on?"

I turn on another light table and Leslie gathers his material.

"Why don't you stay, Leslie," Leaf says. "See how we do things."

Unlike Leaf, I don't care how beautiful Leslie is, I don't want him at *my* meeting. But I proceed to show her my selections for the first residence. Leslie looks over our shoulders. Leaf moves so he can get a better look.

Leslie doesn't say anything until we come to the third residence, a mountain home in Colorado. He points to a photo I've rejected. "This shot really shows the roof line."

"You can see it in the overall shot I selected."

"Yeah, but this really zeroes in."

"We're focusing on the interiors." I hope my voice doesn't express my annoyance. "This isn't an architecture feature."

Leaf moves the photo in question over with the rest of the selected shots. "See if you can work it in, Anthony."

Leslie doesn't comment as I show the remaining residences, but I'm still annoyed.

OCTOBER 31, 1980

The invitation is branded on black leather. There's no RSVP number: Attendance is demanded. The occasion is Christopher Richter's birthday. The fact that he was born on Halloween might explain his demonic appearance.

Timmy also is invited, and we decide to go together.

"What are you wearing?" Timmy asks a few days before the event.

"The Armani jacket Robin Rainbow gave me."

"That's not very butch."

"The invite says 'leather.' There's nothing about 'butch.'"

"It's implied."

"I'm not spending hundreds of dollars on clothes I'll only wear once."

"How do you know? Once you put them on you might become a leather queen. But I guess the jacket will do if you keep it unzipped and don't have on anything underneath. What else are you wearing?"

"Jeans. Probably construction boots."

"No and no. All your jeans are too loose. I'll lend you a pair of mine. And I also have black leather knee-high boots I wore last year when I went to a Halloween party dressed as Cecil B. DeMille. I'm sure they'll fit you, but even if they're a bit tight, it's worth it for a few hours. I'm bring them in on Friday."

"What are you going to wear?"

"You can bet half the guests will be in leather chaps and jockstraps with their ass hanging out, so I have to top that." He giggles. "As Leaf always says, 'Less is more,' so that's what I'll be wearing: Less."

I doubt Timmy realizes the quote is not original to Leaf.

On Friday he gives me the boots and jeans. "Wear a cock ring and *no* underwear. You *do* have a cock ring, don't you?"

I nod.

"I'll come get you at ten-thirty." Timmy glares. "And if I see underwear, you can walk to the party."

In the evening when I slip into the jeans I understand why Timmy would know immediately if I had on underwear: Part of the crotch looks as if it has been deliberately worn away. Eight white horizontal threads play peek-a-boo with the head of my penis.

When Timmy picks me up in his Jeep he's covered in a bulky sweatshirt, a kilt and black boots with six buckles.

"Not what I'd expect to see you wearing."

"Oh this is just the camouflage to not get me arrested driving through Beverly Hills. The real costume is underneath."

The valets at Christopher Richter's are in leather chaps and jockstraps, bubble butts hanging out just as Timmy predicted. "All the guests in the same outfit are going to be furious," he says. "They're a cliché even before they get to the front door." Before handing over the Jeep, Timmy lifts the sweatshirt over his head to reveal a leather harness with chrome rings circling his nipples. A small silver key hangs on a rawhide chain around his neck. He tosses the kilt on the back seat. Timmy's genitals are encased in an extremely brief form-fitting silver chastity belt complete with padlock.

I raise my eyebrows. "You can't get much more less than

that."

The cute valet gives Timmy a claim check, which he hands to me. "I don't have any pockets."

The front door is open. In the foyer is a typical Richter sculpture: a life-size nude bronze of a young lad. This one holds a leather whip.

The house is dark with votive candles in brown lunch bags leading through the living room to the pool area, where everyone is gathered.

There's a large table laden with birthday gifts and a metallic sign reading *Happy 50th*. We add our presents to the grouping. Timmy and I had gone to The Pleasure Chest on our lunch hour, and I bought a black leather mask, though Timmy said our host probably already had one. He purchased a long double-headed dildo, and when I pointed out Christopher certainly has *several* of those, Timmy said you could never have enough at an orgy.

"I can't believe Christopher is admitting to being fifty," I say. "Youth is everything in the gay world."

"It's easy to admit to fifty when you're really fifty-eight," a voice behind us says.

I turn around. "Robin! I didn't know you were in L.A."

"I flew out with a client who wants to buy one of Richter's torsos." Robin eyes move up and down Timmy's nearly naked body. "I'd say that was a sexy outfit but there's not enough there to *be* an outfit."

"Well, you're not wearing *any* leather," Timmy points out.

"Oh, yes I am!" Robin is in a coral nylon jumpsuit, unzipped so three scarves—magenta, purple and azure—flutter in the light breeze. "I've got a *leather* wallet, and that's the most important kind of leather to Richter."

A blond bearded muscled waiter approaches with a tray of Champagne. Of course he too is sporting leather: boots and a motorcycle cap—nothing else—his pubic hair proving he's a natural blond.

Robin caresses his naked butt before taking a glass of bubbly. "They're *actual* twins, you know." When I look at the boy's ass, Robin adds, "Not *those*, although they are *adorable* twin cheeks. The waiters. They're *brothers*."

"Is your client here?" I ask.

Robin looks around. "Oh, he's over there by the *buffet*—the fat one *stuffing* his face. Can you believe he's wearing that leather vest *without* a shirt? No one wants to be exposed to *that* much fat. I don't think it's even *legal* in California."

"Are you going to see Leaf while you're in town?" Timmy wants to know.

"I *already* saw her at lunch today at Barbara Trent's." Robin fluffs his scarves. "And I think I'm on her *merde* list."

There's no need to ask Robin for details; he's eager to tell.

"You know Barbara is *very* chic—always well dressed in *couture* and so are her friends. So Leaf arrives in a *housedress* Mildred Pierce would find homely. Barbara and her *slender* nymphs eat maybe a grape a week. I thought they'd die when Leaf *speared* a baby potato I'd left on *my* plate. And she had *two* pieces of cake.

"Well, as soon as she excused herself to use the *powder* room, these very chic women started yammering as if they couldn't wait one more minute to let it out. One of them said how funny it was that *anytime* someone mentioned *Inside* Leaf yawned. Another said Leaf's dress was *plebeian*. And a third said her jewelry was *bourgeois*. That got me going and I said Leaf's *taste* was all in her mouth. Well, I'm *rather* certain she overheard. Not just me, but everyone. I don't think she went to the powder room *at all*. I think she stood in the hall so she *could* overhear if anyone talked about her."

I ask, "What did she say when she came back in the room?"

"That she was late for another appointment. She politely said goodbye to Barbara—who hadn't said *one* word against her, which is why I think Leaf heard everything. She *ignored* the other ladies, *glared* at me, and left."

"Now I understand why she didn't come back to the office." Timmy pats Robin's arm. "I think this Christmas you better give her *everything* in Tiffany's windows."

I spot Cole Bruin on the other side of the pool. How could I miss him: He's all in white linen. I leave Timmy with Robin and head over.

"I thought leather was the required dress code."

"This isn't my costume. I'm changing just before midnight when Christopher blows out the candles."

"How have you been?"

"Good. I got a bit part on *All My Children*."

"That's wonderful, Cole. Just what you wanted."

"It's just two tiny scenes at Cliff and Nina's wedding, but if there's any audience response, an actor usually gets called back to do more work."

"I've no idea who Cliff and Nina are, but when it airs I'll phone the station to rave about you."

"Don't rave too much or he might leave us," a deep voice says from behind me. Raymond Washington has on brown leather sandals with straps crisscrossing up to his knees and a leather loincloth—just two brown leather flaps, one barely covering his ass, the other hiding his crotch. "Cole's been Selection's top sales rep six months in a row."

"And all the other reps hate me." Cole twists Raymond's nipple. "The only reason I stay there is because of you."

"And that fat commission check you get every two weeks."

Just as I'm wondering if Cole and the showroom manager are having an affair, Raymond inserts a finger between two threads of my shredded jeans. "This is very inviting."

I point to his loincloth. "So is that."

Cole says, "It's made out of samples of Mrs. Cohen's new kid leather collection. If she only knew!"

Raymond rubs my penis. "Oh, I remember you."

"How many guys," I ask, "have put their hand under your flap without asking permission?"

"How many guys are here? But none of them can do what you can."

"What's that?"

He looks at his crotch. "Get a rise out of Ray Junior." The front flap lifts.

Before things get out of hand, Jason Hunt, in black leather pants and a cotton sports coat with a black turtleneck, approaches Cole and points to me. "Your mother is putting the house *this man* rejected on the next cover of *Luxe*."

"Wonderful!" I say. "That's where it belongs."

Timmy walks up and whispers in my ear. "I love when you drink. It stops you from censoring what you say."

Raymond lifts a muscled arm high and snaps his fingers, and one of the naked waiters rushes over with another tray of Champagne. Raymond points to me. "They're all for him."

When I take a glass, Timmy commands, "One gulp."

I swallow every drop. Raymond hands me another glass.

"I'll sip this one," I say. "Otherwise I'll get sick."

A prissy redhead, wearing leather shorts and pierced nipples, comes up to Jason. "Guess who came in the showroom this week?"

"Ed works at Wall-Pride," Jason informs us but doesn't make introductions.

"So guess! No, I'll tell you. Leaf Wyks! I expected her to be as sophisticated as Audrey Hepburn. She wasn't even Audrey Meadows. I thought it was strange that Leaf came in because isn't Sarah Cohen her decorator? Anyway, it turned out Leaf wanted remnants. She said she likes to cover her scrapbook covers with pretty wallpapers. I asked what kind of scrapbooks and she said all the clippings about her and the magazine. I asked if she was going to paste in the clippings and paper the cover herself, but she said she has a flunky to do that."

"Ed, I'd like to introduce you to Timmy, Leaf's flunky."

Ed smiles, either not listening or oblivious.

"Leaf used to dote on us decorators," Jason says. "She would take us to dinner or invite us to tea. She made us feel she was our great supporter. She asked us to show her our designs first, when we could have gone to *House & Garden*. We did everything she wanted. If she didn't like a lamp or a painting in one of our rooms, out it went. But now she doesn't even return our calls."

"All the decorators tell me that Leaf has a"—Ed puffs out his chest—"*liaison* who shields her from them."

I laugh, and he asks me, "Are you in the industry, too?"

"I *am* the industry."

Ed turns to Jason. "What does he mean?"

But Timmy answers. "Ed, let me introduce you to Anthony, the art director of *Inside*—and the *liaison* to the designers."

"Oh, you do the layouts, don't you?"

"You use the jargon but I bet you don't know what it means."

"I don't know what 'jargon' means."

"It means you're so stupid you don't even realize you should be embarrassed." The grand gesture would be to walk away but I'm curious to hear what else this blundering redhead spews out.

Ed points to Raymond's hip where his dark skin is lighter from wearing a Speedo at the beach. "You have a tan line!"

"Yes'r," Raymond says in a deliberate Southern drawl. "We darkies get a tan just like yous white boys."

Mark Romano joins us. Handcuffs dangle from a belt loop of

his very tight leather pants.

Cole says, "Do you promise to use those on me later?"

"Only if you're a *very* naughty boy."

"Where's Burton?" Jason asks.

"Pouting in San Francisco. Believe me, you don't want to see him in leather. Way too many cows would have to be slaughtered. Besides, he never attends parties where he isn't the center of attention."

Raymond moves behind me, puts his arms around my chest and pulls me toward him. Ray Junior presses against my ass.

Timmy says to Mark, "Leaf thinks it's very suspicious that Colette published two homes that you photographed for *Inside*—first Ted Powell's and then Burton's."

"I didn't give Colette any transparencies." He turns to me. "Didn't you say they were stolen out of a locked file cabinet with only one key?"

"Burton's were. The cabinet wasn't locked when Ted's photos were taken."

Mark sighs. "Leaf's never going to give me another assignment, is she?"

"Probably not." I squeeze his hand. "I'm sorry."

"Don't be. Colette promised me more assignments than I can handle and she pays double what I got from *Inside*."

"What's this about a locked file cabinet with only one key and missing photos?" Ed wants to know. "Sounds like an Agatha Christie mystery,"

I can't refrain from another dig. "Don't tell me you *read*?"

"I go to movies."

"I bet you move your lips when you read the credits."

"I don't stay for the credits."

"Ouch!" Timmy screams and turns around to see who pinched his butt.

"Don't expose your *arsch* if you don't want it played with,"

Christopher says.

"That wasn't playful. It hurt."

"It was meant to. And you loved it. So what are you boys gossiping about?"

"Leaf Wyks," says Ed.

"Oh, don't get me started." Christopher makes a face. "You'd think since she's the editor of such a sophisticated magazine, she'd be glamorous, but she always looks like a dowdy house-wife from Iowa."

"She *is* from Iowa," I say.

Robin sashays over.

"Leaf knows I have a lot of prominent clients," Christo-pher says, "and she's always pestering me to invite her to their homes. When I told her she could get into any home she wanted, she said she couldn't care less about their homes. She wants to meet the owners. And when I do take her to some-one's house for dinner, she's always inappropriately dressed."

"Oh I know," says Robin. "One time I took Leaf to a MoMA opening and she wore a blouse cut way too low for a woman of her age and weight, and four-inch heels with Capri pants, no less. She looked like one of the whores from *Sweet Charity* gone sour."

When Ed giggles, Robin adds, "Shall I show you my imper-sonation of Leaf Wyks teetering on high-heels into '21'?" He gathers his three scarves into two balls over his chest and zips up his jumpsuit so it looks as if he has breasts. He rises up on tiptoe and leans forward as he prances around, nearly tum-bling into the pool. Sweeping his arms wildly and in a voice exactly mimicking Leaf, he says, "All of these stuffed animal heads must be removed before I can give a brunch here."

Everyone laughs. I'm astounded when designers say things about Leaf in front of me. Don't they realize I could repeat what they say to her? Maybe they think because I'm gay I have more allegiance to them than to her.

I notice Cole and Timmy are no longer with our group. When did they disappear? And where? I look around, but they're nowhere to be seen. Maybe they're in a bathroom snorting coke.

When I tune back to the conversation, Christopher is still going on about Leaf. "I think she's desperate to fit into *gesellschaft*—society."

"Leaf is at the top of her field, and she's discovered it's not enough," I say. "I'm no psychiatrist, but I think being an orphan has completely dominated her life. She has the power and the prestige she's coveted, but she still feels empty. She still feels apart from the group she wants to be a part of."

"Oh, so serious," says Mark.

One of the blonds brings another tray of Champagne. "Which one are you?" Christopher asks.

"Axel."

Christopher puts four fingers in the boy's mouth. "You and Arno are such good *schwanzlutshers*."

"What's that mean?" asks Ed.

"*Cocksuckers*."

"Oh I'm good at that too."

I can't resist. "At least you can do *something*."

Christopher consults his watch. "It's time for dessert." He raises his voice so everyone can hear. "Will you all join me in the dining room for birthday cake?"

With blood red walls, the room is centered with a stone table under a crystal chandelier set on dim. Sprawled across the top of the table is Cole. He's nearly nude, only a cluster of purple muscatel grapes shields his genitals. On his torso are perched fifty tall white candles not yet dripping wax on his skin.

Outlining Cole's body are hundreds of miniature cupcakes.

"Everyone!" Christopher announces. "Gather around and help me blow out the candles."

400   Charles L. Ross

Someone shouts, "I'd rather blow the centerpiece."

"That's the real dessert," another person adds.

Everyone sings *Happy Birthday*, and most of the older men blow out a candle taking advantage of the opportunity to touch Cole. I watch his face. A tear slides toward his ear.

Timmy, whom, I'm sure, wishes he were the center of attention, begins plucking the grapes with his lips.

Cole looks frightened, not because of Timmy; other men, especially the older ones, are mauling him—pinching his nipples, clutching and pawing. I move in and with one sweep of my arm knock the candles off Cole. He takes my hand and jumps down from the table.

"What's going on?" Christopher shouts.

"Where are your clothes?" I ask Cole.

"In the kitchen."

As we dash toward the swing door, I know Christopher won't follow us. He'll act as if it's all planned and move on to the next "entertainment"—probably an intimate performance by Axel and Arno.

While Cole puts on his white linen suit, I dash back to the dining room. Some of the men are smearing cupcake icing on each other's bare chests and licking it off. Fortunately, Christopher's back is toward me, so I quickly hand Timmy the claim check for his Jeep. He tucks it under a leather strap of his harness. "Is Cole okay?"

"He'll be fine as soon as he's out of here."

I exit through the back door, and when I walk around to the driveway, Cole's already in his car.

When we're safely mixed in with the traffic on Sunset, he says, "Thank you."

"You're welcome."

"I'm starving. Want to go to the all-night diner in Hollywood?"

"In this outfit?"

"At this time of night on a Friday, Anthony, you'll fit right in."

"Lead the way."

We order hamburgers and milk shakes.

There are less than a dozen customers: one booth with four shrieking drag queens and another of male teens who look stoned.

"Do you think those guys are hustlers?" I ask Cole.

"Probably."

"I wonder if Halloween is a busy night for them."

"If it was busy, I don't think they'd be in here nursing a cup of coffee."

"I guess you're right."

"You were worried about what you have on, but you fit right in with your ripped jeans. I'm the one who's out of place in this stupid white suit."

"You do look like a misplaced extra from *Saturday Night Fever*. Haven't you heard disco sucks?"

"Christopher insisted I wear it. He wanted me to contrast with all the other guests." He studies water rings on the Formica tabletop as if it's a Rorschach inkblot that will reveal the ultimate secret. Finally he looks at me. "Do you think it was degrading for me to lie naked on the table?"

"Of course it was degrading. It was also erotic. Is that why you did it, because you wanted to be degraded?"

"Maybe."

I expect him to say more, but he doesn't.

"How were the candles stuck to your body?"

"With an invisible gel used in museums and art galleries."

"Timmy helped you get set up, didn't he?"

Cole nods.

"Did he know beforehand that he was going to do this?"

"It was planned more than a week ago. I thought it would be

fun." His palm brushes the water rings off the table. "But then I saw the look in some of their eyes."

"Cannibals, right?"

"I thought they were going to devour me!"

"Like a Tennessee Williams' play."

Cole shrugs. "I wish I knew why I want to do—certain things."

"Even if you knew why, it wouldn't necessarily mean you'd stop doing them."

"You know how one time you said sex wasn't everything and I said to me it was?" When I nod, Cole continues. "Well, I really do enjoy sex, and I was thinking why not get paid for it."

"Have you been hustling again?"

"No. That's too unpredictable. You stand out in the sun all day and most of the guys who stop are not anyone you'd want to go with even if you were as stoned as the boys in that booth. I was thinking of something a little more refined." He smiles as if he's made an incredible discovery. "I've been thinking of joining an escort service. The good ones screen the clients and you only have to go out on a call if you want to. And it pays a lot more."

I munch an onion ring before replying. "It could be risky for your acting career. If it ever got out, a lot of producers and directors wouldn't hire you."

"I bet half the producers and directors use escort services. It's all very hush-hush. It might even *help* my acting career."

"Think what Sarah would do if she found out—and she would find out with all those gossiping gays she hires. You'd be immediately fired."

"But I wouldn't need that job. I'm telling you being an escort pays a lot."

"But you don't really *need* money, do you? You don't *have* to work at Selection. You don't *have* to be an escort. Your mom will give you anything you want. She gave you a condo!"

"I do get an allowance, but if I want a larger amount, I have to ask her, and I *hate* doing that. My trust fund doesn't kick in until I'm twenty-one. Besides, Anthony, I have to *do* something! I can't just sit around like the 'idle rich.' So I might as well do something I enjoy."

"Have you done any research?"

Cole smiles. "I've missed you. You never make moral judgments. You only look at things from what's practical and logical." He squeezes my hand. "So far I've only looked in the pink pages of *The Advocate*, but it only lists masseurs and models. I think there must be one or two refined escort services, but I don't know how to find them. And that's where I thought you might be able to help me."

"Me? I don't know the first thing about an escort service."

"Didn't you say that a couple of years ago you went out a few times with Hugh Hefner's valet?"

"*One* of his valets. He has more than one."

"Well, I bet that valet knows what's the best gay escort service in town. And if he doesn't know, he could easily find out. Do you still have his number?"

"I think so."

We eat in silence for a while then Cole says, "I don't think you really enjoy sex."

"Why do you say that?"

"Because except for the first time we did it—on my birthday—it takes you a while to get hard."

"I always worry about what the other person wants, if I'm doing the right thing to please him."

"You should be more concerned about what you want."

"I did that once. I did exactly what I wanted, not concerned about the other guy's needs at all. And afterward, he said it was the best sex he ever had."

"So why don't you do that every time?"

"Fear. Afraid of displeasing the other person. Afraid of being self-centered."

"You know, earlier I got a woody just thinking about being an escort, but I bet you were as limp as—"

"A stale pickle." I pick up the tab. "You ready to go?"

"I'll leave the tip."

As we walk toward the door, one of the stoned boys makes kissing sounds at Cole and one of the drag queen says to me, "Love your boots."

Another queen responds, "Girl, with peak-a-boo jeans like that who's looking at the boots!"

In the parking lot, Cole says, "I'm still wound up from what happened tonight."

"What do you want to do?"

"Have sex."

"With anyone you know?"

"With you, stupid."

NOVEMBER 25, 1980

Leaf makes sure Leslie Manchester attends every meeting. I've gotten use to his *seemingly* shy way of suggesting things. I'm sure Leaf finds it endearing. I don't.

But I try to be fair. When we're going through the photography of homes that have been submitted for possible publication, I listen objectively to Leslie's comments, even when they contradict what I've said. And sometimes he's right.

I notice Leaf frequently touches Leslie. She'll put her hand on his arm as if she's trying to stress a point, but I know she just wants to feel him—merely standing still he radiates a certain sexual energy.

Leaf lights a cigarette. Leslie waves away the smoke, and Leaf quickly extinguishes it. She never did that for me.

"When the meeting is over," she says, "Anthony, come with me."

I follow her down the hall. In her office, she immediately lights a cigarette and remains standing.

"Who's that man?"

"What man?"

"The one at the submissions meeting."

"Joe? He's my assistant. He's been here for a year. You've met him."

"Why was he at the meeting?"

"So it would move faster. He follows behind, picking up the pictures we've reviewed and putting out new ones."

"It's distracting. He's always in my line of vision."

"All right. In the future, I'll tell him we don't need him there after all."

"I want you to fire him."

"Leaf, he's a very conscientious worker. He's wonderfully organized and has been a great help in keeping track of all the photography. Besides, he's done nothing wrong."

"I don't like looking at him."

Joe is not handsome, but he's not the hunchback of Notre Dame either. His looks are average—a perfect five on a scale of ten.

"You can't *fire* someone just because you don't like the way he looks! It's against the law and the company could be sued."

"Well, find some other excuse and get rid of him."

"I will not. We don't *all* hire someone just because he's handsome. For God's sake, Leaf, take another Valium and I'll keep Joe out of your line of vision."

"You watch your step. You can go."

I'm upset the rest of the day. Leaf and I have had disagreements in the past but this is our first real argument—the first time I boldly contradicted her. And what did she mean by saying "you can go"? At first I assumed she was telling me to get out of her office, but could she actually mean that if I don't get rid of Joe she can fire me?

DECEMBER 9, 1980

"**H**ave you started the color separations on Ted Graber's house?" Leaf enters my office without a *good morning*.

"Not yet."

"Good, because we have to change it." She wiggles her fingers in a *give-me* gesture. "Where's the layout?"

I pull out it from a stack on a console.

Leaf quickly glances at it. "That's what I remembered—only four pages. You have to expand it to at least six."

"I already used all the best pictures."

"Well, zero in on a detail and make it a full page like you do, but it *has* to be six pages. Nancy Reagan just appointed Graber to decorate The White House private living quarters."

"I hope he does a better job for them than he did on his own home."

PART FIVE

THE WHITE HOUSE ISSUE

MARCH 3, 1981

"I just got off the phone with Ted Graber," Leaf tells me. "It seems Nancy Reagan is very upset with the criticism she's gotten for mixing china patterns for her first state dinner. He said she had to use china from both the Teddy and Franklin Roosevelt administrations as well as from Woodrow Wilson and Truman—all because there weren't enough place settings in one pattern. So now Nancy wants new White House china."

"After all the flack she's gotten for spending so much money on her clothing," I say, "I don't think the American public is going to like using their tax dollars to buy a hundred place settings for The White House."

"*Two* hundred place settings—plus serving pieces. That's the point. Nancy wants to use private funds to pay for the china. So I'm going to convince Claret to buy the china. That way *Inside* would surely get an exclusive to publish the Reagans' private residence at The White House."

MARCH 6, 1981

Claret Bruin holds the annual sales meeting in Palm Springs at a time when the sales reps in New York, Chicago and Detroit think winter is never going to be over. They have an entire weekend to enjoy the California sunshine. But before that fun and sun, they have to endure two days of pep talks and conferences.

Of course the sales reps really want to hear Leaf speak. "That's not going to happen," she tells me. "I don't have to speak and I won't."

I suggest a Q & A, but Leaf rejects even that as too much effort to expend on "a bunch of boring salesmen."

So I have to give a speech about what *Inside* has planned for the future. I keep the crowd amused with the behind-the-scenes humor at photo shoots. I show slides of residences featured in upcoming issues and present the next foldout cover. Then I get to what I really want to say.

"Everything goes in cycles. Consider television. In 1958 there were more than twenty Westerns on television: *Gunsmoke*, *Maverick*, *The Texan*, *Zane Grey*, *The Rifleman*, *Bat Masterson*, *Wagon Train*, *Have Gun—Will Travel*. Judging by your nods of recognition, I'd say many of you watched most of them. Now the only Western on TV is *Little House on the Prairie*.

"In the sixties the trend was toward medical drama: *Dr. Kildare, Ben Casey, Marcus Welby*. The seventies brought crime shows such as *Charlie's Angels, The Rockford Files, Kojack* and *Hawaii Five-O*. There are still a lot of crime shows on the air. There's also a movie broadcast every night of the week. But as the eighties slowly continue, I see the trend to situation comedies centered around characters who do not read *Inside*. I'm sure the Jeffersons subscribe to *Ebony*. But do you think Archie Bunker, Laverne and Shirley, Mork and Mindy or the dukes of Hazzard read *any* magazine let alone *Inside*? The only character in these sit-coms I see possibly reading a magazine about interior design is Flo. But that magazine is *Trailer Life*."

I get a big laugh then continue.

"The point is: Things go in cycles. Television shows follow a trend. And magazines also go in cycles. Literary magazines such as *The Saturday Evening Post* and *Liberty* were once the rage. Only *The New Yorker* has survived in the mass market. Remember when *Life* was the magazine on every coffee table? Remember *Look*? These big-picture general-interest magazines were the ones to advertise in. But everything peaks. Everything wanes.

"Something becomes popular—a western, a sit-com, a magazine—and soon there are imitators. That's happening right now with shelter magazines. Some try to carve their own niche while others, which shall remain nameless—oh, why not: *Southern Accents*—blatantly copy *Inside*'s format. Now I hear there's another copycat coming from England: *The World of Interiors*.

"But *Inside* is number one. And it will—"

I end the speech with practically an anthem, and the applause reassures me that the audience is behind me, ready to guarantee *Inside* stays not only the top magazine in its field but one of the leading publications in journalism.

But one person looking at me isn't pleased. Leaf glares with anger and—could it be *hatred*? She is furious.

We break for lunch, but before I can attack the buffet table Timmy tells me Leaf wants to see me in her hotel suite. She's seated in a chair with its back to the balcony so that no matter where I sit, the light will shine on my face and not hers.

"How dare you say *Inside* will peak! Not everything follows cycles." Her stare is intense. "*TV Guide* will never peak. *Reader's Digest* will never peak. And *Inside* will never peak! I don't ever want to hear you spouting off your crazy theories again. Nobody's interested."

I could respond that the amount of applause, including from Claret Bruin, who actually stood up, indicates otherwise, but I keep quiet.

"And how dare you say *Luxe* is a better magazine than *Inside*."

"I didn't even mention *Luxe*."

"It was implied!"

There's a knock at the door. Leaf opens it to a bellhop who sets down a suitcase. *My* suitcase.

Leaf tips him then turns back to me.

"This time you've really gone too far, Anthony. You won't be further needed at this conference. Go back L.A. and do your layouts. And in the future that's *all* you will do."

MARCH 9, 1981

"Everyone wondered why you weren't at the dinner reception," Timmy tells me at lunch. "I told them you weren't feeling well."

"After what Leaf said to me, I wasn't!"

"My advice is to lie low, to not even let Leaf *see* you until this blows over. *If* it blows over."

"It was just a speech, Timmy. People will soon forget it."

"It wasn't just the speech. Something else happened that was a lot worse." Timmy takes a bite of his sandwich and a gulp of iced tea. "At the cocktail party, I was talking to Chad—the cute sales rep from Texas—trying to get him away from Steve—the tub of lard from Chicago. I don't think Chad is gay, but with enough liquor I figured he might be amenable to a blowjob. But old Butterball kept interrupting, asking all these boring questions about Leaf and the magazine. Finally I told him that this was a cocktail party and I would gladly answer all his questions during business hours. And he said, and I quote, 'Oh, don't bother. I'll ask Anthony. He's the one who really runs the magazine.' I looked up, and there was Leaf, right behind Butterball, and I'm sure she heard him, because she turned white. I've heard about the blood draining from someone's face, but I've never seen it until then. Leaf was as white as this tablecloth."

APRIL 25, 1981

"**W**ow! That color is fabulous!" The walls in Cole's living room are periwinkle blue.

"Didn't you say this was your favorite shade of blue?" Cole's smile shines.

"It just may be my favorite color of all."

"I had it painted while I was on location. Come see the bedroom."

It's as bright red as a fire engine. "I love it!"

Cole holds his arm next to the wall. "Look how sensuous it makes the skin."

"What made you decide to do this?"

"I got tired of living like a teenager. I thought maybe you could help me finish the rest of it."

"Sure. What do you want to do?"

Moving back into the living room, Cole points to the sofa and chairs. "I like Selection's upholstered pieces, but I don't want my home to look like a decorator did it. I don't want every little thing in exactly the right place, the way Waldo did with my mom's condo. And excuse me for saying so, but I don't want it like your apartment either. It's like there's not one extra thing in it. I want my place to look like someone *lives* here. And I don't want just modern furniture. So I thought maybe we could drive up the coast to Montecito, where I was told there are a lot of antique shops and we can pick out some tables and lamps and things."

"That's a great idea. There are some other shops along the way to Montecito that we can stop at too."

I take measurements of the seating pieces so we'll get the tables at the right height, then we take off in my convertible.

"I love April in L.A. when it's almost subtropical and everyone north of us is still hoping for spring." I'm in jeans; Cole's in shorts; and we both have on t-shirts. "So tell me all about the movie and how it went on location."

"It was very boring and very exciting. Of course the boring part is waiting around for your scene. They call you to the set but nothing's ever ready. They're always readjusting the lights or the sound is off or some other technical problem. And you're in costume and makeup so you can't *do* anything that might mess it up."

"I imagine sitting there while they apply the makeup would be boring too."

"Oh no! That's when you hear all the gossip about who's having sex."

"Were a lot of people messing around?"

"Sometimes it seemed more like a porn film than a made-for-television movie. But I couldn't tell if people were actually doing it or whether everyone was just talking about doing it. The gossip was worse than high school."

"And what about you? Did you 'mess around'?"

"Let's say I got a lot of offers—most of them from straight men. *Fat* straight men. Not a pretty sight."

"There wasn't anyone appealing?"

"Oh, there were plenty of sexy young actors, but they were all interested in advancing their careers, so I had nothing they wanted."

"So you didn't have sex with anyone for three weeks?"

"I didn't say that." Cole plays with my ear. "I had what you might call a 'mini-affair' with the screenwriter."

"So you were trying to advance your career too."

"Not that it did any good. He didn't give me any extra lines. But that's not why I did it. I liked him. He was so unlike everyone else. All the performers were concerned about how they looked and the crew only cared about union regulations and getting exactly what they were due. The director was only interested in working with the actresses, almost totally ignoring the men."

"So what did you like about the screenwriter?"

"He was quiet and not pretentious. And not at all condescending—you know, like how some older guys think they have to give the young kid the benefit of their vast experience."

"Do I do that with you?"

"Sometimes—but in a sweet way. I know you're just trying to help but most of them just want to feel superior." He kisses my cheek. "Anyway, the most appealing thing about the screenwriter was that he liked *me*. We didn't have sex all that often but we hung out a lot, and I liked that."

"Now that you got this part in a movie, are you going to stop working for the escort service?"

"I don't see why I should. I got the part because I met one of the producers through the service."

"You got the part because you auditioned for it and were good."

"Yes, but I wouldn't have gotten the audition if I hadn't tricked with the producer." Cole rubs my crotch. "What about you? Did you have a lot of sex while I was gone?"

"I saw Raymond a couple of times. He's certainly sexually fulfilling—if you get what I mean—but he doesn't have much to say."

"How's it going at the magazine?"

"It's really been unbearable. Leaf's latest ploy is to have Leslie attend all the meetings that before just she and I used to have. I've gotten use to him being there when we review the homes that have been submitted. I'm still furious he's there, but I've accepted it. Last year she had him attend one of the meetings when I show her the photos I think we should use in each residence, but now she has him at every one. Leaf and I have been doing this alone for years, and I resent it. He makes stupid suggestions because he feels he has to say something—and she listens to him! I find it so hard to believe that Leaf would turn against me just because *one* sales rep said I run the magazine. Hell, she was the one who said it first. I was right there in her office when she told your father that I run the magazine."

"Maybe it wasn't just one sales rep. Maybe others have said it too. But maybe it's more than that. Maybe she feels threatened by you."

"What do you mean?"

"Because you *are* the one who's running the magazine, Anthony. How many times has Timmy told you to solve a problem that Leaf didn't want to handle?"

"Practically every day."

"And didn't you tell me you're the one who decides how many pages a feature will be and how the issue is paced. Your layouts dictate how long the text should be, even how long the title should be. I've never heard of an art director having so much power over the editors. I think Leaf is frightened that you could do her job better than she can."

"If I did have her job, I wouldn't publish some of the homes she picks. Lately it seems every issue has at least one home that isn't well designed, but she wants to include because it's some society person she wants in with. She always says, 'You can make this work.'"

"And you do! And that probably frightens her too. She knows she's not as creative as you are."

"She gets all the credit for making *Inside* such a success," I say, "but you know she's not the only one who deserves it. Our former circulation director—the one who's now working for your mom—did a great job building up the subscriber base. And Jake White, the public relations guy, did a tremendous job promoting not just the magazine but Leaf as well. He made Leaf a celebrity."

"Yes, but, Anthony, even with all that promotion, if you hadn't made the magazine so beautiful, people wouldn't have accepted it like they have. I've heard many people say they don't throw away a single issue. And I've told them what you said in that *Advocate* article— that you design *Inside* like a book and people keep books."

"That's one of the things wrong with *Luxe*. It has the right paper and superior printing, but it's designed like a throw-away."

"My mom asked me to critique the latest issue. I told her she always picks the wrong photo to make a two-page spread. And I pointed to all the ceilings, and said you would have cropped them out." Cole pinches my side. "Then I told her she should hire you as art director."

"Well, if Leaf keeps it up, I might just do it. Not to brag—well, yes, to brag—the only good layouts in *Luxe* have been the ones stolen from me." I give Cole a quick glance. "Did your dad say whether we have any grounds to sue?"

"The lawyer is still checking into it."

"You're in a tough situation, aren't you, Cole? I mean, with your mom and dad owning rival magazines."

"Anthony," he says, "it's even more complicated than you can imagine."

JUNE 16, 1981

"Leaf painted her fingernails the entire time!" I nearly shout at Timmy. "I had to spread each layout across her desk, wait for her to look up from her nails, and then wait until she nodded before putting out the next layout. It was humiliating." I toss the layout boards on my console. "The only good thing was she seemed determined not to speak to me."

"Why is that a good thing?"

"She couldn't ask me to change any of the layouts. She thinks she's being clever and spiteful, but if she were really trying to hurt me she'd criticize my layouts and make me redo them."

"Leaf flew up to San Francisco last weekend to see that doctor she dated two years ago. Maybe she was hoping to rekindle the relationship and it didn't work out, so she's in a bad mood and taking it out on you."

"Maybe, but I think she's still angry about my speech at the sales meeting."

"I've seen her get like this with others. My advice is to just do your job. If you push her she gets more hostile."

"I don't know how much more I can take. Not if she treats me like this."

JULY 8, 1981

Timmy rushes into my office and looks behind the door. I think he's going to spill the latest gossip, but he says, "Oh, good. You still have your tie and jacket here."

"I always have them in case something comes up last minute."

"Good. Be ready by 1:00. Leaf wants you to join her for lunch at Perino's."

"Am I being fired?"

"Maybe we all are. Claret told Leaf Colette's decided to divorce him after all. And she's going to take back ownership of the company and shut down *Inside*."

At the appointed time, I walk down to Leaf's office. She's reading *W*. "Hadn't we better be going?"

She looks at her watch. "Colette will be deliberately late. So we'll be later."

In her car, Leaf seems to have forgotten she's barely speaking to me. "I thought Claret at least had some stake in *Inside*, but it turns out Colette owns it outright. But with California's community property laws they have to split everything else down the middle. He seemed more concerned about losing his Rolls-Royce than the magazine."

"So all along Colette has been using *Inside*'s profits to subsidize *Luxe*. She can't seriously think that if she kills *Inside Luxe* would take its place. It doesn't stand a chance."

"Maybe not as it is now, but Claret said Colette asked you to be art director."

So that's why Leaf wants me along. "First time I've heard of it."

Leaf gives me a skeptical glance, but I don't know if she doubts what I said or what Claret told her. At a stoplight, she reapplies lipstick. "I'm not worried about me. I can call up Si Newhouse and be editor of *House & Garden* tomorrow."

We arrive at the restaurant a half-hour late but we still have to wait another ten minutes for Colette.

She's outfitted in Ann Taylor black; a small oval hat with one purple feather makes her look very East Coast. Leaf is wearing a cotton ecru dress, topped with a rough-weave taupe poncho draped with a triangular navy blue scarf. She probably thinks the layers hide her extra pounds, but they only create a larger mass. Colette is as chic as her photograph that accompanies her editorial. Leaf looks nothing like her picture. It's been re-touched to erase fifteen years and thirty pounds.

Their pleasantries last one sentence each. No one orders an alcoholic drink. We sip Evian sans ice.

"I'll get right to the point, Colette," Leaf begins. "You simply cannot shut it down."

"Of course I can. I own it."

"But think of the readers. They—"

"What readers? We've never had any substantial readers."

"Oh my god!" I immediately grasp what's going on, but Leaf hasn't got it.

She practically shouts, "But it's the number one shelter magazine in the world!"

"What are you talking about? I'm shutting down *Luxe*, not *Inside*."

"But Claret said—" And Leaf gets it. She signals a waiter. "I'll have a Jack Daniels. Double. Neat. *Now.*"

Colette orders a French chardonnay. I ask for a vodka tonic.

Colette shakes her head. "So the thimble of my love has done it again."

"Why does he do it?" Leaf wails. "He's not even here to see me humiliated."

I wonder if she is hearing the same voice I am: the psychic saying a man is going to betray her.

"Claret's a very sick man." Colette's lipstick doesn't stain her glass the way Leaf's does. Probably Chanel. "Listen to me, Leaf, because this is the truth. The main reason I left Claret was because of his lying. It's pathological. His lies are very elaborate. He thinks the whole thing through. They're not spur of the moment. He knows he's lying and he does it deliberately. He really needs psychiatric help."

Leaf reapplies her lipstick—again—and orders another drink. I wonder if we're actually going to eat.

"So are you really getting a divorce?" I ask Colette.

"Yes. And if I had any doubts about it, this little incident makes me all the more certain I want that man out of my life. I'm making a lot of changes. Now that I'm closing *Luxe*, I've decided to take a more active role not just in the property I own but also erecting new buildings. There's going to be a real estate boom, and I want to be part of it."

I doubt Leaf has heard a word. She seems lost in her own thoughts.

"Colette, would you do me a favor? When your lawyers are going through the property settlement with Claret, would you make sure he doesn't get to keep the Rolls-Royce?"

SEPTEMBER 14, 1981

"We got The White House." Leaf struts into my office like a student with an all-*A* report card. "I saw it yesterday. Considering that Ted Graber did the interiors, it's surprisingly good. Nothing innovative or dramatic, but simple understated design. Everyone wants to show it, but we've got an exclusive—not just over other shelter magazines but *Time* and *Newsweek* as well. But only if we do it right away. How soon can we get it in?"

I take a schedule out of my drawer. "The October issue goes to the bindery on Monday. The middle-of-the-book for the November issue is being color proofed. Of course, I've already laid out the next three issues after that, but—yes, we could get it into December, but it's going to be a major project. Walter will go crazy. But if we get the photography right away, we could do it. Are we going to show the entire White House?"

"Oh no. Most of the public rooms haven't been changed. It's the Reagans' private apartments on the second floor that we're interested in. That's what everyone wants to see. But I had to agree to show the third floor too. That's where the guest bedrooms are and the solarium, where Reagan recuperated after the assassination attempt. There's lots of Americana—needlepoint by little old ladies, that sort of thing—but it'll be okay."

"How soon can we photograph it?"

"Sunday. I think we should use Derry Moore."

"But he's British! The British burned The White House. Don't you think we should use an American?"

"No. Let's use Derry. He's so well connected. Tell him he can fly over on the Concorde so he won't suffer from jet lag."

"How many pages?"

"As many as we need. And the cover, of course. The cover has to be special, Anthony."

"Okay. I'll go over the current December issue and see what we can drop. This is going to be a lot of work, not just for me but also for the editors. We'll probably have to adjust three issues that are already in production."

"It'll be worth it. Walking through there I got chills. I didn't think it would affect me, but when I entered the Oval Office, I got very emotional. When you think of all the presidents who've worked there, who've decided our future, it's inspiring."

An hour later I hand Leaf revised contents sheets. "I've worked it out. I've taken out Sarah Cohen's home since it was the December cover. I moved it to March so we can keep Lee Radziwill on the January cover."

"Yes, Lee needs the publicity. She hasn't been getting too many jobs lately. Sarah's not going to be pleased. But, hey, it took her years to finish designing her own home. She can wait a few more months. What's on the cover for February?"

"The beach house that Angelo Donghia designed."

"Oh, right."

"Okay, so taking Sarah out of December gives us twelve pages; then we can move de Kooning to January, since that's 'At Home with . . .' and we'll be visiting the Reagans instead."

"That's wonderful, Anthony! I hadn't thought of calling it 'At Home with President and Mrs. Ronald Reagan.' That makes it more personal."

"Yes. So that's eight more pages. I just hope de Kooning's still alive in January. Also, Leaf, we probably shouldn't publish that San Francisco basement apartment in the same issue as The White House."

"Why? It's so eclectic it would make a nice contrast."

"Do you know what's located above it?"

"What?"

"A gay porno theater."

"Oh, God! I bet every designer in San Francisco knows. Hell, they've probably all been there. Let's put it on hold for a while." She lights a cigarette. "We have to be extra careful with the December issue. It will be studied with a magnifying glass."

"So I've taken out twenty-six pages. We need a contemporary to replace Sarah's project, so I've moved Larry Laslo's place from January to December. That leaves eighteen pages for The White House."

"That should be plenty. Have you given any thought to the cover?"

"Yes. Of course, I haven't seen any of The White House rooms, but even if they're beautiful, they'll still be just rooms—they could be anywhere—so I think we should do an exterior with the American flag waving on top of the portico."

"It's corny, but you're right. We want everyone to know immediately that *Inside*'s got The White House."

SEPTEMBER 11, 1981

"The first batch of transparencies of The White House hasn't arrived." I'm sure Timmy can see the anguish on my face. "I phoned Derry, and he said they were sent yesterday. I asked him if he sent them himself and he said, no, he gave them to an usher, who supposedly sent them. Federal Express guarantees next-day delivery, so they should be here. Could you try to find someone in The White House who knows what's going on?"

About a half hour later Timmy comes to my office with a sour look. "I finally was able to speak to an assistant in The White House mailroom. The photos had been *mailed*."

"Shit!"

"I guess they used the postal system because it wouldn't cost The White House anything. I told him from now on he was to send them Federal Express and charge it to *Inside*. So the *second* batch of photos should be here first thing in the morning."

"Who knows when we'll get the first batch."

SEPTEMBER 12, 1981

"I got the second batch of transparencies, but there's no cover shot," I tell Derry over the phone. "Is it in the first batch—which still hasn't arrived."

"I haven't shot it yet."

"Derry! I *told* you to shoot it first, that the cover is printed before the rest of the magazine. We're on a very tight deadline, and if I don't get the issue to the printer on schedule, it won't be on the newsstands on time. You simply *have* to shoot the cover today."

"There are always too many people milling around the grounds. I can't get a clear view."

I try to keep my voice calm. "I want you to get up at dawn and take the shot. There won't be anyone about then. Do it straight on, one-point perspective, like we discussed. I don't care what it takes, but get that shot."

SEPTEMBER 15, 1981

All the transparencies of The White House finally arrive—including the cover shot of the portico with Nancy Reagan-red flowers encircling the fountain. Derry Moore has taken one-hundred-and-sixty-four exposures. I spend four hours editing, choosing the best color and angles. Then I spread out my selection on the light table for Leaf to see.

She studies the First Lady's dressing table with a magnifying glass. "Nancy has a photo of Jerry Zipkin. I won't have that moth in my magazine. Have it air-brushed so that he's unrecognizable."

See what happens, Mr. Zipkin, when you decline Leaf's request to publish your home.

I point to another silver picture frame on the table. "Did you notice this one doesn't have a photo in it? Isn't is strange to have a frame with no photo in it?"

"You'd think Derry would have removed it."

In the afternoon I lay out the eighteen-page feature. Walter has already received Russell Lynes' text, and it's been sent to the typesetter. I work late to paste up the Photostats so I can show the layout to Leaf in the morning and Walter can write captions. I take a deep breath. We're going to make it.

SEPTEMBER 20, 1981

Claret Bruin invites me to lunch at The Brown Derby in Hollywood for my birthday. He's never acknowledged my special day in the past, and the fact that it falls on a Sunday this year makes his gesture even more surprising. Naturally I accept the invitation but, because of how he lied to Leaf, I promise myself to be skeptical about everything he says.

He downs a Chivas Regal and orders another before we order. "I've decided to give out company bonuses this year. I continue to hear a lot of good things about you, but I need to ask a few questions about your responsibilities. I want you to answer with absolute candor. Everything you say will be in the strictest confidence."

"What do you want to know, Mr. Bruin?" I sip a glass of chardonnay.

"What exactly does being an art director entail besides laying out the magazine?"

You would think after all these years he'd know. Or is he just playing dumb? "First Leaf and I plan the issue—choosing what homes to feature—though a couple of times I've done it myself. I show Leaf what photos I think we should use, and she makes changes if she disagrees, but usually she doesn't. Then I do the layouts."

"Who determines how long a feature will be?"

"I do, but sometimes Leaf will want them longer."

"Do you do all the layouts?"

"I do all of the middle-of-the-book features. One of my assistants does the departments, which I formatted, and I supervise two people who do paste-up."

"And what happens after the layouts are finished?"

"I show them to Leaf, who usually approves them without change, then I work with the production director on the color separations checking the proofs."

He signals the waiter for another Chivas. "What else do you do?"

"Well, there wouldn't be anything to lay out if we didn't have photography, so I assign all the photography. Whenever any pictures come in, either commissioned or unrequested, Joe, another assistant logs them in, and I screen them for Leaf to review."

"Do you ever scout homes?"

"Sometimes, if Leaf doesn't want to go."

"She obviously has a lot of confidence in you."

I wonder if he knows Leaf has been rather distant with me for more than six months. "The past two weeks working on The White House has been invigorating. It was a lot of work—I had to rearrange three issues—but I got everything accomplished on schedule."

"And Leaf had let you handle it all." He picks up a shrimp from his salad with his fingers. "I'm concerned for Leaf. She told me she met Nancy Reagan at The White House, but when Leaf was in Washington the Reagans were in Santa Barbara at their ranch. Leaf *did not* meet Nancy Reagan. She has to be very insecure to lie like that. Sometimes she's like a little waif. The other day when I saw her I commented how nice her hair looked—and she immediately had it cut! That's a perverse thing to do. Has she ever acted strange with you? Remember, Anthony, nothing you tell me will go beyond this room."

"I have no complaints, Mr. Bruin. About my work or Leaf." I concentrate on my heart of romaine salad.

"I think you are extremely creative, Anthony. Your covers continue to be interesting, and I like the way there's always a pleasant surprise when a foldout cover is opened."

"There's no point in having it fold out if there isn't a treat."

He waves for another drink. Four. But who's counting?

"I worry that you might leave the magazine. If you ever think of quitting, come see me first." His care *seems* sincere; his smile *appears* genuine. He's charismatic and it's difficult to resist his charm. "What's your career fantasy, Anthony?"

"What do you mean?"

"I'm sure you don't always want to be art director of *Inside*. You must have a dream you hope one day to fulfill. All creative people do."

"Do you?" I ask, giving myself time to think.

"I'm not creative like you, but, yes, I do have a career fantasy. One magazine isn't enough for me. I'd like to have a whole empire of magazines. As a matter of fact, I'm currently investigating the purchase of another periodical. I hope to make an announcement before the end of the year. So, I've told you mine, now you tell me yours."

"Well, you're right. Being art director, even if it's art director of one of America's most successful magazines, isn't my ultimate fantasy. I'd like to be both art director and editor of a high-gloss gay magazine—sort of a combination of *Esquire* and *Gentleman's Quarterly* but for gay men. I think the time may be right."

Claret smiles again. "I can't promise you a gay magazine, Anthony, but if this deal goes through, I might be able to make *most* of your fantasy come true."

SEPTEMBER 21, 1981

Leaf is out of the office, so I sit chatting in Timmy's office while he opens the mail. He slits an envelope and removes a single sheet of paper. "They have got to be kidding! This is an invoice from The White House. *Inside* is billed $770.81 'for the labor of ushers, maids, movers and others who had assisted in readying the personal residence of the President and Mrs. Reagan for photography.'"

"Don't you think the ushers, maids and every White House employee are paid regular salaries? This seems like someone's trying to bilk *Inside*."

"There's more. Are you ready for what they're charging the magazine for the floral arrangement? $3,329.45!"

"That's a lot cheaper than the Queen paid for Princess Di's wedding bouquet."

"Yeah, well Nancy Reagan isn't the Queen."

"Not yet."

SEPTEMBER 23, 1981

Timmy quietly approaches my drawing board and whispers although I'm the only one in earshot. "Brace yourself. Mr. Bruin told Leaf you want to be editor of *Inside*."

I don't even bother to explain that is not what I told him. I just hold my head in my hands.

"Leaf has assembled practically all the editors in the viewing room to plan the next issue."

I pick up a folder, rub my forehead and walk down the hall. Ever since Ivory was fired, I've planned the issue alone with Leaf. She invited Leslie Manchester to one meeting but realized he had little to contribute. The meeting usually lasts ten minutes because I prepare a proposed contents and Leaf merely makes sure I haven't left out a home that she wants included.

Walter and Leslie are seated on either side of Leaf. Other editors stand in the background. I hand Leaf a sheet of paper with my suggestions for the April issue.

She doesn't look at it. "Shall we begin?"

Silence fills the room.

I stand in the doorway and wait. I look at each editor but none of them dare speak. Finally I say, "We should put in the Montana ranch because there's a bit of snow in the exterior shots and this is our last opportunity to publish it until next winter."

Leaf stares at the bulletin boards with its three-by-five cards designating the residences. "Let's put in the Montana ranch," she says as if the idea has just occurred to her. "Timmy, will you move its card under 'April'?"

None of the editors know the decor of the unscheduled homes so they can't possibly make any informed suggestions, and most of them are wise enough to be silent. Leaf continues to ignore me, and I think of leaving the room but decide to remain pleasant not wanting to antagonize her further. One by one I propose the residences on my list, and one by one Timmy, after a silent nod from Leaf, moves the corresponding card to the April column.

After the meeting, which lasts nearly a half hour, Leaf brushes past me without speaking.

I follow her into her office and sit on the banquette before she realizes I'm even there. I won't have her desk create a further separation between us.

"Leaf, do you have a minute to talk?"

She looks started but quickly recovers. "*A* minute."

She joins me on the banquette.

"I know why you're angry with me and I think we should talk before the situation gets even worse."

Leaf looks directly into my eyes. "I don't like it when someone goes behind my back. I don't like it when someone *who works for me* tells Claret that he's running the magazine and that he should be editor."

"I never said that, Leaf. I can't believe you would believe *anything* Mr. Bruin says after what he said about Colette wanting to kill *Inside*. But let me clarify my conversation with him. He said we were going to receive bonuses this year and he asked a lot of questions about my duties. I answered truthfully.

I never *once* implied I was running the magazine. He also said he was planning to expand the company, to buy a new magazine. He asked if I had a career fantasy, as he called it, and I said one day I would like to be both editor and art director of a magazine. But I never said I wanted to be editor of *Inside*. I said I would like to start a high-gloss gay magazine, but that was way down the road—just a fantasy. Up until recently, I've been very happy at *Inside*."

"All right, Anthony, what you're saying is probably true. Claret's lied before. He has a history of it." Leaf's lips smile but her voice remains tense. "I'm glad you're happy here, and I hope you'll remain happy, but there are going to be a few changes. First, from now on, I will be the sole contact with the designers. You will have nothing further to do with the designers—no lunches, no phone calls."

She looks at me as if expecting me to respond. I just stare at her, my face, I hope, as stony as I feel.

"Second, I've decided," she continues, "to put Joe—that assistant you're so fond of—in charge of the photographers. He will be the one to stay in contact with them and to schedule their assignments. All you are to do, Anthony, is design the magazine. And you mark my words: As long as I am here, *I* am the only person who will be editor of any magazine at this company, whether we buy one already in existence or start one of our own. And if anyone goes against me, there will be no transfers to another department or to another magazine. There will be no protection from someone else in the company. If anyone tries to undermine me, that person is gone. I take no prisoners."

SEPTEMBER 25, 1981

"The backlash has already started," Timmy says during lunch at a deli restaurant. "Did you read Judy Berlin's column today?"

"No, what'd she say?"

"She said the 'general news media' is upset they're denied access to photograph The White House presidential quarters. She went on to question why *Inside* should have an exclusive and she felt the magazine was exploiting the public by raising the cover price for the issue to $4.95. She also said that in the text for the article Nancy Reagan is quoted as saying, 'This house belongs to all Americans, and I want it to be something of which they can be proud,' but Judy points out they can only see it if they fork over five dollars."

"I wonder how Judy got an advance copy of the text."

Timmy smiles.

"You didn't!"

"I like Judy. And I think Leaf gave her a raw deal."

"You better be careful, Timmy. Leaf is on the warpath, and not just with me."

"I imagine it's too soon to tell if things have gotten any better since you had your little talk with her."

"I don't think things are going to improve. Today when I

showed her the pictures I selected for the April features she had Leslie at the meeting and listened to his comments more than mine. I used to enjoy my meetings with Leaf. We'd gossip and talk about personal things, but that hasn't happened in quite a while. I think it's over. It's just a matter of time before she fires me."

"How can she fire you? You run the magazine."

"I wish people would stop saying that." I take a sip of matzo ball soup. "Tom showed us the photography for the early California paintings we're running in April. Leaf thought they were wonderful, but they look rather mediocre to me."

"Of course she thinks they're wonderful. Don't you know why we're publishing that feature?"

I shake my head.

"Because Leaf bought half a dozen early California paintings! She thinks if *Inside* does a story on these same artists, the prices will increase and she can sell them for a big profit." Timmy chomps into a Rueben sandwich.

"She better hope no one finds out."

"I'm surprised she came into the office today after what happened yesterday. I like when she's out—I get so much more work done. I pretty much know what she wants so I often answer her mail. I have her sign the letters, but if it's just an interoffice memo I usually sign her name. No one's the wiser and things get done a lot quicker."

"What happened yesterday?"

"I thought you heard. I thought the whole office heard." Timmy wipes sauerkraut juice off his mouth. "About three o'clock I get a call from Sarah Cohen asking me if Leaf's in, and before I can transfer her, Sarah hangs up. Well, she must have been calling from the pay phone in the lobby, because within five minutes she's barging into Leaf's office without me announcing her. And she starts right in: 'How dare you move my house from the December issue and not tell me!'"

"Oops!"

"I don't know how Sarah found out she was moved to March. It wasn't me who blabbed this time."

"I told Raymond Washington and he probably told her."

"Aren't you the Chatty Cathy?"

"After the way Leaf has treated me, I don't regret it. So what else did Sarah say?"

"It seems that since it was her own home, which she'd taken *years* to finish, she had sent out invitations to a big party at her house on the day the issue comes out. So she carried on about how embarrassing it will be to tell all her friends but especially her business associates that now it wasn't going to be published for nearly four months.

"Leaf tried to placate her, saying she'd never had done it, but it was The White House, and surely Sarah could understand. But Sarah was having none of it. She started screaming that Leaf didn't have any talent and that she feeds off of the work of others and that she couldn't decorate a *dog*house. She said Leaf didn't even go to the photo shoots, that all she did was look at pictures and say 'yes' or 'no.' Then she added the kicker. She said there are people in this world who are so blind that they don't realize how *un*talented they are, but Leaf knows she hasn't got *one ounce* of talent and she never will! And you know what, Anthony. Sarah's right. Leaf doesn't have a single talent."

Before I comment, Timmy excuses himself to use the restroom. When he returns he leans across the table and whispers. "You won't believe who's sitting in the booth right behind us. Maxine."

"Claret's secretary?"

"Yes, and she's eating alone, so you can be sure she heard every word we said."

When Timmy and I return to the building, Maxine is leaning against a wall by the elevators in the lobby. She's holding an open cardboard box with various items—including a brass Tiffany lantern clock.

She walks up to Timmy. "Leaf said you're not to come upstairs. She said your services are no longer needed." She pushes the box toward him. "Here are your things."

Timmy grabs the Tiffany clock and throws it against the marble wall.

OCTOBER 19, 1981

The White House issue goes to press at one o'clock. At two the secretary to Rich West, head of personnel, says he wants to see me at four.

I bundle my April layouts in a large sturdy envelope. I add the layouts I've done for future issues—all the homes for which I art directed the photo shoots. Then I address the envelope to myself.

"Joe, make sure that this is mailed today. I'm going to be fired at four o'clock."

"They can't fire you," he says. "You run the magazine."

"Not anymore."

I mix up all the selected photos of each April residence with the duplicate exposures; let the new art director figure out what to use. I copy phone numbers I might need from my Rolodex. Then I stack all my personal items on my desk.

I decide the least amount of severance pay I'll accept is $20,000.

A minute before four I go down to the personnel office. I see —before I enter West's office—Leaf's foot swinging in the air.

I sit opposite her and stare.

"The company is being streamlined and the job of art director of *Inside* is being restructured." She's obviously been coached what to say. "There will now be fewer responsibilities and therefore a much lower salary. It's clear that you do not qualify for the new position."

I don't point out the blatant contradiction that if there's less to do I'd be more than qualified. It's all bullshit. "How much severance will I receive?"

West picks up a check from his desk. "It's for $32,726.78. It includes vacation time due you." He hands me a single sheet of paper. "You'll have to sign this standard termination form saying you will not reveal company secrets."

"I refuse."

"Then we can't give you the check."

"Oh, give it to him." Leaf stands. "Let's get this over with." She turns to me. "I'm sorry that it had to happen like this."

"I don't believe you're sorry at all."

"You don't know what I feel."

"Oh, but I do, Leaf. I know you like an open book."

PART SIX
THE LETTER

NOVEMBER 6, 1981

"Anthony," Leaf announces in a groggy voice. "I need you over here. *Now.*"

She hangs up. She doesn't have to say who it is. Or where I'm to go. I recognize that voice. No one but Leaf Wyks would summon me to her home at midnight, not concerned that I may be sleeping or with someone. And of course, she knows I'll go, even though she fired me just last month.

Twenty minutes later, I press her doorbell, but there's no response. The sliding glass front door is not locked.

"Leaf?" I call softly, entering the black-mirrored foyer. "Are you still up?"

On the living room coffee table are a liqueur bottle and two glasses. *Tiffany*, I think. In the adjacent dining area, the table is cluttered with chocolate-stained dessert dishes and empty cups.

I turn toward her bedroom.

"Are you asleep?"

She's propped up in a mist of pink silk pillows. A Daum lamp glows on the Art Deco nightstand, illuminating a magazine on the bed. It is, of course, *Inside*. Just off the press, it's The White House issue—which I haven't seen—and I'm tempted to grab it.

Leaf's eyes are closed, her lips parted.

She may be annoyed if I wake her, but if I slide out, I'll have to deal with her anger tomorrow when she accuses me of not showing up. Do I even care?

"Leaf." I touch her shoulder. Her head slumps forward.

I put two fingers on her neck. No pulse.

I stare, unable to move. I don't think I even breathe.

And then the unwanted thought registers. *I'm glad she's dead.*

What should I do? Leaf is dead, and I've found the body. How is that going to look? Should I leave and hope no one finds out I've been here? But if, for some reason, the police are involved, won't it look bad if I slip out?

My hand shakes as I reach for the phone on the nightstand.

"I need the police." Aware of how rapidly my heart is beating, I'm surprised at how calm I sound. I relay all the pertinent information, and when I put down the phone I notice a pink envelope—addressed to me.

My eyes zoom in like a movie camera: I recognize Leaf's handwriting. I pick the envelope up but don't open it. Maybe I stare at it so intently in order not to look at her lifeless body.

The police will be here any moment. Suddenly I run to my car, pop the trunk and bury the envelope under the spare tire. I dash back inside and slow my breathing as police lights color the night blue and red.

NOVEMBER 7, 1981

Anthony,

I'm writing to you because I've always felt that—no matter what—I could trust you. You're ambitious, but you're also honest—an unusual combination, but one I can rely on. I know—without a doubt—you will come here tonight when I call. And even though I fired you, I know I can trust you to carry out what I want done. And I want—I need—someone to know the truth.

It all started—and ends—with a bottle of framboise. Do you know it? It's a raspberry liqueur. Taylor Allen—the editor of <u>Inside</u> before me—was once given a bottle for Christmas, with a card that said, "Because I can't forget." He was found dead next to a glass with a trace of framboise—and poison. In his hand he clutched the gift card, and the police assumed it was a suicide note.

Taylor did not kill himself. He was murdered. And I—not the police—figured it out. On Christmas Eve, the day before he died, Taylor told me who gave him the liqueur and about the card—what could not be forgotten.

One night Taylor and Claret got drunk and ended up in bed together. Taylor told me that from then on, whenever he wanted something—a raise, a new car—all he had to do was threaten to reveal their sexual escapade and Claret would grant Taylor's wish. But Claret got tired of being blackmailed. <u>So Claret murdered Taylor.</u> He thought his secret was safe. He didn't know that Taylor had told me everything.

I told Claret I knew the truth, but that I wouldn't blackmail him as Taylor had. All he had to do was make me editor of <u>Inside</u>. Of course, I also told him that if I died under unusual circumstances, my attorney would open a letter I had given him revealing all that I knew about Taylor's death.

I invited three guests to dinner tonight to celebrate The White House issue—what a laugh! "The White House issue." The hoopla will be over in a week. It will have meant nothing—like everything else. Anyway, I invited Sarah, Claret and Ted Powell. I told them the dinner wasn't merely to celebrate the issue but to forget the past and make a fresh start.

After dinner I showed them the new Tiffany liqueur glasses I'd bought. I passed the glasses around and everyone touched them. Unfortunately, I said, I had forgotten to buy any liqueur.

I arranged it so Claret stayed a few minutes after Sarah and Ted left. Then once Claret was gone, I washed Sarah and Ted's liqueur glasses but kept the one with Claret's fingerprints all over it. I actually did have a bottle of liqueur—framboise, which Ted had given to me. I didn't like the taste, but I saved the bottle. And after Claret left, I filled the two glasses. Using only a clean napkin to touch Claret's glass, I poured out the liquid. Then I drank the other glass, which contained an overdose of sleeping pills.

Yes, Anthony, I've planned my own murder.

I'm not insane. I don't want to die. But I'm going to, much sooner than I thought. In June I went to San Francisco to consult a cancer doctor. The prognosis, as they say, is not good: less than a year. He suggested chemotherapy, but when pushed he admitted that even the best treatment can be worse than the disease. So I've opted out in my own dramatic way.

How perfect to do this with the publication of The White House issue. The media will go crazy. Nancy Reagan—who didn't have the graciousness to meet me at The White House—will be livid. It will *overshadow her redecoration.*

I am getting so tired —

But I will have my revenge.

Last week I made out a new will, naming Claret my sole beneficiary. I also made a point of letting him know he would inherit should I die.

If you, Anthony, are accused of murdering me, I realize you will show the police this letter in order to free yourself. I understand that. If Sarah or Ted is arrested, do not let anyone see this letter. At least not right away. Not until they have suffered. I <u>want</u> them to suffer. Like I have. Let them feel the panic. It will do them good to suffer, to panic.

But there should be only one real suspect. When my attorney opens the letter I wrote about Claret murdering Taylor and the police discover his prints on one of the glasses — well, there can be only one conclusion — that Claret murdered me just like he did Taylor. If you have any qualms about keeping silent about my death, remember that Claret <u>did</u> murder Taylor. So if he is found guilty of murdering me, and I'm sure he will, let the bastard burn in Hell.

—Leaf

NOVEMBER 11, 1981

It all goes just as Leaf thought it would. Claret's fingerprints are on the liqueur glass, making him the prime suspect. Then Leaf's attorney gives the police her letter naming Claret the murderer of Taylor Allen. Claret is arrested.

I keep silent.

But not inside. Inside I'm a wreck. I'm unable to think about anything else. I don't know what to do.

And my doorbell rings.

"I just came from the police station." Cole seems out of breath. "I have to tell you what my father just told me."

I bring him a 7UP, and we sit in the living room.

He swallows half the contents. "For a long time I've had my suspicions about who gave my mom the Burton Fisher and Ted Powell photographs to publish in her magazine, and now I know for sure: my dad."

"Your father gave the photographs—and my layouts—to *Inside*'s competition?"

"Yes. He just admitted it."

"How did he do it when I was the only one who had a key to the filing cabinet?"

"As he said—rather smugly—it's easy to get a duplicate key made when you own the company."

"That man is unbelievable!"

"He wants to see you. He says he has something vital to tell you."

I don't want to see him. I want him to hang. But I'm not certain California even has the death penalty for murder.

Claret Bruin looks as if he hasn't slept in a while, but he doesn't appear worried—about anything. "I didn't murder Leaf and I didn't murder Taylor Allen. All these years she thought she had something over me about Taylor, and I let her think she had the upper hand, but I did, because I knew the truth."

"And what's the truth?"

"It's true that a man did give Taylor a bottle of framboise to commemorate the sexual trysts they had. Taylor, because he was a wicked bitch, told Leaf I was that man because he had, shall we say, offered himself to me—more than once—but I always turned him down. You homos may think every straight man can be had, but Claret Bruin is not to be had."

Homos? I assume he wants me to help save his life, but calling me a 'homo' isn't going to endear him. I guess I'm supposed to ask him who *did* give Taylor the liqueur. But at this point I don't care. I don't say anything. And I stay silent until it registers that I'm not going to ask him.

"Taylor told me he and Ted Powell had done it a couple of times but when Ted had broken it off, Taylor threatened to tell everyone Ted was a homo." Claret smirks. "Taylor told me Ted gave him the bottle of framboise. Only Taylor didn't know it was poisoned."

I think back to Thanksgiving dinner at Jason Hunt's in Rancho Mirage. Someone had brought a bottle of framboise but no one admitted it—it must have been Ted. And what about Geraldo Cortez? I remember Cole said he smelled raspberries on Geraldo's breath when he found him dead. Did Ted poison him too?

"So you knew Ted Powell murdered Taylor Allen and you did nothing about it?"

Claret shrugs. "People make choices."

"Why are you telling me all this?"

"Because I want you to help me."

Surely he doesn't know about the letter Leaf left me. "What could I possibly do?"

"You're an attractive man, Anthony. Seduce Ted Powell and get him to confess."

"So that he can poison me because I know too much?"

"What I can give you will make it worth the risk. I can give you the magazine you want. I can make you editor-in-chief and art director just like you want."

I stare at him. "I'm sure you've heard the story of 'The Boy Who Cried Wolf'—about a boy who repeatedly lies about a wolf devouring his sheep so that he gets attention. Then when he finally tells the truth no one believes him. So tell me, Mr. Bruin, after all the lies you've told, why do you think I should believe you now?"

People make choices. I can clear Claret with Leaf's letter. Or I can let him stand accused—and likely be convicted—of murdering both Taylor and Leaf.

It's up to me.

ABOUT THE AUTHOR

Charles L. Ross was the art director of *Architectural Digest* from 1978-1985. In 1987 he was the founding art director of *Veranda*, which grew in status to compete with *Architectural Digest*. Besides designing the magazine, he also edited the text and had his own column until he retired in 2004. His writing has been also published in *GQ*, *Christopher Street* and *The Advocate*, as well as a short story in a gay anthology. He is currently at work on another novel.

Follow on Facebook:
Charles L. Ross, author

www.facebook.com/CharlesLRossInside

11545130R00256

Made in the USA
San Bernardino, CA
22 May 2014